by ROBERT ROBIN

SOMETHING IN COMMON

Simon and Schuster NEW YORK

Library of Congress Cataloging in Publication Data

Robin, Robert.
  Something in common.

  I. Title.
PS3568.0273S6   1985   813'.54   85-1894
ISBN: 0-671-54769-0

Grateful acknowledgment is made to The Welk Music
Group for permission to reprint an excerpt from
LONG AGO (AND FAR AWAY) by Jerome Kern and Ira Gershwin.
Copyright © 1944 T. B. Harms Company. Copyright Renewed
(c/o The Welk Music Group, Santa Monica, CA 90401).
International Copyright Secured. All Rights Reserved.
Used By Permission.

Acknowledgments

EVEN SOMETHING as solitary as writing is connected to people who have cared: to Patricia Soliman, my editor; to Karen Klein, Kirsten Olson, and Alice Rosengard; to my friends over many years who were encouraging from the start; to Alan Hergott and Hugh van Dusen; to my literary agent, Joy Harris, and Robby Lantz, Marion Rosenberg, Ken Sherman, and the people of the Lantz Office; to Rosemary Janisch and finally, and always, to my friend and counselor, George H. Pollock, who provided the "click."

To my family

PART

1

1

OUR BREAKFAST room was in a magazine once. The decorator had knocked out a wall between it and the kitchen and put shining red Portuguese tiles on the floor and glassed in two walls. A third of the ceiling had been opened up as well. It had been filled with skylights so it felt like a conservatory, and when you looked up, you could see the huge shade tree overhead. The room was full of light, and in the mornings, it seemed as though you were eating outdoors.

The mud room, which was not done by a decorator, was just off the kitchen. It was full of lawn mowers, snow shovels, Judd's skateboards, pegs for dripping clothes, and we had put a drain in the tile floor so we could hose the whole thing down. Andy had pulled his knapsack off a shelf and was stuffing his chemistry workbook into it. Cath had just told him he would be grounded if he missed curfew again. He had gotten out half a "Je-sus Ch-rist" before he thought better of it.

As soon as Juddy entered the kitchen, he sniffed bacon but turned toward the wedges of cheese on the rotating tray and went through his usual ritual of trying to decide if he wanted an omelet or eggs and bacon. Of the two boys, Juddy was the neat one. His clothes were always pressed and he even had a sense of color. It hadn't progressed much past cream going with brown, but that was light-years ahead of Andy. He sat down at the table and put a napkin across his lap. "Mom, I'll have eggs, I think." Judd was the younger of the two, and he looked like Catherine. He had her long face and her sweet eyes. He was a beautiful child and was taking on her love of music and puzzles, but his pleasure in mechanical toys was his own. He said words like "yum" and "gulp" instead of making the sounds and he still hid candy in his night-table drawer, but in terms of judgment, he was Andy's equal.

Andy walked back from the mud room into the kitchen, carefully adjusting his leather jacket. When he saw Judd, there was a glint in his eye as if he had spotted prey.

"What are you smiling about, stain!"

Judd shifted his chair and drank his orange juice, eyeing Andy all the time. "Andy, you barf me out!" he said.

"Yawn," Andy answered. He stood with his arms crossed, massaging both shoulders.

Judd giggled, apparently satisfied, and continued his breakfast.

What had started as a nice cheerful morning would have looked to the outsider to be rapidly disintegrating, but that wasn't so. The smiles and the goodwill were still there, subdued under the tension of the moment, I'd admit, but operative. Tranquillity was rarely found in our household. There was always too much going on.

Andy bent down to tie his shoes when the phone rang. "These things are thrashed," he said. "Can I get boots Saturday?"

He was almost fourteen with a voice that had changed a

year ahead of time, and he had a strange need to dress as if he worked in a gas station. He wore the Levi's he had slashed when Cath wasn't looking and said "fuck" and "shit" to his friends on the phone, but by any measure, he rated as a good-hearted kid. When he was twelve, he had taken Judd to Wrigley Field on his own, and since he had started high school that spring, he had taken him along to night basketball games, but no one really expected that Judd's role as Andy's companion would continue much longer. Cath knew Andy was my own personal thug who could do no wrong, but nevertheless, she had said privately to me that she could see a revolt coming, and that we had better start enforcing the rules early. Hence, the curfew argument of that morning.

Andy reached for the phone, but Judd beat him to it.

"Stern residence," Judd said, sounding what he must have thought, at eleven, was worldly.

Cath, who stands five foot seven in sneakers, stood over him, shaking her head. "Judd, don't answer the phone like that." Then she laughed a little in spite of herself and Judd caught the spirit. He covered the mouthpiece.

"He told me to," he said, pointing to Andy.

"I did not."

"Calmness, boys," I said. "I want calmness."

"Stern residence." Judd repeated. He pulled the phone away from his ear, and the caller's voice carried across the room. I was pretty sure who it was.

Judd stole a look at the clock. "We're fine," Juddy said, "and how are you this fine day?" Andy made his puke face. "It's Mr. Ingram," Judd whispered. "He talks *very* loud." Judd wiggled his finger in his ear. I took the phone and covered the mouthpiece. "No, he doesn't. He's just enthusiastic," I said.

"Hello," I said.

"Joel! How are you!" Ken Ingram was our firm's senior part-

ner, and he said hello to everyone as if he had waited all day
to do so. He was a charming man, but he could easily appear
as a comic opera figure because he bellowed so much. What
few knew was that it was an act, a way for a very shy man to
appear outgoing. I looked at Juddy, who still seemed puzzled,
and I wondered why I had contradicted him on the loudness-
of-voice issue.

"I'll be brief," Ken went on. "I'm supposed to interview all
day, but my schedule's in the toilet. Can you cover for me this
afternoon? I'm in the middle of a deal that's going speedily
down a down staircase."

"Sure," I said. Sixteen years with this guy and his lingo still
sent me for a loop. The hellos were over, and it was just the
two of us, so he softened his voice. "It's some youngster from
Columbia. He asked for you anyway, they tell me."

"He did?" I said. "What's his name?"

"O'Connor, I think, something like that," he said, with a
Midwesterner's way of mixing up ethnic names that you ignored after a while.

"Doesn't strike a bell," I said.

"By the way, I'm against renting more space. You?"

"I agree. Two floors is enough."

"I won't be at the partners' meeting," he said. "Cast my
vote."

"Done," I said, and of course there would be no more space.

By then, Andy stood at the back door, ready to leave. "What
do you want new boots for?" I asked. "I thought you liked
your clothes thrashed." He turned the collar of his leather
jacket again trying to get it to stand halfway up. "Jesus, Dad!"
He walked across the kitchen, having completed construction
of his straight-from-the-gutter look. He kissed Cath good-bye,
then me. He would kiss me at home, but no longer in public.

"I'm supposed to cover an interview," I said to Cath. "Do

you believe it? That's what Ken called about at eight o'clock in the morning. Sometimes," I said, "I don't understand that man." Cath leaned back and looked up through the broad glass windows at the oak tree over our heads. The leaves were turning and in a week or so, they would be yellow.

"Well, stain," Andy said to Judd, "it's been a slice."

"Don't slam"—it was too late—"the door."

One down, two to go, Cath must have thought. She poured coffee for me and then stood at the stove, making Judd his eggs and bacon, her white robe tied over her nightshirt. She whipped up his eggs like an expert and poured a little cream in while he was busy reading the sports page.

"Jesus, did you see what the Cubs did?" he said. "I don't believe it. Why couldn't they play like that last June?"

"You mean Bowa to Sandberg to Buckner?" she asked.

"You bet."

"Hot, huh?" she said as she put the plate in front of him. Coming from above, the sunlight cast a yellow glow on almost every item in the room, especially the metal gadgets and the window trim. If we had had water outside instead of grass, it would have sparkled like the Mediterranean. Cath walked back to the stove, a special smile on her face. It was always there when she talked sports with Juddy. "Do you want toast?" she asked. He nodded. "You still on that cinnamon kick?"

"Tastes yum," he said, a big smile for his mother.

When Cath smiles, she beams, and I'd say if she had wanted to put it all together again, the Diane Sawyer voice, the smile and the looks, she might have moved successfully back into a spot as a TV reporter. The hour format on public television had opened a job, but Cath didn't go for it. It had been years since she had done any of that. She sat down. "Juddy, may I have part of the paper?" she asked. In that moment, it was possible to see that she once had been a little girl talking baseball with her father.

"Sure, Mom," and he gave her the sports section.

North School started at nine, not eight thirty, and Juddy wasn't quite used to his mornings alone with us or walking to school on his own. He had played outside last night in the rain and came in wet to his underwear. He howled when I told him I wanted to take his temperature again before he left.

"Feel my forehead. I'm fine. I'm fine," he said.

"Could 'fine' have anything to do with basketball practice?" I asked.

"Not a thing," he said.

"Let me do this," Cath offered, and Juddy tilted his head toward his mother.

"He's fine," she said.

"See!" He scraped his chair against the tile and pushed away from the table.

I listened to him say grunt as he put on his galoshes. Judd knew the sky had cleared as well as we did, but he was pulling those rubber goliaths over his basketball shoes anyway. One controversy a morning was enough, no doubt. Cath would dress later; I was ready to go.

The folder for a report Cath was working on was on the floor next to her chair. As soon as she had the house to herself, she would sit in the breakfast room sunshine in her white robe, and spread the report of the Landmark Preservation Commission before her. She had a yellow pad full of notes near the bread plate and in her nightshirt pocket a thin Lamy ball-point pen that wrote in three colors.

The mornings were first too noisy and then too suddenly quiet to say anything unless you desperately wanted to. Besides that, you were always timed; so when Judd left, we watched him walk up the driveway, and we didn't say anything. We saw Judd look at the sky, stick his hand out, palm up, to feel for rain that wasn't there and then march off in his galoshes.

"He really didn't need those things today," Cath said.

"I suppose not," I answered. "When is the Commission hearing?"

"Next week. There'll be TV coverage," she said.

"Really," I answered as we kissed good-bye.

Cath held her pen aloft and I pictured her posed as a flutist, hearing inner music.

"You're seeing me as something strange again," she said. "I can tell."

"You're Jean-Pierre Rampal."

"He's a he." She was generally good-natured about my make-believe. "Can't I be Eugenia Zuckerman?" She rearranged a small bunch of yellow tulips that were in an old water pitcher on the breakfast room table and smiled at me.

"I've got to go," I said, and kissed her good-bye again. I decided to sketch her with a flute, playing Mozart, as soon as I found the time.

THE KID was blond, almost too good-looking. Ken Ingram called those types "pretty boys," and this kid, like the rest of them, would never be offered a job at our shop. He had not taken a seat, but had waited to be offered one. He stood, his back to the door, looking closely at the Art Deco desk clock Catherine had given me when I became a partner.

"Mr. O'Connor?" I said. "I'm Joel Stern. I'm sorry Mr. Ingram couldn't see you."

He turned around. "It's a very handsome clock," he said. We shook hands. "About 1920?"

"Yes, and it's a striker." He had good eyes—they stayed

with you—and a good voice, a little high-pitched yet, but that would change.

He wanted to be a deal lawyer, do takeovers, leveraged buy-outs, all the complicated news media stuff, but he parted company with others who promoted themselves for the fast-track work. "I'm not sure how much of it is dazzle," he said. He looked out the window. "I realize a firm makes an investment in training, but in all honesty, I can't provide a commitment that I'd stay with that specialty. I'm not really sure what it is."

"We don't hear that from a lot of people," I said. "They want what they want and that's usually all there is to it."

"It's only a question of being fair, I guess." He looked embarrassed.

From where we were in the room, we could see the railroad yards, the shoreline curving to Hyde Park, and west, in the distance, the International Amphitheatre and the empty spaces where the stockyards once stood. I had intentionally chosen an office that looked across the back end of the city. It was easy to sit at the top of the Sears Tower and forget where you came from, but not if you always had your old neighborhood in front of you. It was a kind of comfort for me. He wasn't from Chicago, but he seemed to know what he was looking at: the yellow bungalows, Catholic churches every eight blocks, the railroad yards and the precincts that held four Democratic votes for every two people.

"This is a beautiful city," he mumbled. "I think I'd like to live here."

"Out there," I said, almost daydreaming, "that's the tough side of town. That's where people with muscle come from," I said.

"I know. I grew up, too, where the women worked." I turned around in my chair. He looked at me for a moment and then turned away.

I gave him every opportunity to put on a canned show, but he never did. He refused to turn himself into an exhibit. On the other hand, he interviewed; he told me about himself and tooted his own horn a little, but never nonstop. Instead, he talked about his degree in fine arts from Columbia, and his switch to law so he could earn a living without having to teach. Every time we talked law, we stayed with it only long enough to be sure one of us was ready to go on to something else. His eyes lit when he talked about Renaissance drawings, and it was obvious that art meant a great deal to him. Cath wanted me to paint more, but certain things got away as life went on. I knew he would never be happy here.

"With your record, Paul, I'm surprised you're not interviewing in New York."

"I have been interviewing there. That's really why I asked to see you. I think you know Ted Stackler. I told him I was coming here and he asked to be remembered to you." I looked out the window again, unnerved.

"You know, it's funny," he said. "You two are a lot alike."

My first impulse was to cover up and ask a lot of questions about Ted, but I didn't. I hadn't really thought about him, and Cath had said nothing nor asked about him since Andy was born and the birth announcement came back undelivered.

"He said you were law school roommates."

"Pardon?"

"You look like you're a million miles away," he said.

"I guess I am," I admitted. "We were very good friends."

"He said the same thing."

I looked at Catherine's picture. It was in a silver frame on my desk.

In all her photographs, she was smiling, and there was always a lot of activity going on around her. They were mostly candid shots with the inevitable golf course behind her, and later, as time passed, the backgrounds moved indoors and became grinning co-workers in sensational clothes gathered around a copy machine at the Junior League.

In the picture on my desk, Cath was dressed in a tailored blue suit, stepping onto the train at the Glencoe station. The morning the picture was taken was her first day as president of the Junior League, and we were going downtown together, like colleagues. She had no idea I was going to whip out my camera and yell "hold it" as she stood on the platform in front of the train doors. She looked at me and hesitated a second. Then she caught herself and waved like a presidential candidate. Her smile itself was eight by ten. Watching her through ground glass, dressed for business, I realized she had a face that looked like her father's face.

"Paul, who do you see when you're through with me?" I wanted him out.

"I take it that I'm being hosted—is that the word?"

"That's the word."

"—by Mr. Stanton."

"Well, Paul, the hiring partner himself."

After he left, the office was quiet and all you could hear was the creak in the window joints when the building flexed in the wind. There were no street sounds that high up, and the city seemed innocent.

I realized I had relied on Cath's picture as if I were holding the cross outstretched to protect me against evil. I didn't want to think about what was going on. I just wanted to get home.

AFTER DINNER that night, Cath asked me about the interview. She put the question casually, more for conversation than information.

"Just another job hopeful. Too creative for us," I said, covering up.

"Then how did you get in?" she asked smiling, and without waiting for an answer, Cath changed the subject. She told me that Andy was right, that his desert boots were thrashed, and he would get a kick out of it if I were to take him shopping, maybe at Eddie Bauer, for the Wellingtons he wanted.

Despite all the activity each of us engaged in and the acquaintances that came with all our running around, home was not a place that was full of outsiders. Noisy, I'd grant you, but it was, for us, an oasis. There were very few people outside of our family whom we cared deeply about. There were one or two halves of a couple we were close to (Cath and I rarely liked both), and when they visited, they became part of us, and if they wanted to use the bathroom, they felt as free going upstairs as we did. Nothing in the house was off limits, and it was that way even when Andy was a baby and we had lived in a small apartment on Lakeview in Lincoln Park. Our home was never full of furniture you couldn't flop on or tables with polished surfaces you couldn't eat off of. Cath was never a compulsive housekeeper, and at that point in our lives, her league work had become her career. Not to the exclusion of the boys or me, but she preferred it to the whitest-wash-on-the-block activities most women her age still suffered out of habit or barrenness.

Years later, when this all started, she was not happy about the way she looked. She felt she looked her age and that I didn't. She was, she would admit, attractive, although she really was much more than that. Within reason, she spent time and money on her appearance, but she had her own limits. Her hair had darkened and what was once red turned raisin, but she never touched it up to get it back to its original brightness. Time had taken little away from her, but she thought it had, although she rarely spoke about the issue out loud.

If there was one way in which she liked the way she looked, it was dressed up as she looked in the picture. I remembered

sneaking looks at her smiling as she tied her floppy bow ties
from Brooks Brothers. She was lively and more brilliant in
conversation than I was, but the reverse had been true when
we were first married. At that time, I was in my hometown
and she was the stranger. Ebullient and ambitious was the way
I was then. Sixteen years had gone by, and later, as she found
herself a significant place in civic activities, and I had learned
to mask my reactions, she had scored in the fascinating-in-
public department. She had become daring, self-possessed and
high-spirited, and I had come to like staying in the background. The league work had placed her in the middle—half
housewife, half workingwoman. At least, it provided her with
half of what she wanted. When she was ten, she had told her
father, "When I grow up, I'm going to have a lunch box and
a penis."

I felt an immense amount of distance between the life I was
then living, complete with Andy and his argot ("stain" being
the latest catchword), and the lives Cath, Ted and I had led
in Cambridge. Cath had almost completed her master's when
six of my classmates tired of the food at Harkness Commons
and decided to eat off campus. We had placed a notice on the
Radcliffe bulletin board describing the job. We needed someone to cook for six Harvard Law School students at the apartment Ted and I shared, Monday through Thursday, in at five,
out at seven. She had come to our place on the second floor at
44 Brattle Street, carrying the ad in her hand. It looked like a
scene out of a Depression movie. We were glad to see her because the first cook had quit after a week.

Cath was a real maverick then, sort of a Barbra Streisand,
The Way We Were type, but without the frizzed-out hair.
She was almost too tall, had an intense look on her face as if
she would die for modern art, and everybody said she looked
as if she should play the flute. But somehow, I had felt for her

more than anyone else. I always had luck hitting it right off the bat with people who would be in my life for life. Cath was that way, and when we were all together at school, I had hopes that it would always be that way for the three of us. Of course, that was not the way it turned out.

After the interview, I had one other word about Ted and that took up half a paragraph in a letter I had received from Paul O'Connor. He had written a very thoughtful thank-you note. That kind of courtesy wasn't usual anymore, and given the buyer's market in jobs, I was surprised the firm wasn't flooded with such proprieties. I was disturbed, however, by his last paragraph. He said Ted had been out of the office, that his secretary was a little mysterious about it, but that he would pass on my regards as soon as Ted returned.

That wasn't Ted, or, at least it never used to be. The plague could pass through Cambridge Common and somehow Ted would make his classes at Langdell, especially if Henry Hart was teaching. That was the way I remembered him, and that was why the tossed-away piece of information that he was out for a week was alarming. I thought about saying something to Cath, but I wasn't quite sure how to bring it to her attention without provoking a barrage of questions. So I kept my concerns to myself.

Then came the day when the issue of hiding Ted's attempt to reestablish contact didn't matter anymore.

IT WAS a week later, on a Tuesday or a Wednesday. I can't be more accurate because many of the details of that time are clouded in my mind. Cath had called before lunch. I had seen the message, but I didn't return the call until I came back from swimming. She began by saying, "You've been busy, I gather."

"Interviews. Three straight weeks of interviews. Ugh! Garbage."

"You sound like Andy." Her laugh sounded like a disguise.

"I should have called back right away," I said. "Sorry."

"Ted's father called." She had said Ted, not Ted Stackler, just as if we had seen him yesterday. "I suppose I should just say it. Ted had a heart attack during the middle of the night." There was a sudden dimming in her voice and then total silence on the line. "He's not all right, Joel. He didn't make it."

Even though you know two seconds before bad news hits, it doesn't help. My eyes burned behind my glasses. I took them off and cleaned them. "I don't want to talk now," was all I could say, but I didn't hang up.

I know I should have thought of her and asked how she was doing, but I didn't. Instead, I walked back and forth in front of the window. The cord was long enough to let me cross the room to the end of the sofa, circle my conference table, head for the door and finally double back on myself until I stood in front of the window again. I dragged the phone behind me.

"The funeral is tomorrow," she said quietly. "They've got to do it before Friday night." I sat down, exhausted, as if there were two tons of me. "It's going to be at his father's temple in New York. Temple Isaiah," she said. I felt her voice reach out to me. "That' a great honor, you know," she added, and then there was a long silence.

I sensed the role reversal; she was taking care of me, but it should have been the other way around. I was not making the right moves.

"There was something else," she said. She hesitated for a long time. "His father asked for you," she said. "He said Ted would have wanted you there."

Then, with no life in her voice at all, Cath said, "I haven't heard anyone call you 'Buddy' for years."

I pulled the house key out of my pocket and toyed with it. "Buddy?" It was the first word I had said, and I wished my voice had sounded stronger.

"His dad called you 'Buddy,' " she said. I sat silently for a long time with my eyes closed. I blocked what I was thinking until her voice intruded.

"I don't know what to do," she said, "I mean about going. I'm not supposed to care anything about him." Then there was no more Diane Sawyer voice; the strength was gone. "Why the fuck after all these years did he have to come back into our lives like this?"

I put the keys back in my pocket.

"I'm the talker," she said, "you're not. I suppose I should learn a lesson from you and just shut up."

I pulled out my drawer, looked at the train schedule and checked my watch. "I'll make the three ten," I said.

"That's okay," she said, "you really don't have to."

"I want to."

"Joel," she hesitated, "it's been awful here."

"Cath? Still there?"

"Yes."

"Was Ted . . . I mean, was someone with him . . . when he . . ."

"I don't know," Catherine said. "I didn't ask," and her voice ran down like a neglected clock.

2

THE TRAIN I usually took, the 5:40, made one stop between the North Western Station and Glencoe. The 3:10 felt more like the El, making a stop, it seemed, every eight or ten blocks. I sat on the narrow upper deck where there was a single line of faded brown benches on each side of the car. The train swayed and clicked through the neighborhoods of Chicago, and I liked it up there where I could sit by myself.

You didn't smoke or drink when I was a kid, that was for later. What you did is you went over to somebody's house for lunch. There was always some cool kid that everyone wanted to have lunch with. He had a playroom and a pool table in his basement, and he knew all the smooth moves. At law school, when being a kid was supposed to end, Ted had liked me on the spot. I could never get over that.

The train slowed at Green Bay Road, and just before the car door slid open, I saw my sons through the glass—Andy, seeming so tall, and Judd, so far behind him that they no longer looked like brothers. It was still light out and I was

coming home and what were the boys doing out of school?
Then it dawned on me that I was the one out of sync. The
door was sucked back into its sleeve, and I stood on the bottom step, alone for a moment.

"Hi, Dad." Andy squinted, the afternoon sun in his eyes,
and then he stretched out his arms upward to hug me, something he hadn't done for over a year. I tried to lift him up, and
I hugged him hard.

"Mom told us your roommate from law school . . . well . . . ,"
said Andy, ". . . so we thought . . ."

"Me, too," said Judd.

Judd squeezed my hand. I looked at him, then quickly up
at the sky. I bit my tongue and forced tears back so my boys
wouldn't be upset. Why? Why do we hide that? Maybe it's
okay for a daddy to hide his tears from his boys. And maybe
it isn't.

I put my hand on the back of my Andy's head, and I
pressed his cheek to mine. "Dad, I'm sorry," he said. I felt a
hand pulling at me.

"Daddy, me, too," said Judd, looking a little left out. His
blond hair had fallen over his eyes, and he pushed his small
hand across his forehead so he could see. I put Andy down but
I wouldn't let go of his hand. Juddy took my other hand, and
I walked with my sons, my boys.

"Well," I cleared my throat a few times. "Thanks, you guys,
for coming to meet me."

"You're welcome," said Andy. "We needed the exercise,"
he said, pulling his hand free, and we all laughed.

"That, for sure, is one thing you guys don't get enough of."

"Well, tell him," ordered Andy.

"Tell him what?" asked Judd, annoyed.

"Yeah, tell me what?"

"I had my picture taken," Juddy said, embarrassed. "All the

kids did. You know. Looking studious. And, well, here . . . I brought it for you."

My number two sat at a desk, a book opened before him, looking up with a big smile, a patch of his blond hair falling over his forehead and his green eyes, his mother's eyes, twinkling. "Juddy! You look great," I said. He really did. "Hey, Judd, can I have one for my office?"

"Sure! You really want it? For down there?" he said, puzzled and pleased at the same time. We crossed Lincoln Drive and cut kitty-corner under the trees in the small park, in front of the red jungle gym.

"You bet I do!" I said.

"You can have this one. I'll get another."

"*Another* one!" said Andy, baiting his brother. "He's got fourteen million zillion of them already."

"I do not," he snapped.

"Oh, yes, you do!" Andy was moving in for the kill.

"Barf," Juddy said.

"Calmness! Boys, I want calmness." Everything was returning to normal again.

"Okay, okay. So I have a few," admitted Judd. "So what?" He stopped in his tracks.

"Meshuggener," said Andy.

Judd stared at him, startled, and I burst out laughing. "Where did you pick that up? You know what it means?"

"Sure, I do," said Andy. "You send me to two Sunday schools, don't you?" he said, rolling his eyes.

"Andy . . ." I laughed, "your mother will kill you . . ."

"She already has," announced Judd, folding his arms across his chest. Andy scowled at Judd and then blew the hair off his forehead.

"What have you guys been up to?" I asked.

"You're a stain, Judd." Andy glared.

"All right, Andrew," I said, "let's have it."

"Dad, it's nothing. She blew her stack . . . well, she didn't do that either." He flicked an imaginary insect off his sleeve. "Judd, go take a bong hit," he said. "She just—well, she looked a little upset and asked me, very intenselike, if I knew what the word meant, just like you did, and where did I get it, and to use the word 'crazy' instead. And Dad . . ." and at this point, Andy looked up at me, his eyes shining, "that is . . . the bottom line." He had picked up that phrase from me the year before and, he was telling me, through the haze of his junior macho period, that it was still okay for him to be my son forever. He waited for me to smile.

"You two are making fun of Mom," said Judd.

"No, we're not," I said. I tried to think as fast as I could. Andy might be the tough guy, but Judd could spring a verbal trap faster than most adults.

"You meshuggener!" Judd said to Andy.

It had become colder, and clouds blocked the sun and the grass around us had turned a deep brown for a moment until the sun came out again. I kicked dead leaves with my loafers and the boys did the same. Judd wore his basketball shoes and Andy, my apprentice hoodlum, still had his thrashed desert boots and leather jacket, the collar finally disciplined to stand halfway up around his neck. Judd's slacks were still pressed but Andy had slashed a fresh hole in his jeans. They'd make a fortune with preslashed Levi's, I thought.

He pulled a tennis ball out of his pocket, tossed it to Judd, who tossed it to me. Andy had tilted his baseball cap at his shoes to keep what was left of the sun out of his eyes, and Juddy put his cap in the pocket of his baseball jacket, the jacket with stern written on the back of it. Judd pitched the ball underhand to Andy who whipped it over to me, bending his throwing arm behind his back. We tossed the ball back and forth as we walked. Burning leaves was illegal, so if that was what you smelled, it was out of your memory—make-believe, nothing real. I never wanted to work again. I wanted to stay home all my life and be with my guys.

Judd tried a behind-the-back shot, like Andy's, but it went astray and he ran after it. After that, he stuck to underhand. We covered about a half a block when Andy said, "Dad, I've never heard you talk about your friend who died." He tossed the ball to Judd and looked at me. "Who was he?"

"I guess I don't know how to answer you, son." I picked up Judd's toss and pitched the ball back to him. "I'm still trying to get used to thinking of Ted as someone who 'was.' "

"But Mom said you haven't even seen him since you were married." A gust of lake wind lifted the ball and Juddy had to reach for it.

"Yes, that's right."

"But doesn't that make him a person who 'was' even before he . . ." Andy stopped in midsentence and looked at me as we walked. "I'm sorry, Dad." He put both hands, red from the cold, inside his leather jacket, but then held one out for me to hold. Judd did the same, pocketing Andy's tennis ball, and the three of us walked together, holding hands.

We crossed the narrow bridge over the ravine that flowed down from Lake Forest. It tinkled on pebbles below us. Our house was just around the corner, set back from Crescent Drive with a broad lawn in front, and in back, behind the sunroom, out past Catherine's rose garden, there was more lawn, over fifty yards of it. Then, the woods began and the land sloped down to the ravine where you could hear the water rushing even in winter except for the few days when it was frozen over. I wanted to keep both boys' hands in mine forever, and I felt tears in my eyes again.

Catherine waited for us on the broad raised terrace, a soft yellow cardigan sweater draped over her shoulders, one leg placed in front of the other, planted with the strength of a tree.

I thought of how Cath looked that day and how she had appeared sixteen years before when the three of us were still in Cambridge. Uncertain had turned into elegant, and flutes no longer suggested themselves to anyone. Her hair was sleek now and pulled back tight with a deep blue ribbon. If the way she looked had changed over the years, it was subtle, and you had to know her both times to really see the difference. She still asked, as was her ritual, "Well, how shall we improve our morning," except she asked it of the boys and not me alone. She still liked surprises, especially creating them for others, but down deep, she was beginning to want life to become a bit more tranquil (to which, I agreed—after all, we weren't twenty-four any longer). Her eyes, still lineless at the corners, always seemed to be opened wide, as if the sense that saw you would hear you too.

"How're my boys?" she asked, looking worried, like rain was coming.

"We're okay," answered Andy.

We walked up the five stone stairs to the terrace outside our front door where Catherine stood. Cath and I hugged each other for a long time. The boys remained near us, but said nothing.

CATH HAD plopped down in one of the two easy chairs we had in front of the bedroom fireplace where we read at night. She packed herself into the corner of the cushions. She was used to my cross-examining and went over the text of the call, reciting her own words as well as those of Ted's father. She did so with great precision, but she had dropped the "Buddy" part and the "Ted would have wanted me" part, and when that happened, I knew it was time to stop. As soon as she was sure the questioning was over, she moved to her desk.

"Well, you'll need a dark suit for tomorrow," she said,

"probably a white shirt and a quiet tie, and black shoes. For God's sake, don't wear brown loafers."

"Why don't we just take the crack-of-dawn flight, go to the funeral, and turn right around and come back? Why are we going tonight?"

She shook her head. "Joel, I can't."

She stood up and walked toward the window. "Are you going to stay for shivah?" she asked.

"That's a whole week anyway, I think," I said. "I'm not sure anymore."

"That starts after the cemetery. Right?" she asked.

I closed the suitcase and sat on the edge of the bed. "Cath, I get the feeling you think I should make a real production out of this trip—that I ought to stay for the whole works." She didn't reply.

"We haven't seen Ted since we were married," I said. "The last time we saw him, he wasn't particularly thrilled to be around either of us."

"I remember," she said quietly. She took up a pencil that needed sharpening and began working on it. "I was stealing his best friend," she said, almost to herself. Then she walked over to the window and looked out at the yard. She had acquired the stance of a princess. "I don't belong there," she said. The sun was setting and in the half-light, I saw her reflection in the glass, and her eyes were closed.

The door opened, and Judd peeked in. "Are we far from dinner?" Andy stood at the doorway behind him, his hands in his pockets.

"Boys, we'll eat in a short while," I said, letting the annoyance show. "Mom and I are talking."

Andy said, "Come on, Judd," and started to lead him out of the room.

"Hey, guys," said Catherine. She went over to the boys and

put one hand on each of their shoulders. For just an instant, I felt jealous. "Dad didn't mean it. You may come back in." The boys looked tentatively into my eyes. I nodded, and then I realized Catherine had welcomed the interruption. I studied her, trying to see inside. I hadn't noticed Judd standing on the bed until I heard him yell "whoop." I turned around just before he flew into my arms.

"I'm hungry," Judd whispered as he hung around my neck. I kissed his ear and hugged him.

"Yeah, me, too," announced Andy.

Cath headed downstairs, maybe a little too much in a hurry.

"Dad, you want your shaving stuff?" asked Andy, as he watched Cath move down the hallway.

"Sure, son," I answered, distracted.

"I'll get your ties," Judd said, not to be outdone.

"Dark ones," I called after him as he disappeared into the closet.

"Brown or blue?"

"Blue. Definitely dark blue," I answered.

"How old was your friend?" Andy asked from the depths of the bathroom. It was the second time he had raised that subject.

"My age, Andy," I said. "Thirty-nine." He came back into the bedroom, very slowly, studying me. He put my razor on the bed.

"Actually, Ted was about three months younger than I am," I said.

"He had a heart attack, huh?" Andy asked tentatively. He moved away, toward the far end of the bay window, still watching me closely. I sat down on the bed and motioned him over. He hesitated, but walked toward me. Judd came too, and we were all at eye level.

"Yes, he had a heart attack. He had it at a young age. Is

that what you're thinking?" Andy nodded without saying anything and Judd looked away. "Well, that's rare," I said. "Very
rare."

The boys looked at me and said nothing. Then Judd's eyes
started to fill with tears. He turned his head away, but I put
my hand on his cheek and turned his face around so I could
look at him.

"I'm not going anywhere, son." He looked into my eyes and
I grinned. "Got it?"

"Yeah, I got it," he said a little weakly.

"Now, you two, out! I'll finish dressing and see you downstairs. Deal?"

"Deal," they said in chorus.

They left and I started to wash. My hands and face were
full of soap when Judd walked into the bathroom a few minutes later. He sat on the toilet, cover down.

"Can I wash my hands in here?" he asked.

"Sure, son."

"Where's the soap?" he asked.

"You can take some off my hands," I said. Juddy came up
to the sink, stood next to me and put his little hands inside
mine. We let our hands touch over and over again, pretending
that washing them was all that was going on.

"Dad, does Andy always look like he dresses in the dark?" I
smiled a little. "No, son, it's part of being that age."

"Andy said I wasn't a man."

"Why was that?"

"Dad, did he have his thing stuffed? Did he have surgery?"
He looked up at me and smiled. Then he looked nervous.
"That's puberty, right?"

"Yes, son, that's right."

We put our fingers under the warm water faucet, then the
cold water for a rinse, and we grinned. I washed soap off my
face, and I was looking in the mirror trying to decide whether

I had to shave again. Judd was looking in the mirror too.

"Dad, do I look like you?"

"You look like both of us, but probably more like Mommy, I think."

"I want to look like you." He rushed the words out, teasing, smiling all the time.

"You will when you comb your hair," I said. He beamed as we used different ends of the same towel to dry our hands.

"I want to see *you* comb *your* hair," he said, and his eyes lit up.

"Juddy!"

"Ha!" he blurted out. "I want to see it!" He started giggling.

"What is this all about?" I couldn't help it, I started to laugh too.

"Mom told Mrs. Maxwell she liked the way you combed your hair."

"Well, that's nice." I felt embarrassed and tried not to look in the mirror.

"So I want to see. Ha!" Light filled the whole room for me.

"Okay, big shot, here's a comb. We'll do it together."

"Gimme the comb," and he grabbed it and held it at the ready.

I started the lesson: "First, you comb the front forward, then over your forehead and to the right. And it flops around. Got it?" It took him two tries, and he still didn't get it, so I combed his hair for him. Then he looked in the mirror, and his eyes shifted from his new hairstyle to a full look at me.

"You're gorgeous," he said, his eyes twinkling.

"Judd!"

"Well, that's what Mom told Mrs. Maxwell," and he stuck out his lower lip. "She said you look like Gary Hart's younger brother."

"Judd . . ." I said. "Oh, Judd, you're as much of a screwball as your mom." For a minute there, it was hard for me to talk. I wanted to pick him up and hug him, but too much affection would make him wonder. He was no dumb kid. "Let's go eat," I said.

AFTER DINNER, I was going upstairs to get my suitcase, and Cath, who had left the table before the rest of us, was coming down. I stopped her on the landing.

"Cath, there's still time for you to pack," I said. "I could call my folks. I'm sure they'd stay with the boys." I touched her arm, but she pulled away.

"They wouldn't arrive on time." Cath shook her head and continued walking down the stairs.

"All right, Cath," I called after her, "God damn it, *don't* go!"

Andy raced past me, climbing the stairs two at a time. He looked at us oddly, but I wasn't sure what he had heard. I was never certain any longer what he knew and what he didn't know. He stopped just short of the top landing and looked up at us. "What time are we going? We'll be late," he said.

That was the second time the boys had given Cath a break, a way out of the trip or a discussion of it. It was clear to me at that juncture she wasn't going—that was all there was to it.

THE RIDE to the airport was quiet. The boys leaned forward with their chins on the front seat, uncharacteristically silent. Catherine turned on the radio so we could listen to more than the roll of tires. We followed traffic into O'Hare and pulled up near the American Airlines departure area. I had expected to take my suitcase out of the trunk, say good-bye to Catherine and the boys, head into the terminal and be on my way. But instead, Catherine said, "Boys, will you stay in the car for a moment? If a policeman comes along, just tell him I walked your father to the gate and that I'll be right back."

"Sure, Mom," said Judd.

"Don't worry. If the cops complain, I'll just move the car." Andy jumped the seat and got behind the wheel, while Judd said, "Zoom, zoom."

The terminal was under construction, and crowds milled everywhere. Trying to watch Cath out of the corner of my eye, I bumped into a large woman searching the arrivals screen. I apologized and wanted to turn back and look straight at Cath, but something told me not to. "Mr. Ingram to an American Airlines White Courtesy Telephone, Mr. Ingram, please." There were twelve million Ingrams, but I wanted to button my jacket and stand up straight, as we used to do when Ken walked into a room. Cath watched me on the sly and smiled, knowing what my mentor had meant to me. We walked through the X-ray check to the gate. We looked around and found two seats together in a corner next to a pillar. There were leftover newspapers and dirty coffee cups all over the place. We looked out of the broad glass expanse at the moving planes.

Then, for the first time, Cath looked directly at me. "I know you wanted me to go with you," she said, "and for a while, this morning, before I talked to you, I thought I might go, but I can't do it."

"I know that. They should have called me first." Four college kids behind us made more noise than a regiment. We stood up, and I hooked my arm around Cath's waist, and we walked toward the other side of the concourse. She reached behind her and touched my hand gently and I let loose of her.

We were in the center of the aisle when she stopped. I remembered as clear as day the scowl we got from a lady in a wheelchair as she was steered suddenly to the side to avoid us. Cath looked at me, sadly, lovingly, almost as if we were alone. "This is between you and Ted. I know you two were lovers in law school."

NOBODY HAD told me to expect that. I shook as if I had a chill, but that occurred inside all the winter clothes, so I didn't think Cath noticed the shudder. On the outside, all Cath saw was what I had wanted her to see—an easygoing, healthy-looking face, and a strong, resonant voice that said, "Huh? I'm not sure I heard you. Say again?" I had spoken as evenly as I could, to make it look like her words produced no stir whatso-ever. It was like a nightmare, a bad "pretend," as Andy used to say. For a minute, I almost got the giggles, and then, as a feeling over all the other feelings, I felt disgrace.

"Joel, don't say anything. Just listen." Her voice was un-steady. "Ted told me. He thought you had said something to me, but you hadn't." Cath looked up pleadingly. "As cruel as this sounds, now that he's gone, I'm relieved." She caught a breath. "He said you couldn't take it any longer, that way of life, or whatever, and . . . well, that you . . . needed . . . loved . . . me . . .   Look. Just go. He's gone, it's over, and this is for the two of you. I have no place there. I want no place there." She took a deep breath and then another while we looked at each other.

Maybe I could fake it, I thought. Maybe I could squirm out of the whole thing. Maybe it was make-believe. *This is the story of a friend—a friend told me*—I could have tried a lie, but I knew there wasn't the tiniest avenue of escape. "Why did you wait until now?" I asked her, and in two seconds, all the years were all out in front of us.

"I'm not sure," she answered. A fat man, puffing and heav-

ing, kicked a vending machine—his coin must have stuck—
and we stared at him. Then we turned to each other again.
"Joel, I'm going back to the car. The boys' bravery will hold
only so long." She offered her cheek.

I bent my head down and kissed her, but she broke away.
She moved down the corridor, and I hurried to catch up with
her.

"Catherine? Cath?"

She turned around, her face impassive.

"Why are you telling me this in a public place?" I finally
asked. She didn't know what to do with her hands, like someone trying to juggle six packages at once. She seemed to be
shaking. "So the words will get lost in the crowd. Corny answer, isn't it?"

"It's okay, Catherine. Everything is fine."

"I know that," she said. She pulled back and smiled, Junior
League style, kissed my cheek and walked down the concourse,
all with a show of great civility.

3

CANCELING THE trip had crossed my mind. I didn't because the boys would have never figured out why I had done it, and of equal importance, I had the feeling Cath wanted me away. Following Cath down the concourse for at least fifty feet or so had also crossed my mind, but I didn't do that either because I had nothing to say. I could have called from the hotel in New York as well, and that was one more thing I didn't do.

Instead, when I arrived, I went right to bed and tried to fall asleep, but every noise seemed to be coming through an amplifier and six sets of speakers. First, a toilet went whoosh two floors away, then a truck went by below, straining in low gear. In New York, dark was never dark; there always seemed to be a gray kind of light in the sky, and some of the halo seeped into the hotel room through the draperies. Then the noises started again. The wind banged the shade hard against the open window, and the sudden crack made me jump. It was too close, too intimate, and I felt it inside my chest, and then the whole scene at the airport returned. I closed my eyes as tightly as I could, like a kid trying to make a bad dream go away, but it didn't work. Every crevice and curve of the ceiling looked as if it were swaying three inches above my head.

Before risking sleep again, I thought it might make sense to sit up for a while. I pictured Cath, alone in the sunroom that night. It would be quiet and only the pin spots which shined on the paintings would be on. She would have sprawled out in the red chair under the oil we had lent once to a museum and she would think about herself and me, her husband. She had married an outcast, she would think. But she would be wrong. If I had wanted to be an outcast, I could have been, but with her, I had become a consummate insider. I turned off my light and tried to fall asleep again.

It would have been easy to plead shipwreck and complain about what a bad night it was for me. Every time I was tempted to seek sympathy from anyone I imagined, I cut off the search and tried to think of Cath instead. While I sat there, in the dark, I felt tears in my eyes. That had not happened even during the worst of the Vietnam War when it was either leave Cath or do what? if my number was drawn.

Her cousin Richard had suspected. I knew he did. He was just finishing Columbia, and some guy Ted had known had gone to bed with him. Ted had told me. I had disregarded the story because Ted flashed the news just after he knew Cath and I were going to be married. I was cautious anyway. At my stag dinner a week before the wedding, Richard made it a point to introduce himself. As we shook hands, he looked longer into my eyes than he had to. The signal was given, and I knew the story was true. I never said anything to him, obviously, and to my knowledge, he had said nothing to Cath. I hadn't thought those thoughts in sixteen years.

* * *

THE NEXT morning when I woke up, it dawned on me that I didn't know the time of the memorial service. The phone rang several times at Temple Isaiah. Finally, a man with a thick Yiddish accent answered it.

"What time? Wait a minute, I don't know. I'll look it up. You'll hold on?"

"Thank you, I'll hold on." I could hear papers being shuffled in the background.

"You're a friend?" the man asked as he came back on the line.

"I was his roommate in law school," I answered.

"For that long you were a friend."

"Yes, for that long."

"The service will be at ten o'clock. In the upstairs—the fancy shul. Not in the downstairs. That's not big enough. You hear me?" he shouted. "Ten o'clock?" I looked in the mirror to see what I looked like with tears in my eyes.

All the memories I had fought so long to exclude returned, but not in the clear, to use one of Cath's favorite expressions (in the *clear* . . . let's be *clear* about this . . . are you being *clear*?).

Like the army, the memories came to me by the numbers.

Memory number one took place in Jimmy's Harborside Restaurant on the Boston waterfront. We had taken the subway from Harvard Square to Park Street Under, and then a cab to Jimmy's. There were seven of us: Ted and me and Cath and four other law school classmates. We often went out to dinner as a group, thinking of it as cook's night out. It was the night at Jimmy's that the soft-shell crabs from the Maryland shore (Cath was from Maryland) attacked me and the time when Cath came back to Brattle Street to stay with me.

Memory number two: My first memory was wrong. Ted wasn't with us, and the Jimmy's Harborside incident happened in our third year, not our first, six months before Cath and I were married.

Memory number three: At the beginning of law school, I knew no one and I had no idea who Ted was when he was assigned as my roommate. New York had been last on my geographical preference list, but Harvard housing handed him to me. He was from Sands Point, Long Island, and when I first went east, I had no idea how wealthy a suburb that was. I had written a letter to my unknown roommate-to-be and received an invitation to stop at his home (estate would be more like it) on the way to Cambridge. I met his mother first (a charmer), then his father (a tycoon). His godfather was then a U.S. senator.

Memory number four: I couldn't remember anymore when I slept with Ted for the first time. Things like that are usually fixed in one's mind, but I remembered more about how I felt afterward (guiltless) than what led up to it or how I felt while we were together in bed. As far as guys were concerned, however, it wasn't the first time, but just about. I had thought long and hard about what I was getting myself into. Ted was no lark. I wasn't drunk and I liked him one hell of a lot. I didn't know by sleeping with him if I was a confirmed anything. A lot of guys tried it then. He was there, and we wanted each other, and that's what it was all about that night. The next morning, all I could think about as we walked out of our room was that everyone knew. If I had misgivings about anything physical we did together, I suppressed them. Nothing was forever when you were twenty-two. He showed so many signs of being happy; that was the attraction.

Memory number five: An hour after I had eaten my first soft-shell crab, I excused myself from the table and threw up. Cath felt terrible, as if everything grown in Maryland or near its shores were her responsibility. Pasty-faced and a little weak,

I watched them eat dessert and eventually, thank God, we all went back to Cambridge. The rest of the eating club left us at Harvard Square, but Cath insisted on sticking with me, and we walked home, me leaning on her more than I liked to admit.

We climbed out of the subway exit, past Nini's fruit stand, and walked very slowly up Boylston Street to the point where it curved into Brattle. By the time we passed the movie theater two blocks down, the air and cars whizzing around Harvard Square had revived me, and I started to walk on my own. Cath's dorm was a block west of our apartment, but Cath came upstairs with me, having decided that hot tea would be just the ticket for both of us. She went into the kitchen, which, of course, she knew well, and I went into the bedroom and took off my tie and hung up my jacket. I lay down on the bed, and when I woke up in the morning, Cath was next to me. I guess that's what gave me the idea.

Sixth and most important memory: The idea was that I could be married, have kids, and more than a collection of men who would roll in and out of my life from time to time, which was the extent of my worry then. When I thought of that particular future, which I tried not to do in those days, I saw it, despite Ted's protestations, as sour.

I didn't tell Ted what I was thinking, although the idea crossed my mind. Ted and I were chess players, and he was up more than most on the history and theory of it. He had books on the subject and had learned all about elegant, exquisite, brilliant chess, the use of pawns in a press, and the classic maneuver of Philidor's defense: the sacrifice, in three successive moves, of a pawn, two rooks, and later a queen, to win the game. I had to keep the possibility, the thrill of Cath, to myself. Keeping her private brought her closer to me. Cath made me remember that I had choices. I didn't want to have

lunch with her twenty years later—Cath married, me alone—
and tell her in the corner of a fine restaurant that not being
with her was the most important mistake of my life. From
then on, I could not prevent myself from seeing Cath, and
whenever I was not able to be with her, I thought of her as
life itself.

I WALKED past the brownstones on Seventy-fifth Street, toward Temple Isaiah. It was nine-thirty in the morning, and
the laundry and hardware delivery trucks were already double-
parked. I thought of the fears Cath must have endured over
the years because we had never had this out on the table. The
law wouldn't hold me liable, but I held myself so. I knew I
had let her down, and I wondered when Ted told her, what
he had said, how she had felt, why she even stuck with me.
She hadn't stuck straight though, but I put those first two
winters out of my mind then. All I could imagine was Cath
listening to Ted, trying to digest what he was telling her. She
must have pictured what we did in bed and she must have
blinded herself to what she imagined. What passed between
them only Cath would know.

Perhaps Ted noticed none of her pain when he told her, but
down deep I doubted that. Neither Cath nor I let anyone see
the wheels turn, but he would have known. Of course, I could
have opened my mouth and said something, but I hadn't. I
crossed Seventy-fifth and Park.

MEMORY NUMBER seven was almost as important as six: Cath
had a tougher time of it than she let anyone know. True, her
middle name was the name of a town in Maryland. True, she
lived on a farm that had been in the family since the late

seventeen hundreds, but the fancy family was all a fake. They hadn't had any money for years. Her mother had no respect for her father and her father was sorry he had ever married. He would rather fuss in the fields than talk to his wife or either of his daughters. Love was sparse and education was hit or miss until Cath's high-school math teacher took over and encouraged her to go to Radcliffe where she spent most of her time learning precise English words as if they were numbers.

When Cath was in Cambridge, she was alone a lot of the time, and she couldn't get it through her head that she was beautiful in a way that counted. She was real. She had brown hair with a lot of red in it, occasionally combed, freckles, and green eyes, and skin that glowed. She wore blouses with long, puffed-up sleeves that she sewed herself from pastel cotton cloth that came from Mexico, and she wasn't ashamed to put on her glasses when she watched a movie or walked into a party that was held in a large room.

She had lived by herself in a minuscule two-room dormitory garret, and one room was sloppier than the other. I'd never seen anything like the collection of belts, large beads made into necklaces, earrings to match, cosmetic jars with lids off, hairbrushes, books, poetry magazines, weeks of unread *New York Times*es, records out of their jackets, more red-beaded bracelets, red to match the highlights of Catherine's hair, and assorted junk lying around. Sure, there were dressers of drawers, but they, too, were full; at least one, like the kitchen cabinet, was left ajar, with cloth, again my memory told me powder blue, visible from anywhere in the room. The closets were very small, no more than a foot deep, and they, too, were packed. This was Catherine in her natural state, eyes sparkling, with a bright mind that reached out, wearing a long dress with a high fluffy neckline accented with three or four necklaces of red beads, and bracelets that banged against each other when she walked.

She had brought her junk unaltered to our first apartment in Chicago. She hadn't been there ten minutes before her collected rubble was all over the place. I had some faint memory of standing in the middle of the living room watching her distribute a coat here, a jacket there, her records on the piano, a hair dryer on the floor, a clear plastic bag full of red-beaded necklaces in this place, another bag of something in that place, scooting off to the bedroom to deposit bags and bundles everywhere; so that at the end of ten minutes' worth of tossing stuff around, the place looked lived in. It was as if someone had lit small candles all over, and they flickered yellow and cream and the rooms were alive.

Catherine taught me how to touch, how to feel her body, and how to run my hand through her hair. She had taught me to respect myself. I had always envied my high-school friends who walked down the sidewalks near school with their arms hitched around their girlfriends' waists. I had never had a girlfriend, and if I had, I couldn't imagine putting my arm around her waist, especially in public.

Something in me wished our home was like our first apartment, full of open jars, beads, bottles, newspapers and nail polish. I hated the order. I wanted to walk into our bedroom and toss clothes all over the place and not care if they were ever picked up. I wanted Catherine's clothes to be on the floor in a frantic pile, the way they were when we ran our hands over each other, and when we would have tried, giggling like kids, to get my glasses out of the way so I could kiss her and so we could make love—the real thing.

I CROSSED the planted mall in the middle of Park Avenue, and called Cath from a street phone. It rang three rings before she answered. Traffic was sparse enough to hear inflections, and I heard her voice jump pitch when she said, "Joel!" I put my finger in the coin return to see if there was anything there, and, at the time, I thought it was an omen—my quarter had come back. "The kids just walked out the door, the water is boiling and the other phone is ringing. I'll get rid of whoever it is. Hang on." I could hear her smile and I could see her in the kitchen with her sleeves rolled up washing glasses. It was her voice crowded with life that made me feel so thankful. "Sure," was all I could manage to say. I was so happy I was ready to scale a lamppost like Gene Kelly. I felt as if she had come back from the dead.

She asked me if the hotel was still the same, how the weather was, and had the plane arrived on time. Then it was my turn.

Instead of responding in kind, I told her there were a lot of frivolous and insensitive things that I had done in my life, but by not telling her about Ted and me, not allowing her an informed choice, was an act of omission I'd be ashamed of all my life. I told her I would do anything she wanted me to do and that I loved her.

There were several seconds of silence, and then she spoke: "I'm sorry we said good-bye the way we did . . . at the airport . . . I mean—" I could tell she was fighting to hold back the tears.

"Cath, it was me, not you."

Then, without warning, she said, "We almost didn't make it, you know." She started to say more, but she stopped.

I imagined Cath holding the kitchen wall phone, the screen door I had not yet taken off banging against the house. She would be wearing her terry-cloth robe with the white belt twisted to hold it closed, but it would loosen, and then she would use her free hand to tie it back, hiding her body. She laughed, faking a recovery, and she said I probably needed a hug as much as she did. It was phony and I knew it, but the two of us were connected, at least by wires, and I felt better again.

"Joel, ignore what I said, please . . . about the winters."

"I can't even remember what you're talking about," I said. I realized I was thinking about Ted, not about her at all. "I wish you were here," I said, and the lie frightened me.

"On the street corner? In New York? The way I'm dressed?"

The traffic had picked up and a siren-blaring vehicle sped across the intersection at Seventy-third Street, and I missed some of what she was saying. It didn't make any difference; she was there, that's what counted.

"How are you dressed?"

"My hair's not combed. The boys just left; Juddy cleaned his plate. Andy didn't. He still won't eat the yellow." I heard her chuckle. "My shoes aren't on, and the only act of cleanliness I've undertaken today so far is a fast brushing of my teeth."

"I've had two breakfasts," I said.

"I know," she said, "you always go back to the buffet twice."

"I want to talk to you," I said, repeating myself.

"I suppose it's a mark of something to go to the covered dishes at the Carlyle buffet and know where the eggs are," she said.

4

THE LAST few months in law school were easy for third-year students because the grades didn't matter anymore. You either had a job or you didn't, and if you didn't, a last minute pickup in grade point average wouldn't put you in the big firms where Harvard Law School proclaimed you ought to be. Packing crates appeared outside of dorms and apartment windows, and we loaded up cars and rented vans with records, sneakers, books, goldfish bowls and other odd junk kids in their twenties called belongings.

In the late spring, the Cambridge Common was the place for baseball games, out-of-season touch football which Ted and I used to play, nannies with little kids, and old ladies wearing broad-brimmed hats and cataract glasses, and you could hear the sports chatter and feel sunlight over your shoulder. Some studying went on, more as exams came closer, but for Ted and me there was no ball playing and those last few months were a mess.

I don't know how many times Ted and I went over the same

ground: I didn't want any more of the physical side of our relationship but he didn't want that to end. As corny as it sounded, I wanted us to be friends.

The first night after I told him was also the first night I had slept in my own bed in close to six months when he had the flu. When I went to sleep, I had great thoughts of Ted being our kid's godfather, but I woke up in the middle of the night sweating and afraid. When I finally realized that I hadn't died, which is what happened in the dream, I looked across the room and saw Ted sleeping soundly, and once again I felt enormous relief because he was still with me in the way I wanted him near, but that didn't last very long.

His anger grew as the days went by. He skipped meals with me, and for three consecutive nights during the week after I told him, he didn't come home at all. When two o'clock in the morning came around and the bars had closed and he wasn't home, I knew what was going on. Nothing like that had happened between us ever before. I knew it was supposed to be a common occurrence, promiscuity and all that, but it wasn't our set of rules. I lay awake trying to figure out how I was supposed to feel, and the truth was that I didn't feel anything at all.

By Sunday, which was a week after the big announcement, I walked in before dawn after staying practically all night with Cath. She didn't want me to eat breakfast at her dorm, and I agreed and had left for the apartment. I put my coat in the closet, knowing that Ted sat in the darkened living room watching me. I felt him come up behind me, expecting that he was going to hug me. He didn't do that. Instead, he spun me around, stared into my eyes for just a fraction of a second, as if to make sure that it was me and not a case of mistaken identity, and then he grabbed me by the shoulders and slammed me into the wall. He stepped back and glared at me, the deepest anger I can ever remember seeing sunk in his eyes. He didn't say a word. He put on his jacket and left.

I saw him again at eight or nine that morning, and he looked like death took a holiday. He walked into our bedroom, woke me up and sat on the edge of my bed. "I've been letting people fuck me." I didn't dare move or say a word. His mouth was slack and he turned to look out of the window. "It didn't do any good." As he spoke, he swung his head toward me and I felt his forehead against mine. Then he stood up, and looked around the room as if he were searching for something, and I realized I was in his bed. His gaze fell on my bed and he went over to it and fell asleep without another word, wearing all of his clothes.

Neither of us woke up until late afternoon. He got out of bed first, undressed and showered, all in the bathroom. When he came out, I went in, closed the door and ran the water. I made the shower extra long, thinking that if he wanted time to leave without confronting me, he could. But he was there, seated on the sofa, one foot on the table, calmly reading the Sunday *Times* when I came out.

We had coffee together, but didn't talk much. He asked me if I would have dinner with him, and I told him, without enough hesitation, probably, that I couldn't. What little life there was left went out of him. I quickly told him Cath had set something up with a friend of hers who had been married over spring break, and we were invited to the newlyweds' apartment. It was exactly the wrong thing to say. He muttered that it was okay, but he looked terrible. I realized I was isolating him. I wanted to call Cath and cancel dinner or say something more to him, but I was afraid, so I did nothing. I left at six, I had to, and he just sat there, as if he had been anchored to the same place for the entire afternoon.

The first three days of the next week saw the anger escalate

again, not only on Ted's part, but on mine as well, culminat-
ing with me yelling at him and asking him what the fuck was
so important about sex, demanding to know if that was the
main thing he wanted from me, and goddamn it, what the hell
was so fucking wrong with a friendship? At that point, he said
he was going out for a walk, that he'd be back in an hour.

That was on a hot Wednesday afternoon in late May, two
weeks before he left for New York. An hour or so later, he
returned from his walk. The windows in the bay window of
our bedroom were open, but the shades were pulled down because the sun hit the room directly from the west. There were
packing boxes all over, surrounding our beds. The room was an
obstacle course. Ted lay back on his bed in his cutoffs, his
back against the headboard, watching me as I finished packing, his legs stretched out across the sheet.

"You don't understand sex at all, do you?" he said. His voice
was dark.

"I do my best," I said, stuffing a few more books into a
carton.

"Sex is a way you tell someone you love them," he said.

"I know that."

"So don't ever accuse me of using you for sex unless you
understand what else there is of me that goes along with it."

I folded the ends of a box in on each other, and unwound
from a squatting position. Standing up, I wiped the sweat off
my face with my sleeve. Ted was flushed with anger.

"I know what goes along with you," I said.

"Do you?" He took a step toward me and I backed up, suddenly afraid of him. "You want raw sex?" he said. "You think
that's the ball game?" His voice became metallic, almost with
a cruel edge. He stood up and pushed his hand into my chest.

"What in the hell are you doing?"

"Anything I want." He gave me a push. "It's our bedroom.

If I want to stand right on top of you, I will." Another push.
"I don't really need this shirt. I don't really need this either."
He was inches away from me as he took his clothes off. I
froze. "How about it, big guy?"

"Jesus Christ! Are you nuts?"

"Come on. We'll get it on."

"I'm leaving."

"Why? Got a hard-on you don't want your girlfriend to
know about?"

"Ted, get away from me." I stumbled backward over a box
and ended up with my back to the wall, Ted flush against me.

"I thought so."

"Ted, please—"

"—No, Buddy. You, please. Touch me. Help yourself."

"I don't want to. Just let me go!" I jumped over two boxes.

"Still got that hard-on, huh?" I pulled away from him,
scared to death.

"I get this way with Catherine too," I pleaded.

"Is that an apology or an announcement?"

"Will you put your clothes on now, please?" He wore no
underwear.

"No."

"I'm not going to do anything, Ted," I said, determined.
"I'm telling you. Not anymore."

"We're going to bed, Buddy. We're going to make it. We
can do anything we want. We can make our own rules." He
pushed me, and I fell back on the bed. He was on top of me.

"No!" I rolled over, throwing him off. "I'm not going to
lose the life I want." I shouted so loud my throat hurt.

He grabbed my leg, and I kicked him hard, to be free.

"You can do both," he said, almost begging. His eyes were
vacant, and he held his chest where I had kicked him.

"No, I can't!" I jumped off the bed, and squeezed past two

packing cases until I found an empty piece of the floor I could stand on. Then I saw his face. God, I hurt him. I turned away from him so he wouldn't see my eyes. I heard clothes. First his cutoffs went back on, then his shirt. We didn't look at each other.

"I'm your lover," he said, trying to catch his breath. He stood at the edge of the bed, breathing heavily, his hand still holding his chest. "I know you hate that word, but you're wrong. It's a beautiful word. It means I love you. And that you love me. You know, Buddy, you'll always love me."

I looked at Ted and saw him damaged. "I know," I said. My voice faded, my shoulders collapsed, and I closed my eyes, feeling them almost decay in my skull. I sat down on the edge of the bed next to him. "Please help me," I said to him. "Please. I don't know who else to turn to."

He raised his arm and held it above my shoulder, looking for permission before he let it fall and touch my body. I felt his arm close around me. "What is it you want?" he asked. His voice became tender, and I knew, if it never happened again, that once someone remarkable loved me.

"Cath isn't the only one. I love you too."

"What do you want me to do?"

"I won't have any chance if—if I'm still with you." It came from so far inside. I don't know how I said that to him, but I did. He was silent for a while.

"Am I more of a threat to you than picking up some guy for a fast one if things don't work out?"

"Yes, you are."

"Why?" he asked.

"Because something like that won't mean anything." I swallowed hard. "You will."

He stood up and walked around the room several times, rubbing his breastbone. He stopped circling and sat down next to me. "Thanks for talking," he said. "I think you've taken the anger away." He smiled and it was the first time I had seen him smile in almost a month. "I love you and I want the best for you." He hung his head, and then he looked up.

"Can I hug you, please?" I asked.

"Always," he said.

"Old men cry," Ted said, "when they think life is almost over—it's expected, but it's hard for a young man to let go." I looked up at him. "At our age," he said, "we think it's our manhood rolling down our face if we cry, but it's not. We're not losing anything."

WE WALKED down to the Charles River together. We never touched each other in public, even in those rave times when we first met, but I felt free to poke his elbow or his shoulder whenever I felt like it that day. We joked and laughed and ate hot dogs on the bridge next to the boathouse leading into Harvard Square. I thought we had passed the crisis point, but at night, when it came time to go to sleep in my own bed, I just couldn't hack it; I wanted to be next to him.

I had to go out—I just had to.

"I NEVER thought I'd see you in this seedy bar." It was Jerry Atkins, one of our classmates who was a member of the fraternity.

"Why the fuck not?" I answered. The place was a dark storefront. It smelled like a urinal, but I knew that before I walked in.

"Where's Ted?" Jerry looked sober that night, although he could really tie one on when he wanted to. He had tried a mustache, but it wouldn't grow. He touched my arm, but then took his hand away.

"At Brattle Street. I just left him."

He looked at his watch. "It's the middle of the night. How come you're here?"

"That's a dumb question." We wore the uniform: Levi's, polo shirt, penny loafers. The smoke was brutal, and I felt scum all over my skin.

"Sorry," he said, turning around.

"Jerry," I suddenly felt desperate, "don't walk away."

"These kinds of bars," he said, "aren't for conversation. I'll let you cruise." He raised one eyebrow and leered. "Rumor has it you're going to marry your cook."

"Yes, rumor is right."

"So why are you here?" I looked through the hard brown room that all of a sudden seemed like a tunnel. I looked at the herds of young men standing under black steam pipes that hung from the ceilings, and I decided to tell him precisely why I was there. "To get fucked," I told him.

"That's blunt."

"Why not? One bed, two beds. Do it. Get it done to you. Boys. Girls. Who gives a fuck? Want to fuck me?"

"You're drunk."

"Drunk? Me? I don't even know what drunk is. Oh, yeah. I was drunk once. Ted pulled me out of the middle of the Mass Turnpike after the tax exam. Now that's drunk! This is zip. Okay, down to business. Where can a guy get a good fuck around here? You know, one last night out with the boys?"

He winced. "Go home," he said to me, and Jerry touched my shoulder again.

"I don't care. Anyone will do." I held my fifth beer in one hand and swept my free arm in a broad arc way out to one side, hitting a blond kid in the shoulder. He turned around and smiled at me, looking for a long time.

"Go home," Jerry said to me.

"Just a little drunk." I looked back at the blond kid. "So

what." I leaned against the filthy wall. "Makes it easier, they tell me. Look, there're six faggots in the law school I know of." Jerry hated that word, but I used it anyway. "We've got to stick together. So, if one of us wants to get fucked, the other has got to do it. Right? Right, Jerry?"

"Wrong. Go home."

"You're missing a bet, Jer. This could be the last time for me. And I could be pretty good. A real hot number."

"You're getting yourself into a real box."

"That's very funny. My future wife would appreciate the double entendre. Did I slur that? She's very bright, you know. You're not going to take me home, are you?"

"No, I'm not, but I'll walk you back to your place." We looked at each other for a silent moment. The air was hot and I felt beaten. I wheeled around on the barstool one more time (being dizzy wouldn't hurt, I figured), and then I told Jerry, "I can't go there."

"Why?"

"Because I can't sleep with Ted anymore. I won't do anything with him anymore. Jerry, I can't." Jerry took hold of my arm, and I straightened up. The blond kid held no interest for me anymore.

"Why don't you call Catherine?"

"Ted's been talking to you, hasn't he?" I didn't feel high anymore either.

"No, but everybody knows what you're doing."

"I want another drink," I said.

"No, you don't."

"Yes, I do. And I want a good fuck. If you won't cooperate, big fucking deal. I don't care. Anybody will do." I said it, but I didn't mean it.

* * *

THE LIGHTS in the apartment on Brattle were fuzzy, my bed felt lumpy, and Ted stood over me, dulled and out of focus. "How did I get here?" It hurt to talk.

"Jerry dumped you on the doorstep an hour or so ago." His arms were folded over his chest, and he looked down at me, and then stared at the floor.

"What time is it? My God," I blurted out, "we'll miss federal courts."

"Jerry will take notes for us."

"But that's Henry Hart. You idolize him."

"I'll get you some coffee," he said. "Imagine, offering your body to a law student. They're all diseased, you know." He smiled. He thought he had me back.

I sat up, looked at Ted, and I suddenly felt I could never lose him.

"If you're not sure, just wait," he said. He sounded confident. "You'll do yourselves a favor. Both of you."

"I can't wait. I can't. It won't happen again."

"God damn it, Buddy," he burst out, "you blast out of here at three in the morning. You announce to the world you're out to get fucked. You stagger back at the crack of dawn, and in a matter of weeks you're off to get married. You don't need advice. You need a good doctor."

"No, I don't. I know exactly what I'm doing."

"If you think that going out in the middle of the night and getting yourself drunk so you can do what you never liked to do—playing my game—is going to turn you off guys, you're wrong," he said. "It's like riding a bicycle. Once you learn, you never forget."

"Why are you poisoning me!"

"Because . . . because . . . ," he stared at me, "because I don't know." He looked at the floor. "I don't have all the answers either."

"Ted . . ." I felt myself muttering a prayer. "I want a home, not an apartment. I want a family."

"I want a home, too," he said, "with you." Tears started to fill his eyes. He stopped talking and held the side of his forehead. "Hey, wait. I won't start that again. Let's not get angry. If we do, we'll lose each other for sure." He tried to smile. "Deal?"

"Deal," I answered.

5

MORE MEMORIES (I lost count): It was late May and we were still in Cambridge. Ted would no longer talk to me and he had started to spend all his time at the *Law Review*. He came home from Gannett House only to sleep and always in his own bed. The instant his exam schedule ended, he took off for New York as if he were shot out of a cannon.

After he left, Cath had more or less moved in, and it had taken us the better part of a week to dismantle my half of the apartment. It was the third day of packing. It was hot and sticky, the windows were open, and it was about to be the end of Brattle Street for all three of us. The radio was tuned to WHRB (Harvard had a female announcer even then), and Cath sat on a chair with one foot propped on a packing box, drinking an Orange Fanta. I had just finished stacking what seemed like ten dozen four-hundred-pound crates that were to follow us to Chicago after graduation. She waited for the break between the second and last movement of whatever Mozart they were playing, and then she said, "Ted isn't coming to our wedding."

I sat down, out of breath, and straddled the bench in front of the upright piano Ted and I had painted yellow. "How do you know?" I asked.

"He called while you were in the basement," she said. "He said that the flights to Europe were jammed, and his dad came up with a youth fare seat the day before the wedding and he just had to take it. Elaborate excuse, isn't it?"

"He'll have himself a first-class seat before the plane leaves the runway," I said. She offered me some of her pop, and I shook my head. I decided to sound as calm as I could. "Cath, I don't know that there's anything I can do." I felt like I was living on my nerves and I shut my mouth to keep from talking like a fool.

"Joel, he's your best friend."

"I need more rope." I started to escape through the hallway and reflected on unintentional gallows humor.

She followed. "Will you call him?"

"I'll think about it," I said.

"I'll be glad to give him a call," she said. "Would you mind?" she asked. She pushed the pop bottle at me. "Want some?"

"What good is that going to do? You just talked to him."

"Do you still want him to stand up for you?"

"I think that's up to him."

Cath turned and walked back to the living room, and this time I followed. "Joel, why isn't he coming? What is this all about? Did he ever have an interest in me?" she asked. "Is that what's going on here?"

"Maybe that's it," I said, for the sake of play.

"But how could that be?" She would make a good lawyer's wife, I thought, always able to argue the other side.

"Let me handle this," I said. "I'll get him to come."

"You look very relaxed about this whole thing." She turned

around and looked straight at me, and then at my arm stretched across the chair next to me.

"Why shouldn't I be relaxed? I'll take care of it." Cath sat down next to me, and I put my free arm around her.

"Hello, Mrs. Stackler. This is Buddy."

"Buddy, how nice to hear your voice."

"Nice to hear yours."

"We received the invitation this morning. You couldn't have kept us away. The farm is just outside Annapolis, isn't it?"

"Yes, it is."

"Do you think we can make it down there and back in a day?"

"Oh, don't do that," I said. "You can stay overnight in Annapolis. That way you can have a good time and stay late. Don't run off. Let me make the reservations for you."

"Catherine must be a lovely girl. We only hope Ted finds someone who makes him as happy as Catherine is making you."

I didn't know what to say, but I spoke before my throat closed. "I hope so, too." I took a breath. "Is he there?" I asked.

"Yes, he is. I'll call him." She was always so pleasant to me, I thought. I waited, and then she came back on the line. "I'm sorry, Joel." She sounded uncomfortable. "He's tied up. He says he'll call you back."

"I'm going to be hard to reach later. We're moving, you know. I'll hang on. Will you tell him I'll wait?"

"I don't know how long it will be," she said.

"That's all right. I'll be glad to wait." I paced back and forth, holding the phone to my ear, feeling anxious and uncertain.

"Yes, Buddy, what is it?" He usually sounded good-natured and glad to be where he was, even reciting a dull property case in Casner's class, but that day, over the phone, his voice came across ice-cold. "I'm busy right now," he announced.

"You're really putting me on the spot."

I heard static on the outdoor extension cord. He must have been in the backyard, looking across the water. He liked to sit out there, alone, sprawled in a lawn chair, his feet up, shoes off, in cutoffs if the weather was warm enough, wearing a button-down shirt, with sleeves rolled up past his elbows.

"By doing what?"

"By not coming to the wedding."

"How can you expect me to come?" he asked, the anger out front where anyone could see it.

"I want you to be there," I said. Cath had gone to the basement to collect more junk. I could never have talked to Ted like that if she were within hearing.

"Why?"

"Because you're my best friend."

"Too glib. Why else?" he demanded. "To cover your tracks? Is that the game?" I heard a motorboat go by.

"Yes, Ted. That's right. Absolutely right. To cover my tracks. Any feeling I ever had for you is gone. You're just a pawn to me now. Come to my wedding and help me cover my tracks. And do me a favor, Ted. When you take the knife out, don't twist it."

"I'll think about it."

"Think about what? Twisting the knife or coming to my wedding?"

"Both." Ted would have taken his sunglasses off, jammed them into his shirt pocket and rolled his left sleeve up and down twice by then.

"You know, Cath asked me to call you, too," I said.

"God damn it!" he shouted suddenly. "How much pretense

do you want me to go through? Whatever games you play with yourself are up to you. Whatever games you play with Catherine are between the two of you. But when I'm involved, no deal! Why don't you just tell her?"

"Ted, please, your mother! She'll hear you."

"What if she does?" All at once, he stopped yelling. It sounded like he was cupping his hand over the mouthpiece. "Why don't you just tell Cath? Look, she's no dummy. She can understand that people shift: boys one week, girls the next. She knows people can move back and forth like that all their lives." Then he stopped a moment. "I suppose she can also understand that the shifting stops. I can understand all of that. Don't you think she can?"

"Of course, she can." I found myself whispering. "I just don't want to do it that way," I said.

"That's your privilege. But don't ask indulgences from me," he said softly.

"Will you come?"

"I don't know. I'll think about it."

"I have no right to ask you, but please do."

"That's right. You have no right."

"Call me, Ted, please, one way or the other."

"I will." And he hung up.

But for a justice of the Maryland Supreme Court instead of an Episcopal priest, our wedding was classical. We stood under a large oak on her family's farm, and the bridesmaids walked out of the front door of the gray frame house, down the path and stood on the left side of the old tree. I waited on the right side of it, fingering the bark, and Ted stood next to me. He gave me the ring to give to Cath, and I wanted him to stay, but he didn't. He looked away, and as soon as he could and still be polite, he left. I never saw him after that.

6

———————— THROUGH THE years, Cath had dropped the subject of Ted, and in return, as part of a silent trade-off, I had dropped the subject of her skipping out on me. It had happened not once, but twice, during the first two winters we were married.

The first time she gave the news to me over the phone. I was in New York on my own, without a partner supervising me. It was quite an honor for a first-year associate, and I called to say I would be stuck there for another day. I knew I sounded self-important, but not so much so that I lost the ability to listen. Something in her voice told me it didn't matter if I got stuck there for two years. I asked her if everything was okay. She hesitated, and I could hear that it wasn't. Who was she with that year? Greg. That's who. Every time I thought of it, I became angry and jealous all over again.

"But, Cath, I've only been out of town five days," I said. "Less than a week! Who is this guy?"

"We'll talk about it when you get home," she responded calmly, totally in control.

"I can't get home any more tonight. The last plane left."

"I don't want to talk about it over the phone," she said.

"Cath. We just got married last June! I don't believe it."

"I'll be at home when you get here."

"Well, don't do me any favors."

"All right, I won't."

"No, Cath, I didn't mean that." The panic returned. "Whatever you want. I'll be home in the morning. I'll pick you up at work." By that point, I was begging.

"Joel, that's foolish." I could hear the triumph in her voice. "We'll talk in the evening when we're both home." She had become totally self-satisfied.

That Friday night, I told her that I loved her, that I wanted to spend my life with her, that I was never so happy as when I was with her. I told her I wanted her to tell Greg she'd never see him again. She looked at me, sort of puzzled, as I thought back on it, and all she said was, "If you like." That's all: "If you like." She asked me to leave so she could call Greg in private. Hell, no, was my response. She liked the assertiveness, I supposed, and she smiled at me, but she went out to make the call anyway.

She came back in fifteen minutes looking ashen, and said she had called him. I wanted to hug her, but she moved away from me. She said she had to go shopping, that she knew I'd like to tag along, but she'd prefer to be by herself. I had never been called a "tagalong" before and I had thought about that while she was out. I realized that I hated shopping but that I went just to be with her, to avoid being alone in the apartment on Saturday afternoons. It was the same thing going down to the laundry room, doing the wash together, being with her when she did it, holding the soap and feeding quarters to the dryer.

Cath had been gone about two hours and I had begun to worry. I spent a lot of time wondering what would happen if

she left, but every time I thought about who or what I would
sleep with if she left me, I made my thoughts divert and double
back to Cath. Cath returned, not alone, but with Corinthia
Maxwell (the name astonished me), who had told Cath about
the Junior League. She had a fake patrician accent, and loved
a great story, but the punch line had to be in French. I didn't
like her. Cath was excited but wondered if the league would
ever accept her, and if she did get in, she worried about
whether she could do it and still keep her job at the newspaper. Corinthia suggested she apply and told us a few weeks
later that she had fixed it.

The first winter, I managed to keep Catherine's absence a
secret from the firm. I was ready with a lot of excuses. She was
on a story, or in Maryland or wherever. Anyway, her timing
was good. She was gone only a few weeks and we ironed the
whole thing out in time for the spring dinner dance.

John, she told me; that was his name the second year. It
was almost like an anniversary, starting around Christmas and
going right through New Year's, her second public statement.
It was the second New Year's Eve I spent alone. He lasted
four months, that one, and it felt like forever. Cath was doing
political surveys for the *Tribune* then. She was a star at work.
She had succeeded in getting into the Junior League. She
seemed so much happier, so when something went wrong, it
was a blind-side hit.

That whole winter when she was away was a slow blur for
me. I'd get up at five in the morning and stare at the ceiling.
The anger would roar through my body and I would slam my
fist into her pillow. She had left on a Tuesday and in ten days,
I had lost about ten pounds. Too skinny, Buddy, too skinny,
Dad used to say. The second time, my folks knew; there was
no way to hide it. They thought she was nuts and good rid-
dance—that I was even nuttier than she was to try and hang
on. They worried about me.

I didn't see Cath all winter, but I imagined I saw her every-where. Unconsciously, I called other women by her name. I thought about her and talked about her all the time and my friends looked at me sadly. I was afraid to call her, sure she would hang up. An idea: If she had my thoughts in writing, she could read them and review the ideas more than once; it would give me a second chance in case anything got lost in a single hearing, so I wrote a letter. End of idea: I never mailed it. If I sent the letter, would John tear it up? If she got it, would she read it? My friends told me to leave her be. There was no choice; that was all I could do.

I had done my best to keep up appearances and stick to my work. I had billed more hours than almost any associate at Sydell & Ingram. After all, I had nothing else to do.

"Everything going well, Joel?" I was in Mr. Ingram's office on a Friday afternoon in February. I was "Joel" at the office too. That was my reentry name. Good-bye Buddy. It was too much a kid's name. Mr. Ingram liked me. Mr. Sydell had died the first month I was there, and Mr. Ingram had become the senior partner. He had white, wavy hair and eyebrows that never moved. I was the youngest associate getting assignments directly from him. He had a big, perfectly controlled voice, a rolling tone and a remarkable presence, and he could range from a whisper to a roar. He sounded like Richard Nixon. They said, as the years passed, I had begun to sound like him, which was fine with me, except the last person I wanted to hear myself compared to was Richard Nixon. Mr. Ingram told me ten times to call him Ken, but I kept calling him, "sir" be-cause that's what you did then.

"Yes, sir. Everything's fine."

"You and Catherine want to come out to the house and have dinner with Marge and me tomorrow?"

"I . . . I can't, sir." I turned to look out of the window. Mr. Ingram came over and stood next to me. His arm hovered over my shoulder. *God, don't touch me,* I thought. *Please, dear God, don't let me crack.*

"Joel, is everything really all right?" I kept looking away.

"No, sir. It's not." I moved to one side.

"I didn't think so." He lowered his arm and put his hand into his pocket.

"Well, maybe you'd like to come out for dinner by yourself?"

"How . . . how did you know?"

"Oh, I've been around awhile. Maybe you'd like to talk to our minister."

"No, thank you."

"You know, Joel, men have a way of understanding other men. Women are different. No matter how strong they appear, you still have to take care of them. Men and women live in different worlds. Ever have a close friend, Joel? Someone you could go hunting with? Go out in the country together. It would be good for you, Joel."

"Thank you."

"If you change your mind about dinner, you're always welcome."

"Thank you, sir."

Ted called that winter. My father must have called and told him what was going on. I was away from my desk when Ted phoned, and when I saw his name in the stack of messages that had come in, I closed the door and for the first time in I didn't know how long, the tears started silently. He would always be there, I knew that—he cared. I felt a fear and a prayer at the same time: I would go back to him. Ted would hug me. He would hold me. I stopped crying when I realized what I had thought. I panicked. I didn't return the call.

Ted called again two days later. I knew he would, and for a week I didn't trust myself to answer my phone. My secretary

shortstopped all the calls at work, and every time I saw the
button light up, I held my breath. I was battered and I didn't
want anyone to beat me up anymore. I stayed home every
night, but he didn't call me there. Neither did Catherine. The
truth was simple: I would have gone with either of them then.
Whoever called could have had Joel.

7

As I walked down Seventy-fifth to Temple Isaiah, I saw a school yard across the street, and kids playing baseball. "Hey, that's a chuckin', baby." "Let's see that ball." "Cream the fuckers." The sounds reminded me of the last spring in Cambridge. All that was missing were the little old ladies wearing cataract glasses watching the game and giggling, embarrassed at the ball players' patter, and Ted across the street in our apartment on Brattle.

"YOU CAN'T go in without putting on a tallis." A small man, probably seventy-five if he was a day, shook a finger at me and squinted. His knuckles were red, and he had to strain to see things far away. "There's a rack over there. You'll put one on," he ordered. He wore a white shirt buttoned at the collar but without a tie, and jacket and pants that were both brown, but didn't match. There were only the two of us in the rotunda of Temple Isaiah, and his words echoed across the marble. I told him I was sorry and I walked to one end of the large hall, put a skullcap on my head and took a blue and white prayer shawl from the rack and was about to put it around my shoulders.

"You can't do that without saying a prayer," he ordered. I must have looked helpless. "I'll say it for you," he said as he walked toward me. The room was cold and his voice reverberated again, bouncing off the conical ceiling high above our heads. I looked up and saw the traditional memorial plaques set in concentric circles layered above us, naming the dead. Tiny lamps were switched on next to each of them in anticipation of the memorial service, and together they made the rotunda glow with light.

The old man took the prayer shawl, held it extended between his outstretched arms and sang in a raw but clear tenor voice the Hebrew words woven in blue letters into the tallis. Then he stood on the tips of his toes and put the tallis around my shoulders. I closed my eyes and thanked him.

Rabbi Baruch was to conduct the service. I had met him only once. We had come down to New York when Ted's grandfather had died suddenly, but before we went out to Sands Point, Ted wanted to stop at the temple. I sat outside of the rabbi's study and fidgeted. Ted looked up to Jason Baruch almost more than anyone in the world. Even when Ted was a little boy, they called each other by their first names, and Jason always clamped his arm around Ted's shoulder when they said good-bye. I always wondered if Ted had told him about us, how we were living together and all that. I still censored the word, even in my own mind.

There were two huge staircases that connected the rotunda to the rest of the building. One staircase went upstairs to the large sanctuary and the other led to the school. I walked toward the classrooms to look at the pictures of the confirmation classes of the last thirty years that lined the corridor walls. Ted's pictures were in two or three places, and I wanted to see them again.

Ted at sixteen looked like Ted at twenty-one. He had the same sport coat, the dark brown tweed he wore with gray slacks and a red tie. He always wore a red tie. In the picture, his face was pale, without grain, and his eyes were blue and optimistic. When I first knew him, his eyes seemed to twinkle, amused with life. Ted lived with his eyes and his ears. He was tall, thin and privileged, and he had an innocent love of himself that was nowhere near narcissism. Even at sixteen he had a look of self-possession. He was not like a lot of people who had failed to form a face, but who instead adjusted the features to please an audience. Gray hair had just begun to sprout at twenty-four, and by then, the sizzle in his voice disappeared as did the daffy side of his smile. By then, the rigidity of adolescence had gone out of him; he was flexible, gentle, and he had an aura of strength about him. Even when we met, he knew how to hold everyone in a room by his stillness. He had it all, but he never hit you over the head with it. And yet, if you were close to him, he felt no shame in being the demonstrative kid who could hug you with all his heart. Like most of us, though, he never saw himself the way he was. For example, he described himself as having thick, ugly eyebrows, which, of course, wasn't true at all.

"Buddy?" I heard an unmistakable voice behind me.

"Yes?" The fluorescent lights buzzed overhead, and the corridor seemed narrower than it was a moment ago. Rabbi Baruch had come down the hall and stood beside me. His hair had turned almost white, but remained as curly as it had ever been, and when he stood with you in a small space, you had the sense of being crowded by a giant prophet in a Saville Row suit. We looked at Ted's picture together for a moment.

"Mr. Silverman told me a young man was here early." His

voice still boomed. "Of course, to Mr. Silverman, even I am a young man," he continued. I stared at him. "Do you recognize me?" he asked.

"Of course I do, Rabbi." His eyebrows still bounced as part of his greeting, and he threw his arm around my shoulder.

"Call me Jason. Come. Have a cup of coffee with me. Are you Buddy or Joel these days?"

"Joel," I answered. I glanced sideways at him and he winked.

His study was upstairs and it was lined with books, a sofa, chairs, a desk, and a hot plate on a stand behind the tropical fish tank.

"I didn't know you liked tropical fish," I said.

"I watch them spin stories," he said, "round and round, in and out. Biblical. Talmudic, almost. Joel, sit down. It's good to see you, even under these circumstances."

"I feel the same way." Somehow being with him brought Ted back to me.

"I'm sorry I wasn't downstairs to greet you." He glanced down at the floor as he spoke. "Not much of a welcome, is it?"

"I didn't know what time . . . sometime in the morning was all I knew."

"Mr. Silverman says you're a nice boy, but you should learn about talaysim." He lifted his eyebrows, and that movement alone said, "Nu?" I laughed. So did he. He was the Welcome-in-the-White-House Rabbi, a famous humanist and respected intellectual, but with more than a trace of stubbornness and a taste for exotic skullcaps. The one he had on looked like an Oriental rug.

"How do you like your coffee? It's instant," he said.

"Black is fine." There were five paperweights on his desk, each holding down a stack of printed material that probably never got read. I began to feel nervous. He sat across from me

in a brown leather armchair that went poof as he let his large
body sink into it. "Oy," he said, letting the word last two mu-
sical measures at least. "So, Joel, how are you?" All of a
sudden, he sounded like a Borscht Belt comedian. I remembered how he could imitate a stage immigrant brilliantly, out-
doing Mr. Silverman, whose wandering syntax was at least
real. "I'm fine," I said. He put his feet on a stack of magazines
on the coffee table, looking at me through eyes that appeared
to be half closed.

"And how is your family? Catherine? The boys? Andy and
Judd?" He pulled at the skin above his Adam's apple, but
otherwise, he didn't shift an ounce of his weight.

"They're fine, but—"

"—but how did I know their names?" he finished my question. "Right? Of course, right." He made himself sound like
Tevya from *Fiddler on the Roof.*

"Yeah," I managed to laugh, "that's the question."

"I'm glad Henry called you," he said evenly, and I said
nothing.

"I take it that Henry Stackler told you about my family,"
I said, trying to play what were beginning to feel like bitter
games.

"No, Joel." The Tevya rhythm vanished from his voice.
"Ted told me. He kept up with you, but never so that you
would know. When Ted, may he rest in peace—" The rabbi's
voice left him. He looked at me. Then he went on. "I suggested to Henry that he call the house and ask that you come
out." He paused again. "I did that because I need your help."

The book on his desk was *The Broken Heart.* Stuffed sideways in his bookshelf was a thin, brown corrugated box that
looked like it had held a large pizza.

"What kind of help do you want?" I asked.

He pulled his knees up to his chin with an agility that surprised me. Then, he put his shoes back on the tabletop. "Ted

passed away two nights ago." His voice faltered again, and he cleared his throat. "I knew of events in his life that no one else knew, except those who participated in them. I knew he lived with a young man whom he loved very much."

I looked at the fish tank because I didn't have the courage to look at anything else. Jason Baruch stared at me and I forced myself to meet his eyes. He bit the corner of his lip. "He had asked me several times before he passed away"—the rabbi blinked again—"may he rest in peace, to help him."

"Help him do what?" I didn't recognize my own voice.

"I never met the young man, but Ted wanted him not to be hidden. He wanted his parents to know. I know your question, Joel. Ted was—how old are you? You and Ted?"

"Thirty-nine."

"At thirty-nine," the rabbi continued, "men are not supposed to care what their parents think. Right, but not so right. I had lived through some of his escapades." He frowned disapprovingly. "I didn't like it, but I listened. Five years, for this, his friend—more than a fling. Now, that young man is being excluded."

I listened to him and grew cold.

"I have spoken to Marion and Henry twice—"

Oh, my God, was what I thought.

"—and I must talk with them again. It is a promise I made to Ted, that his lover be accepted." He put a curled hand over his mouth. "It's hard for them. I know. They've had no time. No time." Then he took it away. "I should never have made that promise."

"Why?" I asked.

"Why what?" he asked, the thought apparently having left him.

"Why should you have not made that promise?" I repeated the question.

"Leviticus, Joel, Leviticus: 'Thou shall not lie with man-

kind, as with womankind: it is an abomination.' " He looked
up at the ceiling and continued his recitation, first in Hebrew,
then in English: " 'If a man also lie with mankind, as he lieth
with a woman, both of them have committed an abomination: they shall surely be put to death; their blood shall be
upon them.' "

He looked at the fish tank and traced the flight of the fish
from across the room with his index finger. " '*Toevah*,' Joel,
'*Toevah*.' It means 'abomination.' " His finger followed a blue
and gold angelfish. Then he put his hand down and his palm
rested on his knee.

"Then why did you make that promise?" I asked.

"Because of Ted. I made him the same promise years ago.
For you."

I stood up, polished as steel, and offered my hand. "Rabbi,
you have a lot of work to do this morning and I had best be
going. Thank you for the coffee." He didn't move.

"Joel, I have never been known as a man who beats around
the bush."

"Yes, Rabbi. The burning bush."

"That's very clever."

"Rabbi. Good-bye."

"Joel, sit down. Are you denying your relationship with
Ted?"

"I don't have to admit or deny anything. Your references
are unnecessary and not helpful to anyone. Further I would
expect that you are bound by some priest-penitent rule of con-
fidentiality. Am I correct? And by the way, I prefer to stand,"
I said, giving him a hostile look.

"Yes, of course you are correct, but it is the penitent, the
person who tells the secret, not the priest who hears it, who
decides if it remains a secret. If the priest is released from his
duty by the penitent, or, instructed to act, he is not bound."

I sat down. "But isn't he bound by other considerations?" I asked.

"Of course, and it is those new rules that now apply. So you can relax."

"Look, Rabbi."

"—Jason!"

"Rabbi," I said, annoyed and frightened at the same time, "the only reason I am sticking around is to find out what it is you intend to do. I have a wife, and a family, and in addition to any admissions or denials that you may consider you have just heard, be assured that I will not tolerate any interference by you in any manner which is even slightly disruptive. Do I make myself clear?"

"You are overdoing it, Joel. I am saying nothing to others about you. Ted's statement to me, years ago, was, at best, hearsay."

"I'm glad you appreciate that."

The room became quiet, except for the air bubbling in the fish tank.

"Henry and Marion will be here shortly. You are a link to them."

"Rabbi," my voice left me for a minute. He was in a box. He had put himself there but still I felt for him. "I can't be in this room with you when they come here. You know that. If I were here, my complicity would be clear. I would be presenting a situation to them. I don't know anything about that situation. I would be presenting a person to them. I have no knowledge of that person. If I were here, it would only say something about me. I can't do that." I looked at him, and I knew he understood. The fish tank bubbled again. Perhaps we had a truce.

"Try to put yourself in my place," he said, still trying.

"I can't do that. It isn't my deal."

"Joel, this isn't anybody's deal." He looked at me squarely and I felt defeated.

"What is it you want to do?" I tried to understand him, but I couldn't. "What do you want of Ted's folks? Why are you insisting on handling this right now? What's wrong with two weeks from now?" I asked.

"If Ted's death," he could hardly say it, "passes without that young man's place in his life being clear, it will be wrong."

"*Why* will it be wrong? Why are you jamming all these people into a corner?" I repeated my question slowly, word by word, "What is it you want to do?"

"He will sit in the front row. He is family."

"Jesus Christ, you can't do that!"

"If He can help, I'll take His help too." Back to the Borscht Belt.

"Rabbi, with all due respect, you're being frivolous. You simply cannot plunk some kid down in the middle of the family row at a Jewish funeral and announce to the world what was going on, perhaps to the embarrassment and lifelong sorrow of all concerned."

"I can and I will. Ted would have wanted it."

"Would he? How much damage would he be willing to cause? And to whom? And to further what end? And to make who feel better? And if so, for how long?" I stood up. I walked around the room. Then I sat down again.

"I know Ted meant a lot to you," he said softly.

"Yes, he did." Jason Baruch quietly watched his fish again.

"What do you propose I do?" he asked me.

"I don't know. You're the one with the rituals," I said. He looked up.

"Joel, you wouldn't want it for you. I know that." His voice was quiet and his eyes went through me. "In your day, in

Ted's day, when you both were younger, things were hidden."
I hung my head and looked at his carpet. "Ted's idea of what
he wanted became clearer as he got older. Not all at once, but
gradually, the way changes that mean anything normally come
about." He looked at his fish, one chasing the tail of the other.
Then he looked back to me. "I know it will be hard, but Ted's
folks will get over it. I'll be with them. I'll do what I can. But
if I don't do this for Ted and his lover"—I shuddered at the
sound of the word—"a wound for life will be inflicted on
Ted, on his friend and on me."

"Why is it you want to sanctify what your own Bible says
is sacrilege?"

"Because 'rabbi' means teacher. Sometimes a rabbi has to
learn in order to teach." I stood up before he could see the
tears forming in my eyes. No wonder Ted loved him.

"Rabbi, please understand—" I couldn't finish.

"Joel, do what you can. You will see the time when you can
do what you will do. After all," and he smiled and turned into
Tevya again, ". . . chance favors a prepared mind. Right?"
He walked me to the door and put out his hand. "Now, down
the stairs before they arrive. And thank you."

"For what?" I asked.

"For what you did. You showed me something." He paused
for a moment as we stood on the top of the staircase leading
down to the rotunda, already beginning to hum with voices.
"If those on the inside can't help, those on the outside
should." He nodded his head, up and down, praying almost,
as he spoke. "And for that I thank you because it gives me
strength. Now, go."

8

THE TEMPLE rotunda was packed, and you could hear men mumbling prayers as they covered their shoulders with the blue and white talaysim. I signed my name in Ted's Book of Remembrance and followed the crowds moving upstairs to the large sanctuary. Stalling might have worked for a few more minutes, but I went in, deciding it was useless to put it off any longer. I heard the choir and saw Ted's casket at the same time, and the room seemed to go dark for a moment. The casket was closed, thank God, and it rested on a velvet-covered catafalque next to the rabbi's podium. I imagined seeing Ted through the wood, and I turned away, but I forced myself to look at the casket again. Behind it, Rabbi Baruch sat in a large thronelike chair. His palm rested on his forehead and his fingers fidgeted in his hair under what was now a brilliant white skullcap.

Halfway down the center aisle, I sensed how big the place was. The ceiling seemed miles up, and the choir loft seemed very far behind me. Up front, visible through the sea of skullcaps, I saw Ted's parents. Marion sat in the first seat on the aisle in the front row, and Henry was slumped next to her. A line of fifty or so people stood in the center aisle waiting to extend condolences to them, and I took my place at its end. The room had become noisy, and I felt it was indecent. In the middle of a funeral, people talked, waved hello to each other and seemed to forget why they had come. I didn't like it at all.

The line moved quickly and the front row came up almost too fast. Henry's and Marion's responses were warm, but they seemed rote and rehearsed, and they were always the same.

"Thank you for coming."

"Ted would have been glad you came."

"It was a heart attack. No one expected it."

"It was the middle of the night. He was alone in his apartment."

"Thank you for coming."

"Ted would have been glad you came."

Marion saw me, but it took a second for my face to register. Then, "Oh, Buddy—" Her eyes filled with tears, and she opened her arms. I bent down, and felt her shudder against my arm. A short, wordless sound of a child who was scared and helpless in the middle of the night came out of me. I looked at her and then the words just rolled out involuntarily: "I loved him too." She drew back and looked at me. I had done what I hadn't wanted to do.

I stood up, but her eyes followed me. Then Henry stood up, spun me around and hugged me. "Buddy, please, my son is gone." He wiped his eyes. "You were so important to him. Come home after it's over. Please."

Marion reached up to take Henry's hand, and they looked into each other's eyes for a long time. She forced a smile as she heard her husband say to me, "Come for Ted." I looked at Henry and managed to nod.

"Bud, your yarmulke fell off," he said. Henry picked up the white skullcap, which was just like the one my grandfather had given me when he, Dad and Uncle Mike fought with Mother and insisted that I be Bar Mitzvahed. I bent my head toward Henry, and as he replaced the white skullcap, he let his hand rest on my head as if he were blessing me.

The aisles were still crowded as I looked for a seat, and all at once, the noise got to me. I wanted to punch the gossiping women and yell out loud, "Have respect. This is not a canasta game." Then I remembered that was the same line my father used.

AT THE front of the sanctuary, Jason Baruch, big as a bear, stood up and started to move toward the lectern. In the front rows, those who were paying attention noticed his presence in the pulpit and started to say "shush." He took what appeared to be a picture out of an envelope and put it on the top of the lectern. He looked steadily at the audience, moving his eyes up and down each row, as if he were taking inventory. Some people continued to talk, but more and more, the congregation fell quiet. His eyes came to rest, and just then, somehow, that big burly man looked thin and trapped. He moved forward to the left of the lectern and walked down the stairs into the sanctuary. Given his bulk, he seemed to loom as he stopped at a row nearby. He looked to the person seated, staring ahead, in the fourth seat in from the aisle, and said, "Doug?"

"Yes?" It had taken the young man a moment to answer, and he had looked up, puzzled.

"I'm Jason Baruch. Will you come with me? Ted asked that I ask you."

He looked to be in his late twenties with dark hair, wearing glasses, quiet and alone. A raincoat was on one seat next to him, and the other seat held the coats of the two women who sat on the aisle and who heard the exchange. The young man didn't respond. He sat there, not comprehending. He stared at Baruch as he was spoken to and then he looked away, not moving.

"Doug, please. The service must start," he said urgently. Baruch reached down as if to shake Doug's hand, and seeing the hand, Doug, reactively, put out his right hand to meet Baruch's. Using the hand as a fulcrum, he took Doug's left hand and grasped his right arm just in back of the elbow, lifting him up out of his seat. He pulled Doug after him, and they walked together down the aisle toward the front row.

The crowd hadn't settled down, and still, people were passing the front row. Baruch, still leading Doug, stopped in front of Marion and Henry.

"Doug, this is Marion and Henry Stackler. Marion, Henry, this is Douglas Field. Doug," Baruch paused, "please sit down," he said, and you could see accomplishment in the angle at which he held his hand.

Doug, who had said nothing during all this, sat where he was placed and said nothing. He turned to Henry and Marion and let them see his eyes, which were red, even behind his glasses. He then looked up to Baruch. Doug seemed ready to say something, but he looked up, moved his head up and down in a nod, as if he were saying thank you. Baruch put his hand on Doug's shoulder and then he turned back toward his pulpit covered in mulberry velvet, past Ted's coffin, his hand touching the polished wood.

A RABBI's funeral sermon almost always follows the same pattern. Here are the rabbi's rules of funerals:

First rule: Mention everyone in the family. Example: devoted son of Henry and Marion, beloved grandson of the late Adolph, loving nephew of Helen and her late husband, Sam (a gasp from Helen) . . .

Second rule: Say something nice about the deceased. If you knew him, reminisce with personal stories. If you didn't know him, get to someone in the family before the service starts to pick up some *meinses* (this is the reason all rabbis get to services early, even earlier if they didn't know the deceased at all). If there are no stories, that is, if the deceased was a hermit or otherwise a problem, talk in generalities. Here's a tip-off for funeral audiences: the less anyone knows about the deceased, the more he'll be made to sound like the president of the United States snapped up in the prime of life. "A great lover of mankind, a beneficent protector of the needy." Translation? A putz whom no one knew.

Third rule: Talk about the family's contribution to Judaism. Encourage them to continue their giving and their gifts.

Fourth rule: Induce tears. Jews don't run from sadness. Give it all you've got. Help them get it out.

Fifth rule: Announce where the family will be sitting shivah. "The family will receive friends and condolences at their home on Middle Neck Road in Sands Point beginning from tonight until Friday. As you know, the sitting of shivah is terminated by the joy of the Sabbath."

Sixth rule: Use Hebrew now and then. No one understands it. But everyone feels good when they hear it.

Seventh rule: End with the recitation of the Kaddish and explain that the prayer, although known as a mourner's prayer, is a prayer in praise of God. Don't use the Twenty-third Psalm at the chapel for the congregation. Hold that for the cemetery.

Baruch pretty much followed the rules, including one of the most important ones: never let a memorial service go more than thirty minutes; twenty is better. Baruch went twenty. At the conclusion of the service, Baruch asked the congregation to remain seated until the family left. As they rose, he called the names of those who would be pallbearers, and Doug's name and mine were among them. Marion heard our names, passing through the side door leading out of the sanctuary. She snapped her head and stared at Baruch.

Doug looked at no one as we hauled the casket out of the congregation into the elevator, and out through the fresh air to the hearse, wearing the gray gloves each pallbearer had been given. He walked alone down the narrow alley to the front of the temple and I watched Rabbi Baruch follow him. They disappeared, one after the other, into the crowd in front of the temple. I felt honored that my name had been called; I belonged, I did.

The limousines carrying the family drove past the string of waiting cars. The hearse started forward, and the family cars were interspersed between the hearse and the other cars. In that order, the procession headed for the cemetery. Henry, Marion and others I didn't recognize were in the first car, and more people I didn't know, except for Baruch and Doug in jump seats, rode in the second limousine.

AT THE grave site, the crowd assembled again. The hearse was driven up to the site, the family cars behind. We put on our gray gloves again and moved the coffin from the hearse to the grave, and when it was settled into the chrome machinery by which it would be lowered, the family were led from their cars to the rows of chairs set up under a dark green canopy.

Doug stood with a crowd of maybe one hundred people, but he was again in the front row, about three feet from the head of the coffin. It was a little windy, but the sun was out and in the distance there were no more than a few whitecaps on Long Island Sound. There were cars going by on the expressway miles away and you could see but not hear them. Rabbi Baruch recited prayers in Hebrew, words I hadn't heard since I was a child. Then, white hair moving slightly in the cold wind, no longer bent by uncertainty, but ramrod straight, he spoke, his voice carrying over the creak of bending trees.

"People live in many ways, my friends. They give and take, often in ways that cannot be comprehended by those who do things differently." The wind blew the skullcap off his head, and he bent over to pick it up. He put it back and caught it before it sailed away again. He held the skullcap there, and then he took his hand away as the wind died down.

"And, my children, people love. They love with their hearts. They pick partners mothers and fathers might not pick. But what is important, is that they love. It is important that they have tried to be good, to care, to give, and to be cared for and given to." Jason Baruch looked at Doug, Ted's parents, and then he put himself on the nether side of Leviticus. "And if love happens in ways we cannot understand, that doesn't matter, for we are outsiders to the love of others. It is a secret between them. It is honorable as laughter, as much a miracle as two children, each new on the block, finding they can be friends. Together, they discover a special joy—that after being alone, after moving from the old neighborhood, there is one of their own to be close to."

It was silent now. You could hear the chirp of the last October bird.

Rabbi Baruch recited the Twenty-third Psalm, and Doug cried without shame. I watched Jason Baruch say the words, but never look at the book he held in front of him. He examined faces; when he looked at me, I saw tears in his own eyes, and he slipped on some of the words. When the valley of the shadow of death disappeared in his sorrow, I cried too.

The coffin was lowered, gray gloves on its lid. The family was taken back to the car, which took them away. The others started to leave, but Doug stayed. Only when the family was out of sight and the casket lowered, someone, someone special and close, Baruch had told him as they rode out there, should wait to make sure that the coffin was at rest. So Doug waited, and then he did what Baruch told him tradition dictated was right for Doug and only Doug to do. Doug knelt down, picked up small clods of dirt, and tossed the warm earth on Ted's casket, as it came to rest in the ground.

9

I WENT back to the Stacklers' house after the funeral. After all their announced need for me, Marion and Henry ducked me completely. I wasn't surprised. It didn't take a genius to guess what ideas had entered their minds about me, and ignoring me was their defense. Had they thought of me other than Doug's precursor, I would have been sought out, but that was not the way it was. I wandered through the house alone.

Ted's red and white lounge chair was still in the backyard but next to a new swimming pool. The basketball hoop that had been bolted above the garage door was gone. His old fat-wheel bike, the one he had in Cambridge, was hung upside down from the garage rafters; I could see it through the window, and the chrome was still kept shiny.

Inside, I wanted to be in the library alone. The painting they had done of Ted when he was eighteen was there. He hated sitting for it—felt like a fool, he said. The eyes in the canvas followed anyone who looked at them all over the room. Then my mind went to work: Why was I in the middle of all this? If the self-proclaimed teacher had decided to do the dead favors, that was his business. If Marion was going to ask questions, let her ask Baruch. I should go home. It was a good painting, Ted. It was worth sitting for. I always felt that way. I never told you, though.

The rooms and corridors of the house were packed. I saw Baruch's snowy head bounding up and down in the crowd and then I saw him open the door to the den. He left it open, and, from inside the room, I heard Marion say, "I won't meet him. I don't want him in this house." Her voice penetrated the swarms of jabbering people.

"Marion, please . . ." I heard Baruch say.

"You had no right . . ." It was her voice, shrill and hurt, cut off as she shut the door.

I looked outside and saw a limousine in the driveway that had apparently brought Baruch out to the house. Doug sat alone in the backseat. I walked into the dining room, got a Scotch, drank it and watched the water in the swimming pool. Baruch, how clumsy can you be? I thought. Your promise to the dead has mangled the living. I looked outside again and the limousine was gone. I walked back into the living room, pushing my way through knots of people. I smiled at relatives who thought they half-recognized me, but inside, I was angry with Jason Baruch and distracted. Helen, Marion's sister, was on the move and I grabbed her arm.

"Helen, do you know anyone who is driving back to the city?"

"No, not yet. It's too early. Wait until the minyan. After that, there'll be plenty of rides." She was weaving her way back to the kitchen to fill up a tray.

"That's okay. I'll call a cab."

"Buddy, you have to stay for the minyan. We need ten men."

"There're plenty of men here," I answered.

"Oh, yeah? Count!" she ordered, and then was gone.

Upstairs, I opened the door to Ted's room. We used to stay there when we came into town on weekends. Ted had abandoned his room, as we all do when we leave and go to college, and it still had that high-school look about it. Ted's blond wood desk still stood in front of the window and his red Exeter pennant was thumbtacked on the grass cloth. Behind the dresser was a picture of his young mom and dad, and next to it, an empty fish tank. The room had been frozen twenty-five years ago; time had stopped for it then, and once, in this room, in one of those beds, we had slept together.

There had been times with Ted, and probably only with him, when I could say whatever I wanted to say. There was truth to what people said about me—that I was a cold fish, elegant, good-looking, charming, bright, but a cold fish. I was known to be impatient, demanding and cranky when the pressure got too high, and it was no secret that it was the little things that tripped me up. I forgot Mother's Day or I brought Dad a box of cigars when I knew Mom was nagging him to quit. I competed too hard and I envied someone rich enough not to work or someone who could write a song. The great believer in exposing it all, telling the other guy exactly where you're at when doing a deal, was the world's greatest cover-up artist on the personal side. It was agony for me to touch another person until Ted.

That was long ago, so at best, Ted's time was a "remember," as Andy used to call a memory when he was little. A nice remember. Maybe it was a nice "pretend," too. That was another of Andy's special words: "pretend" stood for a hope or fear; it's what you pretend will happen to you. What were Ted and I pretending? I wasn't sure anymore. Maybe it was practicing law together and sharing an apartment in New York. He thought it would be fun trying to figure out how to cover things up. It wouldn't be much of a problem at first: we could have two beds in one bedroom, or better yet, two bedrooms. We wouldn't have needed two phones. We were young; that wasn't necessary yet. It was no big deal. When we would hit thirty, we would have a choice: elaborate the pretense or say the hell with it. Ted was all for saying the hell with it. The whole world came down to beds: how many and what rooms they were in.

There was never anyone like he was. When he wanted me to be his roommate, me and no one else, I was alive and sometimes thought of crying for joy because I could be close—I could have a pal. We bought books together, and we had our hair cut together and we went record shopping together and we loved each other right there in his bedroom. I sat on the edge of his bed, looking at his criminal law book, remembering times there with him.

"I don't believe you can't tie a bow tie," he once said to me in that house.

"I use clip-ons," I said.

"Not tonight, you don't; not with a tuxedo."

He had hugged me. He always hugged me. We had stood in the tiny bathroom adjoining the bedroom, dressing in dinner jackets for the *Law Review* banquet in New York that year. Ted seemed buoyant and he looked wonderful. I smiled and felt full of happiness as I watched the two of us in the mirror, afraid it would all disappear if I looked at us directly.

"Pretty snappy pair, huh, Bud?" I saw him in the mirror smiling at me. "Come on over here and stand where I can tie this thing. No, not there, you creep. Over here. That's right, now face the mirror." He stood behind me and put his arms in front of me and tied my tie. "See, you take this end and put it around the other end, just like you're tying your shoe. Will you stop laughing? I can't see with you bobbing all around. There we go. See? We look like a million bucks."

"A million bucks apiece," I said, turning around. I reached out, and so did he. But I reached out first and I hugged him first. Being with Ted had taught me to try.

In that room in his parents' home, in the middle of the night, Ted told me I was wrong about loyalty. "So you never had anyone before, big deal. I'm not going anywhere. I'm here," he said. "Sure, the world after school is going to get harder and harder for us to manage, but that's logistics, and that's all it is. Sticking together isn't all family history and it isn't protection against changes. History doesn't always repeat, especially if you understand it. Changes? Sure," Ted said, "they'll happen to us, but if you want to be with me when the changes happen, I want to be with you." He said that to me. He actually did. No one had ever talked that way to me ever.

At the end, I had taken the easy way out and let Ted leave me. I sat in a chair in the kitchen back at school and watched him get ready to go to New York. Both of us had known I wouldn't be there when he returned for commencement. He said good-bye and he hugged me. I sat there and looked out of the big window, counting the rows of garbage cans on Brattle Street until I realized I was counting the same ones over. He stood in the doorway and turned around to look at me. I could see his reflection in the glass, but I wouldn't turn around. I couldn't. I sat there, ice-cold, even after he left the apartment and came back two minutes later to hug me again.

After he had tied my bow tie that night of the *Law Review* banquet, we walked out the front door, dressed in our dinner jackets, headed for the Harvard Club on Forty-fourth Street.

"Hey," he said, beaming, "that's the first time you've hugged me all on your very own without prompting. Congratulations. By the way, Buddy, you look terrific."

"You do too, pal."

He loved it when I called him pal. He had smiled from ear to ear, and his blue eyes had been so bright. I remembered the times we had, and I owed him everything for that.

I PICKED up my bag at the hotel and headed for home, but I didn't want to go there.

I called Cath from the airport and told her the Stacklers had asked me to stay, that I couldn't get out of it, and that I would be home tomorrow. She told me not to rush back.

The unexpected had always brought questions from Cath, a whole collection of how's, why's, and what happened's. Not then. She asked me no questions, and I was spared inadequate answers. That had never happened before.

I hung up the phone, and stood there with my hand remaining on the receiver as if I were about to make another call, until a large man, with boots and a Lyndon Johnson drawl, asked me if the phone was free.

That was two airports in twenty-four hours. I picked up my bag and walked back down the concourse, heading for New York instead of Chicago, pushing opposite noisy crowds moving through the metal detectors. I walked down the stairs toward the cab stand, and I looked up at the electric sign where words went across in dots, telling me what was going on in New York that day. The cab line was nonexistent so I waited. A Peugeot took me to town, and I loved riding in the soft car, looking at the city silhouetted in front of the mid-afternoon sun, and all at once I felt alone, like Doug, a new breed of exile.

10

_____ AN HOUR later, and I wasn't sure why, I stood in front of the building Ted had lived in. It was on a side street just off Fifth Avenue, with a pale green awning that reached from the front door to the curb. The plate over the buzzer for apartment 9E carried both names. The phone system the doorman used to call each apartment was an old one; you shouted into a perforated plate on the wall, and when Doug answered back his voice was broadcast across the lobby: "Joel . . . Stern? . . . Oh . . . Uh . . . Okay." The lock on the downstairs door was released, the doorman pulled the door open, and I walked in, thinking I had received less than half a welcome.

I waited at the threshold, uncertain as hell, and when Doug opened the apartment door, I shook hands and introduced myself. "I'm Joel Stern, Ted's roommate at law school, and I'm very sorry about Ted."

"The place doesn't look very good," he said. He wore a pair of drab-colored slacks and a wrinkled blue shirt with the sleeves rolled up past his elbows. There was a pencil stuck in his shirt pocket and his eyes were empty of color. He seemed dulled and almost mutilated. He asked me to follow him, and we walked through a short hall.

The living room was out of a magazine. There wasn't much furniture in it, but everything counted. It was practically all gray and two fierce-looking Sepik River carvings stood menacingly in a corner, and there was a black grand piano in front of the windows. Outside sprawled Central Park, and you could see all the way from the Plaza Hotel to Tavern on the Green, which from high up looked like a carousel.

"Susan, Jay, this is Joel Stern, Ted's law school roommate. Joel, this is Susan and Jay Cole, and that fellow is my best friend, Allan Kennedy. Susan brought dinner."

"I didn't bring dinner at all," she said. "He made it," she pointed to Doug.

"She wants to make sure I eat," Doug said. The words were polite but his voice was colorless.

"Please join us." Doug looked at me squarely and I said I would stay.

There wasn't much left to the afternoon, and most of the talk involved their lives together in New York. I listened a little, responded when they brought me into the conversation, and surprised myself by not paying strict attention to each tidbit which would have provided a picture of Doug's life with Ted and their lives together with all those people. Somehow, I didn't want to know. I tuned in now and then. At one point, the Coles talked about a new public relations client they were working for, and at another time, at the tail end of what he was saying, I heard Allan Kennedy say something about the Bank of International Settlements in Geneva, and then it clicked. He was a lead Reuters correspondent and had a book out on macro oil economics. He was meant to be a wizard, this fellow.

"I think I know you," I said.

"It happens a lot," Allan smiled. He had small eyes, just visible behind steel wire glasses, the kind privates wore in Vietnam. I felt myself perk up and couldn't resist asking his opinion on whether Brazil could repay its loans. He took fifteen minutes to say who knows? and went on to a caustic analysis of the World Bank, leaving a trail of gossip about the way decisions there were really made.

Dinner brought the smell of Ted Stackler's stew. I heard the sound of knives and forks and the buzz of conversation, but all I thought of was potatoes and carrots and the smell of gravy with garlic that reminded me of many happy times. I could almost see Ted back in the kitchen, and during most of dinner, I felt as if I were in a no-man's-land, a block and a half from anything real.

At eight thirty the Coles left and Allan said he had better be pushing along as well. Doug walked Allan to the door. They talked, first normally, but then in mumbles until the elevator door clanged open. I thought I heard kissing sounds and I flinched. I heard the front door close and the sliding shut of two lock bolts. Doug came back into the living room. All at once, he looked very tired. He sat down and let his head fall back into a sofa cushion. He was quiet for a long time.

"That's a lovely view," I finally said.

"Thank you," he said, staring out the window. Opposite the window, behind us, was a wall of books, records with labels in French and stacks of sheet music.

"You play the piano?" I asked, searching for something to say.

"A little." He looked across the room at the piano. "I don't practice enough," he added, but he seemed too tired to be upset with himself.

"I never did either," I said. "That's why they gave up and bought me a guitar."

"When you were little?" he asked.

"Uh-huh."

He smiled a little, out of one side of his mouth. "They bought me a ukelele," he said.

"And you played the Top Forty hits. All forty, right?" I asked.

"No, just one," he said. " 'I'm Looking Over a Four Leaf Clover.' " We both laughed a little. "I didn't get very far with it," he said. "Well, what can you do?" He began to sound more alive, but he had a cardplayer's face; it told you nothing. "What did you play?" he asked.

"Beatles songs," I told him. "In *A Hard Day's Night*, they were the Marx Brothers all over again. Ringo, when he sat still, reminded me of Harpo. It was the light coming from behind him when he played. His eyes became so quiet." I stopped talking; I felt like a fool.

"That's a very beautiful thing to say."

"You think so?"

"Sure, I do," he said. "Those aren't easy songs, though."

He took two phone calls, one right after the other, and then he pulled the plug out of the wall.

Doug moved his head slightly to one side, and then put his pencil in his mouth.

"I play saloon songs on the piano," he said. He stood up and walked over to the window and looked out of it. "Torch songs, three o'clock in the morning songs. Songs Billie Holiday would sing. Sinatra. Ella Fitzgerald. Rodgers and Hart. Hart was gay, you know." It had to happen, I said to myself, it just had to. "You'll hear different meanings in his lyrics now that you know that," he went on. "Cole Porter, too." He looked across the room at me.

"That's the same kind of music Ted and I used to listen to." I sent him back his message.

"I know."

He went back to the sofa and sat down again, then he stretched out, but his expression betrayed nothing at all.

He was dark complexioned, and even though he had shaved that morning, I could see blue hair under his skin, which meant that he'd have to shave again if he had plans for the evening. He was a jogger, I knew that. There was a red windbreaker on the kitchen chair with a National Jogging Association shoulder patch on it. He had color in his cheeks, like Andy had when he came in from playing football in the fall. He had a long nose that dropped at the end, narrow and almost Roman. His hair was brown, and tangled where he had neglected to comb it or where he had put his hand through it. He did that a lot as we talked. He let his hair fall at an angle across his forehead. When he combed it, it probably looked neater than it did then, sort of half over one ear on one side and behind the ear on the other, down to his collar in the back.

What struck me most, even behind his glasses, were his eyes. Sometimes they looked bewildered, even numb, probably because of what he was going through, but at other moments, they flashed with life. His walk changed the same way: sometimes drooping and sad, maybe just for a second or so, and then bouncy, upright with shoulders straight, then back again.

He tucked his right foot up and sat on it in sort of a half-yoga position. He sat the way Ted used to sit, but that didn't surprise me. After all, they had lived together, I thought, and when Ted and I did, I remember picking up the same habit. The large glass wall with the city behind it creaked, as if it needed oil. You could hear the wind outside the window and a stream of light hit Doug's eyes, but his head didn't move. Then he turned to me.

"There's a bookcase behind you. Take a look at the third shelf, near the plant."

I walked over and held the picture of Ted and me. It was taken outside of Stowhoff, in Vermont, eighteen years ago. I looked at the old print over and over again. Ted used to joke about it when he told the story about how, just as we were ready to leave, we found Gene Mason hiding in the backseat of our car. We had made the mistake of talking about the trip in front of Gene, and he had invited himself along and we couldn't dump him; but at least he was there to take the picture. It was the only one ever taken of Ted and me together.

"I haven't seen that in a long time," I said. Ted and I had worn identical blue duffel coats and I had worn my sunglasses. We had the same shoes on, penny loafers, the ones that had come back into style, the same button-down shirts and chinos.

"I have trouble thinking of you as Joel. Ted always called you 'Buddy,' " Doug said.

I looked at the picture, then back at him. "That was my name then."

"It's easier to look alike now," he said; "that is, if you want to."

"Yes, I know. I saw your names together on the door," I said, feeling very much on the defensive.

"It was Ted's idea. I was to be unknown to his parents, but he didn't want me to be an outsider in our own home." He hesitated. "They would never accept me or anyone, for that matter, as a roommate, so the solution was simple: he never let them come here. He kept them away, but put my name on the door. Something for them and something for me." He glanced my way, but then he turned sideways quickly. "I belong here. And I'll tell you something else. I belonged in that temple too." I felt as if I wanted to stand up when he walked into a room. "I don't think I had to sit in the front row, though. I don't think that helped much," he said, and then he was sad again. "Jason really didn't have to do that."

He walked over to the piano and picked out "Frère Jacques,"

but didn't get the notes quite right. He turned away and looked out the window again; the poker face had returned. The trees on Fifth Avenue swayed as a bus went by, one of its headlights askew, throwing light on the empty benches. Doug sat down and cleared his throat but his voice sounded pinched, the defiance gone.

"It wasn't easy for Ted, but he never hid me. There were only three places we couldn't go together: formal office functions, mine and his, and . . . with them, his parents. He hated those people." He stopped and pulled his pencil out of his pocket and put it back again. "Ted only had two lovers, you and me."

God damn that word. I hated that word. I didn't say anything.

"There were a lot of lonely times between your time and mine. Ted knew what the bars were all about. After you were married, he had to find out." Doug's eyes turned hard.

"This town is full of young kids from Ding-Dong, Iowa, who could have made it through if they stayed home and worked in the John Deere plant. But they had to get out because they were gay. So they mustered all their energy, moved to the big city and had just enough steam left to find a barstool, sit on it and look pretty. They lived from hand to mouth. An aspirin threw their budget off. They carried orange plastic bags full of their treasured teenage belongings, and to deal with the threat of the big city, they longed for a big brother, and Ted was the best." He took a breath. "But that role never gave him anything he could count on."

"I was young, too, but," and the boldness came back, "I was a city kid. He used to call me a street-smart city kid. I didn't know the first thing about livestock, but I knew about subways, how to fake being comfortable with something I'd never seen before and how to follow rather than being dragged. I had a running start. Ted used to say that." Doug's voice trailed off and he walked over to the bookshelf, looked at something, or pretended to, then came back and sat down, just where he was a few seconds ago. He sighed, a pained one with stutters in it, and when he spoke again, his voice had aged.

"It seemed such a long time ago." He paused. "We knew each other before we slept together, and that's the way it should be. We met at a Harvard luncheon, no less." He grinned. "We had lunch quite a few times after that, but never dinner. When we walked together, Ted always put his arm around my shoulder. When we talked, his forehead was close to mine. Then he asked me to come here. I wanted to see how he lived, what his life was like, and then I saw the picture of the two of you on the bookshelf. I got up enough nerve to ask him who you were. He was in the kitchen, and he called back, 'Someone who was very important to me . . . yeah, my roommate at law school.'

"I should have walked in there and asked him, point-blank. Then I could have seen his eyes and I would have known which answer counted. You see, he gave me two answers to my question, and the first answer, I hoped, was the one that meant something. The second, 'the roommate,' was the cover-up.

"It was our first dinner together, and we were here listening to records, sitting across the room from each other. When the first side was over, I just blurted it out, that I was gay and hoped he was. He came over to me and hugged me. I had never been so happy in my life. You see, we knew each other. It wasn't sex out of a bar. We had some idea of who each of us was. It was a good deal."

" 'Deal' was one of Ted's favorite words," I said.

"He got it from you."

I didn't say a thing. I found myself remembering how we made our first deal: allocating expenses for the old green Pontiac his mother gave him which the two of us drove together.

"When I met him," Doug said, "I wore my contact lenses all day even if I bruised my corneas because that's how he first saw me. I put creams on my face because I thought he wanted me only if I looked young. Without my appearance, I didn't know if I was anything to him. Over the years, I grew up, and then I knew all along he loved me for who I was inside. It's because of Ted that I wear these glasses and if I want, I can skip a shave on the weekend. You know something, Joel? I miss him."

Doug had talked for close to an hour, and I knew that was what he should do. That was what shivah was for. I realized that I had performed a ritual, made a certain peace, and that my dad could know that part of me was still his. I felt I had made a double peace, because part of me was here with Ted. It was a feeling of joy from years back.

"What do you think of what I'm doing?" he asked unexpectedly.

"You mean how you're playing with that paperweight?"

"No." He forced a smile. A clock chimed somewhere, probably a big brass ship's clock in a walnut stand on a desk in one of the gray rooms nearby. "I mean about Ted. I'm not sure what the right way is to miss him." He caught a breath, and spoke slowly. "If this were three days ago, I'd be here with Ted, but I'm glad to be here with you now." He took his glasses off and looked straight at me. He made no effort to hide his eyes. "I'm sorry," he said.

"I shouldn't be here."

"That's not so. I don't think anyone could possibly object. Including Ted. In a way, the people who were here today are more strangers to me than you are."

"I came to see you and I don't know why," I heard myself tell him.

"We shared a lot. Once removed," he said.

Doug reached into his back pocket, took out a handker-chief, took off his glasses and cleaned them. "I'm glad you came."

"This isn't the greatest time in the world, is it?"

"No, I guess not."

I hesitated, but then I said it. I wanted to be careful and I picked each word. "If there's an extra bedroom, I'd be glad to stay tonight if you'd like."

He had been staring down at the table. He looked up, hesitated and nodded. I told him my bag was at the hotel, and he offered to walk with me up Madison Avenue to get it.

Once we hit the air, he took a deep breath. "Ah, that air feels good." He reminisced, feeling better.

"My old apartment could be a mess at times," Doug said. "I had a roommate and the toothpaste stuck in the bathroom sink was one of his least objectional habits. Ted said it re-minded him of you."

"Of me? I never did that." I paused a minute. "I don't think I did. Believe me. There's a tube of Ipana in it for you."

"Ipana? Oh, yes. Toothpaste of the ancients." He smiled and I laughed out loud, and I was glad I had come to see him.

We returned at about eleven thirty and decided that we were both pretty tired and would go to sleep right away. Doug kidded me about pressed pajamas, and acknowledged that toothpaste in the sink was probably not one of my habits.

"If you'd like to talk some more, that's fine," I said.

"No, that's okay," he said, "I'm just glad . . . Thanks for staying," and he smiled.

He seemed calmer, said good night, went into the bedroom and closed his door. I went to my room, read a magazine for a short time, turned out the light, had a hard time falling asleep, but finally made it.

I had no idea what time it was, but sometime during the night, I heard a plate or a glass break. "You okay?" I called out.

"Yes, I'm okay," his voice echoed down the hallway. I got out of bed, put my robe on over my pajamas and walked toward the kitchen.

I had spent a lot of time with a person I didn't know very well in an alien setting, and I felt out of place, like the outsider I never wanted to be. Questions started rolling in my mind, taking the sound of Catherine's voice and her litany of why's, how come's and what happened's. First panic: What if Catherine called the hotel? Where the hell am I supposed to be? Second panic: What if she called the Stacklers? Another lie. Third panic: Where was I? But there would be no such questions. She had her chance, she didn't ask.

Doug was in the kitchen, pouring cognac into an orange juice glass. He was wearing a red nightshirt, and I didn't know whether to laugh or cry. Then I saw how lost he looked.

"You doing okay?" I asked.

"I was having a bad dream. I can't remember it, though." Doug leaned back against the kitchen cabinets and rubbed his eyes. "I don't believe it," he said quietly. "I can't get it through my head."

"Whatever it was, it was just a dream."

"I know. I know." It was another of Ted's mannerisms, the double repeat. We walked out of the kitchen, and he turned the lights out behind him as we went down the hall.

We stood opposite his door to the bedroom. I said good night and started to walk back to the den.

"Joel, please don't go back there."

I stopped. "Doug . . ." I shook my head in a gentle back and forth no. "I don't do that kind of thing anymore."

He took his glasses off and rubbed the bridge of his nose where his glasses had rested.

"I'm sorry," he said.

I walked toward him and tried to put my arm around his shoulder. He stiffened and pulled away. He walked into his room, turned out his lights, leaving it to me to decide whether to close his door or leave it open.

I walked back to the guest room and tried to fall asleep again.

About fifteen minutes later, Doug pushed my door open as quietly as he could. The lamp was out, but there was enough street light coming in from the window so he could see I was still awake.

"Sorry to bother you, but I need to get something out of the closet. You store paraphernalia anywhere you can in these small apartments."

"That's okay." Doug no longer had the red nightshirt on. He was dressed in a pair of Levi's, a red flannel shirt, and sat down on a chair and began to lace up a pair of field boots.

"What in the hell are you dressed up for?"

"I'm going out."

"At this hour?"

"Why not?" he said, his voice tight.

"It's . . . almost two o'clock in the morning!"

"Well, that's about the right time." He stood up and stretched until his fingertips almost touched the ceiling.

"For what?"

"For me to go out."

I got out of bed and threw my robe on. "Where in the hell are you going?"

"To a bar, if you must know."

Doug stood in front of me, his hair neat now, combed back, but still with a slice of it over his forehead.

"That's your business, but why don't you have a drink here?"

"That's not what I'm going out for."

"Oh, I see."

"Oh, do you?" he asked with a sharp edge to his voice.

"Doug, what do you need to—"

"I'm not going to do anything wrong. I'm just going to go out and get fucked. Okay with you?"

They were all the same, I thought. God, they were all the same. "You do what you want," I hesitated, "but if you want to know the truth, it's not okay with me."

"Sorry, that's your problem," he said. "If I'm not back before you leave in the morning, well, thanks for coming. See ya."

He walked out the door and started to close it. I took a step and held his shoulder.

"Look, just don't touch me. Okay? Remember? You don't do that kind of thing anymore." I kept my hand on his arm. "Joel, just let me go. I want to be with somebody. Anybody. I don't care."

"Well, I do." I took hold of his shoulder. "Doug, I've been down that track." He tried to pull away from me, but I held on. I turned him around and pulled him close to me. I put my arms around him, and a strong light from somewhere fell on his face before he stopped resisting. He raced to catch his breath; he shuddered and then he started to cry.

I heard mumbling, sounds, and it took me a minute to realize that the words I was hearing weren't Doug's, but a replay of Ted talking to Doug; it was Ted's words Doug was saying:

"After the hospital . . . we'll ask my folks to come and see us. No more hiding. Huh, pal?"

Doug looked at me, straight into my eyes. Now he spoke for himself: "Hear that? Dinner with the in-laws after five years."

His smile was forced and full of pain. His eyes were tortured. His arms closed around me and he broke into the staccato cry of a child.

"Why did they make it so *hard* for us?" he asked.

I put my hand behind his head; he bent forward, drained, and he let his forehead fall on my shoulder. He would start to quiet down, but then he would shake and cry again. He lifted his head and looked straight at me. His eyes were red, the tears falling down his cheeks.

"I want to hear his voice. I want him to call me 'pal' again."

Doug looked at me, pleading, without understanding. We stood there, hanging on to each other. I had no answers. I wished I did.

After a while, the rocking stopped and Doug stood on his own. He sat down on the edge of the bed, exhausted, and let himself fall backward until his head rested on the pillow. Through the space between the window shade and the sill, a little light entered the room. There were no horns outside, just the bad coincidence of the faint sound of a siren. Doug's face twitched, and his eyes closed tightly when he heard it. He propped himself up on his elbow and looked where the window was. Then, once again, he let his body collapse, dropping back to the pillow, and he closed his eyes. In a while, I sat down on the edge of the bed and watched him. He opened his eyes again and stared at the ceiling.

"Would you let me sleep here tonight? I mean, just sleep?" he asked, almost in a whisper.

"Only if you take your shoes off," I answered.

He smiled a little weakly, sat up and started to unlace one of his boots. I leaned over and began to unlace the other. "I'll give you a hand."

He sat up and tossed his legs over the side of the bed. He took off his shirt and slipped his pants out from under him. He pulled the blanket back and covered his body. He had turned to the window, his back to me.

In a few minutes I heard his breathing even out, and I knew

he had fallen asleep. I looked at the ceiling. I wanted to turn over on my side, but I didn't want to disturb him. So I looked up and watched the shadows move around the room. He made a wordless sound and then turned over and faced me. He opened his eyes for a minute, and we looked at each other. He smiled, more asleep than not, and closed his eyes. I turned over and cried, not aloud or passionately, but enough to know that part of me had not died completely. I didn't think Doug heard me. He had his own sorrow.

AN HOUR later, the wind was still hammering at the windows and accidentally setting off car alarms which whined into the night. I was still awake, listening, asking myself all the questions Catherine had never asked of me.

First question: "Joel, did you just turn it off one day and never want Ted or anyone like him again?"

Second question: "Did your mother say, 'Joel, you can change if you want to.' Did you believe her and just go out and flick the switch?"

Third question: "How about the last sixteen years, Joel? How about them?"

I felt that I had to get out, so I dressed and sat at the table in Doug's living room, starting three different times to write him some kind of a note. I forgot what I said.

PART

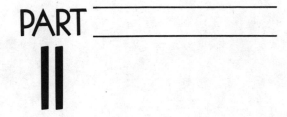

II

11

THE CAB that took me to the Loop was one of the jolting green Checkers that aren't built anymore. It had more Bondo in it than metal and the whole thing rattled and banged like crazy. The Pointer Sisters blared out of the huge ghetto blaster on the seat next to the driver. My head buzzed and my eyes hurt, but none of that would show. I knew my face. I rarely registered fatigue and I never understood how I could look the picture of health and feel lousy inside. The Kennedy Expressway curved east at Addison Street, and in the distance, Sears hadn't moved an inch.

Right there, bouncing in that taxicab, I knew that if I had had a brain in my head, I would have stayed away from Chicago until I had sorted everything out, or at least figured out what to lie about. I had never been good at planned lying. It was my face again. I had known people whose faces never changed no matter what they were up to: choir boys' faces doing mean things and mean faces being nice. The driver slowed down, stuck in traffic, thank heaven. The windshield had yellow smile stickers pasted on it, and I realized, almost proudly, that I could disguise almost anything, including ill health. I had developed the placid healthy look and learned how to stay still so it could radiate. The cab picked up speed, it hit another pothole, and I thought the rear axle was going to fly off before we got downtown.

The cool cookie side of me said wait until tonight to talk to Cath, but she had already called the office and delay had become impossible. I looked at the phone several times, and I wasn't sure what I should do. I got through Ted's funeral service, I thought, trying to give myself advice; I would get through this. I called her at the league.

"I wasn't sure about calling you at the office," she said.

"That's okay. I'm glad to hear from you." I heard muffled voices in the background. It sounded as if she had put her hand over the mouthpiece.

"They're rushing me," she said. "The hearing to save the Bateman School is today and I'm speaking. I have to get over there." I didn't say anything immediately, although I should have. "But it's okay if you miss it. You're probably exhausted."

"No, no," I said, filling the void as fast as I could, "I want to come."

"I'm not taking you away from anything?"

"I want to come."

"They're rushing me."

I stopped at McDonald's under the El tracks on Wells for animal crackers and to see if Catherine's hearing was mentioned in the paper. I was supposed to know where it was, but I didn't. The last Evanston Express of the morning took the tight turn at Harrison sounding like a barrel of loose nuts and bolts. That would make it close to noon. The *Sun-Times* had nothing, but the *Trib* had it: at one o'clock, in the City Council Chamber. There was no picture of Catherine, but there was one of Jack Stewart, the developer, with a model of the apartment building he wanted to put up after he tore down the Bateman. There was absolutely nothing there about the Junior League, its efforts to save the Bateman, the architectural value of the place or anything approaching an even-handed account of the issues before the Preservation Commission.

I remembered thinking that maybe the El would go the way of the Bateman. As a little kid, I always saw the El as a way out, the route to a job downtown. There, I could be where the big guns worked. My El was safe—no developer wanted it, and no one could make a big buck out of wrecking it. After all, selling scrap to North Korea was passé. Cath had a deal with the big downtown architects. They'd get behind the league to save the Bateman (the designer of the proposed building was an unprotected outsider) and she'd put the league behind the El.

THE COUNCIL Chamber was packed and the audience shouted and stamped and the floor shook like a revival meeting. A claque of well-dressed young women stood down front wearing yellow streamers that read SAVE THE BATEMAN. Two members of the Preservation Commission grinned, which encouraged the shouting even more, and then the sole female member, dressed in a plaid jumper, and proud, no doubt, of her sex, beamed as if she had given birth to all women since Dr. Leakey's Lucy.

The chair was a wily old-timer with a stone face like Clint Eastwood. He had integrated Hyde Park single-handedly and could scheme his way through anything. The developer had hired "clout" to make up for the architect's lack of it. The law firm that used to honor the mayor as its senior partner had sent a team of the most Irish-looking lawyers imaginable and they sat all in a row off to one side. Catherine, however, had become a friend of a former mayor's mother, who in her time was also president of the Junior League and had attended the Bateman School in its halcyon days. The league had counterclout.

Cath thought she had the hearing stacked. She had learned a hell of a lot. One doesn't walk into the league and run it without spending time in the drug abuse program or on hot lines for runaways from two to six in the morning. Cath would cry when she came home from night phone duty, and said all she was doing was pissing in the ocean and she felt so helpless. She ate ice cream and read poems silently, until five or six on the worst nights. That was not a good time for Cath. She had learned plenty through those years, but it wasn't enough.

I had expected Cath to go back to television work soon after Judd was born, but certainly not embrace an activity such as the Junior League that promised to fill her days with women. She did not depend on women for anything that mattered to her, but the civic side of the league gave her a special place to be, and admirers far beyond the range of Judd, Andy and me. Then, the controversy over the Bateman flared.

The building was just across the street from league head-quarters. It was the only Stanford White building in Chicago, and somehow, over something, Cath got mad. That building simply was not going to be torn down; that was all there was to it. She was young again, she was fighting the good fight, and unlike the phone-line help effort, on this one, it was no holds barred.

"Ladies and gentlemen—" The announcement boomed and reverberated. We were at the 1940 Democratic Convention.

Ripping through the rafters, Mayor Kelly's "voice of the servers" was introducing FDR. The voice rose, just like at the stockyards, until the shouts of the audience almost drowned him out. "—May I present to the committee"—huge cheers— "Ladies and gentlemen, Catherine Stern."

Banners waved, applause rang out, and people stamped in rhythm. "Save the Bateman. Save the Bateman." The place shook as Catherine stood at the podium. She wore her blue suit, white blouse and tweed tie. Her hair looked soft, lit by the television arcs. She nodded as if she were royalty. The camera with the red bulb burning, swung around to the audience, boom mike following to catch the applause, then back to Catherine. She looked directly at the lens, a controlled public figure.

Then, she grinned from ear to ear. For an instant, she became the little girl in a pink dress at a piano recital, beaming after tossing off Bach. The applause died down.

From somewhere, I didn't know where, she had picked up the ability to coin trenchant eight-second phrases strung together to fit the evening news slots. She had learned how to signal the TV crews when the quoteable quotes were coming, for without fail, the camera would swing to her, with red light on, at just the right instant.

Her delivery was solid, steady and forceful, yet she was always a lady. Her commitment carried the day. If some people sneered and thought the Junior League was a collection of postdebutantes screeching "How many of us girls will it take to man the booth?" it was clear that Catherine was not part of that image. Chitchat had never been her passion, and a day at the hairdresser's on Oak Street was not one of the activities Cath shared with others she knew. She enjoyed a world of men and she fit. The audience loved her. She was trying to hang on to something worthwhile, and they knew it.

I was guilty as hell for all kinds of things, but I was home, and that's what counted.

AFTER THE speeches, in the cleared hall, the adversaries went down front to do business. They had dropped the blood feud poses, and together, with Cath in the middle of it, they would work it out. The old-timers, looking like Mayor Daley with heavy jowls and pale blue eyes, stood aside, wearing enameled American flags in their lapels, lopsided. They waited until later when deals would be made in private.

Down below, near the podium, Cath looked up and saw me watching her. She was too far away from where I stood for me to hear her, but it seemed like she said "Joel." I saw her touch the elbow of the councilman next to her and gesture in my direction. Thank you, thank you, I could see her say, pushing her way out of a cluster of people.

She stood next to me, a little uncertain.

"I'm glad I came," I said. I hugged her and she smiled, almost embarrassed. "You were great." We stood apart and looked at each other. I pulled at a twisted shirt cuff, trying to straighten out my shirt-sleeve. She gestured toward the huddled politicians. "I've got to go back."

She walked toward the speaker's podium, but a third of the way there, she turned around and headed back to me. "I'm sorry you went to New York by yourself," she said. "I really am."

"Meet me for coffee? A drink?" I asked.

"The Bismarck in twenty minutes?" she said, as she went back toward the center of the room.

Central Casting could have cast Bette Davis as Cath. Both walked the same way: tough, one foot on the floor, bang, then the other. Or Ann Sheridan could have had the part, swaggering with shoulder pads, playing guys' games in old movies. But I would never cast Cath with a harsh face. She would look as if she had just said good night to Juddy. Cath looked up and caught me staring at her. She winked at me, and I winked back.

LA SALLE Street traffic between City Hall and the Bismarck was total anarchy. The mayor's limousine, with the chase car behind it, took up most of the no parking zone, and red Buicks and white Eldorados with license plates like VITO and POOCH took up the rest. Horns blasted and potbellied Chicago cops traded stories with the Democratic faithful leaning against old City Hall, smoking half-chewed cigars, remembering, no doubt, da days of da mayor, da leader, as traffic, left to itself, did the best it could.

Cath was fifteen minutes late. The restaurant at the Bismarck thought it was in the mountains. The napkins and menus had a snow-covered-peak motif, and the back wall was hung with a huge mural of the Grand Tetons. Politicians and labor guys ate there and your importance was measured by how long it took you to work the crowd and finally reach your table. All through the place, there was the smell of old food. Trash it out, as Andy would say.

Catherine was suddenly there. She hurried through the revolving door, spotted the table and pulled a chair out for herself before I could do it. She slowed up momentarily, just enough to set her Hermès briefcase carefully on the floor beside her. Fifteen years was supposed to buy crystal, but it was that black dispatch case she wanted. She had joked about building a coffee table out of the orange shopping bag it came in. She started to talk a blue streak even before she sat down.

"Joel, I think we've blocked them. It will take a lot of soft-

soaping, but if we can find an alternative site for their development, they'll give up the Bateman location and trade." She
could hardly move her lips fast enough as she reported the
deal she was engineering. "The city will condemn the new site
and resell it to them at a bargain price, but no one will see
the link." Like a kid, she crossed both fingers in front of her
and added, "I hope.

"Stanley Rabinowitz called me aside after the hearing. He's
the development company's lawyer. He is really a character.
He carries a beeper with him all the time. It's set to go off if
someone tampers with his Corvette." She looked at the ceiling
and rolled her eyes, still part teenager. She had quick eyes and
they telegraphed when a question was coming. "Do you know
him?"

"No, I don't think so," I said.

"Can you believe that he is still threatening me? He tells
me he was hired for a reason, and that he's sure I knew the
history of his firm and its partners, and he winks at me. I'm
just outraged." Her words flew. "There is no way that man is
going to put that building up there." Her hand, flat out,
sliced the air inches over the table. "He's so dumb he can't
even figure out what we're doing for him. We'll teach him a
lesson and do him a favor at the same time. You know what I
don't understand? I can't imagine how he thought he was
going to get away with it in the first place. I'm sure he still
believes, even after today's hearing, that the league is full of
naive little girls. He's such a nothing. Totally ineffectual. Joel,
have you ordered anything yet? I'm famished."

Halfway through lemon ice, almost as an afterthought, she
asked, "How did it go in New York?" She wasn't smiling anymore, and her face grew tense and maybe a little angry, but
I wasn't sure. She began making little swirls on the tablecloth
with her fingers.

I was wondering when she was going to get around to it. Maybe she didn't want to get around to it at all. Maybe that's why she ran off at the mouth. She was no sharpie. It was nuts to portray her as one. I felt like a kid, ashamed, and put my elbows on the table.

"There were a lot of people at the temple," I said, "and they asked me to be a pallbearer." Catherine looked up from her dish. Her eyes opened wide and she put her hand over her mouth. "I went to the cemetery, and after that to the house. I saw Marion and Henry, and what can you say? It's over." I looked out of the window at the crowds on Randolph Street, not focusing. Cath leaned back in her chair, suddenly paying attention.

"I'm glad that you stayed the extra day," she said.

"I went to the Whitney."

I had lied and I had to make up for it. She had changed the subject and went back to chattering about the Bateman. I tuned her out, but I watched her. As it turned out, I told her the truth with a vengeance. "At the funeral, I learned that Ted had . . . well, he wasn't alone."

She remained still for a moment, and then her voice became warm beyond any reasonable expectation. "I'm glad for him," she said.

Cath leaned over and restacked some of the papers in her case, and then, upright again, she sat silently in her chair for a long time. I was going to be asked a question; her eyes told me. "Was his friend a man?"

"Yes."

We both ate more lemon ice and then she looked up from her spoon. "Did you meet him?" The sound of her voice was careful and far away.

"Um, hmm." I still had the cold mass in my mouth.

"What was he like?" She asked the question as casually as

she could, as if she lived in Peoria and wanted gossip over a back fence. Underneath the country cousin act, she was breathing like a cat.

"His name is Douglas Field," I said. I paused, testing to see if I could conclude, but Cath's eyes still burned in that certain way. "I don't know what possessed me, but I went to the building where Ted lived," I said.

Her face turned slightly pale. I reached over and took her hand. "Cath, he was alone. He didn't have anybody."

Contrary to all childhood instruction, I put my elbows back on the table. Cath sat across the table, suddenly dignified, unreadable, looking at me. "Cath, I don't know what to tell you. I want to tell you everything"—the words ended up rushed— "but I don't think we can sit here that long." I tried to smile.

"I don't mind." She felt her wedding ring. "But on second thought," she said, looking around at the crowd, "at home, though. Please?" I remembered Cath when the shine on that ring was fresh.

Her fingers rested on the handle of her coffee cup. I reached across the table and touched them, and she gave me her hand. She was embarrassed, I could tell, but she didn't pull away, even when I ran my fingers across her wrist and then touched the top of her hand. I slid my hand over hers and covered her hand to the end of her fingertips. "There's nothing now," I said as softly as I could, mindful of the crowds. "There never was. It's over. It was over then."

"Can I have my hand back, please?" she said.

"Sure," I said, letting go of her. I forced a smile. "It's your day and I don't want to spoil your triumphal march."

She looked away, at her watch, out of the window, anywhere. "Act two, scene two," she said. I had read novels with jokes about New York psychiatrists that made me laugh hysterically—"So tell me, Sigmund, it is very interesting. No?"—

but then I couldn't think of anything funny to say. "When did we last see *Aida?*" was all I could come up with.

"A long time ago, I think." She started to nod slowly as she does when an idea is ticking away in her head. She smiled a little. Cath had changed mood on her own. "Don't we have Lyric tickets this week?" she asked. I pushed my chair back with a scrape, relieved at the upswing.

"Yes, tomorrow night, come to think of it." Her hands began to gesticulate once more; the stillness was gone.

"What are they doing?" I asked.

"Boheme."

"Well, that isn't so bad," I said. "Tunes for a change."

Cath reached under the table for her papers. Her face popped back up again with a full podium smile. "Andy has B-ball [more of Andy's argot] practice tonight and you promised you'd go."

"I remember. I wrote it down. See? Andy—Basketball." I showed her my daily diary, a pocket version of a three-ring notebook.

"Since when do you write down your children's activities in your do-it-for-the-client book?" she asked brightly.

That's right, I thought, feeling punched out, since when?

DESCRIPTION OF evening routine at the Stern household:

Six o'clock: My key goes in the door. If not, they call the hospitals.

Six o six: I have finally made my way through Andy and Judd, and I enter the kitchen. The maid cooks. Cath supervises, her one remaining household task. I run.

Seven fifteen: I change. Back to Clark Kent. Or is it the other way around?

Seven thirty. We eat. Speedily. Everyone has to go somewhere. Andy is at the stage where his destination is usually described as "out." No one questions him. Judd does not go "out." He goes to a described destination. Often that means "with Andy." But if one goes, the other goes. Sometimes I think Judd goes out even if he has nowhere to go and that he just walks around. He is torn between being left out versus being a baby and staying home, bored. He is young, but he knows the difference. He is intellectual.

Eight o five. They are out and we are home, just the two of us. It will stay quiet for all of ten seconds. Then the phone takes over. We have three lines now. The phone book says:

Stern, Joel	555-1726
Stern, Catherine	555-1727
Stern, Child	555-1728

Two-seven goes off at least three times. Conversations ensue, each taking up approximately ten minutes folowed by a sigh. Two-eight rings twice. One caller hangs up when I answer and the other says, "Nice to talk to you, Mr. Stern. Ask Andrew to call Sally." I tell Cath and she shrugs her shoulders.

At nine thirty, everyone is home again and still has something going every minute. By ten, the routine subsides, finally.

It always took me at least a half hour to unwind; not after a day's work, but after the three hours after a day's work. Cath could never see what I was talking about until her days started to fill up with league business. The truth was we loved it. There was life in our house, and in that way, we were luckier than most.

FINALLY, THE boys were in bed, and Catherine and I had settled. We were downstairs in the sunroom, alone. She had

picked up her knitting basket and started working on the
needlepoint pillow that was a semisecret present for my big
birthday in December. It had "Joel" written all over it in several kinds of print, and it was going to have a different color
yarn for each typeface. She had designed it. Cath had two late
calls, both short and both about the Bateman project, and
then it was quiet. We read a little.

"You know, the boys really liked you on TV tonight," I
said.

"Did they?"

She had let her hair down at the end of the day and it stood
full, inches away from her face. Body, the shampoo ads called
it. She wore night colors, gray and black, and she seemed to
focus, if on anything at all, on the border stitching for the
pillow, the part close to the edge of the wooden stretcher holding the Joels.

Cath wore fuzzy wool socks that would keep her warm in
an igloo, the ones she had bought in France. She had never
wanted a car in Paris. The key to always being happy there,
she had said when we were there the year before, was to go
everywhere on foot or by Métro. We had spent long nights in
little bistros near the Bourse watching photographers play
Vessel, and then, in the first light of the morning, we walked
through the gardens of the Palais Royal. We roamed the city
and she had called me the boyfriend she would grow old with.
It was there, as she looked in a shop window full of Bazooka
graphics and in clothes that she had the idea for the pillow.

Cath pushed one shoe off her foot and maneuvered herself
into a squat. She hugged her knees, feet tucked under her, and
she looked like Katharine Hepburn. Then she unwound and
wrote something down on a note pad. She had them all over
the house, near places where she liked to hang out as Andy put
it, and at the end of the day, after she had taken note of her

notes, so to speak, the wastebaskets were full of balled-up scraps. She held the needlepoint frame to the light, gave it a quarter turn and started another row.

It was the first quiet I remembered in days. I thought of the cure we had found for the commotion of acrobats, sword swallowers and fire-eaters in the square west of the Pompidou Center in the Baubourg. We would take an "old building" walk along the silent streets and blind alleys of the Marais, and somehow end up across the Seine in the tiny Place de Furstenberg near the Rue du Bac, eating comic ice-cream balls shaped like the head of the president of France.

I sat there looking at Cath. I realized that before we met, when I thought of a woman, I thought of shoes, not feet, and a fuzzy sweater instead of what was under it. It took time for me to think of women's hose as stuffed with flesh and where a woman's legs joined, it was smooth and not bulky—different than a man.

"It's almost eleven," I said. "Do you have any interest in going upstairs?" She shook her head no. "In a while," she said. "Go ahead if you like." Intricate, like a filament in a light bulb, I thought. The key to Cath was patience; wait, she would talk in her own time.

DOWNSTAIRS, AT three o'clock that morning, Cath sat in the shadows of the breakfast nook, pushing a spoon around in a teacup. Outside the darkened room, I stared at her hair, changed once again, pulled up tight aaginst her head, held together in a bun by a rubber band. She wore her white terry-cloth robe and one end of the belt touched the tile floor, leaving the placket loose.

"I know you're there, Joel," she said without turning her head.

"No wonder you can't sleep," I said. "That stuff has caffeine in it." I walked across the room and my feet felt cold against the tile floor.

"What was going on in New York?" she asked. She had picked her time and her place. She looked at me, waiting for an answer.

"I've already told you." I sat down across from her.

"You haven't told me much." She looked down at her lap.

"I was waiting for you," I said. "I always do that."

"You don't have to wait for me. Just tell me what you want to tell me."

"I thought you were the one who liked public places so things would get lost in a crowd." She blinked. "If you want to know, fine—just ask."

She took a deep breath. "Okay, I'm asking."

"Two things happened. First, the rabbi who ran Ted's service wanted me to help him tell Ted's folks that Ted was living with this Field kid and I said I wouldn't. He said he would have done that for Ted and me and I should do that for Ted and Doug. Are you happy now?"

Every time I tried to make her a villain, it fell through. I kept seeing her in a different way, the way she was when we were first married. She had small, soft white breasts that almost disappeared when she lay down, and they had hurt her when Andy nursed, so much that she sometimes cried, but she went on with it anyway.

"I don't want to hear any more," she said. She stood up and moved toward the door, and I stood up to get out of her glare. I caught her and put my hand inside her robe, and I could feel her body tense.

"Cath, please, let's have this over with."

"You only got to 'one' on your list, Joel."

"There is no 'two'." I told her nothing of seeing Doug.

She walked toward the window and looked outside for a very long time. I said nothing and several minutes passed. It was silent between us, like the times we walked along the river on the path next to the Louvre before they ripped it out and put in a motorway. Cath's most riveting feature was her eyes. It wasn't the green color; it was something else about them. They told you everything if you could only see. She wasn't looking at me. She was still looking outside. "Ted told me he loved you," she said. "He called you his lover. He wanted you to stay, but you wouldn't."

"I wouldn't stay with him," I said softly. "That's right."

She turned around and I followed her. We walked single file through the upstairs hall, quietly so as not to wake the boys. In bed, her eyes were open and she stared at the ceiling. We used a flowered chintz comforter during the winter. It was soft and full of down, and when I touched it, I liked to imagine what things would have been like if I had lived my life differently, on a farm, in the country, where the covers came handed down from great-grandparents.

"I can't sleep with you tonight," she said.

"Why?"

"I'm going downstairs."

"That's out of the movies."

She sat up in bed, in the dark, and looked out of the one unshaded window we left opened so the air would come in.

"I'm tired of behaving well," she said. "I'm sick of your on-the-button timing. Here," she threw open her robe, "touch me. Help yourself."

Her next words would be "Fuck me, Joel." There were no words when we were first married; no "yes," no "no," no "you're good," no "you're awful"; not a peep. Alone with me at midnight, she was better guarded than in a living room with twenty people present. It had all changed after Greg, more after John.

It was the words she had picked up from them, the whip-hand demands, that got to me.

"Don't talk that way. It takes it all away."

She turned her head.

"Maybe it reminds you of someone else," she said. She huddled on the far side of the bed, and then she pulled the comforter away and stood over me. "Maybe Ted talked to you like that." She took a deep breath and turned on the lamp. "Did he say, 'Fuck me, Buddy'?"

I shuddered and felt the veins in my neck punch out.

I got out of bed slowly and stood in the middle of the room, naked, my chest heaving. I went into the closet, and stood there buying time, trying to calm down. I grabbed the first thing I could find to cover my body before I came back into the light.

"No, Cath." I could hardly talk. "Ted never said, 'Fuck me, Buddy.' That's something he never said."

"But you did that, didn't you?"

"That's none of your business."

"Well, well, well! An assertion of precious privacy after all these years. Now I don't have to wonder anymore."

"That was your choice."

"No, it wasn't," she said. My stomach gave a long rumble, and I was embarrassed.

"Tell me, Joel"—breathless a second ago, she was now elegantly controlled; she purred—"was Ted a good fuck? Or did he fuck you?"

It was the first time she had said those words with the lights on. Maybe she was testing the female equivalent of locker room lingo where the guys yelled, "Hand me the fuckin' towel"; "Where's the fuckin' soap." Or the gas station: "Fix the fuckin' carburetor"; "Fill the fuckin' tire." Before she had talked that way only in the dark. Now it was ladies' macho, girl power. I receive you, I make you, fuck me, fulfill me. I call the shots.

It looked as if her skin were ratcheted tight by a vice behind her head. Then, plop, her face came free again and went slack. Her eyes weren't wild anymore and her shoulders fell slightly and she moved easily.

She walked over to the desk, her robe swirling, rearranged a stack of papers, and then sat down in her reading chair, moving the cushions around her. Her eyes had become the color of a faded dollar bill. I went toward her, but she motioned me away. She sat still for quite a while, and went back to the bed and sat on the edge of the mattress.

"Ted meant a lot to me too, you know," she said. "Maybe we could have all been friends if we had been a little smarter."

"I'm not sure smarts had anything to do with it," I said.

I ran my fingers through her hair, and she moved under the covers. I went to my side of the bed, put my robe on a pile of magazines and pushed between the sheets. They were still warm.

"I've had no hidden life," I told her. "I've never wanted one."

"I hope Ted's friend isn't a gold digger," she said. I realized her thoughts were on an entirely different track.

"That happens a lot, you know," she said.

"You sound expert." I watched her, as if she were a face on television, unable to look back.

"I found out from the kids at Northwestern who helped us with the Bateman. There are some couples. Men. They talked to me."

"What about?"

"Nothing in particular. I just listen, I guess. Young men use older men," she said, touching her fingers to my forehead. "I guess young men and young women are capable of doing the same things."

"They can be." I leaned back on the pillow and looked off into the darkened room. "Doug told me Ted was used by kids like that," I said. "When Ted was alone, after me," I swallowed hard, "that's what happened."

"That wasn't your fault," she said, and her forgiveness almost made me cry.

"I learned," she said, "to say fuck me a long time ago when I wanted sex. The words made it more exciting for me somehow."

"I know."

"I meant the words for you," she said, "not anyone else."

"I know."

We held hands for a while and then her fingers went limp. I looked at the ceiling and recalled a priest at Saint Chrysostom's strutting his way through a sermon on Saint Mark, and the organ Cath had wanted to hear playing Bach vibrating with such energy that the flowers rattled in the vase on the console.

My legs began to sweat and Cath put her hand underneath the cover and started to collect the perspiration between her fingers. I turned over and moved her leg under mine. "I feel sheltered when you're there," she said, barely whispering. I put my hand behind her head, lifted her face off the pillow and kissed her. "Sheltered. I like that," I said. "It makes me feel good when you say that."

Then she moved out from under me and kneeled, tilting us toward her side of the bed. She lifted her nightgown as she straddled my body. I watched her hips come around as she lowered herself onto my cock until it disappeared inside of her. She rose and fell on me. "Now, now, now," she said.

12

By the week before Thanksgiving, we wore parkas one day and light sweaters the next. Andy rode his bike and paced me on my predinner runs, and Cath did her usual mock "I'm angry, you're late" numbers when we finally came in. It seemed like dinners had been moved to eight and then eight thirty, but it was really the early darkness that made it seem so late. After-dinner time semed compressed, out of whack as well, and the seasons were changing, finally.

My train rides home were taken up with think sessions. Not that I decided anything, because in personal matters, I was not the most decisive person ever to set foot on the globe. The reason Cath had a new car and mine was nine years old was not because we couldn't afford another new one, but because I didn't know what I wanted. It seemed that I displaced all my indecisiveness onto a car. If something wasn't going right with my life and I didn't know what it was, I'd tinker with my new car project. Down deep, I really wanted a 1947 Buick Roadmaster Convertible, Series 70. I had bought books about them (Harley Earl designed it and 11,503 were made) and I had several pictures of them, with their long, tapering pontoon front fenders, wide vertical grille and gunsight hood ornament. It was an armful to drive, but I could handle it; parts were the problem. That's what I thought about as the train rumbled up the tracks at night and down the morning.

Routine had been also broken by another unexpected event that occurred within days after I returned from Ted's funeral, but I didn't say anything to Cath right away. I could have woven it into the narrative of what has happened so far, but my mind didn't work that way. Instead of saying anything to Catherine right away, I thought I'd let one thing settle at a time. What happened was what anyone in his right mind would expect: receipt of a letter from another old friend also thrown out of whack by what happened to Ted.

The envelope I carried in my pocket was addressed to the office. It was marked Personal and the handwritten note inside was from Jerry Atkins on a sheet of Justice Department stationery, postmarked Washington, D.C.

Dear Buddy,

I've just heard that Ted passed away, and I don't know what to do. It's probably out of line for me to write to you, but I have to say something to somebody. I'm a little unnerved, but I have to tell you that he cared for me with a generosity and open-mindedness I shall never forget. I know of no one else to write to except you, and perhaps with all of this, you will understand that it gives me real pain to think that through the negligence of the last sixteen years, I have lost touch with you as well, someone who also meant so much to me in those days when we had only the few of us to turn to.

My wife and I will be in Chicago November 18, and if it is not an intrusion, I would like to see you again.

As always,
Jerry

He gave his phone number, marked private.

I wanted to see him very much, and as the day for lunch with Jerry came closer, I had to abandon thoughts of my make-believe Buick and I decided, finally, not to tell Cath about the letter and that Jerry and I were going to see each other again.

"I GOT married too, you know." Jerry emphasized the word "too," as if we had been competing. He spoke softly, as if he wanted people to strain to hear him. A lot of husky people did that. His suit was rumpled, and he looked more like a professor than a government lawyer. We were at the Metropolitan Club on the sixty-seventh floor of the Sears Tower.

"No, I didn't know," I said.

Our table was at the window off in a corner, and he looked at me for a long time without saying anything. His right eye had been hit by a squash ball during our second year in law school and there was a speck of the ruptured blood vessel near the center of the pupil that had never dissolved. I hadn't thought of Jerry's red dot in twenty years, and I had to look in the other eye and try not to let him know I had noticed. He had finally managed the mustache he couldn't grow when he was younger. It sat square in the middle of his face, which was full of strong angles, no longer round and sweet like a boy's. Maybe it was that he looked thirty-nine and I didn't, I wasn't sure. We made a little more conversation, so stilted and uneasy that I wanted to leave.

"The last time I saw you," he said, "was at Sporter's, in Boston, when you were still with Ted. Right?"

"I guess so."

He toyed with the knives and forks on the tabletop, moving them back and forth and then lining them up like battle tanks.

"Another Scotch?" he asked.

"Sure."

He leaned forward in his chair and looked out of the large window at his right elbow, straining to see the street sixty-seven floors below. "There were barricades in front of the Wacker Drive entrance when I came in. Why was that?" he asked, changing the subject.

"Sometimes ice forms at the top of the building during a storm. The pedestrians are supposed to steer clear of the west facade."

"Oh," he said, the word meaning nothing. He looked away from me, across the room. The waiter brought two Scotches. I told him I had only ordered one.

"You don't want to drink alone, do you?" Jerry said.

"No, I guess not."

"It's pretty here when it snows," he said, avoiding me, looking again out of the window.

"The first snow came early this year," I said, "but it won't be on the ground long."

"Is that the planetarium out there?" He pointed across the table. I twisted my neck and looked over my shoulder, glad to have the chance to move.

"No, that's the Shedd Aquarium," I said. "The Adler Planetarium is at the end of the point of land. It's right there, just where the DC-3 is landing. That's Meigs Field, our downtown airport."

"It's just like National."

"National can take commercial flights. Meigs is for private aircrafts mostly." I had contradicted him with too much enthusiasm. He turned away, and once again we looked anywhere but directly at each other.

"Buddy, I'm sorry I came to see you. It's an intrusion." He became perfectly still. It was late and the room had pretty much emptied out.

"There's just been a lot going on—with Ted and all that," I said. It was hearing him call me Buddy that made the anger go away. I took a drink of water and there was a damp circle in the tablecloth where my glass was.

"Did you see Ted after you and Cath were married?" he asked quietly.

"No. Did you?" I hadn't even thought about the question. It just came out.

"He came to Washington during the Carter years. He was seeing someone." My throat tightened. "A White House aide. A very bright young man—"

"That's impressive," I said.

"—but not too stable. His name was Alexander, but everyone called him Sandy. He was twenty-four then. He had covered the campaign for the *Atlanta Constitution* at twenty-one, and left to go with the Boss before anyone thought he had a chance. Sandy was in a special liaison job, and he had an office in the West Wing. They tried to move him to the East Wing, but he had himself moved right back to his old office. He was a tough kid. He signed the moving order himself. The president let him stay there."

"How the hell did he get a security clearance?" I asked.

For the first time since we said hello before lunch, Jerry smiled. He still had a smile that made anyone near him smile. There was more of Jerry, maybe twenty pounds or so, but he could still look like a blushing kid. His hair was almost all gray at the temples, but when he laughed, he seemed young again.

"Sandy told us there was nothing to it. He simply had two sets of everything: two sets of friends, two sets of vacation places and two doctors. He went to one doctor and told him everything was fine, and then to another who cured all his ailments. The FBI got the name of the one with the thin file."

"Two doctors? He had two doctors?"

"I keep forgetting what a mimic you were," he said. "Strei-sand would weep."

I kept it up, and he laughed. It felt good to play again. I hadn't had an audience like that in years. Jerry grinned across the table and ran his spoon around the inside of his empty ice-cream dish. "Buddy, I feel so much better. An hour ago I thought this was the biggest mistake I ever made."

"I thought so too," I said.

"I didn't know if you wanted me to talk about Ted or not," he said.

"Well, it's better than making war with the silverware."

"I don't have the slightest idea what you've done with your life."

"Sometimes I don't know either, but nothing like I did with it then."

"I hear you," he paused and lowered his voice, "no boys."

"That's right." It was odd, I thought, when you're around a woman you have to be strong; when you're around a man you know, it's okay if you're not. It was your turn to be sheltered. I toyed with my glasses. The room was almost empty, except for a few tables at the far end. You could see the spills made on the tablecloths during lunch, and the busboys were setting a white porcelain turkey in the center of the long buffet. "I've never said even that much, out loud, Jerry—to anybody." I found myself whispering and exposed. "You know me. Ha-ha. I always had to be the jock who whistled in the men's room."

"Are you nervous talking about it now?"

"Do birds fly?" I imitated the Brooklyn half of his accent and he broke into a wide smile.

"Sandy was a good kid," he said. "He was good for Ted." There was an easy sound to his voice as he reminisced. "We have a big guest room over the garage, and Ted used to stay with us when he came down from New York. Sandy came to our house; it was safe there." Absentmindedly, he took memo paper marked Department of Justice out of his pocket, folded it in half twice and then put it back in a different place.

He hesitated a moment. "I would like Marie to meet Catherine. Buddy, is that possible? We're going to be here for a week. It's the Bar Association Anti-Trust Section annual meeting."

I was caught off balance, and I didn't know what to say, so the only thing that came out was, "You won't be able to call me 'Buddy.' "

"I understand. I'll call you Max!"

"I don't know what's come over me," I said, trying to apologize to him. "It's all these memories coming back after all these years."

"When you see me, you can't forget, can you?"

"I guess not."

Maybe it was the wrinkles around his eyes or the line or two across his forehead that appeared when he strained to hear you if you mumbled. It made him look as if he were really listening.

Riding on the moment, I decided to tell him. "Catherine knew all along," I said. "She told me at the airport when I left for Ted's funeral."

His eyebrows rose. "Not before?"

"No." I shook my head. "Not before."

I watched his face, but there was no reaction. All he did was lean forward across the table. Two waiters at the busing station joked loudly about something, and Jerry leaned back again. "Buddy, I don't know if it was easier that way for you or not."

"I should have said something and I didn't. You make a choice. If it's an informed choice, fine. If not, the choice doesn't mean anything." My friend looked at me, as he had once done in Cambridge.

"The time," he said, "when that choice was made is gone. You've got to start now; you've got to start with where you're at." Then he smiled.

I wondered who this was across the table from me. Then I had the answer. It had come to me so slowly.

He was the judge who had decided the case before I had to decide it; he was the lawyer who tried the case before I had to try it; he was precedent.

"And Marie?" I asked. "What did you say to Marie?"

"I told her," he said evenly. "I told her right away."

He paused for a second. "I continued to go out, though. Marie knew. She still knows."

"How do you do that?" I hesitated. "I mean how do you arrange it?"

"It's okay to judge, Buddy."

"No, it's not."

"I try never to hurt her." He looked sad. "I succeed most of the time."

"I'm sure of that," I said.

After a while, Jerry started to talk again. "Marie knew about Ted," he said. "Ted wouldn't have stayed with us when he came to Washington if she hadn't known. He had the same set of rules about those things as he had when we were all together. People he cared for had to know who he was. He was the one who told her."

"What did she say?"

"Not much. She just hoped Sandy wouldn't hurt him. She's really an unusual person. We sleep together. We have sex together. She knows I go out, and I'm careful, but I never go anywhere when Noah is home. I love him too, and she knows that. I was involved with someone once. Marie and I talked about it first. Our lives went on. We were honest about the events in our lives. It's not that easy for most people, though. But it works for us."

It's hard to tell you how close I felt to Jerry that day. I think if I tell you about that feeling, I'll destroy it. It was there, though; it was really there.

As if he had been to a Sunday brunch back in Cambridge, Jerry called the next day to thank me for a nice time. In one way or another, the stubborn life we had led clung to us, like paint on a wall ten colors ago. After I spoke with Jerry, I called Cath. If Ted couldn't come to my home, Jerry could. I never put it to Cath that way, but I think she understood. That night she called him. They spoke a long time, and then she set the date with Marie, for Saturday night.

THE BELL rang downstairs. It was a chimer, and if it were just a trifle more elaborate, it would have sounded like the 20th Century-Fox theme music. Cath and I were upstairs dressing and there was no way either of us was going to run downstairs. We simply weren't dressed.

"Andy!"

"Yo!" he called back. He was downstairs studying, reading, as he put it, Your Top Greeks, but I could hear the TV and I had to shout.

"Andy, get the door, please?"

"They can't be here! They're twenty minutes early," Cath said. She finished adjusting her suit jacket. I loved to see her dressed up. It was her dark purple suit again, although I was sure there was some fancier name for the color than purple. The beads were pearls, and as formal as she looked that night, a little of her looked like a kid.

"You would think doorbells and telephones belong to anyone except our boys," she said. "Here, button this, will you?"

"Do I look all right?" I asked.

"You look wonderful," she said, "but you don't have to be all that nervous."

"I'm not."

"Tell me about it."

"It's Mr. and Mrs. Atkins!" Andy yelled.

"We were supposed to call from the station, but we rented a car!" It was Jerry's voice, obviously not used to being raised, joining in the mélange. The closet doors in the hall downstairs banged open and Cath and I just shook our heads as we heard the sound of the metal hangers clanking and banging from one side of the rack to the other. Only Andy was able to make so much noise accomplishing that simple chore.

I went to the top of the stairs and in deference to Catherine's cautioning, spoke in a most reasonable tone. "Andy, get Mr. and Mrs. Atkins something, will you, please?"

"Can they have liquor?" he answered back in clarion voice.

"I'll bet he's dressed like he's about to change a tire," Cath said. "What will they think of us?"

Cath finished dressing, and we came downstairs a few moments later. "I'm terribly sorry," Cath said as she strode into the living room, her hand extended toward Marie.

"These are my parents, Mr. and Mrs. Stern." Andy stood in his hiking boots, and put on his serious face. "Folks, these are Mr. and Mrs.—"

"Andy, stop!" I said.

"Right, Andy. Stop," echoed Judd.

"Yawn," Andy said.

Cath shook hands with Marie, and then turned to Jerry. She stopped in front of him and looked at a face she hadn't seen in sixteen years. She smiled and her eyes seemed to fill with tears. "Oh, Jerry," she said as she put both arms around him.

Jerry put one arm around Cath's waist and he held her silently, his eyes closed.

I smiled at Jerry, happy Marie had called me Joel right off. She had a round face, and she wore a necklace that looked strong enough to hold up a saxophone. She had to be older than Jerry.

"Jerry's been looking forward to this for a long time," she said.

"I'm really embarrassed," said Cath. "We should have been at the door." Cath pulled her suit jacket around her. "Well, come in. Please come in."

"We should have called," Marie said. Cath turned around to beam at Jerry, unable to take her eyes off him. I watched Catherine watching him, and eventually, she noticed the red dot in his eye. Once she had done so, she turned her head ever so slightly when she looked at Jerry, and one time, when she looked my way, she winked.

Under the candlelight at Carlos, Cath's face became younger, gentler, and it seemed to date from the last time Jerry was with us. She had taken her wedding ring off, and it sat next to her coffee cup. The buzz of the conversation faded, and it felt more and more like we were the only ones in the restaurant. Cath unbuttoned the top button of her blouse, and I saw that she had worn her mother's necklace with the pendant watch. She sometimes fingered it while we had our coffee. It was like the old days. Cath was happy without being charming. She wore little or no makeup. The laugh lines around her eyes jumped as she smiled. There were no creams or powders. It was not a prepared face.

On the way home, I drove past Moraine Park next to Lake Michigan. Cath knew I was going out of my way. She glanced sideways as we passed Central Avenue and went straight instead of turning left, but she didn't say anything. The park had a small carillon which played bells every quarter hour until midnight on the weekends, and at that time of year, the music was for Christmas. We reached the park just at the beginning of the quarter hour. There wasn't a footstep in the snow around the tower. I stopped the car and the bells chimed, "I'll Be Home for Christmas." Toward the end of the second verse, Cath was humming.

As we rode home, it was Marie's voice we heard in the darkness of our car. "Jerry didn't find out about Ted until after the funeral. He would have gone if he had known about it in time." We drove along for a few blocks in silence. Then Cath said, almost proudly, "Joel went."

"Jerry told me," Marie answered. "That was a fine thing to do. I told Jerry, in a way, that you went for him too." Other than our voices, there were no other sounds, just the muffled sound of the tires on the snow. "Were others there from school?" Marie asked.

"I didn't see anyone," I said quietly.

"Ted hadn't seen many of the old group," Jerry said into the side window. "You know how the people you see change over the years," he said, almost inaudibly.

"Were things at all good for Ted?" Cath asked. "God, I hope so."

"They were all right," Jerry said.

"It was all so abrupt," Cath went on; "one minute he was there at our wedding and the next minute he was gone and we never saw him again." There was a catch in her voice.

It wasn't until we were back home, having a drink in the sunroom, that Cath asked Marie about Ted again. "When Ted was visiting Washington, was he seeing someone?" she asked.

Jerry touched his wife's hand and she bought time by opening her purse. Jerry looked at me seeking instructions. I nodded.

"Yes, he was," Jerry said.

"Who?" Cath asked anyone in the room.

It was my turn to speak up. "Jerry told me at lunch that Ted was seeing a young man who worked at the White House. They would see each other at Jerry's house."

"It was a security problem, I guess," said Marie. Her words were matter-of-fact, but she appeared flushed.

Cath looked around the room and then at me. "Joel, may I have a refill?"

"He stayed in our guest room when Sandy came to visit," said Marie, looking gently at Cath. "We have a few rooms over the garage. There was a separate entrance and they could come and go as they pleased." Other than our voices, there were no sounds in the room at all, unless one of us shifted position, in which event, a joint in a chair or a floor plank creaked. "It bothered me for a while," Marie added; "I felt like I was giving secrets to the Russians or something like that," and she smiled a little.

"You know what I don't understand?" Cath posed the question standing next to the breakfront where all the fancy glasses were. I knew that particular innocent look. "All of you seem to be directing this explanation toward me. Why is that?" A smile crept across her face. She twisted her fingers, and then, she didn't smile anymore. Cath walked back to the sofa, and, as was her custom, she scooted into a corner and packed herself, almost protectively, it seemed, into the down pillows.

"Ted hid none of his life from us," Jerry said, "and he would have wanted none of it hidden from either of you." His voice was solid and confident.

"Did his relationship with Sandy, is that his name—?" Cath hesitated.

"—Yes, Sandy," said Jerry.

"—Did it go on for quite a while?"

"About a year," answered Jerry.

"Is that when it ended?" she asked. "Or was it only an interruption?"

"Sandy ran out on him," Marie said. Cath stared into her glass. She looked around the room, but avoided me completely.

"Ted would arrive at our house," Marie said, "and perhaps an hour before he was due, Sandy would call to say he couldn't make it. Ted shrugged it off, on the outside anyway. He used to joke and say, 'Anything for the National Interest.' Then he wouldn't hear a thing from Sandy; no message at all. He allowed that twice. Sandy would call us two weeks later to apologize, but Ted had left his instructions: "no more." Catherine bit her lower lip. Jerry had reached for one of our picture albums and was flipping pages. "Then we didn't see Ted for quite a while," Marie said.

"It was probably a year or so," Jerry said as he looked up from the family picture we had taken at the boys' summer camp last year. "He came down for a weekend, but instead of meeting someone in Washington, he asked if he could bring a friend. We had to ask him to wait until the week after Thanksgiving when Noah would be back at school, but then, Ted's trip was delayed a week anyway because a building Doug was working on was being topped out and he couldn't get away."

I studied every inch of Cath, but there was little movement, just the faintest retreat into her pillows.

"He came down with his new friend." Marie beamed as she said "new friend." Jerry had known Doug, I realized.

"Now that guy, Marie liked," Jerry said smiling.

Cath looked up, and that same know-it-all smile came across her face. "Was that Doug Field?"

"Yes, it was," said Marie.

"Joel met him when he was in New York," Cath said, and Jerry's eyes narrowed.

"I saw him," I answered, "at the . . . temple."

"Joel liked him very much too," I heard Cath say.

"He seemed to be the right guy," Marie smiled. "Just perfect for Ted. He once told us that relationships in the gay world didn't last long. I think Ted had been disappointed so many times that he never permitted his expectations to rise to the point of seeking anything permanent. Doug surprised him. Doug would have a career whether Ted got involved in it or not. Doug was self-standing; he brought so much to the table. It was wonderful to watch."

"You really cared for Ted, Marie, didn't you?" Cath said. Her eyes seemed bright.

"Doug made him very happy. He was an anchor for Ted's life. He brought Ted something that most couples, couples of any mix, rarely know: the feeling that the person who loves you will never leave you." Catherine's eyes filled with tears, and she struggled to hold them back. Jerry moved the ashtray from one side of the table to the other. I was afraid to make a sound.

"I feel so badly," Cath said, clearing her throat, "that we lost touch. I would have liked very much to have seen him happy." Cath's voice was without self-pity or blame. She looked up and took my hand.

Marie asked, "This must be very hard for Doug. Is he doing all right?"

"Not really," I said quietly. "He was with friends. At least he wasn't alone."

"Was that Reuters fellow there?" asked Marie.

"Yes," I said, surprised she knew so much about him. "I can't remember his name, but he was there." The sound of two men kissing came into my mind and I wanted out; I was afraid.

"Well, look," said Jerry, "it's getting late, and we have to drive back into town." He stood up, and the mood was broken. Cath said they could sleep in the guest room and drive downtown in the morning if they liked, but Jerry said he had an early meeting.

WE WALKED out to the car and Jerry and I had a few moments alone.

"They gave you a new Cougar. How do you like it?" I said.

"It's not a bad-handling car," he answered. He turned around and watched Catherine and Marie silhouetted against the light, still standing inside. "The best car I've driven is Doug's. He has an old Alfa Romeo, a Giulietta from the fifties. It looks like the day it came out of the showroom. He drives it like Mario Andretti," he said as he smiled at me.

"You knew him pretty well, didn't you?" I said.

"Not intimately," he said. "Only when he came to Washington with Ted."

"Jerry, when Ted died, you could have written to Doug. Why did you write to me?"

He ran his fingers over the steering wheel and looked away from me, concentrating on the dashboard. "I don't know. It was an excuse, I guess. Doug didn't go back to those days. You did." He looked up at me. "It went all right tonight, didn't it?"

"It went fine." The car door was open, and I put my arm around his shoulder.

"It's a different life than the one you lead," he said. "I wasn't able to stop where you did."

I squeezed his shoulder, and he smiled like an embarrassed twelve-year-old.

"I've thought about you on and off," he said, "wondering if you'd done what I did. Buddy, I'm happy for you." I didn't mind his calling me Buddy. It made me feel good. "It's not that I'm ashamed of the way I live, or even the relationship I had with Bryan last year. It was a love in addition to my marriage. It's you I've wondered about: the absoluteness with which you suppressed it all. It implies such extreme effort to keep it that way. I hope you're okay."

"I'm fine." I should have felt intruded upon, but I felt exactly the opposite, and I told him so. "Thanks for thinking about me, Jer."

"Doug Field is due in Chicago in two weeks," he said.

I squatted next to the open car door. "Is he?" Jerry cleared his throat. "What's he going to be doing here?" I asked.

"He'll be here for a meeting," he said. "Buddy, I called him when Ted passed away. I had to."

"I'm not surprised."

"I didn't think you would be. I didn't go up and see him. He was very glad, however, that you did. It meant a lot to him. When I knew that you had been there, and he was the one who told me you had gone to the funeral—well, getting in touch with you was something I had wanted to do for a long time." He turned the steering wheel, or tried to; but it was still immobile because the lock linked to the ignition was still engaged. "But that's off the track. You know, he comes to Chicago on and off."

"And I go to New York on and off. So what?"

"You sound angry," he said.

I stood up and looked at the house. Cath and Marie were still inside, although the door was now wide open.

"No, there's no reason to be," he said. "Doug doesn't travel because of you."

"You sound jealous," I said.

I stood up and looked over the top of the car toward the house. Cath and Marie were walking down the stairs, close to each other. Jerry closed the car door, started the engine, moved the steering wheel to unlock it and reached over to open the right door for Marie. He rolled down the window, motioned to me, and I bent down and moved my head close to his.

"You're not so hard to think about, Bud," he said. "Give people a chance."

CATH WASHED and I wiped the glasses, and we went upstairs together. We undressed, passing each other silently as we walked in and out of the bathroom.

"Joel, I'm wide awake. Will it bother you if I read?"

"No." I turned over, away from the light on Cath's side of the bed. "What are you reading?" I mumbled into the pillow.

"*Portrait of a Marriage*. It just came out in paper. The wife had an affair with Virginia Woolf, and the husband had affairs with several men."

I turned toward her and propped my head up on the pillow. "Cath, when did you start reading that?"

"Not long ago. I'm learning. That's what I'm trying to do." She closed the book gently and turned to me, our faces close together. "Marie is wonderful, isn't she?" Cath said. "She didn't back away from Ted or any relationship he had. She put no distance between them because of that; there was no disgust." Cath's last word made me wince.

"Is that how you felt?" I asked.

"Disgust?" she asked. I nodded.

"Yes," she answered, without reluctance, "that's how I felt."

"I hope we're all through with this now," I said.

"Look at Marie." Catherine sighed, and for a moment nothing was said. "That's the way I'd like to be." I felt the bed shift as Cath pulled the comforter over her legs. Then she spoke in a small voice. "That's the way I used to be. I never used to have the rules I have now," she said quietly. Then she turned to me, the moment gone, and said, the Junior League charm returning, "See how silly I get?"

"That's not silly." I moved and tried to hug her.

"Joel, not tonight," she said. She held her book in her lap, pretending to read, her eyes on the page, but not focusing. "I don't feel like anything physical tonight," she said.

I don't know how I knew, but I was sure she was watching me as I crossed the room. There was a small box on one of the top shelves of the closet that I had discovered a year or so back. Rummaging around in it, I found her red beads, the ones she wore years ago. I hid them in my hand as I came back to bed, throwing the covers over me. Her body tightened. Perhaps she thought I was getting a prophylactic. She shook her head no from side to side. "Joel, let me read my book," she said, a little annoyed. I smiled to myself.

"Do you ever think of wearing these?" I handed her the beads. She put the book down slowly, and she held the beads up to the light and smiled with the corners of her mouth.

Cath continued looking at her book, but I didn't hear a page turn. She looked at the wall across the room, the book lying open in her lap, its contents ignored. "Jerry hadn't seen you for years, but he knew you well enough to know that we would still be together," she said, a little pride in her voice.

"There are stories," I said, "about Jerry and me that I've never told you; things I've said to him, times he helped me when we were all still in school. He knew how I felt." Cath sucked in her cheeks, trying to hold back her emotions. Then she held my hand. "I didn't have rules then either," she said, repeating herself.

I reached over and turned off the light on her night table, my arm sliding against her body. She let me take the book from her lap, and it was the gentlest making of love I remembered in a long time.

13

Doug had not only told me the name of his hotel, but had also given me his room number. I knew I didn't have the resources to start a friendship with a stranger, but I went anyway. As I looked back on it, I didn't think friendship had anything to do with it. The driver ran a red light and hit the brakes hard as we came to a stop in front of the Park Hyatt. Doug waited in the crowded lobby, twenty feet on the other side of the revolving door. He sat in a chair that gave him an unobstructed view of everyone who walked through the main entrance. In the midst of the commotion, he looked calm and relaxed. He made no move to get up; he simply sat there, smiling at me. Then he tossed off a wave. Still, he sat there. I walked toward him, and only as I reached his chair did he lift himself out of it. He took a step toward me, arm extended, ready to shake my hand.

"I recognize you from your pictures," I said and he laughed.

"It sure didn't take you long. You must have flown."

"I didn't. The cab did," I said.

He was taller than I had remembered. He was as tall as I was. He wore a dark blue suit with a white handkerchief in his breast pocket, and a gold pocket watch on a gold chain that crossed from one vest pocket to the other. He looked more like a lawyer or an investment banker than an architect.

"We can have drinks here, or we can go into the bar," he said. He was all smiles. "There were three people there the last time I looked, and that was a few moments ago."

"Let's go there," I said. We walked through a blue glazed door into the bar. He was right. The place was empty.

"We beat out Murphy-Jahn," he said, full of excitement. He had not wasted a minute on small talk. "And guess whose design it is?" We took two stools near one end of the bar.

"I have absolutely no idea," I told him, beaming to beat the band.

"I like Helmut. He's good—if not the best, certainly one of the best—but I'm really very proud. I really am."

"You look it," I said.

"Architecture is one place—there are others, but not many— where you can make it without being middle-aged."

"Now *that* hurt!"

"We'll be on Wacker and Jackson, across from Sears."

"Oh, my God, the pounding!"

"We're not going that high. Nowhere near ninety. I wish I could describe the building, but I'm not good enough with my words yet. Most architects obscure their designs with their description of them, Philip Johnson in particular. It's a tradition, since the days of Frank Lloyd Wright."

"Is that who you want to be?"

"Not necessarily. But I would like my work to last."

"Do you think that will happen?"

"I hope so." He paused. "I don't know," he said and he looked around the room. "Someone higher up will want to put his name on the plans, but I'll fight him. I've put in my time. They kept me going back and forth to Montreal for a year on one project, but I learned from that. The French eye can accept more complexity than ours can. That gave me the guts to do the Wacker Center design."

"You care about what you do, don't you?" I said.

"Yes," he said. "Don't you?"

"When did you get into town?" I asked.

"Monday."

"That's almost a week ago. Were you going to call?"

"I wasn't sure."

"I wouldn't have blamed you," I said. "I never should have said good-bye by leaving a note."

"That's right. You shouldn't have done that." He took a sip of his drink. "If my friend Allan had his way, you would have two busted kneecaps by now, New Jersey style." His smile was thin, but at least it was there.

"You showed him the note?"

"No. He was the one who found it. I mean," he grinned, "you could have pinned it to my pillow." He paused. "Well, let's not talk about that."

"That's fine with me." My throat muscles had tightened and the normal resonance in my voice had gradually disappeared. To make a sound as close to normal as possible, I had lowered pitch and spoke slowly. When I did that, I could still sound somewhat like me, but Doug had trouble hearing me because I couldn't produce a lot of volume when I worked on all of those artificial adjustments. I kept clearing my throat. Doug asked if I had a cold.

"I'm sorry about leaving that note for you—" I said.

"You've said that. Don't beat yourself up on that score."

There is power in a fresh friendship when you're young, I thought. You talk all night; you use the darkness to let someone know you. It takes time, the kind of time you will never have again.

At four in the morning, Ted once told me he wanted to teach high school. He wanted to be where he could make a difference, where he could give and not take. It was dark in our bedroom back then, so he didn't see the tears that were stinging me. I was quiet a long time and he asked me what I was feeling. Not what I was *thinking*, mind you, but what I was feeling. I told him that what counted to me was someone who could write a song, or someone who could sing. He told me he felt like a loser. I wasn't doing what I wanted to do either. It was middle-of-the-night talk, and he trusted me as I had never been trusted before. I learned love from him.

When the time came when I would want to sleep with a man again I wondered if I would actually be ready to do it. I had always thought that I would be torn by conflict and experience all kinds of shame and feel more or less like a sneak and a traitor. I felt none of that. Perhaps I had rehearsed the feelings so often that when the real event occurred, the feelings belonged to another time and simply did not come to the fore.

"I made a lot of mistakes that night," I said. "I wanted to stay with you and I didn't."

His eyes widened. "That's too elliptical. What do you mean?" he asked.

"That I should have gone to bed with you." His body stiffened.

"You did go to bed with me," he said, almost in a whisper. "I was very much alone then."

"That's not what I mean," I said.

"Then what do you mean?"

"I shouldn't have put the brakes on. I should have let go, if that's what you had wanted."

"It was. It is." The piano player wasn't playing dreamy music, but he might as well have been. He grinned like Bobby Short and played an upbeat tune from an old Broadway show. Maybe it was escape from something I had brought upon myself, but I wanted to hum. Doug looked away into the middle of the room, then turned back to me.

"Married men go to bars and some tell you they're married, so no one is misled. Others lie, but I can usually spot them. It's a feeling, I guess, of belonging to someone else. It's funny," he said, "it's easier for me to spot a man who belongs to a woman than a man who has a lover. I wonder why that is? Well," he smiled, "I'll add that to the list of ten thousand things I'll never understand, huh?"

"You say 'huh' all the time just like Ted did," I said.

"So do you," he answered.

"I haven't done anything—"

"—Since Ted?" He stopped me in midsentence; his voice was flat, but his eyes knew.

"That's right," I said.

I asked the barman for our check and paid it. Doug took his room key out of his pocket. He looked at me as he did that. Whether he had a thought just then or not, I didn't know, but all at once, the seriousness left him and he looked relieved.

We waited for the elevator doors to open, and we were in the cab by ourselves. He took hold of my wrist and turned my watch so he could see the face of it. "What time is it?" he asked.

"Don't worry," I said. I put my arm behind his lower back. It was not a clamp on the shoulder, locker room style. There was nothing at all resembling the golf club, and Doug didn't pull away.

Inside his room, he stood next to the frosted window, looking out. "Joel, go do it with some stranger." He turned around and his face was contorted. "I'm not new to your life. Ted told me how much it all means to you."

"You're thinking of yourself as well, and you should. You're thinking of how much pain I caused Ted and you don't want any repetition of that."

"You're goddamn right. You blew the roof off Ted's life. You're not going to do that to me. The last thing I am, baby, is naive." Doug stood taller, and his strong brown hair fell over his forehead. "Some guys have sex like peanuts." He shook his head no and frowned. "That's just not me." He hung his head. "I wish it were."

"You ought to celebrate that attitude, not bemoan it." I didn't know where the force in my voice came from. He looked at me, and his eyes misted. "Let's not and say we did."

Doug walked over to the dresser where I was standing. He stood next to me and put his arms around me. His head fell on my shoulder. We stayed there. He didn't move, but then I felt his hand on the back of my neck, and I moved my body close to his, to let him know I felt for him also.

It was different with a man. What happened at the end was the same, but it was how you felt, what you did before you got there that was different. It wasn't better, it wasn't worse, it was different. I wanted to touch old bases, but I didn't do it.

THE BARTENDER downstairs, as if he heard a silent prayer, put a Scotch in front of me. I closed my eyes, which was one way to rest them. I had just left Doug's room and stopped in the hotel bar for a drink because I needed one. My back and chest sweated and my hands were cold enough for anyone who touched me to feel the fear in them. It was a delayed reaction.

There were never impromptu bouts of sex in my life. I never wanted them. In that sense, I was the same before, during and

after Ted. Jerry wondered how I had turned it all off. Easy.
You did it because you wanted to. No. Not easy at all. I didn't
want a life of looking at men and hoping Cath wouldn't notice. I wanted Cath to have all of me, because maybe that way
I would have all of her. It didn't work that way, but she was
away a short enough time not to do any real damage. Besides
that, my impulses were all too dangerous; they were all di-
rected toward Ted, and he was alive then.

Some guy sat down a few seats away from me. He put his
hand on the backrest of the barstool and his wedding ring
flashed. The piano player was at it again and you could hear
the clanking of silver and dishes as the busboys set up the
buffet for the dinner hour. Friday must have been the big
night. Every table in the place was set. The bartender, a nice-
looking dark-haired college kid, brought a bourbon to the guy
down the bar. "Nice to see you again, Mr. Walters." He didn't
speak; he insinuated. "You too, Bill," the man said. If Jerry
were here, he would miss nothing. He would see the winks and
take full note of older gentlemen putting the make on the kid,
and the cash register smile on the kid's face. What a knockout
life that is, I thought. I asked myself if I was headed for anything better.

I crossed Chicago Avenue and headed up Michigan Boulevard. The buses rolled, nose to tail, like herds of green metal
elephants. It had turned colder and the exhaust seemed to
freeze solid and hang there as soon as it hit the air. No one
knew me at this end of the Loop. Our firm represented a big
advertising agency that had offices in the Hancock Building,
but I never did any work for them. You always knew when
those clients were at our place: they looked happy and wore
sport coats. There were headlights sneaking up from behind
and the cabs hissed by on the slippery pavement.

Two blocks south was Stuart Brent's bookstore, and I decided to stop there because it was a bookstore that was still run by people who actually read books. Between this place and a few on Madison Avenue, like Books & Co. and the Madison Avenue Bookshop and even our own Kroch's, I knew the world was still safe. I fumbled through the art book department, wearing the white gloves Stuart provided for browsers. I was almost through with the book I bought a few weeks ago and needed another. He suggested a new study on short stories and I bought it. Stuart rang up the sale himself, a gesture of courtesy to a friend, and I was appreciative.

A young kid in the railroad station begged change. She looked lousy. I gave her a couple of quarters, but she moved on to the next sucker before I could ask her what the trouble was. I ran into my partner in the law firm, Ed Flynn, at the newspaper stand and as we walked to the long row of double-decked yellow cars, I was depressed by the thought of sitting next to him and having to make casual conversation all the way out to Glencoe.

"I haven't kicked the habit yet," he called out and abruptly turned to jump the steps of the smoking car.

"Keep trying, Ed. Good to see ya." I was tired of being hearty. The head of the train would let me out on the northernmost end of the Glencoe station, where I would be closer to the house. I knew why people commute, I thought. It gives them time alone. Same reason for jogging. The train would not arrive until seven ten. Maybe I should have called home. A few years ago, Cath had asked me not to call if I couldn't make the usual train every day. She didn't like the idea of me checking in. After all, she wasn't my mother waiting with cookies and milk at three o'clock, she had said. How do you love your wife without having her turn into your mother because she's a woman? I asked myself. Love your boyfriend, that's how.

I was really a smart aleck. I had all the answers, I thought. The train rumbled along and seemed to sway more than usual when it hit the switches at Davis Street, Evanston. What if the thing toppled over the embankment smack onto the parking lot next to the Marshall Field's branch? A mess, that's what would happen. Gar-bage. I never worried about buying it in a plane, but at that instant, I could see it happening to me in beautiful downtown Evanston.

14

THERE WAS no dressing for work the next morning; it was Saturday. It was still dark outside when I started to run. The boys were asleep when I walked past their rooms. Juddy still slept rolled up in a ball and he had left a huge, partly assembled puzzle on the console in the hallway just outside his door. It was probably the only large clear surface within miles of his room. I looked inside, and sure enough, there were the characteristic stacks of books and games and the boxes his puzzles came in. The room was as neat as he was. I always liked the house best when it was quiet, when you could hear it creak.

The runners in the block have a deal. There is a meeting place we worked out. It's the bench at the top of the gravel beach just off Park Avenue, and we meet there on the hour. If anyone else wants to run, the drill is to be there. We run together, but there is no obligation to talk, unless you want to. That morning the lake was gray but there were no whitecaps. Running on the beach was for Saturday only. It was very special to me—a kind of private yet active time, not like sitting on the North Western, which was one, but not the other.

Runs, even the energetic ones, never lasted more than an hour for me. Cool-down took about ten minutes and I timed it so the tenth minute was over just as I sat down on the stool in the mud room and took my shoes off. Inside, at the breakfast table, Cath and Andy were going at each other. He had stayed out past curfew again the night before, and Cath had laid into him for what seemed to me to be a few minutes' infraction. I refused to ground him. I tried to joke about it, reminding Cath how we used to tell him that God is good to those who eat vegetables. She didn't smile at all. She was angry and he was joyful. Frankly, I didn't give a damn. Sometimes the boys wore me out. Sometimes the whole thing did. The minute Andy had figured out that his lenient sentence was due to disinterest, he sulked. I wanted to go to him, but I had other things on my mind.

Andy had just picked up the phone. If, in person, his voice sounded like a tugboat, amplified, over the phone it was worse, especially when he had just come off a good squabble and was in a bad mood. God help the ears of whomever he was talking to.

"Yeah?" he barked. "Sure, this is Andy. Who are you?"

Cath corrected him sweetly. "Andrew, be cordial."

She reached for the phone, but he took a step away and the receiver went with him. He sweetened his tone. "Well, isn't that nice. Good to hear your voice." He cupped his hand over the mouthpiece and asked Cath, "Is that better?" his tone so sarcastic I wanted to slug him. Then he exposed the mouthpiece and continued talking.

"Well, he's fine. How are you?" He shrugged his shoulders. "She's fine too."

Judd pulled Andy's arm. "Who is it?" Judd piped up.

"Slimeboat," Andy said to him, and then, sweetly, back into the phone, "Would you care to converse with Father?" Mouthpiece covered: "This guy's nuts. He's taking everybody's temperature." Mouthpiece free: "Well, I don't know. Maybe. Here. You can talk to my mom," he said, stumbling over his exit line. He handed the phone to Catherine.

"Hello?" she said. "Why, yes. How are you!" she said. You could tell she didn't know who she was talking to. I knew her taken-off-guard look, but that was quickly erased. "We're quite well, thank you." She turned to me and shrugged. Her gesture was the same as Andy's. "Where are you?" she asked and there was a short pause. "In Chicago?" she said. "Why that's wonderful!"

Where her enthusiasm came from, I didn't know. There was another pause. "Well, of course, he's fine." She looked puzzled. "He looks a little tired, though." She smiled at me, and then her expression changed. There was a long pause again during which time she looked straight at me as she listened.

"I simply won't hear of it," she said. "It's very nice of you to ask, but you're in our city. You must come here." She was turning the telephone cord in her fingers.

"Who the hell *is* that?" I asked.

Cath put her hand over the mouthpiece. "It's Doug Field. It's Chanukah tonight," she said to me, her hand still covering the phone. "We can't leave him alone."

She turned her attention fully back to the phone. "We insist that you come here. One moment. Joel will check the train schedules for you." Cath turned to me: "Joel, it's in the drawer just next to you."

In the dream I had the night before, I had taken a taxi from the office to the North Western Station, something I never did in real life. The driver took a shortcut through a parking lot, but the owner slammed the gate down before we could

escape. No pay. No leave. I wanted the police; they appeared
by magic and the gate rose. We drove through all kinds of expressway overpasses and underpasses that didn't exist in reality. The cab fell in the Chicago River, but I wasn't in it. Instead, I sat peacefully on the bank of a green and fresh stream
in the country. The taxi was floating in the stream and the
driver was sitting on top, smiling. He was young with curly
hair and he had his shirt off. He called to me and I headed
into the water toward him. Then I froze. Back on the bank,
a girl had a blue phone, but she was talking and wouldn't give
it to me. I was frantic. "Police!" I shouted. "I need to call the
police!" I ripped the phone out of her hand, and the two girls
next to her glanced unperturbed at me, polishing their nails.
I woke up sweating, uneasy, wondering what had happened to
me. I always liked to bug my own dreams and knew that in a
dream, you're really everybody; you play all the characters. In
the taxi, I was the passenger who ended up on the riverbank
trying to save the driver, and part of me was the driver on top
of the sinking cab with my shirt off, out to destroy myself.

Cath read off the departure and arrival times to Doug, and
I stood at the sink, looking out across the backyard as I heard
them agree. Cath hung up the phone. The refrigerator motor
clicked on and hummed. "He was all alone," she said, "and he
called to wish us a Happy Chanukah, and to ask how you
were, and how I was. He asked about the kids, too."

"Well, it was nice of him to include everybody."

"Joel! You're heartless." I was glad she didn't speak to me
that way in front of the boys. "Be nice to him. He's alone,"
she said.

IT SHOCKED the hell out of everyone there to see me at the office that Saturday afternoon. One of the pleasures of partner-
ship was the avoidance of paperwork, but it also meant you

got stale. There was drafting to do for a private placement, and I decided to do it myself. The teaching I received and the teaching I provided had a basic tenet: you never know what the deal is until you try to draft it. Sitting at my desk with paper clips, Scotch tape and a scissors made me feel young again, like a kid out of law school. When I finished, I was proud of myself. The agreement was twenty-eight pages and it was so tight that when you held it up and snapped your finger at the corner, it rang like crystal.

I ran again several miles late that afternoon. I didn't feel the cold and I seemed to float over the ice patches and cracks next to the beach. It was a stall to buy time and keep from going home, and I knew it.

It was dark—close to five and pitch-black—and the house seemed to loom in front of me, the lights in the rooms making it look like a face. For an instant, I felt as if the stone the house was made of had a grudge against me. Doug and Juddy were playing on the living-room floor. They were so involved that for a moment, they didn't notice me. I cleared my throat and Doug looked up. I hadn't started to take off my sweat shirt when Judd bounced up, full of excitement, talking so fast he could hardly get the words out.

"Dad, look what Doug brought me. Look. It has these two towers and a wire that goes between them. You set up the towers, tie the wire between them, and put the plane on the wire. You press this button, and the plane flies on the wire over the target and then you press this button, and pow! the plane drops its bombs."

Doug was looking up at me, his eyes wide and soft, and his hair fell over his forehead.

"It looks as if you found a friend," I said to Doug.

Cath turned the corner, coming down the staircase. You could tell by the cast of her features that she was satisfied, proud that she had asked Doug to be with us. She was the perfect Junior League samaritan. "Doug walked into the house as if it were Christmas," she said. "You should see Andy's football. Regulation and it might even stay clean for a minute and a quarter. Doug also brought both boys an aquarium. He knew just what to bring."

Catherine spoke of him as if he were not in the room, and he looked at the floor. There were times when those Junior League manners drove me nuts; the way she smiled like a demented jack-in-the-box whenever someone new entered her life. We had always led our lives with a certain amount of high finish, and anyone who knew the rule to bring gifts for the children was a hit.

"How was your train ride?" I asked him.

"Fine," he said. Doug was seated cross-legged next to Judd. He unwound himself and stood up. His hair seemed a little longer, I thought, or maybe he had lost a pound or two. Not in twenty-four hours, I told myself. People just look different when you see them in different places, I thought.

"Joel, want something to drink?" Catherine asked.

"I need to change first." I started up the stairs.

"Doug can take a Scotch to you," Cath said. I didn't want to hear that; I didn't. "I'm busy with dinner," she said.

"I'd be glad to," he said. There was nothing else he could say.

"Joel takes a light Scotch. Leave it for him in the guest room, where we put your menorah." I was halfway up the stairs when I heard that.

"Where we put your what?" I said.

"I wasn't sure you'd have one." He looked up to the landing. "I brought ours." Bang, he turned on his smile again— playful, questioning, forgiving, warm, glad to be back, all at once. He pushed his hair off his forehead and straightened his tie.

The small guest room was at the far end of the upstairs hall.

We stored our old furniture there, including the stand-up desk I bought in Cambridge at our fifth reunion (Felix Frankfurter had worked at one). Cath and I had not talked about whether Ted would show up for that reunion; it was a moot point, he didn't. I felt comfortable with all that old stuff and I liked being in that room. It had a leaky steam radiator that hissed, and the sound, especially on cold mornings, reminded me of my old room on the South Side when I was a kid. Doug looked at a collection of certificates Cath had elaborately framed. His schoolboy blazer and long hair made him seem young and soft. The cold weather had made his skin glow. Cath's sense of humor had prevailed, and the gaudy airline million-miler documents had been hung above the Harvard diploma, and he had taken note of that.

"I hate to fly," he said. "I get through it by being unconscious," he said. He grinned and I didn't want to realize that I was glad to see him. "I sleep on airplanes," he said. "Do you?"

"You must have a clear conscience," I said. I took a sip of the Scotch he had brought.

He walked as far away from me as he could get in that little room. "I feel as trapped being here as you are having me. Catherine didn't ask me to come here; she insisted. I didn't need that crack about conscience." He bent over to look at the snapshots under the slanted writing surface of the desk, but there was no one there he would know. When he raised his head, his face was flushed. "Let's make the best of it, okay?"

"It wasn't meant as a crack," I said.

"Oh, yes, it was."

"Will you wait a second? Stand still," I said. "Your shirt collar is standing up." I walked over to him and folded his collar down around his tie until it lay flat. "Good, that's better," I said. He started to reach up, but he stopped and his arms fell back to his sides. I stepped back and looked at him. "Yes, that does look better," I said.

"It's all right that I'm here, isn't it?" he asked. The adversary tone had disappeared.

"Sure it is," I said.

"Don't just say it"—he snapped his fingers—"like that. Think about it before you say it." He turned quickly toward the door, apparently afraid our words had carried. "I'm sorry," he said. He spoke softly. "I shouldn't have called. I just wanted to make sure you were okay. Yesterday should have been the end of it." He walked over to the desk and studied the pictures again.

"Listen," I said, "Cath isn't going to have time to walk with me to get a paper," I said. "We usually do that every night."

Cath was in the wine storage room in the basement and I called down to tell her I was walking to the village for the paper and asked if she wanted to come. "No, take Doug," is what she told me. I walked down the back stairs to talk with her. Doug sensed that I wanted to speak to her on my own and he waited in the hall.

"There is more dust in this wine bin than you can shake a stick at," she said, "but, I guess that's good." It was dark down there, and Cath had a flashlight and she was shining it across the rows of bottles, turning them, checking labels. "We're supposed to have red," she said, "but how about a Montrachet for good measure?"

"Sure you don't want to take a walk?"

"If I wanted to, how could I?" she asked. "Arlene is off. It's her mother's birthday."

"I'm sorry. I didn't think to ask. We don't have to go. I can help."

She turned to me and smiled, and for no reason at all, she hugged me. "Now go show our guest a good time." When my ear was close to her mouth, she said, "Remember how we used to walk into the village in the winter? And if it was warm enough, we'd sit on the bench—"

"—in front of the drugstore," I said, "and we'd listen to the clock chime and the trucks two miles away on Edens Highway."

"I'm glad he's here," she said. "You didn't see him when he came in. He looked lost. Somehow, in a way, he could be like a godfather to our kids, like Ted might have been."

"You miss Ted," I said, "don't you?"

"In an odd way, I always did," she said. I held her hand tightly. "Doug's waiting," she said. "And I've got to finish this." She started turning the bottles over again, checking labels.

"YOU KNOW," Doug said, "it's colder than I thought." The breath shone from our mouths and noses.

"Well, we can walk fast," I said.

"Okay."

Doug pulled gloves out of his pockets and put them on. He wrapped a bright red scarf around his neck and buttoned his coat.

We passed the park just south of the Crescent Drive bridge, and he took a cap out of his pocket and pulled it down tight over his forehead. We cut west across Lincoln Drive and crossed over to the gravel roadbed where the old North Shore line tracks used to be, parallel to those of the North Western.

As we rounded the curve in the road, the trees stopped and gave way to the open park, and railroad tracks and beyond. The wooden platform where the train stopped was empty and whoever was waiting for a train was inside the old brick station house. The traffic on Green Bay Road, on the other side of the station, was muffled by a tall hedgerow between the road and the train tracks. The trees were set up, as they were in Europe, to break the wind.

"I've got the money for the paper," he said. He pulled out a pocket full of change and dropped coins into my hand, without looking at how much was there. I put two dimes in the vending machine chained to the lamppost and gave the rest back. He took the paper out and let the door clang shut.

"I'm sorry for making you uncomfortable," he said. "Am I forgiven?" We turned around and started to walk back to the house.

"I made Ted very happy," he said. "I really did."

"I have no doubt of that."

"When I moved into his house, when I knew it would last, you know what he did?" I shook my head. "He played the piano and even sang a few bars."

"Long Ago and Far Away," I said.

"That's right," and he spoke the lyrics:

> Long ago and far away,
> I dreamed a dream one day.
> And now that dream is here
> beside me.

I watched his cap, perched on his head, not daring to look directly at him.

"Love gets lost on people who live on the line," he said. He looked straight at me.

"What if you're different than you appear?" I asked him. "What if you don't want to live on the line all the time?"

"You'd always want to step up to the line," he said, "and if someone didn't step up to the line with you, you'd be bored."

We crossed Crescent Park. "You ever try that jungle gym

over there?" he asked. He headed toward the maze of colored poles and threw his right arm over the top one. He hoisted himself up, one pole after the other, and stretched horizontally, poised over the top, grinning like Superman, looking as if he could fly. He somersaulted, and ended up, feet first fortunately, on the ground, standing inches in front of me. He was breathing fast, and his face was full of color. His hair had fallen all over his face and he looked as if he didn't care about anything in the world except being right where he was. He bent down and picked up his cap, which had fallen to the ground. It smelled like ferns, deep in the forest. He stood up, put the cap on his head and reached over and touched the collar on my coat.

"I worry sometimes about the way I like you," he said.

"Come on, we'd better get home." I cleared my throat, and I smiled as if the whole thing had been a joke and started walking. He bent down to tie his shoe, then caught up and walked next to me. I knew I would lie awake that night, wondering how I could beg him not to tell anyone.

15

ALTHOUGH THERE would only be five of us, the table was pulled out to its full length, as if we were expecting a crowd. The east wall of the room was almost all glass, and you could see Catherine's garden, right under the window. Beyond that, all the way out fifty yards or so to the tree line was where the lawn dropped off into the wooded ravine. Six months from then, in the early summer, Cath would be busy with her Junior League roses, but that Saturday night, the lawn was covered with snow, which had started to fall as we walked back into the house.

The good dishes were out. The good silver—the set Catherine received from her mother which had been in her family for aeons—was set in five places, the forks and spoons upside down, European style. The tablecloth was folded over the sides of the table past knee height, and there was a pad under it, so that when you picked up your knife, you felt softness rather than a chunk of wood. Two places faced the window, and across, there was a place for one. The center of the table was reserved for two banged-up old brass candlesticks. They had belonged to my father's mother. They were her Shabbas candlesticks.

Catherine had learned how to use them during the first year of our marriage. My grandmother was still alive at the time, a small woman, then in her eighties. The day she came to our apartment had been no more than two or three weeks after we had returned from our honeymoon. Grandma wore a dark green dress, and she still used her pince-nez which, when not on her nose, hung from a small gold chain pinned to the collar of her dress. Her eyes sparkled and danced, the same way they had years before when I was a child and she insisted on dealing with me as an adult. There was no baby talk from her when I was a kid. Instead, at five, she sat me down, facing her, and asked, quite firmly, "Tell me, young man, what do you think of President Eisenhower?" She wanted my opinion, not an evasion.

It had been the same way that day. She had marched into that little apartment on Addison Street, conveyed her greetings and had seated Catherine across from her as she spoke. "Now, Catherine dear. I know you are not Jewish, and I do not wish to impose anything on you, but there is something I want to give you. Here are two candlesticks. They are old. Even older than I am! They belonged to my mother. The women of a Jewish household light candles every Friday night to usher in the Sabbath. Here is a box of candles. A Jewish woman sets the table and prepares a Sabbath meal, and as the sun sets, she lights the candles and says a woman's Sabbath prayer. I will teach you the prayer, so that you may use it if you want to. In fact, Joel's mother rarely used these candles, but perhaps you will use them more. Joel's mother wasn't Jewish either, but people respond differently to such rituals."

Catherine had sat silent during this. Mom's refusal to make

any attempt to acknowledge Dad's heritage had hurt Grandma. So, now, with Catherine, she would try again. I sat and listened as Grandma went on.

"So, Catherine, here are the candles. You put them here. Sometimes you have to force them to fit. They're supposed to be lit as the sun sets, but, my sweetheart, wait. Wait until he comes home, and when you have children, wait until they are all at the table. Wait, even though the sun has set. Wait until they, your family, are ready to sit down and eat on Friday. Have the table set; make it white. Use the best of what you have. It is the Sabbath. Make it special. And if they want to eat and the candles have not been lighted, make them wait. The Sabbath begins with the candles, and that means the Sabbath begins with you. Seat them at the table. Bring the candles to the table. Say nothing. The room will be silent. You will see. No, do not turn the lights down. Keep them bright. The Sabbath is bright and happy. Come into the room with your candles. They, your Joel and your family, someday, will be seated in their chairs. You will stand. The candles will be in the center of the white table. You will, with your arms in front of you, sweep them around the candles, then lift your hands to your eyes. You will cover your eyes, as you will have covered your head."

"But, Grandma," Catherine asked, "what will I say?"

"What you want."

"Aren't there prayers? In Hebrew?" Catherine had asked in fear.

"Of course," said Grandma, "but let's not try everything at once!"

Catherine and I both laughed, and Catherine asked again, "But what do I say?"

"What your heart tells you. God will understand."

"Will He?"

"My sweetheart, of course, He will. I promise." Grandma put her hand on top of Catherine's hand.

Catherine had arranged the table in our dining room so many years later just as Grandma had instructed. Catherine didn't practice the Sabbath candle ritual more than twice a year, Passover and Chanukah, and she did that only when Andy started going to Jewish Sunday school and asked if she would do it. Thank heaven for my Andy. I was so glad he asked. I had not.

The boys, Doug and I came down the stairs together. The living room was visible through the railing on our right. The lamps were faintly lit, and all the rooms were dusted with light except the dining room, which was bright and strong in contrast to the rest of the house. The tablecloth was white, the china and silver sparkled, and the room drew us to it. Andy and Judd, on their own and without being told, had put on their blazers, white shirts, gray slacks and rep ties. I had on a sport coat and tie, as did Doug. The four of us walked into the room together.

"Wow," said Judd. "Isn't it beautiful!"

"It sure is," answered Doug, who then put his arm around Judd's shoulder. No one said anything. We just stood there, at the double doorway to the dining room. Catherine walked through the other door that connected to the kitchen. Her gray jacket was placed over the back of one of the side chairs, and her white collar, soft and intentionally loose, exposed her slender neck. She saw us, all four of us, standing there.

"Happy Chanukah," she said.

"Where do we sit?" honked Andy.

"Anywhere you want," she answered.

"I get to sit next to Doug!" shouted Judd.

"Let's not go through that again!" I said. "One of you can sit next to Doug, and one of you can sit across and look at him. Okay?" Doug turned red. Doug and Judd sat together, and Andy sat by himself on the other side of the table. Doug took the chair closest to Catherine's, rather than the one near me. Catherine had gone back to the kitchen while we seated ourselves, spaced far apart around the big table.

Catherine nudged the kick plate on the kitchen side of the swinging door to the dining room and came in carrying Grandma's banged-up candlesticks and an old tray to put them on. She walked over to Andy's side of the table and stood next to him. She placed the candlesticks on the tray and put the assembly in the center of the table. She put two Sabbath candles, now holiday candles, in the candleholders, then stood back. She put a white shawl over her head and her shoulders, her back visible in the reflection in the window behind her. She extended her arms, molded the space above the candles into a protective dome, and pulled her hands, palms forward, to her face, and covered her eyes with her hands. Catherine stood there silently, her head in her hands, while we lowered our heads. She finished the silence by saying, "Amen."

"Well, that's that. Happy Chanukah, all," she said, sighing relief.

"Wait, wait," said Andy.

"Yeah, wait, wait," said Judd.

"What are you? Little Sir Echo?" teased Andy.

"I am not . . . whatever that is."

"We still have the Chanukah candles," said Andy.

"Catherine, with your permission," said Doug, "I would like that to be my department."

"Joel?" asked Catherine, looking at me.

"Of course," I said.

"Good, I'll be right back," said Doug.

Doug came down the stairs a few minutes later carrying his and Ted's Chanukah menorah. It was silver and about ten inches tall. The center column stood on a rounded base, about

three inches in diameter. The stem branched off into eight
smaller columns on one level and a ninth, on a higher level,
holding a single candle, guarding the rest.

"Come on, guys, we'll light them together. Andy," Doug
called out, "come on over here." Andy pushed his chair back
and went over to Doug. Doug had pushed his chair back behind him, as did Judd. The three of them stood together at
the side of the table, their faces reflected in the window looking out over the snow on the lawn. The light from Catherine's
Sabbath candles bounced off the windows and the boys' faces.

Doug stood between my two sons. He gave Andy and Judd
each a candle, one blue, one white. Without instruction, Andy
held his candle ready to be lit for the *shammesh*, the guarding
candle, and Judd placed his candle in the holder farthest left
on the menorah, it being the candle for the first night. Doug
took three skullcaps out of his jacket pocket. They were all
white. He put one on his head and handed one each to Andy
and Judd who did the same. Doug lit Andy's *shammesh* candle
and placed his hand over Andy's smaller hand, and the two of
them guided the *shammesh* to pass the flame to Judd's candle,
the first candle of Chanukah, the Festival of Lights.

"Juddy, give me your hand too." Doug took Judd's hand,
and with his right hand over Judd's in turn holding the first
night's candle and his left hand over Andy's hand holding the
shammesh, the two candles were lit, and the boys, my two
sons, and Doug, without books to read from, sang, not spoke,
but sang:

"*Baruch Atah Adonnay, Ellohaynu Melach Hoalom,
Asher kidishownu Be'mitsvoh sov. Vitsivohnu, l'had lik
Ner, sh'ell Hanukah.*"

In Hebrew. In my house.

The candles stood alone now and each burned with a yellow flame. Andy went back to his seat, and Doug and Judd sat down again. No one said a word. Doug reached over to a horizontal lever that was on the base of the menorah. He swung it over to one side. There was a music box in the base of the menorah, and it played a song, a Chanukah song I hadn't heard since my mom and dad used to argue about sending me to temple as a kid to learn about those things. The song was "Rock of Ages." The Jewish version.

The music box made a sound like small bells. Then Andy started to hum the tune. He started to blush and he seemed embarrassed, but to keep him going, Doug joined in. They looked at each other, intensely, into each other's eyes, the way it is okay for men to do when they sing. Judd smiled, and I almost cried I was so happy. I looked over to her, but Catherine was staring out the window.

No MATTER what happened during the rest of my life, I was sure, as the door closed behind Doug as he went to his taxi, that I would always remember that night. Catherine wore the gift Doug had given her. She had opened the blue Tiffany box with a note attached to it. She had leaned back, the firelight reaching her face, and read the note out loud, " 'To Catherine, with my love. Always, Doug.' "

"Oh, oh, he's in love with my mother," Judd had piped up.

Catherine had taken a beautiful gold pin in the form of a beetle out of the box. It was about three inches long and had small red stones representing the beetle's eyes. She put the pin on her blouse right at that moment, leaned over, kissed Doug and thanked him.

"Now he's kissing her," said Judd.

"Soon you'll be the child of a divorcée," popped Andy.

"Joel, it's your turn," Catherine said, looking oddly at Andy.

"I see another little box there that looks suspiciously like the one Cath just opened," said Doug, the same impish smile still with him. "Why don't you try it?" he had said to me.

I looked at Doug, raised my eyebrows, asking without words if it was okay. He looked back and nodded. There was a small blue felt bag in the box, held closed by a drawstring. I pulled it open, and a pair of gold cuff links fell into my hand. They were oval, and they had my initials on them: JLS.

Since when, I thought, does Tiffany's work overnight?

"Dad, they made a mistake," Andy had pointed and as he picked them up. "The initials aren't the same. It says 'JLS' on one side and something else on the other side."

"It says 'DTF' on the other side," Doug had said.

"Huh?"

"It says 'JLS' on one side," Doug explained. "That's the side that's worn on the outside of the cuff, the side that people can see. The inside of each link has the initials 'DTF' on it. That's private."

"That's so Dad won't forget that you gave them to him. Right?" asked Andy.

"Well, sort of," said Doug.

"Read the note," said Catherine.

"Yeah, read the note," echoed Judd.

"Okay, okay. It says: 'To Joel, with all my love. Always, Doug.'" I read it slowly. The room was quiet, and the firewood popped and crackled here and there.

"It's the same note as Catherine's," Doug said, almost in a whisper. "After all," he said slowly, "I couldn't discriminate." He hesitated. "You have made things much easier for me. Both of you. You mean . . . a lot." He rubbed his fingers through the carpet, looked into the fire, then to the boys—to Catherine, and finally to me. He had started to speak, then stopped. He cleared his throat. I had to interrupt.

"We're all very glad you're with us," I said. Doug looked at me.

"I mean, after all," said Andy, "who else would sing Hebrew with me?"

Doug put his hand on Andy's shoulder. He looked at Catherine and let Andy look into his eyes and see that there were tears in them. Andy looked directly at Doug; he didn't flinch or pull away. Doug stood up, cleared his throat and said he would be back in a minute. He left the living room and headed for the bathroom at the end of the hall. We were all quiet.

"Are you going to be Doug's best friend now?" Judd asked.

"I don't know," I had said, staring into the fireplace, avoiding my son's eyes.

"You'd make a good best friend, Dad," said Judd.

"Yeah," said Andy. "I suppose Doug could do worse."

"Do worse than what?" Doug asked as he walked back into the room and folded himself next to Andy.

"That's for me to know and for you to find out," said Andy.

"You're a stain," Doug said as Juddy cheered.

"You're worried about something, I can tell," Cath said.

"You're right, I am." I turned over and pulled the cover with me.

"Don't worry about me, if that's what it is," she sighed. She leaned over and put her arm across my chest. "I felt a little left out at the table tonight, but that's because I don't speak Hebrew!" I felt her body move as she laughed.

"That whole thing meant so much to me," I said, "and I'm not sure why."

"It's part of you, Joel. It should mean something to you. The boys go to both Sunday schools not because it's trendy, but because it means something to you, even if you don't show it a lot."

"The more the evening went on, the more I saw you on the outside—"

"I wasn't."

"—and the cuff links didn't help either." I turned around to look at her.

"They're beautiful," she said. "He really must have thought a lot about them. It was certainly no spur-of-the-moment gift."

"I know."

"What did you two talk about when you went to the village?" She sat up and wrapped her arms around her legs.

"Oh, you know, career problems."

"That's odd," she said. "He doesn't strike me as that kind of person at all." She leaned over and turned out the light.

WHEN CATHERINE came into the bedroom, three or four nights later, I was ashamed that the room was not neat. I didn't realize I could make such a mess in one day. I was sprawled all over the bed, half dressed. Magazines and books were strewn all over the bed and on the floor. She walked into the long corridorlike closet, a windowless room with clothes hung on either side, and disappeared. Cath's side had rows and rows of shoes stacked on wire supports that rose almost three feet from the floor. Three feet of feet. Funny, I thought. The closet, the room, the bed, my side anyway, were sloppy as hell.

She came out of the closet and turned on WFMT. Lawrence Winters was singing Porgy in the 1951 Columbia recording.

"Joel, are you all right?"

"Yeah, I'm okay," and we went to sleep.

IT WASN'T unusual for me to wake up in the middle of the night, somewhere between four and five. It wasn't a symptom of midlife. I'd always been like that. I tried to move out of bed quietly. I liked being in the house alone at night. It was the quiet I liked. When you get married, you pack two people into a small apartment and there's no place to be by yourself, except the toilet. You escape by going inside. You're there and yet you're not. You're a character in your own tale.

My white socks were in the bathroom. I sat down on the toilet and put them on. I found my loafers and a robe and walked out of our room and closed the door quietly. My mother walked all over the house too. She opened windows, closed the windows; put the bed covers on, took them off. It was 3:00 A.M., negligee sweepstakes. It was as much an excuse for me as it was for her. I could walk into Andy's room first, then Judd's—see if the window was open or closed, or if the blankets were on or had been kicked off. I could kiss Andy first, then Judd, and whisper to each of them, out loud, "I love you."

I thought I was hungry, but decided I wasn't and went into the sunroom without a stop at the kitchen. There was a glow bouncing off the clouds that came in through the glass walls. No other light was needed. I sat down, put my feet up on the coffee table and dozed off.

"Test patterns." Cath's shadow, slanted and gigantic in front of her, disappeared as she moved in front of me.

"Huh?"

"You're supposed to be watching test patterns," she said. She was a tall figure standing next to me in the dark. "I have it on the very best authority." She drew her robe around her and sat down in her red chair.

"Is there anything about me you don't know?" I asked. She rustled around in the dark and reached for a lamp. "Please don't," I said. She pulled her hand back. "How come you're up?" I asked.

"I'm not," she said. "I'm sleepwalking." I started to smile.

We sat in our places and didn't say much at all. She stood and stretched, throwing her arms out to the sides. She started up the two stairs that led up out of the room. Then she turned back and switched on the TV set. She turned the channel selector until she found a test pattern.

"Ah, there we are," she said.

"I didn't know they still had those things."

She started to leave the room again, but hesitated. "You want a glass of anything?" she said.

"No, thanks. That's okay, but if you want some, please—"

She turned and walked out.

I didn't expect her to come back; I thought she had gone back to bed, but she came back and put two glasses of milk on the coffee table and sat down.

"You're really a very quiet man, aren't you?" she said.

"I'm not known for being quiet."

"I'm not talking about the press you put out," she said.

"Okay, I'm quiet. Left to my own devices, that is."

"Do you know what time it is?" she asked.

"About four thirty?"

"Joel, where is all this going to take us?" She looked at me, hurting.

"Where is what going to take us?"

"The dinner at the Stacklers' in New York," she said.

"What dinner at the Stacklers'?"

"Marion Stackler called and said they had asked Doug to dinner at their house; that he and, what's his name, Jason Baruch, thought if you were in town, you would like to come too, and that she said I should feel welcome as well."

"No one said a thing to me about it."

"I'd like to go. I didn't go before. I'd like to go now."

PART

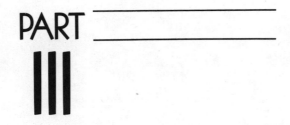

III

16

THE STACKLER house was always more imposing at night than it was during the day. Somehow it looked bigger and more formidable in the dark. It sat on the top of a low hill in Sands Point, and as you drove up the road to the courtyard you saw the lights in the windows long before the outline of the house became visible. It was an established house; it didn't look like the first strong wind would blow it away. The edges of it were blurred against the night and there were two other cars in the drive. I had to be careful as I backed an oversized rented car which I was not used to driving against the stone retaining wall, the gravel spitting out from under the rear tires.

The night was clear and the temperature had dropped to the teens. Cath and I stood chilled in front of the large fountain, now waterless, in the center of the circular drive. Cath smoothed the wrinkles out of her coat, and I folded my arms against the cold. Henry's car was parked next to the house (I could tell by the license plates which had his initials on them), and there was a fifties Alfa Romeo next to it, probably Doug's.

There was no car belonging to the rabbi, and as I was to find out shortly, he had decided not to be there. "You were coming," Doug would whisper to me later, "so there wasn't any reason for him to come. He said something about chance favoring a prepared mind." I guessed the rabbi had figured it was finally my turn.

Every light in the house seemed to be blazing. It felt as if the living room were lined with lamps, blue ones and green ones with white pleated shades, all lit full blast. There wasn't a shadow in the room. It looked almost whited out. At the threshold, looking into the living room, we saw three people, spread out as far away from each other as they could manage and still be under the same roof. Doug and Henry Stackler sat at opposite ends of the room. They stood when they saw Cath. Henry was smoking a cigar, squinting through the smoke. He looked thinner, gaunt in a way, and his face somehow had gone from round to triangle. He looked like Anthony Quinn in a crew cut. His eyes were far from his chin, a long way for tears to fall. Marion was seated in a wing chair at a midpoint. She made no effort to move, not even a finger. She remained where she was, completely still. Catherine hesitated a moment, then she took my arm, and we walked into the room.

With a step that was terrifyingly direct, Cath went immediately over to Marion. Seated in the chair in which she took up little room, she surveyed Cath coming toward her. She pressed her feet against the floor as if she were trying to push the huge chair farther back to gain more space. Catherine continued, crossing the room, undaunted.

"I'm Catherine Stern, Mrs. Stackler. Please accept my condolences."

Marion's eyes glazed over. "That was weeks ago," she said.

You had to know Cath to detect the slight freezing of her body, but she extended her hand and Marion took it. Cath sat next to her. She would not back away.

"Thank you for coming," Henry Stackler's voice boomed out from the other side of the bright whitewashed room. I had heard that voice years ago, resonating then as it did that night. Resonating was Ted's word. His father had told him that he did it on purpose; it made him seem powerful. When he was a little boy, Ted could hear that voice all the way up to his room. He heard it in the middle of the night during the years when they had lived in the city and when Marion complained about her husband being away on one business trip after the other, but at the same time joyously ready to spend every penny he earned. "Don't spend less, earn more," Ted's father used to say. That was his task. She had spent the profit of a deal before the check had passed through his hands.

Why was it, I thought, that I had adopted, without independent investigation, Ted's picture of his mother as destructive, at least insofar as his father was concerned? Maybe Ted thought he would have made a better husband to his mother: put her in her place, make her devote herself to him, stop a minute and care rather than demand. Maybe he thought he, instead of his father, could have brought out the best rather than the worst in her.

"Drinks anyone?" Henry asked. "Catherine, what can I get for you?" He seemed to laugh between syllables out of nervousness rather than joy.

"Yes," said Cath, looking relieved, "I think a drink would be a wonderful idea."

"You name it," Henry Stackler said. "May I call you Cath? Or do you prefer Catherine?"

"I'm called both," she answered.

"Buddy, how about you?" he asked, turning toward me. Cath, hearing my old name, my Ted name, turned her head quickly away.

Cath's eyes searched the room after she had sat down. She folded her leg across her ankle, and then she did the same thing again in reverse. She seemed sprung on a hair trigger, but outwardly, she knew what she was doing. She held her hands up against the lamp and you could see the red lines in them.

Cath turned to Marion Stackler, who sat regally not two feet away. Cath had schooled herself in the old Jewish traditions. The impetus had come from my grandmother. Cath had taken to her and felt safe in her kindness. The candles for the Sabbath were just the beginning. Cath had had wonderful times with Grandma, and after those first two winters away, they had lunch together every Thursday. Grandma was old, but she was the only mother Cath had really had. If we were ever to have a girl, Cath would name her Sara, after Grandma. Cath had learned from Grandma. I was not surprised when I heard what Cath said to Marion. "There's an old Jewish proverb: It's sad to lose a parent, but it's a tragedy to lose a child." Cath held her breath, knowing she had taken a huge risk.

Tears stood in Marion Stackler's eyes. "Oh, my dear, how did you know that." It was a statement of gratitude for a special sympathy, not a question, and she seemed to soften, and she held out her hand and Cath took it. The two women looked at each other, separated from the three of us standing on the other side of the vast, silent living room.

"Buddy isn't called Buddy anymore," Doug said nervously. "He's Joel now."

"Well," Henry said (he seemed to speak so loudly, but it only seemed that way because everyone else was talking practically in whispers), "I'll try, but it may be hard for an old man to break a habit."

"That's all right," Catherine said, raising her voice to a normal level, "Buddy is fine," and she looked at me, a mist in her own eyes. Then Cath turned back to Marion. "I'm glad we're here," she said. "I'm glad you've let us all come."

Marion turned to her husband. "Henry, I'd think I'd like a small sherry," and her eyes brightened, "as long as you're pouring." Then she looked across the room. "Douglas, what would you like?" Marion rose from her chair. "I can't believe," she said, with a smile rising from the corners of her mouth, "that Henry has allowed you to be with us and not offered you a drink." She moved slowly at first. "Henry, do get Douglas something. I'll be back in a moment." She left the room and I thought I heard a taffeta skirt squishing back and forth as she walked, the kind great ladies used to wear years ago.

Marion came back a few moments later, her face shining as if she had scrubbed it. "Well now, that's better." She did not head back to her wing chair, but instead sat next to Catherine in the center of the sofa, no longer far away from the men. "Tell me, did you have a good trip?" she asked Catherine.

"It's been too long since Joel and I have been here. He goes all the time, but it seems I never am able to make any trips with him, what with our boys and all."

"Yes, you have two boys, don't you?" Marion said.

"Andy and Judd. Andy is almost fourteen. Judd is eleven," Doug said.

"Are they anything like their father?" she asked. "Buddy was always quite handsome as a youngster."

"Joel, dear," Henry said to his wife, "it's Joel."

MARION SAT in state at the head of the dinner table. Henry had pulled out the chair for her and Doug had done the same for Cath. I stood quietly behind my place facing the window. The room, lit by candles, was as dark and full of shadows as the living room had been bright white. The walls were painted a deep enamel red, there was a burgundy Persian carpet on the floor, and the table, covered in white lace, gleamed in the center of the room. It was like a glistening china lacquer box.

Marion enjoyed the attention, and it was obvious she had placed herself in the position of deserving it. She was the parent still grieving for the child. The father had recovered, the boy lover had recovered, but Marion was still mourning the son she had lost, not to mention the daughter-in-law and grandchildren she would never know. Her grief covered the generations. The more she went back to putting on her act, the easier it was to skip the core of genuine feeling that was undoubtedly inside her. Yuck, as Juddy would say.

We continued to cater to her, and I was beginning to find it a little wearing. Henry had no choice. He had to live with the woman before dinner and after. Catherine and I were subjected to no such requirements. And Doug? Or Douglas, as she so pointedly called him? Would he see more of her? Was that the objective of this gathering? I thought of this dinner with Marion at the head of the table, and it reminded me of Al Capone at the New Michigan Hotel on Twenty-third Street presiding over a sit-down to give out the contract on a hit. Jason Baruch had achieved his goal. We were all here.

I couldn't help but wonder what our presence had accomplished, that is, Cath's presence and mine—me with the two names. It probably kept them civilized. Probably more than that, I guessed. We probably enabled the event to occur. Without the rabbi to shame them into it or Cath and me to provide the buffers, would this dinner have occurred? Did my presence with Cath prove to Marion Stackler that Doug was an aberration and that Ted was, down deep, just like me, who also, but for some trick of fate, would have been sitting here along with his wife who would have also been Junior League material? What was Marion thinking?

Cath had warmed her up. She had done more than that. She had established contact with her. There was another woman in her house, a woman who knew what she knew and, therefore, a special person who could feel what she felt. She was not alone. It was not Cath and me as a couple who had made this occur for Doug. It was Cath as a woman who had made it happen.

During dinner, Henry alternated between silence and making jokes at his own expense. His eyes would twinkle during those instances in which he permitted himself to come alive. He told one story after another, all featuring the great man making little but understandable slips. He wanted so much, it seemed, to show himself human. One could imagine him in a bank boardroom, telling one of his stories and endearing himself to an eavesdropping waiter who was serving coffee or another self-made member of the board who likewise refused to forget where he came from. He enjoyed showing, in a pleasant way, that his journey had not made him infallible. You couldn't help but like the guy. Nor could you miss his message: Ted's life-style was not *his* fault. He was not, repeat, not, the powerhouse-but-distant father who had failed to give his son the strength to resist seduction and remove himself from Mommy, the true loved one. Little phrases seeped into his conversation, words like "awareness," "fantasy" and the like. You could tell he had been to see a counselor or therapist.

Doug had turned melancholy. One could only guess that he wanted the other half of himself, his Ted, at this table with him. It was ironic, maybe he thought to himself, that the two of them could never be together at this place, in life or death. Occasionally, when he was sure she wasn't looking, Doug would steal a glance at Marion, trying, no doubt, to see through the careful facade, to understand what it was inside that had suddenly raised the gate to this house. One could understand that it was reasonable for Doug to sit there and count his losses.

There was not an inward, provincial person at the table. We all complimented ourselves on being Easterners, even though

Cath and I lived elsewhere. We read *The New York Times*, shopped at Bottega Veneta (or, if not, knew where on Madison Avenue it was), and thought of Washington gossip as our own because we knew so many people who worked there, no matter who was in the White House. Well, I wondered while passing the salt, if we all were so smart, why were we here?

Catherine, inevitably the charmer, had broken the ice, I realized, not less than two hours ago. She had practically had to do it with an ice pick. Marion had been ready to sit in that old wing chair, her throne of suffering, and rule the evening. Perhaps she had expected the rest of us to eat in her vermilion box dining room while she remained in a seated position, ancient Chinese style, awaiting a meal to be brought to her on an ebony tray by a servant with bangles on his ankles. Cath had punched through all that, drawing on a background that was learned but wasn't hers, the Jewish anecdote pulled out of a hat, that served to melt Marion.

The thought kept running through my mind that they were two women amidst men and that there was some silent alliance or at least understanding between them that changed the course of the evening. It was clear to me that if Cath had not been there and somehow managed to connect with Marion, things would have gone sour. But there were times, when Marion lapsed and when Henry wasn't entertaining us, trying to lift the dinner table, as it were, on his shoulders, and shake the pall off with a laugh when we felt sad.

Cath must have known she could accomplish a breakthrough because she never resisted coming to that dinner. She screened her anxiety by telling me with a smile that she would accept any excuse to visit New York but underneath, I felt a sense of purpose in her voice when she said yes, she would come.

I found myself wondering about women more and more, not only that night, but ever since Ted had died. I wondered

how women differed from men. Not physically, because I
knew that. When I had that thought, I realized I had it without shame. Constitutionally, however, I wondered how women
were different, or if they were not, why they thought they
were—why it took one woman to get through to another when
a man would never be allowed to do so. Like that night.

"Joel, would you like another helping of dessert? I'm sure
Esphera would be delighted to bring some more strawberries
for you." Marion looked at me from the head of the table, and
I realized my desert plate was clean while the others were still
full. I always ate fast when I was withdrawn and thinking on
my own, and I was embarrassed to have been caught at it.

"No, thanks, Mrs. Stackler. This was just fine. A wonderful
dinner. Thank you."

"Yes, Marion, it was excellent," Catherine added. I felt like
laughing to myself. Cath called her Marion, and I was still
stuck firmly in boyhood calling her Mrs. Stackler, although I
had managed Henry.

Maybe fathers and mothers were different, I thought. A
father became a man to a man, and because the way the world
was organized, you saw him as a man in other settings. You
could deal with men and see them not always as fathers, yours
or somebody else's. A woman was different. She was always a
caretaker somehow, always a mother.

"Yes, Mrs. Stackler," Doug said, "thank you very much."
See? He did it too.

"Right, Mom," added Henry. "You outdid yourself."

"Well, thank you all," she said, and we seemed to see the
first genuine smile of the evening from Marion Stackler.

"Catherine?" Henry asked. "Marion is used to it, but I
thought I would ask you, Do you mind if I smoke a cigar at
the table?"

"That's very thoughtful. Of course, I don't mind," she said.

Henry looked at Marion as he lit his cigar, smiling, proud probably of his manners. Then she said, "Why don't we all go into the library? I'm sure Douglas has something to say to us."

Her smile had been an ambush. Doug looked as if he had been punched.

"No, not really. I really don't have anything to say. I'm just glad to be here," and he looked first at Henry and then at Marion to whom he said, "with you," and then he smiled and brushed his hair off his forehead. Marion took a sip of her coffee and said nothing. Henry boomed, "Doug, that's very nice of you."

"I mean it," he answered. He took his glasses off and started to clean them.

We left the dining room, and Henry led the five of us down the long wide hall across the atrium that looked out over the Sound, beyond the living room, moving deeper into the private sector of their home.

Once in the library, quieter than the rest of the house because of its carpets, dark woods, and floor-to-ceiling books, all five of us seemed to stand in the middle of the room, wondering where to sit, each looking for a protective nest.

There was a huge mahogany partner's desk across from the fireplace, and from the way his eyes darted toward it, Henry must have thought of taking his accustomed seat behind it, but he veered toward a leather reading chair, leaving empty the most obvious situs of authority. There were two sofas flanking the fireplace and the two women sat together on one of them. You could see, as the evening progressed, that they had moved closer together. At that moment, fearing lord knows what from Doug, they had allied. Doug placed himself on the other sofa opposite Marion and Cath. The leather was dark green and the light made the cracks in the cushions stand out, making it appear well-worn and comfortable. Doug backed into a corner, leaving room for me and an army, but I pulled an armless chair up to the coffee table, completing the circle, but leaving Doug on his own. The room was quiet except for the sound of kindling breaking occasionally in the fire and a low wind outside. The swimming pool, empty of water, had a blue cover over it, and the entire backyard, all the way out to the pier jutting out into the channel, was softly lit.

"I guess I do have something to say, although it wasn't what I thought I'd say when I first met you. But then, I never thought I'd meet you without Ted." He looked at me and I wanted to show the respect I felt for him. "Ted loved both of you very much," he said to Marion and Henry, "and if he didn't see as much of you as you would have wanted him to, it was because of me." Marion closed her eyes for just a second, but otherwise there was stillness. "He couldn't bring me here, not because of your prejudice, but because of your intelligence. You would suspect who I was no matter what false identity he created for me. To have lied about me would have done violence to Ted and me and the way he always believed in handling our side of his life."

I wanted to say "that's right" or "you bet" or sing an anthem.

"I'm glad you allowed me to come here tonight. It was a visit Ted had promised me," he said.

Henry knocked an ashtray off the table in front of him. He clamped his cigar between his teeth and rubbed the ashes into the carpet with his shoe. Marion's eyes followed his soles gnashing the white powder into her Aubusson rug, but she said nothing.

Some thought must have passed through Doug's mind at that point because he became quiet as well. Marion's eyes turned toward him, expecting him to continue according to his own scenario, but he looked as if he had no script at all. He looked lost.

Henry would have been a great friend of Warren Harding.

He found everything jovial, and at that moment, apropos of nothing, except perhaps his own discomfort, Henry roared with laughter, walked over to Doug, slapped him on the shoulder and bellowed, "Well, it's good to have you here," in his best bowling-league voice. There was a small pucker between Doug's eyebrows, apparently all he could manage. And then, out of nowhere Cath spoke, looking directly at Doug. "Would it have meant a lot if Ted were here with you?"

Tears came to Doug's eyes, as he said, "The world."

Speaking at the same time, Marion said harshly, "I'm sure it would have."

Cath's question astonished me more than Marion's gratuitous response. It was too personal, too intimate, and then I realized what I was really thinking: it was none of her business. What was between Ted, Doug and me was becoming their property. She was stealing from me.

"Well, Henry" (I almost called him Warren), "I sure as hell would like that drink. Henry, do they ever call you Hank?" If he was bowling for a spare, I was out for a strike. I couldn't remember myself ever sounding so locker room. No wonder Andy aped my macho side.

"Haven't been called Hank for years," Henry boomed back. "When I played baseball, they called me Hank. Left field."

"I played shortstop." I was resonating to match him. "I was short, but fast. It was before I grew. Ha! Ha!"

"Well, folks," Henry said, his voice bombarding the room, "Buddy sure has made up for lost time." He looked up my full length, calling attention to my height. I turned to Doug, a smile on my face, but he just stared at me, appalled.

I was breaking his mood, or more accurately, helping Henry to do it, and I was sure that this was not the reason I was asked to be here with him tonight. Nor had Catherine come to watch me in an act of destruction. I realized I had made alliance with Henry. Why had I done that? I asked myself, and I didn't know the answer. And how had Doug, finding himself deserted, felt about sharing his sensitivity with the ladies and not with me?

Why did I do that? I wondered, and then I knew. Doug had pushed me into it. He had told them the truth and he was accepted, if you could judge by the look on their faces. Well, well, the modern age begins in Sands Point. I thought it and I wanted to say it, but I didn't because it was too cruel for public consumption. Doug was in, and after all those years, I was out.

Doug seemed physically to have retreated. He slouched in his chair and his back became rounded. Cath's eyes fell on him as she said, "You look like you're a million miles away."

"I was for a minute," and then he forced a smile and sat up straight, "until the boys' baseball team brought me back."

Marion cleared her throat. "What do you think would have happened if my son had brought you here?" she asked. "Or if we had come to visit the two of you?" The library went dead quiet and any visions of baseball camaraderie vanished.

"I don't know, Mrs. Stackler. Those are two different settings, and often, the space you're in makes a difference in the way things happen."

"You *are* an architect, Douglas, aren't you?" she said.

"I suppose I am." He leaned forward and reached for a candy, taking the top off the crystal dish on the table in front of him, choosing carefully a particular chocolate that suited him. He never ate sweets—he was buying time, considering his next sentence. "You've never been to our home. We would have liked very much to have you," he said. Then he smiled, that wonderful warm, I really mean it, no bullshit smile. I knew he used "our" and "we" intentionally, and they must have known it too.

"Oh, I've been there," Marion Stackler said. Doug covered his surprise well.

"When was that?"

"Apparently when you were away," she said.

He paused a moment. "Did you like it?"

"Yes, very much. I knew Ted didn't have that talent."

"What do you think it would have been like to visit us there?" Doug asked. Henry started to stand up as if he were ready to intervene, but Marion's eyes sent him back to his cushion.

"I don't know. My imagination won't take me that far," she said.

"Well, no one's an oracle," said Cath, and all of our eyes turned to her. She shifted positions several times as if trying to find a place without taint. You can never acquire anyone else's mind, no matter how well you know him, or her, as the case may be, I thought as I looked at Cath. Why did she come here? Why did I? As of a week ago, we could have spared ourselves this. How did we decide our way into tonight? I asked myself. Marion fixed a steady smile on her, and the room was hushed.

Then after taking another drink from the Stacklers' barware decorated with colored ducks, Catherine said, "Anyone can visit anyone. After all, no one's in a cage."

17

CATH AND I didn't talk much on the ride back to town. We followed the small taillights of Doug's Alfa back into town, across the Triborough bridge, down FDR Drive and out the Ninety-sixth Street turnoff. We lost him at the light at Second Avenue. Between there and Seventy-fifth Street, where we turned west, all Cath said was, "I'm glad that's over." I turned north at Madison Avenue and right at Seventy-sixth Street to the Carlyle garage. At the desk, Mr. Hector said how nice it must be for me to have Mrs. Stern along and he hoped we were comfortable. We had a room next to Richard Widmark, and I told him we saw him in the corridor. Both he and Mr. Goldenberg smiled from behind the desk.

I remembered sitting on the stiff red bench in the lobby one morning waiting for a client who was late. I wondered what it would be like if I stopped working for a living. It was a question Doug had suggested I think about once in a while. If I quit, I would never be able to afford this place again, I decided. How would I feel? Would I miss it? Or had I had enough?

We rode upstairs to 3306. The south wall of the room was all glass, and it had a huge, king-sized bed. It had been André Meyer's kitchen before the hotel bought the room back after his death, and it had become the best in the house. Would Cath want to have sex tonight? Would I have to prove something? I hoped not.

Cath was always a faster undresser than I was. Her father used to bounce into her room without knocking to say good night. She loved it when she was eight, was confused about it when she was nine and frightened for some reason she didn't understand when she was twelve. She said she didn't understand. I doubted that. My mother used to undress in the closet. I used to say I never understood that either.

Cath looked like she belonged at the Carlyle. Some fancy New York decorator must have had a thing for painterly colors which he designed in the swirls of the carpet and bedspreads on both soft beds and headboards to match. It embarrassed me that I liked all the softness, but that was all right. Remember Matisse, I thought. Cath looked like a woman in one of his paintings. I could imagine her with a narrow edge of her profile edged in a wonderful soft yellow and her eyebrows in a blue that radiated. There would be times when she could look like the south of France, even though we were nowhere near the place. She turned over and propped her head up on her palm, watching me undress with the lights on, as she had done since we first went to bed together.

"I haven't seen you wear pajamas in years," she said.

"Only when I'm out of town."

"Oh." I should have smiled. Cath turned away. She half sat up and looked out of the window. The Tiffany building was lit up and so were the Empire State and the Chrysler.

"Do they still have the miniature bars in the rooms?" she asked.

"Yes, it's in the night-table stand next to you."

"Here?"

"No, the one on the other side of the bed."

"Oh, that's a long way," she smiled.

"Yes, I guess it is." I walked around the bed and pulled open the door in front of the cabinet next to the bed. It was covered in some kind of orange silk and I was always concerned about getting fingerprints on it when I had this room. "They've got almost everything in here."

"Want to split a split?" she smiled as she lay across the bed stretched out, her hand poking around the open cabinet door.

"Sure," I said. "It's the only hotel in the world that gives you real champagne flutes."

"Joel, you never get over this place, do you?"

It was the second time in ten minutes that I should have smiled, but failed to do so. Instead, I felt embarrassed about making such a fuss over such things out loud. Cath took the bottle and opened it. There were two chairs and a small table in front of the picture window, and we sat there, drinking champagne silently. Cath had turned the lights off.

"Did Doug ever race cars?" she asked.

"No, I don't think so. Why do you ask?"

"It takes talent to lose a skilled driver like you," she said, looking at me quickly.

"No, not really." The wine was too cold but I didn't want to wait. "We were almost at the hotel anyway, Cath."

"Isn't Levine conducting *Tristan* tomorrow night?" she asked.

"I don't know. I can get the paper," I said, starting to stand up.

"No, don't turn on the lights," she said.

"Okay."

We sat silently, each in our chair with a table between us, looking south into the city. I held my glass in my hand so that the champagne would warm up. It was like ice. Cath put her glass down after each sip. I think she liked the clink against the marble.

"Somehow," she said, "I thought Doug was going to stop back here and have a drink with us."

"Why do you want me to be sore at Doug?"

"That's out of left field," she said.

I felt like squeezing the glass in my hands. "Sorry," I said. The city looked the way it looked before daybreak, but that was hours away.

"It's water over the dam," she said, putting an end to it.

As she finished her drink and returned to bed, Cath asked several questions:

Do you want to stay tomorrow night or go home in the afternoon?

It's Wednesday tomorrow. Do you want to see *Tristan?* (That hint for the second time.)

Why do you have to work? I'm sure someone else can be found. Are you the only one in that office? Or is there something else you want to do?

I had no satisfactory answers except that I had to stay on. I realized how cut off I was from her now and how committed I was to lying.

FATE, THE next day, produced a balmy afternoon. It was an out-of-place December eleventh, almost sixty degrees and a clear sky. I looked at my watch. Cath had left for the airport an hour and a half ago; she was going home on her own. There are no colleges for forty-year-olds, Jung said. You've got to figure out the second half on your own.

After my meeting, I decided to call Doug to say good-bye. The phone was answered, "Mr. Field's studio," and I was impressed. An assistant told me that Doug had left but she sounded as though she had been alerted to my name. She said that Doug had taken the afternoon off and was at home, and gave me the number.

His home phone rang three times, and then it was answered. "Doug?"

"Who is this?" It was a male voice, but not Doug's.

"Is Doug there?" My throat tightened, and a whole set of feelings went down the toilet.

"Yes, he is." It sounded like a college kid. "May I know who's calling?" the voice continued, with immense formality. I hung up.

Proposition: Doug was as flighty as the rest of the fucking faggots. I allowed myself to replay the voice that had answered the phone, once again. It was not the voice of a college kid; it was simply a younger voice, a voice younger than mine. Doug's voice should have sounded that way, I caught myself thinking, but it didn't. It sounded older. Sometimes voices let you see the people who belong to them. The picture came to me easily. The voice belonged to Doug's boyfriend who was, let us say, twenty-three, and it came from inside an average chest through an average windpipe through just so-so vocal chords, but out through a mouth in an unmatchable face with gray eyes that made love to Doug night and day.

The hotel operator rang. "Mr. Stern. I know you wanted your calls held, but there's a Mr. Field on the phone. He says it's urgent."

I wondered how Doug and his boyfriend made love. I blocked the pictures that came to mind, and the only thing I allowed myself to acknowledge was that they made love a lot. Perhaps Doug had met him at four in the morning wearing Levi's, flannel shirt and work boots, the ones stored in the closet in the room I slept in. I walked over to the window and imagined myself looking out of my office window at Al Capone's hotel. Maybe I could call up Al: "Hi, Big Al. Break a few kneecaps for a pal? Huh, Al?" And he would answer, "Anything you say, Joey baby. Who's the hit?" I would tell him, "A New York faggot, Al," I would say. "Easy job, Joey baby," Al would answer, his cigar clamped in his mouth.

No fucked-up faggot was going to send me around the bend. I had not invaded his life with some fruitcake, limp-wristed queer lying nude next to me. A man takes calls—he doesn't duck them.

"Hello, this is Joel Stern," I said.

"You called here a minute ago, didn't you?" Doug said.

"What is it I can do for you?"

"What is it I have done to you?" he responded.

"How did your boyfriend know it was me?"

"He didn't. It was my guess."

"So he is your boyfriend?"

"Joel, what is this all about? Glenn is a friend of mine from Boston, and he's spending the weekend with me."

"This is Thursday."

"I know. We both took a day off."

"You don't have to account to me."

"I don't intend to."

"Good."

"I missed you," he said, his voice suddenly softer. "Glenn went shopping."

"That's a non sequitur."

"I know, but I wanted you to know that no one was here. I miss you. It's the second time I've had to say it and I mean it!" I saw him in his jockey shorts. "I hope you're okay," he said, his voice appealing, "but please tell me how I'm doing?" There was silence for a moment.

"You're okay," I whispered. I heard both of us breathing. I stood up and stared down at the papers on the hotel bed.

"I pay attention to wedding rings, Joel. I always have. If you want a fling, I'm sure you can find some disco bunny and get him a nice apartment at Marina Towers with two keys."

"What the hell do you think I am?"

"That's just the point. I don't *know*," he said.

"Well, I'm not sure it's worth the effort to find out."

"What's that supposed to mean?"

"You're wound up in yourself, that's what that means. You have as much ability to listen to the needs of others as a piece of furniture. You tease, Doug. That's what you do. Big speeches about who listens to *me*? Who do I tell how much I need to earn? Who do I tell how I want to spend my days? I was cracked open once before. I know you're involved in your own life. You should be. You've sustained a great loss. I'm sorry. I have a theory."

"What's that?"

"People don't mind being wrong—they mind being embarrassed."

"And you're embarrassed."

"Yes," I said.

"Because I didn't pick up on the first signal of need you've sent out in sixteen years?" There was silence on the line for a moment. "I'm not going to talk now," he said. "I would like to see you. It's a nice day. Let's go for a bike ride."

"A bike ride?"

"The four most important words in the English language are so what and why not."

I hadn't meant for things to go that far.

HE WAS waiting in the lobby and there were two bikes leaning against the wall.

"Glenn will not be back. I didn't think you'd want to see him in a social context."

"Thank you."

"Joel, I do try."

"I can't ride in a suit."

"I know, there're jeans upstairs for you. Here's the key. I'll wait here."

When I came down, Doug pulled his red baseball cap tight over his forehead, and he gave me a yellow one to wear. We crossed over a block west to Fifth, and headed downtown, the big co-op buildings on our left and Central Park on our right. I pedaled a little faster and caught up with him. We rode in parallel down the wide bike path on the west side of Fifth Avenue, the green benches whizzing past us. "I've always wanted to do this, but never had the chance," I remembered, puffing, not in quite the shape I used to be. We pedaled together, lifting our feet to the top and bottom of our crankshafts in tandem.

"How come?"

"Never knew anybody here who had a bike!" I took a deep breath. "Come on. I'll race you to Sixty-second." I was off.

"Cheat," I heard the voice from behind. "Unfair start." The voice got weaker as I sped away. Pump those pedals. Wind in my face. "Catch up if you can," I yelled, and ripped the cap off my head and waved it in the air.

"If I can . . ." I remembered hearing Doug's voice. The sound was still behind me, but not as faint. Dogs in the park barked as we whipped past. I turned around fast and saw him gaining on me. Now. Sprint! I forced my chest down into the bars and hunched over to hide from the wind. "Ouch! Ted was taller than I am," I yelled. I heard a laugh from not too far behind. Then the laugh passed me, and I saw the back of a red cap spurt five yards out in front. I leaned into my bike again, making it part of me, so I could fly.

"I hope this thing has brakes—so I—can stop—when I catch you," I yelled between breaths.

"Don't worry," he called back.

We rode like that, parallel, one ahead of the other, then an exchange of lead.

"Here comes Sixty-second Street," I yelled. "A last dash?"

"Challenge accepted."

We rode, steered, pumped pedals, stood on them for power and crunched down to duck resistance. We stopped at Sixty-second Street, flushed, laughing, and out of breath.

"See? I—let you—win!" Doug forced out his words.

"Oh—you did—did you?"

I reached over and yanked the brim of his cap down over his eyes. He lunged toward me, still straddling the bicycle, and with the cap blocking his vision, he fell into me. I caught him across the chest and felt him hang on to me. He stood up, pushed his cap to the back of his head and spun the brim backward, like a catcher for the Yankees.

On down Fifth Avenue, a choir of brass players stood outdoors on a deck of the Trump Tower, playing "Hark the Herald Angels Sing." A woman, overdressed for the weather, carried her coat over her arm, and we waved to little girls from out of town who went by in a carriage, laughing at us on our bicycles. Standing beside me, Doug took my hand for a moment and then let go. I knew I shouldn't have been, but I was entirely happy. I faintly remembered passing by the traffic lights, shop windows, neon signs, and all those people rushing around.

We pedaled past Grand Central and steered clear of the tunnel under Park Avenue South. On the south side of Gramercy Park, we rode past several old mansions in various states of fashionable shabbiness. At 16 Gramercy Park South was The Players, the club of Cole Porter, Richard Rodgers and John Travolta, among others.

Past the front double doors, on the mezzanine, just beyond the grand staircase, we saw the oversize, full-length oil portrait of Edwin Booth. We walked in with our red and yellow base-ball caps, bicycle clips on our right legs, and bounced our bikes up the marble stairs to confront the startled clerk. He was a young kid, with an open shirt, and he wore a large cross around his neck. "Hey, man, you want to park the bikes? Why not? Put them up there under Booth. He won't mind." We all smiled.

The bar in the basement had planked floors, old wooden tables and covering every inch of the walls, framed auto-graphed cartoons of theatrical greats. Doug picked up the beers; I gave my club number and he gave me half in cash. We walked upstairs past Booth to the first floor and out the French doors from the library, to a tiny, almost private terrace. We sat at one of the small, white, marble-topped tables and metal chairs, ice-cream-parlor style, circa 1900.

"What do you want to do tonight?" he asked.

"I don't know that I can stay," I said.

"You're the guest. Whatever you like."

A taxi pulled up to the house next door to the club. It was a private house and I liked to watch and see what kind of peo-ple lived in places like that, private houses on Gramercy Park. The Art Deco lights at the tip of the Chrysler Building had just been lit and Doug blinked. You could tell he loved that sight.

"When I was twenty, I thought I would get married and have children," he said. "I hoped, I prayed. Then I became comfortable with myself. It took me three or four years to do it."

He stopped talking and looked at me, then the skyline and then at me again. He went downstairs and brought back two more beers apiece. "No reason to run back and forth," he said as he put his half in cash on the tabletop. We drank silently. He invited me to see him as a dazzled young architecture stu-dent being met by Ted at the shuttle from Boston. "This handsome man would meet me, put me in his BMW and take me to his sailboat . . . and he loved me." With that tag, he let me know he could be vulnerable. The sky had darkened and I could feel him saying it, asking the question young men must ask when they got involved, as Doug did, with someone older: What if I wake up one morning and wonder what I'm doing with this old man? Will I still love him?

"It was never a shady deal between Ted and me," he said quietly. "Ted lived a life that was beyond me—the people he knew, the fast track he was on. I dreamed of all that, but what could I give back? What could I mean to him? A decoration? Sex? An adoring wife? If Ted didn't give a good life to me, I would have made it myself. I'm really not a lightweight, Joel."

WE TOOK the bikes up in the service elevator and put them in the storage room on the third floor.

"I suppose I should be doubled over with guilt for spending the afternoon with you, but I'm not," I said. He had put his bike up on the rack and reached over to get mine and put it up on the one adjacent.

"Oof, this is heavy," he said. "Not guilty, huh?" he said.

"That's right. None."

"Anything else going on?" he asked, looking me straight in the eye.

"If there is, I can't feel it," I answered.

"Ted said that was always one of your problems." He took his cap off and put it in the back pocket of his Levi's. "He said you couldn't feel things. Come upstairs, if you want to."

He turned on a few lights in the living room. We looked out the window and it seemed that people all over town were doing the same thing. Across Central Park, there were little pinpoints of light appearing, almost an apartment at a time.

"You know, this is the first time since I've been married that

I've been in a home by myself." Then I remembered the truth. "Well, that's not really so," I said.

"You mean the winters when Catherine left you?"

"You knew about that?"

"Sure. Of course, I knew," he said.

"Did Ted tell you?"

"Only after we knew each other for a long time. He wanted to go to you then."

Doug stood up and walked into the kitchen, and I followed him. He put some water in a kettle and started the flame. We looked at it for a while.

"Will you jump if I reach over and hug you?" he asked.

"Do I look like I need one?" I didn't jump, and I hugged him back.

"Yes, you do."

There was a small table next to the stove. He sat down, leaned forward and ran his hand through his hair, messing it. "I don't want to go back to spending every other evening at the gym so I'll look hot at Fire Island or in a polo shirt at a bar. I don't want to think about whether to grow a mustache or cut my hair or get contact lenses. I don't want my time tied up in all of that. You want to know the truth? I'm afraid. I'm afraid of the whole process again—the dressing, the scheduled appearances, timing the bar nights, seeking the crowds or avoiding them. Things have changed. You pass a stage from being hot to being a type. Joel, I don't want to go back to any of that."

"I didn't want that either," I said, "the bars and the baths, and the brunches and the meager chance of finding continuity," I heard myself say.

"Did you walk out because you thought Ted wouldn't stick?"

"I guess so. Yes, that was one reason," I said.

"Then you made a mistake. He would have stuck. He was that kind of guy."

"If you say so."

"What nerve did I hit? The one that says Ted was the kind of guy who would have stuck? And that now, after all those years, you think you might have been wrong?"

"No," I answered. "Part of what you said is right. Ted probably would have stuck. I wouldn't. Sooner or later it would have been me, Doug, not Ted." He looked at me and ran his hand through his hair again. "Can we get off this subject, please?" He watched me and then nodded. I looked away from Doug, but I knew he was still studying me.

"You want to know the truth?" I said. "I don't know if I ever would have done it with anyone other than Ted."

"You loved him, Joel, didn't you?"

I wrapped my jacket around my chest and then I put my hands in my pockets. "Yes, I did," I said.

"Is sixteen years enough time? Does it pass in sixteen years?"

"I always thought, somehow, that we'd have a second chance." I felt a sting in my eyes. "Sometimes, when you give too much, you get back more than you really want."

"You two are very much alike," he said.

"No, we're not. You want to see me as Ted. But I'm not— he was the giver, not the taker."

"I know you're not Ted. He was fine and kind to me, enormously so, and so are you."

"I am not a rebound object for you."

We walked back to the living room. He took long steps that put him just enough ahead of me to create some distance. I let him stay out front, but then, after a few paces, I decided to catch up.

"Well, I guess you don't feel like dancing in the streets do you?" I said looking at him sideways.

He smiled sadly. "No, I guess not."

We walked down a long corridor hung with old maps into a large, high-ceilinged den lined with books, old English prints and more maps. A television set was in one of the bookcases, and at the opposite end of the room was a low, long tweed sofa with a coffee table in front of it. There were three large pillows on top of the table, obviously for feet. I sat down on the sofa. Doug brought a bottle of port and two glasses to the table. He sat down on the chair next to the sofa, poured drinks and handed me a glass. A storm outside had started to rage and then the ice came, ringing against the windows. The seasons were back where they belonged, I thought. I looked at Doug, sitting in his chair, and then I laughed, first to myself and then out loud.

"I'm glad we rode bikes today and not tomorrow," he said.

"I've lived on the line all my life," I said. "I don't know how much longer I can do it." He squinted for a moment, then simply looked at me questioningly. I took my shoes off, one at a time.

I REMEMBERED what happened next less as a series of acts, but as a long set of slow movements: a touch of hands when sofa pillows were moved, a home to ourselves and a neon sign across the park that glowed a crazy blue behind Doug's shoulder, and fingers that were ice-cold at first that traced my spine, then turned sharply into my shoulders. I remember exploring the outline of Doug's body with my fingers and pushing the hair away from his forehead. I felt Doug's palms rub my temples. There was no hurry, and I felt safe. It seemed like it once was: gentle and with honor. I felt I could let go; the bones could leave my body, but I could still be strong, and I could trust my eyes to the fingers above them.

But later, in bed, the good feelings slipped away. It became harsh, and somehow, it had all gone wrong. It went bam-bam fast. The end took seconds, and when it was over, the earth had turned to cracked clay.

AN HOUR passed, and we listened in the dark bedroom to each other's breathing. Doug broke the silence, "Do you want to talk?"

"I'm not sure," I answered.

"It didn't go very well, did it?" he said.

"Oh, I don't know."

"Have we wrecked everything?" he asked. He had the squint lines of a seventy-year-old man.

"I don't know," I said.

"Two guys meet in a bar," he said. He sat up, his chest uncovered, staring at the traffic moving through Central Park. "They exchange nine words. They go home and if sex works three times in a row, they're an item. Then they talk, and what they learn usually puts an end to the whole thing. We reversed it. We learned something about each other first. What we learned was good; it was glue, good glue. But then, did we wreck it?"

"Answers, Doug. Do you always have to have answers?" My throat hurt. "What if I don't *have* the answers?"

"You were afraid, weren't you?"

"Yes." I heard my own voice, and it had gone flat.

"But not right away. You can't deny that."

"No, not right away." I let myself hear the truth.

"I was glad of that." Doug folded one leg under him, and turned to face me. His back was shoved against the window next to the left side of the bed.

"Are you sure the window is shut?" I asked.

"I'm not your kid, you know." His voice seemed to fall apart. "God damn it, Joel, what went wrong?"

"I'm sorry, I don't know."

'Rush. Panic. Get it over with. Why, Joel?" he demanded. "You did that. I didn't do that. Why?"

"The parking meter was running out! That's why."

"If you don't want to talk, you don't have to," he said, giving up.

"I'll straighten it out," I said. "Just give me some time. After all, it's been a long time between boys."

"Jesus Christ," he whispered.

"Remember, I haven't been chasing guys for sixteen years," I said, thinking of Jerry Atkins, who would leer at me if I told him what happened and who could have carried off an affair with Doug like a master.

Doug stared out the window a long time. "You think that's the only way the issue comes up?"

I stared back at him.

"Suppose it has less to do with a parade of boys than caring for one. Or maybe even two? And maybe they're not boys. Maybe they're men."

All I could do was look at him and wonder why I felt like holding him again.

"Just about everybody understands that," he said, "except you." I sat dead still, forcing my eyes away from him. "Suppose it's not like you read in the papers? Or as you've frozen it shut in your own mind?"

"Doug, please," I begged. We sat in that bed and neither of us moved an inch. "I can't take the risk," I said.

"You've already taken it."

I turned my eyes away from the window and looked at him. The snow had turned to rain and the drops zigzagged down the windows. He was right, I thought. It was always one person for me, never a parade.

"I'm sorry," I said, "I'm a little screwed up right now. Don't pay any attention to me."

He took a handkerchief out of the night table, cleaned his glasses and put them on again. He spoke very softly: "I guess you've had years of practice going off by yourself when something happens that throws you off balance," he said. "I'm asking you to stop doing that." He pulled the covers over him. "Joel, you can't spend most of your love on your children. They'll never be able to give it back to you, and they shouldn't. It's too much to ask of them."

I turned my head and I suddenly yelled at him. "What do you think I'm thinking of?" I tried to catch my breath. He got out of bed and started to dress. "Doug, don't you know I'm scared? How can you ask me for answers?"

"Maybe I need them more than you do."

He put his shirt on and tossed my trousers across the bed.

"I want you to be the person you want to be," I said. "I want you to win the race you're running."

"Don't give me that avuncular bullshit," he said. "You love your children because they're *not* your equals. What will happen to you when you love someone at your own eye level?"

I decided to dress. "I don't know that either of us should talk the way we've been talking," I said.

"We should try to be realistic, right?" There was anger in his voice, but I tried to ignore it.

"Yes, to the extent we can be," I said.

"Does that mean the issue is whether you extend yourself to something as sleazy as me?" Doug's eyes hardened.

"Doug, it's not like that at all. Don't look at yourself that way."

"Why not, Uncle Joel? You do."

"Doug, stop."

"No, *you* stop," he said. "If you're trying to be realistic, why don't you start at home rather than giving me lectures? You're a married man, married to a woman. With kids. I've slept with a woman twice. And Ted. And pretty much only Ted. And I like that. I think I'm used to that world. What world are you used to? Do you know?"

I thought of the Reinheimers' house next door to ours, their yard and the red wheelbarrow covered with snow; the one that's full of Cokes for the kids during our summer picnics.

"Joel, have you heard anything I've said?" Doug asked.

"Yes. We have to be careful with each other," I said. Doug looked at me, but said nothing.

"I don't want to be your boyfriend just to see if you want one," he continued, and his eyes were wet.

"Who asked you?" I bit my tongue.

"No one." In those days, I didn't cry, I had theories: one was that friends since school weren't friends—they were competitors. You didn't share your dreams with them because the dreams would be stolen. Your girl you courted; your wife you protected and impressed with victories in order to retain. Being vulnerable was for Mommy—then never again. Other than that, you were alone, save for kids, if you were lucky. When it was over, baby, it was over. Unless it came back once again.

"That isn't what this is all about."

"Well then, what *is* this all about?"

"I don't know," I said, trying to tie my tie. "I get excited when I hear your voice, when I picture you in the shower, when I'm on my way to you, but I mess up when I'm with you. Doug, I don't know what this is all about," I said, trying hard not to cry. People told me that life is once and it's fast and in a way, nothing made any difference. I never believed it.

"You look like you're off somewhere," he said.

"I don't know what I'm going to say to Catherine."

"How about telling her the truth?" he offered. He walked

into the bathroom and came out a moment later. "What's the sense of it, Joel? It all seems so out of reach." He took another deep breath. "I didn't want it to go the way it did tonight. I care for you. I wouldn't embarrass you, you know that, and you wouldn't have to be Walter Cronkite for me. Ted and I lived through that. I think I—I know we can't go any further—"

"Doug, wait a minute, will you?" I took hold of his arm. He stopped. "I didn't want anything to go wrong either," I said. I was suddenly as short of breath as he was, my words tumbling out in pieces. "I didn't know . . . I mean . . ."

Doug put his hand gently on my arm. "This isn't good for either of us," he said calmly. He pushed the door and went back into the bathroom. I put my hand on his shoulder, needing to reach him. He turned to me, smiled, but put his index finger up to his lips.

"It's best if you leave," he whispered as we stood in front of the door. "Good night. You know the way out. It was good to be with you," he said, closing the door quietly behind him. But just before it shut, I saw that his eyes were glazed with tears.

I reached for the knob and caught it in my hand, but it was held tight from the other side. I pulled until my chest hurt. Then I gave up and walked, it seemed, in slow motion, back into the bedroom and finished dressing.

18

_____ AND THEN, having cast a shadow on the altar, I came home. The house was hellish, claustrophobic, and I felt I had made it decay.

"Dad's daydreaming," said Andy. "That's what they call a glazed look, isn't it, Mom?"

I heard him baiting me, but I kept staring out the kitchen window anyway. I watched reflections in the glass, Cath looking at me and then turning to Andy. "Yes, Andy, that's what they call a glazed look."

Judd wouldn't eat his spinach and wrapped it in his napkin. It made me sick when he did that, especially when he had that self-satisfied, sneaky look on his face.

"Any more coffee?" I asked.

"Has the stove moved to Evanston?" Catherine asked.

"No," I said.

The date was December 18, my fortieth birthday, and ten minutes earlier all had been sunshine and smiles. Andy had given me a soccer ball, and Judd had tendered a box of preserved apricots, the result of some school project. Catherine delivered the Joel pillow she had been working on for months. She handed it to me across the table, wrapped in tissue with a ribbon. She watched me as I opened it, her eyes cast down on the tabletop, like a bashful boy's.

Andy and Judd fell silent and looked at us without a sound. I didn't move or say anything and Cath somehow didn't expect me to. When we exchanged gifts, the drill was to make a fuss over the donor who would wait shyly for a kiss and a thank you. Not then. We just sat there. "I've always liked that name," she said, "best of all." Cath and I looked at each other. Then Andy looked up. "Can we please open the window?" he sighed, which was when I started staring out of it.

THE CHRISTMAS parties had started, and we were supposed to go to one every night. I had begged off three earlier that week, and Cath went alone, but there was no way I could avoid the Kellogs' tree-trimming party later that evening. Maury Kellog spelled his first name in that unusual way because his mother wanted a girl named Mary, so when she had a boy she added a *U* and got part of what she wanted. He looked like the dark Everly brother with a mustache, had a boneless handshake and together, he and Grace, with her auburn bangs, greeted all effusively at their door, noses already red, like reindeer.

The place was packed. It was a true Rolodex party, and the living room smelled of fireplaces and spoiling cold cuts by the time we arrived. Maury's family life was complicated by his wife and a barely hidden mistress; he supported eleven people, and didn't need much encouragement to have a drink. The well-informed had brought discreet ornaments, knowing that the creative entries won a prize. He was in real estate, a natural looter, and why we went to these parties, I never knew.

"Happy Birthday" sung out loud was all I needed, and I missed blowing out the last candle. I looked up across the cake and saw Cath, standing in a corner, hand over her mouth, suppressing a laugh. Our friends formed a receiving line, because others, when you're forty, and they're not, like to mark the event. I protested, but down deep I liked the attention, and I thought that perhaps I should not have objected so strenuously when Cath and the boys offered to throw a big party for me. I would have liked that even more, and maybe they would have too.

About eleven, Cath and I left the tweezer perfect crowd. We sat by ourselves in the Kellogs' library, propped up by pillows in the window seat, nests made, drinking champagne. There were candles on the mantel, flickering along with the fire, and Christmas carol recordings playing in the background. The room was lined with leather books, filling shelves all around us, and only one door let you in or out, so those who poked their noses in would tend to say an embarrassed "Hi" and then retreat. Why it happened, I never knew, but somehow we talked politics. Years ago, as Government 101 prodigies, we had each supported Gene McCarthy, but secretly I had been pleased when Bobby pulled out front. I had no respect for people who sought power vowing not to use it. Cath disagreed. Where was the power now? I wondered as we clinked glasses.

Earlier in the evening, in the middle of all those people, I had felt alone and Cath sensed it. She had come over to me, reindeer and snowflakes covering her cardigan, and we stood together next to the tree. She put her elbow on my shoulder, and the bone dug in as she crossed one leg behind the other, leaning on me. "It's no fun to be forty, is it?" she said, her voice a notch or two warmer than normal. "You'll survive. You felt the same way when you were thirty."

The little tree lights snapped on and off.

"That was different," I said. "It was the beginning of something. It was twenty-nine that was lousy."

"I remember," she said.

Our knees touched. "And nineteen?" she asked, "How was nineteen?"

"Who remembers nineteen?" I said. "I don't even know how to spell it." She smiled. What I did recall was twenty-five and twenty-six. She was gone the winters of those years. "What was that place you took me to for my thirtieth?" I asked. "The Blue Banana? Or something like that?"

"No, *that* wasn't it," she laughed, "but I don't remember what it was called," she said. "It was a disco place—you wanted to learn how to boogie then, remember?"

"It was a new era," I said.

The Hemmers came in to talk about sending Mike Junior to camp that summer and asked if we might consider letting Judd go along. Mike Senior was forty-five minutes late because his yoga class ran over, and she was a stitch. "It's so goyishe, Cynthia," she said to Cynthia Mitchell, who understood no New York argot whatsoever. We liked the Hemmers and it was nice that our kids got along. Grace Kellog interrupted, calling the Hemmers out to accept the ornament award. Neither Cath nor I wanted to go, so we stayed, parked in the window seat, our backs against the dark green cushions, listening to muffled laughter and applause that came from the front of the house.

"When you were twenty-six," Cath said, "I wasn't with you on Christmas."

"I know. You picked a hell of time to go," I said.

"You thought his name was John," she said. "It wasn't."

I cleared my throat. "What was his name?"

"Gary," she said, and Cath closed both her eyes.

"What was he like?" I asked, knowing my voice had gone high and thin.

"Different." She hesitated. "Different than you were." I hung my head. "But you were nicer." She smiled, and turned her head against the firelight, and the shadows made her chin seem long, a Joycean Irish chin. She touched my hand as she moved.

She leaned back once again, and let her long legs hang down over the seat cushion. "He was from Indianapolis and he sang Shubert *lieder*. I still have some of his music, along with an old yellow chemistry book he forgot."

She even knew the color. "Do you want to see him again?" I asked.

"No. Not really, but I'd like him to have his music back. It was his performing copy, the one he had marked up when he studied with Eileen Farrell at Indiana."

"He must have been very good." I forced the words out, but Cath didn't notice the difficulty I had in saying them, and I didn't want her to.

"He was. His top notes rang out." Cath turned to look out the window, her back to me. She put her hand behind her head and moved her hair around the back of her neck. "I could never tell you before Ted died. I don't know why," she said.

"Maybe you would like to send his music back to him," I said. She turned around to face me.

"I don't know where he is."

"He never kept in touch?" I asked.

"No, he didn't. I wrote a postcard to him once," she said, "maybe ten years ago. I don't know why, and I don't know what sparked it."

"What did you say to him?" I asked.

"It was just a postcard. You and I were in New York for

New Year's. Remember when your folks took us?" she said.
"He never answered."

"Cath?"

"Um-hmm."

"Is he here tonight? Is that why you're thinking of him?"

"No, no, he's not here." I didn't know if that was the truth
or not.

"Is there another reason?" I asked.

"I don't know." She hesitated a moment, and interrupted
her own thought by shaking her head. "Maybe it's Christmas
and then New Year's coming up and all that."

"I thought loneliness at this time of year never meant anything to you," I said.

"It did."

"When I was away," she said, "even with him, I thought
of you. I wanted someone stronger than you, and," she
laughed, "look what I picked! See?" she smiled. "You were
the strongest one all along."

A door could have banged open and broken the mood. We
sat there silently, avoiding each other's eyes.

LATER THAT evening, we talked. We sat in our chairs in front
of the fireplace, and the rule was you could talk to the fire;
you never had to look at the other person. It was free time.
The house creaked, and we heard the same wind leak whis-
tling through the window frame.

I looked at Catherine, tacked into her pillows in the chair
in front of the fireplace, the lamp behind. There was almost
too much concentration. Then she read something that made
her smile, and she said, "Mmm." Without looking up, Cath
went to a subject that she knew would interest me. She said
Andy was becoming wilder, and although independence was

what growing up was all about, he wasn't quite as grown up as he thought he was and that a slap now and then coming from me would do the trick. "You've got to join me in this. I don't want to be the heavy all the time," she said, looking away.

I listened to her and thought of how unfulfilled she was. She had no career, but she was better than half the men she dealt with. Her career was being my wife, and all she was allowed to do was dabble in falling-down buildings, albeit at the highest levels.

"Andy needs a slap now and then. It's really best for him, Joel. You can't always encourage his independence. He's not who he thinks he is. He can't do what you can do." She looked at me. "You put a premium on being honest with him, but he puts a premium on imitation."

Now life was even worse for Cath, I thought. She has a bogus marriage and a bogus demicareer, and being the plaintiff in a lawsuit may be her most independent revenue-producing status.

"Don't you think so? Don't you think I'm right?"

Being bogus is unjust, an insult and unsatisfying, and being a plaintiff publicly seeking compensation is at best embarrassing, I thought. I've learned plenty from being a father, but I don't know that I've benefited by it.

"Joel, you look like you're a million miles away."

"No, I'm listening."

What would be her version, I asked myself, about our marriage, our infant marriage, when it was all so new to us? Would she admit that in the early days I was the one who was restless and made all the noise in the house, played WFMT, invited our friends over and blew up the pressure cooker making stew? When she left to go with Gary and the one before him, whoever that was, how would she know there were no sounds in the house? How would she explain those departures? What would she say? Would she say that no matter what she accomplished, all Joel did was practice his La Salle Street laugh, a sort of low-pitched "ha-ha," and gave nothing of himself; that he did nothing but drop big names he met in New York, display new friends none of whom dated from his boyhood, trumpet his success and wear a white handkerchief in his breast pocket with three points showing? After all, she could say, "I couldn't fuck a handkerchief, now could I?"

Gary. So his name was Gary, I thought. Was he tall? Was he strong? Was he better in bed with her than I was? Was that so hard to do?

"Joel, I didn't want to tell you this, but I'd better," she said.

Now it was my turn to say "Mmm."

"Andy, that little sweetheart of yours, is gambling, you know."

"Oh?"

"Poker. While you were in New York."

"Did he win?" I asked, grinning her into the ground. She found one of her hands fussing with her hair. Ditch me and your children, see if I care, she probably thought.

Catherine sat still in her chair, closed her book and laid it down in her lap.

"You did see Gary tonight, didn't you?" I said.

"No," she said, perfectly calm. "No, I didn't. But I wanted to." A stick of wood collapsed in the fireplace.

"I know what you mean," I said, thinking of Ted or Doug—whichever one it was, I wasn't sure and I didn't care.

She let her head sink to the top of her chair. "What's the advantage of growing up?" she said to the ceiling. "Sometimes you end up back where you started: dependent."

"Would you have been dependent on Gary?"

She looked at me and laughed. "No chance of that! If anything, it would have been the other way round. He would have been dependent on me." Then she allowed her head to fall back once again, staring upward. "He lived where he shouldn't have lived, on Lake Shore Drive, because he wanted the address. He had an apartment he shouldn't have had and the trucks and the buses went by all night." I bit my tongue and closed my eyes, not wanting to see her there. "He tried so hard, but no matter what he did, he would lose, and it would be my shoulder, not his, that would hold us up. I didn't want to be a prop. That was Daddy and Momma all over again. I couldn't be the real estate lady she was forced to be."

"Why did you take up with Gary?"

"I hated the way you stopped living. I hated the way you gave yourself up." She looked into my eyes. "Who the hell knows?"

"Why is it that what goes unsaid between us makes us talk?" I asked.

"What do you mean? " she asked.

"I don't know. Forget it," I answered, thinking that maybe, in my absence, Catherine would flourish.

Cath said the name "Gary" twice in her sleep that night.

THE NEXT evening, Andy grabbed my sleeve as I was getting ready to leave for a convenient school board meeting.

"Dad, I have been trying to tell you for three days—"

"—Tell me what!"

"You don't have to sound so annoyed." Why was it always at the dinner table? I wondered. I leaned back, smiled, tossed my arm around the chair next to me and looked at Andy, waiting for him to go on. He didn't.

"Well, son?"

"Don't treat me like a reluctant client," he said as he

pushed his chair back and left the table, but not without first throwing his napkin down on his plate in the middle of his chicken gravy.

"What the hell was *that* all about?" I asked, looking at Cath. Judd looked down at the tabletop, his head still.

"It's his glasses," Juddy said into his milk.

"His what?" I asked.

"His coach, Mr. Fricker, said he should get glasses. He told you twice," Judd said sheepishly.

"He did?"

"Yes, he did." Judd drank his milk, but kept his eyes glued to his glass.

"Did he?" I asked Catherine.

"I don't remember," she said.

"You weren't listening either," Judd said, and then he got up and left the table.

"Judd! You didn't ask to be excused," Catherine said. Judd stood still, his back to us. A moment passed. Then he turned around, and said, "May I be excused?" I reached over to his shoulder.

"Please don't touch me," he said, and he turned and left us alone.

I gritted my teeth and waited until he went upstairs. "Excuse me, Catherine."

I followed Andy downstairs to the basement. He was at the pool table. He had broken balls with such force that three of them skipped over the rail and bounced on the hard floor. He didn't make a move to retrieve them. I didn't even think he knew I was there. I walked over to the other side of the room and picked them up as they rolled toward the drain. He looked at me, then turned away.

"What's this about the coach and glasses?"

"It's not important."

"Come on, son. Sure it is."

"I'm supposed to get glasses. I can't see far away anymore."

"Did you just notice it?" I asked.

"I didn't notice it at all. He did."

"Is he right?"

Andy took hold of the seven ball with his fingers, aimed and lodged it in a corner pocket. "I guess so."

"Well, there's nothing wrong with wearing glasses. A lot of people do."

"I know," he barely whispered. I stood next to him and put my arm around his shoulder. "Dad, I don't want to be defective." He threw his leather jacket over his shoulder and charged up the stairs.

"Andy!" I called out. He kept going. I had to think fast. "How tall are you now?" I called out. He spun around.

"That's not important either." I knew he would be angry.

"Let me put a case to you. A hypothetical."

"Fuck your hypotheticals," he said. He turned around, giving me his back. He headed up the stairs, but I kept talking.

"I'm tall and your mom is tall. It's likely you'll be the six feet tall you want to be."

He stopped two stairs below the landing, but he still had his back to me. "So what's the hypothetical?"

"If you're not six feet tall, are you at fault?"

He turned around again, and faced me, but he didn't move an inch off his territory.

"What's that supposed to mean?" he asked. "That it's your fault?"

"No, not at all."

It gave him a sense of power to be up there, towering over me. A year or two from now, I thought, with my luck, he would be six-six, and he would tower over me all the time. But for now, he needed a staircase to do it. "It means," I said, "that who you are, you are, and that what you turn out to be doesn't make you defective."

"That's bullshit. I don't want to be five-two and I don't want to wear glasses and that's all there is to it."

"What's wrong with contacts?"

"Not while we're in a game. It's too dangerous."

"Why is that?"

The edge came off his voice as he repeated his coach's explanation. I didn't remember a tenth of what he said, and I didn't care, really. What I cared about was that Andy had moved back down the stairs.

"Andy, we're going through all this, and you haven't even been to the eye doctor yet. You may not need glasses."

He stood in front of me. "Dad, I need them."

"Then I guess you'll have to have them."

"I don't want them."

"I'd give you my eyes, but then you'd be in worse shape!"

"You're trying to get me to laugh," he said. "Don't." He started up the stairs again. He put his jacket on. He had found a white silk aviator's scarf to go with it. He looked like a junior Bob Dylan. "I'll work it out," he said.

Cath was still in the breakfast room. She looked at her watch as I walked into the room. It was close to curfew and Andy had just gone out the front door. She had done nothing to stop him. Oddly enough, there was no look of concern on her face. Our sons were mine. She had left them to me just the same as if she had died.

Once I saw it: the look of a woman losing her husband as he went back to boys. It was at a dinner party as the man gave all his attention and energy to a handsome young man seated next to him, leaving his wife to watch the two of them across the table. The husband had turned his entire body toward his conquest, bending the ear which was farthest away close to the

young man's lips as if he couldn't hear with the ear that was
closer. As they reached for salad, she noticed their arms touch
accidentally in the cunning manner of those about to be se-
duced. She looked at him helplessly, as if she had a wasting
disease.

I wondered about being a father, what right I had to that
position. Cath had been happy with two boys. "Boys and girls
never bring the same price," she used to say, proud of her production. For the first time, I wondered how she felt being the
only female in the house. Someday we should talk about it,
I thought. In a year or two from now, Andy would be wearing
a sport coat and baggy chinos and stopping at the stereo store
after school. I wanted to be around then; I belonged there. It
was not an accident that Andy and Judd were born; it was not
some experiment by a fucked-up faggot playing false to his
nature. It was not an accident, do you hear me?

19

CATHERINE MUST have thought I was a real lum-mox. I was lying on the sofa, stretched out like a drunk, listening to Fauré through Andy's earphones. I hadn't shaved, and I probably looked like a felon. The Midwest's most prestigious New Year's Eve party was about to begin, a mere three blocks away. All year long, people looked forward to going to the Mr. and Mrs. Hernando Bustamantes'. You'd have thought the pope was hosting it, in the middle of Glencoe, yet. What the Bustamantes didn't consume, they gave away, and everyone went there to learn how to be rich. It was a case of the blind leading the dazzled.

The boys hovered somewhere about the house, on the way to Tommy Sullivan's for a New Year's Eve party of their own. Juddy somehow magically got himself invited without Andy's objection, even though all the other boys were Andy's age, except for one other younger boy, Craig Stewart, whom Juddy didn't particularly like. Everything seemed insanely funny to me: Catherine's hairdo, on which she had spent all day, not to mention close to a hundred dollars to make it look casual, the purple shirt I wanted to wear under my tuxedo jacket, and the Rockefeller Center of a house where the festivities were to be held. It was all topped by the force-fed excitement of New Year's, but none of it had anything to do with time passing or sober realizations of knowing where you wanted to be this time of year and weren't. I simply didn't want to go, and for my money, I could have stayed sprawled out on Catherine's virgin wool sofa in the sunroom until death or the next party did us part.

Lying there, the main question I put to myself was why in the hierarchy of worry was fatherhood first? Why was it only second that I worried about our marriage? Why did Cath marry me? Did she need men less than most? That would be a fine insult. Of course, it wouldn't explain John or whatever the name of the second one was.

I had always wanted to breakfast comfortably with Henry Kissinger. He would sit there, Nancy towering over him, congratulating him on staying home on New Year's Eve. Ted and I never went anywhere New Year's either. That was for the goyim, Ted used to say, even though when he said that, it hurt me because he was talking about my mother. But, then again, no one was perfect.

THE PARTY came and went. Cath had mingled joyously, and I watched who she mingled with, wondering which one was Gary, which one John. Sunday morning the weather had changed. It was raw and the sky was cold.

We were having breakfast with the family, not the Kissingers, and I noticed Andy's nails. They were as long as daggers. "Andy, when was the last time you filed your nails?"

"I'll do it this minute, your majesty," and he bowed deeply from the waist. All of a sudden, the little wiseass got to me.

I raised my arm to slug him, but I didn't. He left his chair
and stood in the center of the room. Blood rushed to his face
and he stared at me in silence, his eyes black holes. He squared
his shoulders and walked out of the room. Judd looked at his
brother's back and at me, then followed Andy out of the
room. I felt as if I were sliding down a wall of ice.

Without a word, Cath started to wash the dishes. I muttered something about helping her and she said she would just
stack them in the machine. I went into the sunroom and tried
to read a damp *New York Times*. Cath came in a few minutes
later with her coat on, and told me she was going to the store.
Cath straightened things out when she went shopping. I
looked at the bleeding newsprint and I thought of Kafka: "I
have completed the construction of my burrow and it seems to
be successful."

I managed to sit still another ten minutes and then I wandered around the house. During that week between Christmas
and New Year's, I had lived as if I had Alzheimer's. I was turning on the stove and forgetting what I wanted to cook and
wondering suddenly, when she was always there, how and
when Cath had ended up in the same room I was in.

Andy's door was closed. I wanted to open it, but we had
been given a lecture a month or so ago on how important his
privacy was to him, and how he thought he had earned it now
he was soon to be fourteen. I thought of how solemn he looked
as he spoke and how well he had stated his case, so I passed
his door and walked down the hall and looked into Juddy's
room.

He was sitting at his worktable, the top polished and the
surface clear of everything except the jigsaw puzzle he was
completing. We had offered him a new desk, but he liked the
small table he had used since he was seven, even if it was beginning to get a bit tiny, even for him. He had moved it in
front of the window, and its position gave him a wide view

across the backyard through the trees, down to the ravine.

"I know you're there," he said, bent over the puzzle. "You can come in if you want." He didn't look up at me, but kept his head close to the desk. He leaned back and held a brightly colored cardboard piece up to the morning light and looked at it sideways, as if a new perspective might show him where it would fit. I pulled out the child's chair on the other side of the low table and squeezed into it. Judd's architect's lamp was bent on its hinged arm directly over the puzzle and threw light between us. I didn't say anything for a while. Neither did he.

"Where do you think this piece goes?" he asked.

"I don't know, son. Let's take a look."

"You'll never be able to figure it out upside down," he said.

"You want me to come over there?" I asked, needing him so much.

He nodded.

I hauled myself out of the chair, walked over and stood behind him. He turned around, and without looking up, stretched his arm out high and handed me another piece that dovetailed perfectly into the one he had given me before, but the question was where the two of them went. He had put the puzzle together from the outside in. I looked down at him, and he seemed so small sitting there.

"Maybe I should have put it together the other way," he said.

"I don't know that it would have made any difference," I said. "What is it supposed to be when it's all done?"

"Can't you tell?" His little voice was clear treble; it sounded like singing.

"I guess not," I answered.

"It's an angelfish, like the one Doug gave me."

"Oh? Did he buy the puzzle for you too?"

"I wouldn't let him do that, not after the aquarium and the dive bomber. I bought it with my own money. Do you like fish?" With his head, he gestured to the other side of his room. I looked at the aquarium, sitting on a stand, next to Judd's chest of drawers, the life inside it lit from above by a long fluorescent bulb mounted directly over the water. "Neat, huh!" he said.

"Did you and Mom have a good time at the museum yesterday?" I asked. "Did you get to the coal mine?"

"It wasn't yesterday. It was last week." He scratched the side of his head. "That reminds me," he said, "where're our presents from Grandpa?"

I had forgotten. "Oh, Juddy, I'm sorry."

"When will you get them?" he asked.

"Probably tomorrow," I said, "I promise."

"Doug was nice to give us presents. Do you like him?" he asked, still pushing pieces of puzzle around on his shiny table.

"Yes," I said.

"I like him, too."

Judd took the two interlocked pieces of puzzle out of my hand and tried to find the right place for them by moving them around inside the frame he had already put together.

"Wanna help?" he asked. I huddled on my knees next to the low table. Our hands touched as we moved the assembly around, trying to work it into place.

"It doesn't fit, not quite yet, Juddy. I think we have to get farther into the part of the fish where the gills are before we'll see where this goes."

"Probably," he answered, using the word I used just before. I loved it when he did that. I raised myself up off the floor. My right knee clicked and he giggled. I stood all the way up and the other one clicked as well. He giggled again, but at least cupped his hand over his mouth.

"Where did you eat yesterday?" I asked, embarrassed that my knees sounded like castanets.

"I told you it wasn't yesterday," he smiled. "You silly

Daddy," using a phrase he hadn't used in years. "It was last week!" He giggled. "We ate at Hamburger Hamlet. We had to wait a long time."

"Was it worth it?"

He shrugged his shoulders, then turned back to the puzzle. "Mom said you used to have another name," he said absent-mindedly. "We had a waiter named 'Buddy.' Mom said that used to be your name." Juddy scratched his cheek. "Andy said he was a homo."

"Don't make fun of those people, son. They're people too."

"I wasn't making fun." He pushed the piece into a corner. "Do you think the piece fits here?" Then he pulled it out and shook his head no.

"Grandpa and Grandma called me 'Buddy' sometimes," I said. "That's really no surprise, is it?"

"I guess not." My eyes fell on Judd's sketch pad with a sleek, long-hooded red convertible drawn across two spiral-bound sheets. I saw Cath hurry past the doorway. He had looked up and seen her also. "I want to talk to Mom, son. See you later."

"Daddy, remember when we all used to take showers together?" I stood in the doorway and nodded. "I guess we're all a little old for that now, huh?"

"I guess so." I started to walk out of Juddy's room.

"Will you take me with you to get the presents?" Judd called after me. "Just me? Not Andy."

I turned around and smiled at him. "We'll see, son."

"That's what you always say, 'We'll see.'" I bent down and hugged my Juddy. "I love you, son."

"You're so gooey."

"Only around New Year's." I tried to laugh. Sometimes I wished I could live in his time, not mine.

I walked back through the hallway. Cath must have been

in and out of our bedroom in seconds because she was gone when I got there. While I was in the shower, I heard Andy's toilet flush, so I knew he was alive. As I soaped myself, I thought of Doug's bathroom down a hall a thousand miles away, and I tried to block the picture of him in a shower that began to form in my mind, but I couldn't. My cock started to get hard. I wanted to hit it.

20

AT NOON, after the boys left for hockey practice, we sat still, Cath and I, in the just-turned-silent house. Our spoons sounded against the sides of the cups and made a ringing sound when they touched the saucer. Catherine looked up from a tattered *Vogue* that lay open on the kitchen table and gave me a smile as if she were on the cover. It was an open-eyed, bright-cheeked smile, pretty enough to put on paper, but she said nothing.

"Catherine, we've got to say something to each other."

"Say whatever it is you have to say," she said.

"Why all the room, Cath? Why have you given me all the room?"

The kitchen was dead quiet. Cath stared at Andy's skis standing against the mud room door. She toyed with her hair, then turned her head toward me. I put a fresh cup of coffee in front of her, and she waved it off. "Joel, what's going on with Doug?" She answered a question with a question, and then the old habits came back.

"You'll have to ask him," I said.

"I'm asking you and he's not here," she said bitterly.

"Well, let's pretend he's here," I said. There were times when I went a little nuts. She sighed and looked bored. "Not that act again," she said. I called it dialoguing. You took parts, that's what you did. Any part you wanted.

"I see by your face," I said, "that you don't believe me." I started to grin. "Let's dialogue it. I can play Doug." I began to enjoy myself as someone fiery and reckless. She had brought my sons into this and I had a grudge to settle. I passed into some kind of never-never land and took her with me. I was mad as hell. I held off a second for effect, but I didn't have her attention.

"Ready?" I asked the question as if I were talking to a two-year-old. I snapped my fingers. "Here we go," I said, making the words sound like whoopee! She stared at me.

"First, the doorbell rings." I stared back at her. "Dingdong," I said to the ceiling. Then to her: "That's the doorbell. Do you hear it?"

"Stop being strange," she said.

"Well, answer me," I demanded. I knew I sounded demonic. "Do you hear the doorbell?"

"Yes," she said, humoring me, but her eyes were frightened. "I hear the doorbell."

"Good," I said, "I'm soothed." I let a pause go by. "Do you go to the door or do I?" Another pause. "Of course, I do. Doug is my friend, not yours." Pause. "So I go." I hunched toward her, whispering. "You hear me walk down the hall. I open the door and shout 'Doug!'" I pulled away when I yelled, and after I shouted his name, I waited.

"Isn't this an intriguing play? We can make it go anywhere we want to."

Cath answered, "Ask Doug if he loves Joel." Her face and

her voice said it all too clearly—use a strategy to stop a strategy.

"Doug, do you love Joel?" I asked the question and cupped my ear listening for the person who wasn't there to give me an answer, and then I turned to Catherine. "Yes, he says he loves Joel." She sat silently, her eyes very large.

"Wait," I said. "Let me ask him another question for you. 'Doug, what do you think Joel is up to?'" I said, once again to the ceiling. Then I turned back to Cath. "He says this isn't going to be very good, and he wants to know if you really want to hear it."

"Tell him I want to hear it," she said, her face blank.

"Okay, he says, here goes: 'First of all, a few facts,' Doug says. 'It took Joel three tries—'" Cath put her hands to her ears. I stopped cold. I let my breath out and put my elbows down on the table, propped my chin in the palms of my hands, and I looked at Catherine. It had dawned on me that the transformation into the feared rival was worse than weird. I cut it out.

Cath turned her chair around backward, and sat down again, her legs straddling the seat. Her eyes came to rest quietly on me, as if she were staring at a stuffed animal at the Field Museum.

"Is the play over?" she asked, barely audible.

"Yes, Cath. It's over." I took another breath. "Why did you say anything to the kids?"

She stopped for an instant. "I didn't." She raised her eyebrows and her mouth remained open.

"Judd asked me about being called 'Buddy.'"

"Well, you were, weren't you?"

"Don't use that tone."

"I'll use any tone I want." Her color rose. "The waiter pranced all over the place and wore a badge that said 'Buddy.'

Even Andy knew what he was," she grimaced. "Can you fault me for making the connection?" She turned away so she wouldn't have to look at me.

"Joel, please." Her cadence had changed. "You're so good at making me feel I don't have a choice." She folded her arms across her chest and sat there, and I suddenly felt as if we were in the harsh, intoxicating silence of a courtroom. "I don't want to discuss this any further. I simply don't have the strength to talk to you." She pushed away from the table and walked through the front hallway, upstairs to our bedroom and closed the door. I sat quietly for a moment, then I followed her and stood outside our bedroom door.

I crossed the hall, knocked on Andy's door, but then I remembered he had gone. I sat down on his bed, rubbed my face and ran my fingers through my hair, which I had let grow long because Catherine liked it that way. The room was full of basketballs, skates, pennants, model airplanes, a television set and his stereo, including an amplifier he had also built by himself. I could still see the brown line he had made on his desk top with the soldering iron. He wouldn't let me help him with it, except for the power supply.

I lay down on Andy's bed. From there, I looked across the hall to the door to our room and watched for Catherine. I turned on my side, but made sure I could still see the door. Andy wouldn't mind if I messed up his bed a little, I thought. I put my head on his pillow, next to the tattered panda. Far off, somebody slammed a car door, and the echo seemed to go up and down the quiet street. I let my eyes close.

It was probably no more than twenty minutes later when a noise startled me. The door across the hall had opened, and Catherine stood in the doorway, twisting a pencil.

"Joel, what are you doing? Have you taken to sleeping with pandas as well?"

I bought time by stretching and then I sat up in Andy's bed. "Have you been in there for a long time?" I asked.

"You mean in 'our room'?" The singsong sarcasm was killing me. "Oh, no, not too long." Catherine walked into Andy's room and stood next to his bed.

"Cath, sit down here, please."

"I can do that," she allowed. She sat down on a chair next to the bed. I shoved my back against the headboard and reached out to touch her shoulders.

"No, Joel." She twitched free. "I know what's been going on with or without your Edgar Bergen–Charley McCarthy act, and if that's what you and Doug do, that's what you do." She pushed her chair back from the bed and balanced herself on its back two legs. "I thought the risk was over when I called to tell you about Ted. I didn't see that kid as starting it all over again. I guess down deep you wanted one or the other." She halted. Her eyes fixed on me, but then they let go. "It seemed like the right thing to do, to ask Doug to come here." Her voice had softened. "He was alone. It was the holiday and— he had lost someone he loved. He had lost his lover"—she swallowed, but managed to get past the word—"and you seemed closer to him than anyone . . . any friend he might ever have had."

She walked over to the window and stared out at the snow-covered yard. "It was like Ted losing you. Who took care of Ted? Ted wasn't a stranger to me, you know." She turned around. Tears stood in her eyes, but she held them back. "Ted wasn't here, but Doug was, and you were going to run after him. I could see that. If you wanted to go, I would let you. You had to figure it out: whether you wanted a wife or a first mate.

"And there was something else." Her eyes opened wide, revealing the deepest sadness I think I have ever seen. "I needed to know where I was." Her voice had become almost too strong when she started to talk again. "I can't live like the other North Shore dollies, wondering what's going to happen to me next. I had the—balls—yes, that's just the right word, balls— to set the stage and see what was going to happen. And now I know."

"You didn't need to set anything up. Why didn't you just ask me?"

"And what would you have answered? More make-believe?" Her eyes drilled into mine. Then all at once, she shuddered and her shoulders fell. "I have no desire to hurt you," she said. "Joel," she said softly, "if you want to go with him, you ought to go."

"Is that what you want?" I asked quietly.

Her eyes asked for help, but then the plea was gone.

"Joel, it's my integrity."

She focused on the ceiling, summoning her strength. It looked like she was hunting for rehearsed words. "I am not able, I have decided, to sit by." She took two deep breaths, regained control and went on. "I have a place in this community. I have a place as the mother of your two sons. If you want to leave, that's your business, but your decision has consequences." Her words clicked away. "I will expect a divorce, and I will expect adequate alimony and child support for the children." She was on a roll. "I will not change the way the three of us live to suit an indulgence." She sat down in Andy's chair next to the window, looking at me, satisfied.

I could see her with the lawyer, the North Shore dolly divorce lawyer. "Baby," he'd hiss, with a fat cigar in his mouth, "if you catch him with some guy's hand on his you-know, we'll take him for every penny he's got and then some." He would lean across the desk, scrunch down, put his face close to hers and whisper, "Hey, sweetheart, baby, the old man been playing around with boys long? It's okay, you can trust me. It'll help your case." She'd look at the crumb, and say, "Well, counselor, you know . . ." "Don't worry honey," says the lawyer, "we'll take him for all he's got and then some. Hey, honey, what are you doing for dinner tonight?"

"That's a canned speech," I said. "It isn't what either of us wants, and you know it."

"What do you want me to do," she asked, "spread my legs when he doesn't?"

She turned her head, suddenly looking all over the room, as if she were trying to find something to throw at me. "Is it hard for you to go to bed with me? If it is, you don't have to, you know." Her voice rose. "You can go to bed with him if you want to." She egged herself on. "I'm sure that adding Vaseline won't slow you down. I mean, you've done it before." The blood swooped to her head and her face flushed. "Wait a minute. I'm sure there's some here." She began to fling open Andy's bathroom cabinets, one after the other, then the draw-ers. "I'm sure there's some here, one place or another." Her words seemed to come from several angles of the room at once. She bent down and opened the cabinet under the sink. "Will Three-in-One Oil do?" She spit the words into the drainpipes. She stood up and stared at me. "Or is that too hard to wash off?" Her eyes were glazed.

The sun hit her eyes, and she squinted. It seemed to break the momentum and she hesitated. Her arms hung lifeless at her sides, and her head seemed to float, almost disconnected. She looked like a broken doll.

Cheerio, the neighbor's dog, barked just under the window, but Cath looked straight ahead, not reacting to the noise at all. She seemed to be frozen still, and from then on I didn't take my eyes off her. Her eyes widened until there was white completely around her green irises. I opened the window to give her air and the cold dried my sweat and made me cough. It was the only sound in the room. Her forehead was still drawn tight, as if some invisible twisting device were tightening a clamp behind her head, but then she relaxed. A few seconds later, she sat down on the corner of Andy's other bed.

"I'm fine now," she murmured.

I TOOK her hand and we went downstairs. Her walk was shaky, but by the time we had reached the kitchen, a little color had returned to her cheeks. The water was in the kettle and we waited for it to boil. Cath sat silently in one of the chairs in the breakfast nook and I stood over the stove, looking out the window into the backyard. After a while, the whistle in the kettle blew. Her faraway look was gone, and Cath managed a smile while she held out her coffee cup. When she said, "It's good. Thanks," her voice began to sound a little like her own again. She took another sip from her cup and traced a circle on the Vogue cover with her finger, then rubbed it out.

She folded the fingers of one hand into the fingers of the other, like the church steeple we made with our fingers when we were kids. She closed her eyes, but just for a second, and then she said to me, "All my life I wanted someone who was alive, someone who had power, ambition and brains—someone I didn't have to be wife and mother to at the same time. I fell for you, all those years ago. I don't know if it was right, back then, to bust you two up. Maybe you should have had your chance." She sat up straight, and put her folded hands on the edge of the table like a kindergartener.

"You didn't bust up anything without an accomplice," I said. I remembered how free I had felt—all the dreams had come true. Cath looked down at the table, then up into my eyes without hatred.

"Maybe miracles don't last forever," I heard her say. "Maybe the days of love are short."

"You allowed something that was part of me to happen,"

I said. "Sometimes, one wants a person, not a gender."

She turned her head away from me and spoke to the window. "When Ted told me, I felt lost." She swallowed hard. "There was nothing I could do."

"Did you think of telling me?" I asked.

Suddenly, her voice became as firm as I've ever heard it. "Not for a moment," she announced. "What would have happened if I had told you? We were kids then. Would we have had the courage to try? Would the knowledge have helped or hurt us? I don't think we would have gotten through sixteen years if your relationship with Ted had been out in the open. One way or another, wouldn't Ted have been part of our lives? You knew Ted. Everything had to be in neon for him. Look what's happened when Doug—" She stopped. "I'm sorry." She took a deep breath, then tried to smile. "Forget that," she paused. "I guess I've made my point."

"Why did you tell me when Ted died?"

"I've told you that, Joel, because I thought the risk was over. I thought you'd see me as I am, not as I was when we were young, as your savior."

I put my cup in the sink, rinsed and refilled it.

"You feel you've missed out on something with Ted," Cath said softly. "That's right, isn't it?"

I hoisted myself up and sat on the counter top. The light came in low and strong, and it reached almost all the way back to the kitchen cabinets.

"Joel"—her voice was so soft, I could hardly hear it—"you know I hardly even cried?" She moved over to the refrigerator and stood there. "I knew what it was like to have men prefer me stupid. I was afraid I would have to make the compromise. You never asked that of me. The stronger I was, the happier you were. Sometimes there was the lure of someone I didn't know. I tried that twice and it meant nothing. I think to myself that if you played around now, it was only tit for tat. I wouldn't criticize you. You never confronted me when I did it. You never once walked out. You waited. I kept thinking that if I had my winters, you were entitled to yours. . . . And that maybe this was your winter." Her eyes were empty.

I felt fear rise in me, and I realized that the only words going around in my head were those that would gloss over the instant. "Cath, this isn't my winter," I could have said. I didn't say that, because I didn't know if it was true. I stood there. I looked at her and resolved never again to lie out of fear, so I didn't say a thing.

"I'm stronger now than I was sixteen years ago," she said. "Time was on my side."

I swallowed coffee too fast and my mouth hurt from the burn. Cath winced in sympathy and brought a glass of cold water to the table. I drank it, and after the glass had been replaced on the table, we sat still a long time. I saw her for an instant as a double exposure in the shutter of a camera, old and young at the same time. I became conscious of the distant shouts of children calling "you're it" as they played in the snow at the bottom of the wooded ravine.

"You don't want to decide anything, do you, Joel?"

"A few days before Ted died, I was in the middle of an interview. Remember that?" Cath nodded. "The kid was so handsome, I hated him. The point is, I noticed."

"I won't make the decision for you. I did that the last time."

"I knew why you left those winters. You weren't sure of me. You should have been. We should have talked, but you and I were never willing to accept messes."

"Sometimes I think," she said, "you fathered the boys first and married me later." She looked around. Cath stared at the oak at the edge of the backyard for a long time, then she blinked and focused on the ground closer to the house, the place where she grew her roses. Finally, she looked inside the room again. "I could never muster enough courage to talk to you before. After the winters when I was away, I tried to make it up to you. I tried all kinds of achievements to get your attention, and then I realized that all I had to do was be myself and be with you."

"Why did you come back?" I asked.

"I didn't like where I was," she said quietly, almost in a rustle.

I hardly noticed when the old memory had entered my mind. I could feel Cambridge all around me, the school buildings, the record stores in Harvard Square, the baseball games and the haircuts with Ted. But it wasn't Cambridge in general or even Ted in general that broke through. It was a day of no strategies, no constructions. It was a day of no defenses, and it felt good to be reunited with that day long ago.

"Cath, can I tell you a story?" She nodded, but she was afraid of another make-believe dialogue. I could tell. "It's not a once upon a time," I said. "I promise."

"Will I want to hear it?" I took her hand for a moment, then let go.

"A long time ago, Ted stuck a poster for a gay dance in our kitchen window on Brattle Street. I never even knew it was there. The next day, we received an eviction notice from our landlady. Alice Harrington owned half the property in Cambridge. Next to Harvard, she was the single largest landowner in town. I had met her when I signed the lease. Ted never knew who she was. She lived in a huge duplex and surrounded herself with every opulent possession money could buy. She had layers of Oriental rugs, overstuffed antiques, padded silk on the walls, and crystal chandeliers, and she drove an ancient, listing De Soto and I think her license plate frame said FAMILY PRAYER CHRYSLER-PLYMOUTH or something like that." Cath smiled, just a little, and it made me feel somehow stronger.

"Ted asked me to talk to her, to get her to let us stay. 'I will speak with you, Mr. Stern, but not Mr. Stackler.'" she told me over the phone.

"Ted had curled up on the living-room sofa as I put on my three-piece suit and I made sure I had a calling card because I knew Mrs. Harrington went for that. 'I'm not worried about me,' he said, 'but if you go in there, I'm afraid I've compromised you.' He didn't need a future, I did. But he had done what I couldn't do; he had put that sign in the window. He had stood up for me, because that's who I was then.

"When I walked in, Mrs. Harrington was all business. 'You may sit here, Mr. Stern,' she said to me, and I sat on a pillow made out of an Oriental rug. 'I'm sorry, but I must ask you two to leave. Advertising is not permitted on the premises. You may, of course, have a month, if you like, provided you remove the advertisement immediately.' I thanked her for her courtesy, but then I said, 'I don't believe, Mrs. Harrington, that the sign is really the issue, do you?' 'Would you care for some tea, Mr. Stern?' 'Yes, thank you, Mrs. Harrington.' An Irish maid dressed by M-G-M's wardrobe department brought tea, and during it, I told her about various holdings in constitutional law cases, and she, in turn, quoted Holmes to the effect that there were limits to free speech. 'You recall his words, Mr. Stern: one cannot scream fire in a crowded theater.' 'I do recall, Mrs. Harrington, but our kitchen window is hardly a theater and the text of the sign is hardly a fire.' 'I notice you refer to the window as our window?' she said. 'Do you support him in this?' she asked. 'I must, of course, make a record of your response. You understand that, do you not.' 'Yes, I do,' I told her, 'and I do support him in this.' 'Are you sympathetic to his cause, Mr. Stern?' 'Yes, I am, Mrs. Harrington.'"

Cath hadn't a taut muscle in her body, nor a slack one either. I interrupted the story and told her I read once that sin was outlawing yourself from God and that I read somewhere else that when people feel the hopelessness of their position, they give up seeking one and instead say what they believe. Then I went on.

"Ted asked how it went and I told him we'd better pack. That afternoon, however, we received a note from Alice Harrington rescinding the eviction notice. It was addressed to both of us. A handwritten postscript was attached for me. It said, 'Thank you for the lesson in civil rights. I trust I contributed as well. You should be quite proud of your honesty.'

"That day was special, Cath. It was a festival."

Cath handed me her handkerchief and I wiped my eyes. She ran her hand through her hair. "It's not so hard to believe in you, Joel. You know, you were the real hero."

She walked to the window and looked out at what would be her rose garden. Cath hesitated, touching her fingers together on the windowpane. Then she turned around and looked at me with her family's green eyes: "I guess there was always more for us than knowing you'd have sex only with me or the female of the species." She lowered her hand. "But I have a question," she said. "If Doug wasn't Ted all over again, would anything have happened?"

I started to talk, but Cath interrupted: "Don't say anything, Joel. Just think about it."

IT WAS the last New Year's I spent in the suburbs. I always made it my business to get the hell out of there right after Christmas. Not that the example of Jerry and Marie did us much good either. At one time, Cath accused me of arranging that whole experience in order to display them to her as some kind of emblematic solution. It wasn't true. People always thought I had the ability to look around corners, to figure out what move to make and get what was wanted before anyone knew what was happening. No matter how I tried to tell Cath I didn't plan it all out, I didn't succeed.

It was true, however, that I was good at logistics. There would be no North Shore dolly divorce lawyer because there would be no divorce. There would be no humiliation or even the slightest embarrassment to Cath, at least on a public level, nor, until it became necessary, would there be any explanations to the boys. We would stay where we were. That was my proposal.

Cath, at that time, was big on all-or-nothing deals. The Bateman had stayed up; the developer had found another site. Cath could move buildings. Why settle for less elsewhere? What stopped a pitched battle between us was the sincere pleasure I took in her success. It revived, as she put it, the singularity of a man who loved her and who wanted her to be as strong as she could be. It was Cath's sense of her own strength and my respect for it that rekindled what we had felt for each other close to sixteen, seventeen years before. We were unique to each other, and since we both knew it, there was no reason to force ourselves into conventionality. And there was another plus. This time, our decision was informed. The full meaning of my life's hero was out of the bag.

The talks we had and the silences that followed (and believe me, it was a process, not an event) enabled us to become closer than we had ever been. We started doing things again, just the two of us. We bought fresh fish together downtown at Burhop's and took the 5:40 train home together, and we figured out how to move Andy and Judd to their various sports events (until Andy started to drive) without splitting up and leaving Cath or me alone, each wondering where the other was. It was not business as usual for Cath; it was better. She enabled us to stay together, to hand each other the truth, and at a stage in our lives when we could handle it and had accumulated enough love for each other to honor it.

Cath finally came to believe me about the Atkinses, and we saw a great deal of them. There were other couples we saw as well, and from the look of it, we had a lot in common, more than anyone was willing to talk about out loud.

Doug visited occasionally. Once, we went to a huge Bustamante-type party together, the three of us, and Cath spent the whole evening with him talking architecture, as if he were her date, or to put it in more adult terms, as if she were having an affair with him. It was the one time when things got too close to the edge for me.

Big buildings take a long time to put up, and his eighty-odd-story sliced facade anodyne to postmodernism (I could feel him wince when he described it on Kup's Show) took several years from start to finish. Obviously, he was here. Those were extraordinary days, and the three of us just let things happen as they happened because there was no way we could do anything else. I kept reliving a lot of events in my mind—things like the thrill of loving again, as if for the first time, or realizing that life is lived more fully when it's not mapped out. At Chanukah, when the boys sing the blessing for the candles, Andy looks at me and I can see in his eyes that he senses something. He supplies the smile when he chants the Hebrew, and I believe he hears Doug singing along with him. Instead of being ashamed, although I am a little sad, I am also alive, for I too have become, if not a singer, at least one who steps into the scenery without trying to move the trees around.

As for Catherine, people didn't know her, what really went on inside her, who she was, and the lengths she would go to care for those she loved. In many ways, her appearance was her disguise. People said she was as she looked. Look again, I'd say.

Robert Robin lives in Chicago where he is a practicing lawyer with the firm of Robin & Tyler. He is a graduate of Harvard Law School and has lectured at the Kennedy Institute at Harvard and other universities. He writes in his spare time and is currently at work on his second novel.

PERHAPS
I'LL DREAM OF
DARKNESS

PERHAPS
I'LL DREAM OF
DARKNESS

MARY
SHELDON

RANDOM HOUSE
NEW YORK

Grateful acknowledgment is made to the following for permission to reprint previously published material:

Harcourt Brace Jovanovich, Inc., and Faber & Faber Limited: Excerpt from "Ash Wednesday" in *Collected Poems 1909–1962* by T. S. Eliot. Copyright 1936 by Harcourt Brace Jovanovich, Inc. Copyright © 1963, 1964 by T. S. Eliot. Reprinted by permission of the publishers.

Library of Congress Cataloging in Publication Data

Sheldon, Mary, 1955-
Perhaps I'll dream of darkness.

I. Title.
PS3569.H392266P4   813'.54   81-40217
ISBN 0-394-51175-1   AACR2

Manufactured in the United States of America

24689753

First Edition

*For Mama, Papa
and Barry*

Acknowledgments

I would like to express my gratitude to Jason Epstein, Gary Fisketjon, Morton Janklow and Anne Sibbald for the guidance and encouragement they have given me throughout the writing of this book. And thank you, Greta Verdin, David Coombs and Ralph Hewitt—my best-beloved English teachers.

Effie

Quiet. I feel quiet. Thick. Full.

What am I supposed to feel? There is nothing from that life before left in this one.

I'm in Effie's room. I couldn't imagine myself being here, but I'm here. I just came up the way the two of us always did after church. Also, the reporters are downstairs.

I don't feel like doing anything.

You'll be all right. I must have heard that forty times today. You'll be all right. You have to take care of your mother. Sure, sure. We'll both be fine.

Six blue Bic pens, three schoolbooks with *Effie Daniels* written along the sides, the candy necklace from how many Halloweens ago, the Santa made of stones, three straws, the crewel owl she was working on, a jar of honey. Effie always did keep a messy desk.

I'm hurrying through her things as if she's about to come in at any second. "Susan, *why* are you going through *my* drawer?" What could I say?

I hear them leaving downstairs. The door shutting. Coffee cups being washed out. So now what happens? Are Mom and I supposed to go out to dinner? Goddamn, I don't know. I've only been to one funeral in my life. And what do you know? This was Effie's first.

It's like being in a black box where everything shuts.

What I keep thinking about. For the last year and a half

she's been after me to apply to Northwestern so she could visit me and see the art museum. Well, if that was so damned important to you, Effie, couldn't you wait until I got accepted to kill yourself?

March 25

Here's a picture of Effie and me at the Santa Monica pier, two years ago. I am pretty and fade into the background. Effie, who isn't pretty at all, comes right out of the picture. She is riding the black carousel horse and wearing her blue-and-white shirt. She is smiling on her way up to the brass ring. Bitten nails, but they don't show in the picture. Her hair is curly over her ears like breakers on the shore. Her white face. Her arm stretched out. You see, I try hard to concentrate on the details, as if missing something would be deadly.

Yesterday, after the service, we walked by a music store. It had one of those television scanners outside, and you could see people in the street on the screen. This young woman walked by the set. She was blond, too skinny and sort of waxy-looking. I thought she looked the way I might look in ten years if I'm not careful.

"Oh, look, Susan." Aunt Kate pointed. "You're on television."

Effie, Effie, have you left me with *anything?*

The wake was last night. Mom invited a lot of people, but some came without being asked. No one telephoned condolences. I guess they thought the ringing of the phone would be unseemly.

No one rang the doorbell either. Mom and I went crazy,

hearing all those hushed, apologetic knocks on the door. A few were so anxious not to disturb us that they stood in Mom's flower bed and tapped on the living-room window to get our attention.

Finally, Aunt Kate just put the door on the latch.

A woman and a little boy appeared in the driveway. She was tall and pale—everything about her seemed black and white. But the little boy had yellow hair. They didn't try to come in or anything, just stood out there. Every time I saw them I nearly screamed because they looked so much like the creatures from *The Turn of the Screw* that gave me nightmares.

I pulled Aunt Kate's sweater, and whimpered to her about them. She said they were just poor people who thrived on funerals and other people's sadness.

I ran outside before I lost my nerve and told the woman to get lost. She turned away the moment I spoke, but first she pushed a hard package into my hand. By the time I jumped away, she and her little boy were gone. The package was wrapped in bright-orange tissue paper. Weird, weird, weird. It was a book, one of those tracts, called *Death and Beyond*.

I was sure I threw it away in the bushes—but when I went inside again I found it was still in my hand.

I wish I could have spent more time with Aunt Kate at the wake. She kept massaging my shoulders. She brought a cake. She makes wonderful date cookies, but Effie was always the one who liked them the best. Maybe Aunt Kate remembered that.

Dad's been here since day before yesterday, but he's gone now. He wasn't any help. I kept saying to myself that once Daddy got here he would make the holes go away, and that I wouldn't think about it until Daddy got here. Dad

just cried into my mother's neck when he did come, and
the holes have gotten meaner and deeper. I was glad to
see him leave this evening. He's looking fat. It meant
nothing to see him go.

Stanley came also, but only for a short time. He was
one of those who didn't get an invitation. He cried more
than almost anybody. That would have pleased Effie.

I was glad when Peter and the fan club came, and I spent
most of my time with them.

Everyone talked about my sister. Nobody wanted to
bring up what happened Friday, so it just wasn't mentioned. They told stories they remembered about her. I
didn't really listen. The ones that included me I knew already, and the ones I didn't know I didn't want to hear.
They made Effie seem farther away.

Everyone left by seven, and Mom and I went to dinner
at a hamburger stand in Santa Monica. It had nothing in
the world to do with Effie.

When we came back to the house, there was the dull-
ness and quiet. All over the hall table and in the refrigerator were footballs of tin foil—cakes and breads that people had brought over. I wouldn't touch them. They made
me sick, like the flowers at the service.

Mom and I went to bed around one. She asked if I
wanted to stay in her room, but I said no. Where I ended
up staying was Effie's bedroom. Crazy. I guess I was thinking that if Effie were anywhere, she would be in there. I
slept on top of the covers, not under them. If Mom were
to notice that Effie's bed had been slept in, I don't know
what she'd believe.

I slept a little and had short, quick dreams about Effie.
Mostly, though, I stayed awake. I'd shut my eyes and concentrate on breathing in Effie off the pillow. But the linens
have already stopped smelling like her. In my mind, I'd

get a vague image of something to do with Effie, just a color or a shape, and bit by bit it would develop into a picture—like the cameras that make the photo before your eyes. Except that until the picture was finished, I wouldn't even know what it was I'd been thinking about. I got a clear image of the pennant Effie brought home from a trip to the Seattle World's Fair; it was as if I had it in my hand. And I could see the flowered enamel wrist watch Grandma brought her from Switzerland. I was frightened and excited, seeing these things in my mind.

At the very last, I could visualize the autograph David Angel sent Effie, even the smudge on the corner. Then nothing would do for me but to go and get the real thing to see how closely I'd imagined it. I got out of bed and went to the desk. Effie always used to keep the autograph tacked up over her calendar. The pin holes were still there in the wall, but she or someone else had taken the paper down.

I looked through a few of Effie's drawers and the bottom of the closet, but I gave up after a little while. Mom's room is right down the hall, so I couldn't make too much noise.

I got upset, not being able to find what I was looking for. I began imagining all kinds of things—Effie actually eating the autograph, letter by letter. I saw it so clearly in my mind, Effie with the inky print on her lips; and that kept me up for the rest of the night.

March 26

The fuss is dying down.

It's bad. I miss her so much. Writing does make it better. She's never not there when I'm writing. And it feels good to write about her, even just her name. Effie, Effie, Effie.

I'll write about her until there's nothing left to write.

I was three when Effie was born. We were living in a little house near Malibu Beach in Southern California, and Dad was trying to start his own ad company. He wasn't making very much money. When I first heard that there was going to be a new baby, I went around cheering. I didn't know anything about the facts of life, but I'd been after my parents for months to get me a baby sister, so naturally I assumed that I was the one responsible for their finally doing it. I was dancing around when Mom slapped me on the face and ran to her room. At the time I was pretty confused, but I understand now that Effie wasn't exactly planned.

I remember something else from the time before she was born. Although I had always wanted a little sister to play with, now that one was actually coming, I was jealous. I had my own room already, and Mom was going to convert the dining room into a nursery for the baby. I got it into my head that the dining room was closer to my parents' bedroom than my room was, and that the baby would be closer to Mom and Dad than I would be. I made Dad measure the distances between all the rooms over and over; finally I was satisfied that I was closest, and I stayed in my old room.

But after Effie was born and when we were little, people were always amazed by how well the two of us got along. I see now that it was mainly Effie's doing.

From the time she could talk, she made me feel I was the cleverest person in the world and, irresistibly, she wanted to be in on every mischief I invented. If she knew it was wrong, she went along with me anyway, never squealed to Mom beforehand, and never cried when Dad spanked her afterward.

I sometimes still feel bad about the time I played dietitian and made her lunch off peanuts and two bottles of aspirin. She had to have her stomach pumped and wasn't allowed to watch television for a month. But I don't think Effie ever held it against me.

She also made me feel that I was as big and powerful in her eyes as Dad was.

I think I knew, even when I was seven, that Effie had to be protected.

Effie and I were California kids. Up until I was fourteen and she was eleven, we lived in that same house near Malibu. It was too small, but it was filled with everything we liked: all our collections, a Ping-Pong table with a warp in it which made playing ten times as much fun, stairs with banisters, a front stoop, an attic. There was a small yard in back where Mom planted a vegetable garden and a fig tree, where Effie and I used to sit by the hour, getting fat and sleepy. In front of the house was the ocean— and so half the time we could feel like farmers in a field, and half the time like sea captains.

I can remember Effie very clearly in that house. She didn't like the cliffs in front after a while because of her nightmares about falling over them. So she used to spend most of her time in the backyard. Every day she'd have a picnic with tomato juice, pistachio nuts, American cheese, a Hostess cupcake, and an imaginary friend, Johnny Appleseed. He was her very first crush.

Effie's favorite room in the house was the upstairs bathroom. She liked it because of the wallpaper and because the roof sloped down to a point in the corner where only she was small enough to fit. There were pandas on the wallpaper, and Mom let Effie crayon clothes on the ones

in that little sloped corner. She used to store her foreign
coins and paper dolls there. It never occurred to Effie that
if my parents or I wanted to steal her things, all we would
have had to do was lean down and stretch out an arm.

Effie: a whole civilization springs up. Soft cloth books
she read as a baby, trimming on her christening gown, the
three-tiered Jell-O she was always after Mom to make.
Right from the beginning she loved to hear stories—Dad
used to brag that her favorite was *Rebecca*. As I remember, he made up his own ending because he knew the real
one would scare her. Effie also loved records, though she
never took the slightest care of them. *Peter Pan* would
play, the needle skipping and sliding, sometimes sticking
on a phrase for minutes on end, but Effie didn't mind.

She also had a passion for butterflies. I remember once
when she was around five, she put an empty jar outside on
the lawn, saying it was a butterfly trap. I laughed at her
and explained that no butterfly could fit in there, and even
if one could, she had to put some grass or clover as bait.
Effie turned stubborn and said that there would be a butterfly. When we came outside an hour later, I swear to God
we found the most splendid monarch you've ever seen
sitting in Effie's jar. Throughout her life, little things like
that would happen to her.

I used to laugh at some of the passions my sister had.
The smell of nail-polish remover. Pale purple and dark
orange. Effie also adored, God knows why, Mitch Miller.
She used to go around the house bawling out "Don't Fence
Me In" until we were crazy.

She was also, from the time she was four, an art buff. I
don't mean illustrations, either. Although Dad did ad work
for a living, he was a painter in his spare time, and over
the years he had gotten together quite an art library. One
day I was playing outside when I heard Effie screaming. I
ran into the library, expecting to see her lying on the floor

dead, but all she was doing was staring at a book, at a painting Monet had done of Rouen Cathedral. I have no idea why this painting frightened her so, but it did, and my parents finally had to cut it out of the book before Effie would even go in the room again.

She was frightened by a lot of odd things. Fireflies, water towers, the mask of Comedy, and especially the sight of anything melting, even butter.

One thing about Effie was how cuddly she always was. Thinking about it now, I'm crying a little. But she always liked to sit on your lap to hear a story, or to massage your hand when you'd been writing too long. And she would walk backward on top of your feet, or give you what she called butterfly kisses, or brush your hair so terribly gently, the way she did her baby-doll's hair.

Still, still! Wait a minute.

I remember once when I was about eight, the two of us were fooling around with some modeling clay. Effie was making an animal of some unrecognizable species, and I was constructing this complicated bird cage, one of those Victorian things with a little bird inside. I was pretty proud of it. When I finished, Effie asked if she could take it into the other room for a minute. I said all right, and Effie took my cage away. The next thing I knew, she came back into the room, her face white and red with anger. The cage was smashed into a huge multicolored lump in her hand.

But all in all, my sister and I were close. And happy. We were happy.

It seems incredible that I could still write that. All the same it's true. Everyone knew it. They even said so at the wake, how Effie was such a happy girl. I keep rerunning all the moments I remember about her as a child, and it seems that for every spanking or bad dream Effie had, there were six or seven good times. But looking back, you can't help searching for hidden warnings, for signposts, for little dangers that you should have seen, and if you had, maybe she wouldn't have ended up doing what she did. But I can only come up with three possible clues, and they're so isolated and unrelated.

The first was something that happened when I was eight and Effie was five. Effie liked bicycling, and I talked her into riding down the coast with me one day. We rode quite a ways and finally found a very flat stretch of beach with one enormous white dune in the middle. For some reason, we pretended that this was Gethsemane, and we took turns playing Jesus, getting on our knees and saying prayers. The one who wasn't Jesus was the chief soldier, walking around the dune and making threats. It was Effie's turn to be the soldier; she was walking alongside the dune when she lost her tennis shoe in the sand. It just pulled off her foot, she said. We stopped playing and looked for her sneaker the rest of the afternoon. Effie knew exactly where she had lost it, and the sand was only a few inches deep at that point, but we never did find the shoe. Effie got it into her head that she was being punished for pretending to hate Christ, and that the missing sneaker was God's way of telling her. I teased her about it, saying that God wouldn't waste His time on anything like that, but Effie never got it out of her head that she had made God angry, and for months afterward she would wake up with those nightmares about falling off the cliffs and dying.

The second thing about Effie was how hard she found it to make friends. It should have been the easiest thing in the world for her—she was such a kind little girl. I kept telling her the old saw about just being herself and then everyone would like her, but somehow it never worked out. Not that anyone ever hated Effie—it was just that she was always the odd one, the one with no partner in dancing class. And she got bullied a lot. Maybe she was shy. Maybe the other kids resented her always being the teacher's pet. Maybe she was a little different. But Effie always tried so hard to be liked.

I remember one Sunday School class. It was a few days after Effie's seventh birthday, and she had been given, besides thousands of dolls and books, a whole set of those awful tiny plastic statues called Disneykins. Effie just went crazy over them, and for three days after her birthday she locked herself in the bedroom and played with her Disneykins endlessly.

On the way to Sunday School that week I saw that Effie was carrying her book bag, which she didn't usually do. I figured she had a show and tell of some sort. We got to class, and she raised her hand and told the teacher that she had a surprise. She said that Wednesday had been her birthday and that she wanted everyone in the class to have a present. The teacher just fell over herself saying how charitable and unselfish Effie was being. Effie opened the book bag and out popped the whole set of Disneykins. She got up from her seat and started passing them out to all the kids in the class.

When Mom came to pick us up she saw right away that something unusual had happened. Effie was pink and triumphant, surrounded by about thirty kids, each one inviting her to a party or asking her to come play. Mom asked what on earth had happened, and the teacher came over and told her. Mom's face started to get very red, and she told the teacher and all the kids who were there that Effie had no right to give away her toys without permission, and that they would have to be returned.

Looking back, I can see Mom's point, but I'll never forget Effie just then, going around to each child and taking away the Disneykin. No one looked at her. Pretty soon, Effie, Mom and I were alone with a full book bag and an empty room.

The last thing about Effie was the one that maybe Mom and Dad and I should have paid some real attention to. But we never thought twice about it.

Effie kept getting crushes. Not only on her teachers, the way little girls always do, but on everybody; the mailman, the owner of the hardware store, the lady who worked at the soda shop, the boy who rented out surfboards at the beach. The crushes would come on all of a sudden, and Effie would write letters and tear them up, and follow the people around for blocks and blocks. Then a week or two would pass, the crush would drop off, and there would be someone else.

The biggest crush Effie had was, I suppose, the most normal. It was on Dad. This hurts a little to write about, because I loved Dad too. I was always so proud of the way he looked—golden and strong. Once, when my parents came to a school open house, I pretended to the gym teacher that Mom wasn't my mother. Not because I didn't love her, but because of aesthetic reasons I couldn't begin to explain. Mom, almost plain, with her bony body and faded face and hair, simply didn't belong by the side of my father.

Dad always used to introduce Effie and me like this: "This is Susan, my big one, and this is Effie, my shrimp." I used to hate being the big one because Dad said "my shrimp" with such love. I used to scrunch down, buckling my knees and slumping my back so I would look smaller.

Effie. Dad adored her. She'd flirt with him, asking him to marry her when she grew up. And he'd flirt with her, too, almost. He'd bring her flowers and grown-up presents like high-heeled shoes and a little rabbit-fur wrap.

I remember being really upset having to start school every autumn. I would sit in class, gloomily thinking of Effie having a good time at home with Dad. She would see him off every morning before he went to work. Dad would be taking his shower, Effie would sit on the toilet seat, and the two of them would sing songs Dad had taught her from the Swing Era. Dad was naked, of course, but Effie was so young that it didn't matter. Then when she was five, she asked Dad something about "his little finger," and Daddy got so embarrassed that he wouldn't let her come sing in his bathroom anymore. You can bet that was fine with me!

Of course, on the other hand, I was always Mom's favorite, but the fringe benefits of that weren't so terrific. Whom Mom loves, she chasteneth. Still, it made things a little more equal, I guess.

When I was fourteen and Effie was eleven, Dad and Mom split up. There were a lot of reasons, and there were a lot of fights. I guess there always had been, but when I was little I took them for granted and assumed that every family was like ours. I remember the first time I spent the night at my friend Claudia Koper's house, I was amazed at how happy her mother was to see her father when he came home from work. He didn't bring her a present or anything, but she dropped what she was doing and went flying to him.

Of course, Mom and Dad flew to each other, too—but only after fights. The worst ones when Daddy would scream that he was going to leave, and Mom would cry like the dog I saw catch its tail in the side door. The funny thing was that seeing Mom and Dad hugging and kissing afterward didn't make me feel any better.

They broke up over a woman. Effie and I had met her once. Dad picked us up from school one day, something

he had never done before, and took us over to this lady's
apartment for milk and donuts. She had a pretty apartment. I don't really remember what she looked like,
though, because I was busy with the donuts. We got back
home around five, and Mom was nearly out of her mind.
She thought Effie and I had been kidnapped. When she
asked where we'd been, Dad said he'd picked us up at
school as a surprise, and that we'd had a flat tire on the
way home. Effie and I agreed that that was what happened. Mom kept asking, and Effie and I kept sticking to
the story. After a while, it seemed that the lady and her
donuts had been a dream, and that there really had been a
flat tire.

When Effie and I came home from camp that summer,
Dad was gone.

Someone once wrote that every unhappy family is unhappy in its own way, but that isn't true. Every show on
television that deals with divorce, every novel about a
family breaking down, every friend's story about a father
leaving or a mother having to find a job, hits me in the
center of myself; and it's the four of us on television, in the
novel, in the story. Dad moved out to the Valley in August.
Mom, Effie and I moved to a split-level apartment in
Westwood.

Effie took it the hardest. She didn't really understand
about the woman, and she loved Dad so much. She told me
she wanted to live with him, but I told her that Mom
wouldn't be able to take that.

We had to change schools, of course, which was all right
with me since I make friends pretty easily. But it was awful
for Effie. She had loved our old school and had been the
smartest in her class. Also, she was just entering the seventh
grade, which is a killer year anyway, even if you know

everyone in your class and they adore you. But it's worse in a new school, and Shaftsbury was hell for my sister.

The other girls scared Effie, the teachers terrified her. She kept getting lost in the halls, she kept getting tardy warnings. She couldn't find her locker. She would throw up in the cafeteria. She didn't understand the homework, she was sure she was going to fail. I remember one October night I found her standing naked at the open window, wetting her body with a sponge. She told me she was trying to get pneumonia so she wouldn't have to go to school the next day.

And there was another night. I woke up sharp at one in the morning because I thought someone was calling my name. I had the feeling something was wrong with Effie. I rushed into her room. She or someone else had tied the top of her pajamas around a pillow and made it look like a person was in the bed, but the room was empty.

I ran to Mom and woke her. She began to scream when she heard Effie was gone. I went outside to get help. Halfway down the block I saw this white thing. It was Effie, in her pajama bottoms. She was walking in her sleep. There was a ruler in her hands—when we woke her up later, she told us she thought she was going to school.

Mom went to the principal and told him what a terrible time Effie was having. He promised he would talk to her teachers about it, and a few days later he called back. It seemed Effie was doing very well, brilliantly, in school, and that all her teachers thought she was the greatest kid they'd ever seen.

I don't remember too many other isolated things from those first months at Shaftsbury. They are chilly and dead in my mind. But funnily enough, November 16 is very alive to me. I knew in advance that it would be a turning point —not because I could sense the importance it was going to have for Effie, but because it was the day of my first school dance.

I'll stop writing. It's very late. I'm hungry. I'm so hungry my stomach is filled with joy. I hate to eat because afterward the joy will go away.

March 27

Today was my first day back at school. When I woke up this morning, it was cold and I didn't want to move. But I was afraid to tell my mother that I wasn't going to school. I didn't want to have to stay with her.

School wasn't horrible. Everyone did his best to ignore me. I kept thinking of Ellen Sansom, though. When we were in the sixth grade, her father was killed in a canoe accident. When Ellen came back to school a few days later, she was wearing a yellow raincoat which she wouldn't take off for anything. She'd talk normally enough, answer questions in class, but she kept that raincoat on for weeks and weeks. I understand. I found myself wanting to carry something of Effie's today. It was even drizzling, but I'd be damned if I'd come to school wearing my raincoat.

Classes were pointless, and I cannot put myself back into a frame of mind where I ever found a point in them.

We had an all-school assembly this afternoon and I played a game, pretending I was God's messenger with orders to kill one person in this room as a sacrifice. I imagined going around asking everyone why they deserved to live.

The principal didn't mention Effie. I had been afraid that he would.

I was also afraid that they would leave Effie's seat in the

auditorium empty. They didn't. A little girl with black hair was moved into her chair. I also had this ridiculous fear that Effie's name would be on the absent list: *Effie Daniels, Deceased.*

Mom came to pick me up at three, but I told her I was walking home. I made myself walk slowly—to punish Mom, I guess, for coming. But I wanted to get back to this writing so badly I shook.

Throw off the day, throw it off. Today is unimportant, it's safe in the past. It feels so good to write the past.

I was very irritated that November 16th, the night of my first dance. I had come home from school early that day to allow myself enough time to dress, and so I'd had to cut my eighth-period French class. I didn't usually do this sort of thing, and it made me feel guilty. And when I got home I had to lie about it to Mom, saying that class had been canceled.

Dinner was another pain. Ever since Dad moved out, Mom had been preparing intricate dinners for Effie and me, to cheer us up, I suppose, or to fill up Mom's time. That night she had made chicken cordon bleu, which I usually love, but the thought of the dance had taken my hunger away. Mom went promptly into Lecture Number Three about the importance of proteins in the diet, on and on and on.

It was almost seven o'clock before I got upstairs to dress, and the luxury I'd been so looking forward to just wasn't there. I took a bubble bath, but it made me itch and I got out of the tub after only a few minutes. Also, I'd hung my new patchwork skirt on a wire hanger instead of a wooden one, and so it had a big wrinkle across the middle. When I ironed it out, the steam from the iron made my hair go kinky. I ended up in a horrible mood.

At seven forty-five I was finally dressed and made up

and combed, and I began to dread the evening ahead. The usual things—what I would do if nobody asked me to dance, what I would do if some boy asked me to go out with him to the bushes.

To calm myself, I went to sit in the living room, my favorite part of the new apartment. It was all pale furniture, yellow-and-white striped upholstery, and Portuguese porcelain that only I knew Mom got at Pier 1 Imports. The room always made me feel fresh and happy.

But when I opened the door that evening, I was hit by a stampede of music. Effie was watching television, the volume way past the level a human ear can stand. I remember the way she looked: lying on her stomach in front of the set, her green-and-white striped top twisted around her waist. Her arms were propping up her chin, which was white from the pressure put on it, and her legs bent back up onto the sofa behind her. I kept track of one bare foot as it bobbed in rhythm to the music. Effie's toenail was bitten, bitten to the quick. I was shocked by it—I have never seen a toenail mangled like that. In those trying days, I guess biting only her fingernails wasn't enough of a relief.

I looked down at her as she was looking up at the set, and I told her to please lower the volume. Her hair was pulled back in loose pigtails tied with yarn, so I could see her face clearly. She looked far away, mesmerized. I thought she was just being difficult, so I asked her again to lower the volume and gave her a little nudge with my foot. Effie rolled up like a green worm will when you touch it, and as she spoke she was smiling, with no resentment in her voice at all.

"Look, Susan," she said. "Here's someone."

It is difficult to sort out my first impression of David Angel on television that night, for of course it's been buried by thousands of posters, records, newspaper clippings and

Effie's fantasies. I do remember being surprised that Effie
would even be watching such a program; ever loyal to
Mitch Miller, she was never much of a rock music fan.
Other than that, I guess I remember thinking that David
Angel looked a little different from the other singers
around—he was clean-shaven, for one thing, and more
simply dressed; minus the usual feathers and beads. Also,
he looked kind of shy, as if he should be someone's kid
brother who writes poetry safely hidden from sight in the
garage, and not a rock singer shoving his guts out to the
crowd in front of him. But he had very large, dark eyes
which made him look bad-hearted. Like a highwayman,
as Effie used to say.

Come to think of it, it's amazing to realize that there
actually was a "first time" Effie saw David Angel. After a
while, all of us came to accept him as one who had always
been there—like Shakespeare, or Mickey Mouse, or even
Effie herself.

She still hadn't turned the volume down, and the way
she was just sitting there smiling at me was getting on my
nerves. Her pupils were enormous sparkling discs, like two
total eclipses of the sun. They gave me the creeps.

I went over to the set and changed the channel. In half
a second, Effie was on her feet and she changed it back
again. She still had the smile on. I got more furious by
the moment.

"Why are you watching this trash?" I started to goad
her. "You're supposed to be doing your homework."

I changed the channel again and held Effie off so she
couldn't get at the television. It was easy—she was so
much smaller than I was.

"Put him back!" she cried out, and she kept crying out
while I teased her.

"Or is he tonight's homework? Are you studying the
habits of the domestic rock singer in your science class?"

I don't know why I was so mean about it. I guess I was nervous about the dance. But the more Effie squirmed, the more I enjoyed keeping her away from the television set. Then, in the middle of it all, she did something incredible. She hit me. She had never in her life hit me. I yelled and jumped away. Without looking at me, Effie switched the channel back. David Angel was beginning another song.

My big evening was a total zero. I didn't listen to the band, I didn't eat, I didn't even put myself in the way of getting asked to dance.

All I did was sit and think about Effie. I just couldn't get over her hitting me. I decided that all the tensions of school and our parents' separation had started to change her. Tonight's punch was only the beginning. Soon she'd be showing all kinds of sibling hate and rivalry, and in a little while we'd be exactly like all the other sisters I knew. She'd even start to blame me for making her eat all those peanuts and aspirins. I couldn't stand it.

Feeling outraged and sorry for myself by the time I got home, as well as pretty damned mad that Effie had spoiled my evening, I charged up to her room, intending to wake her if she was asleep. She wasn't, though. She was lying on her side, facing the door. As if she'd been waiting for me. She looked dreamier and calmer than I'd seen her look since school began.

"How was the dance?" she asked me.

"Just great," I said, pure sarcasm. "Except that no one could touch me on the arm without it hurting like hell."

Effie pushed the covers off with her foot. She walked over to me and stroked my sore arm. She was in embroidered baby-doll pajamas, and her hair was flat to her face where she'd been lying on it. "Oh, Susan," she said, "I'm really sorry about that," and I knew she was. "But I couldn't stand you turning off David Angel like that. You see"—and she said it so proudly and awed, as if nothing of the sort had ever happened to her before—"I've got a crush on him."

No other single sentence in the world could have reassured me more that Effie hadn't changed—not in the least little bit.

I whacked her bottom.

She stuck her tongue out at me.

We went to sleep.

When I look back on those first few months, I separate them in my mind from what happened afterward, and they *should* be separated. At the beginning, Mom and I called Effie's crush on David Angel a blessing. She had been lethargic and unhappy for so long, and now she was buoyed up and secure. She got a comfort from his records that all Mom's tears and hugs couldn't give her.

I used to use David Angel as a barometer for measuring Effie's moods. In fact, it got to the point where, when I had spent the evening at a friend's house, I could judge, the instant I came in the front door, what the hours at home had been like. If I walked in to silence, it meant everything was all right. If David Angel was playing softly, it meant something minor had gone wrong—like a homework assignment Effie had had trouble with. If he was playing medium strength, it meant something more major—an argument between Mom and Effie, maybe. But if he played at full volume, I knew Mom had been yelling over the phone at Dad again.

But always, by the time I got upstairs to Effie's room to see if she was all right, David Angel's songs would already have worked their magic, leaving Effie soft and unharmed.

David Angel colored her life completely—in shades of neon. Effie bought her idol's records, she ransacked poster shops for his image. She hung David Angel in every room Mom would allow. David Angel on a surfboard above the toilet, David Angel sitting gloomily on a fire escape above the dinette, David Angel shirtless in Watts above Effie's desk. And she used to sing his songs out the car window whenever we went on a long drive. I cannot describe how tired I became of David Angel's pulpy lyrics. I used to have a nightmare that I was shackled in a slave ship, and all around me the men were singing "Perhaps I'll Dream of Darkness."

Even when we were playing backgammon, Effie wouldn't let him rest—before every roll of the dice she'd holler in this reverent voice, "This is for David Angel!" She also began reading those flashy pre-teen magazines, looking for mentions of him and taking every fabrication, innuendo or misquote for truth. One ill-starred afternoon she discovered what his favorite recipe was supposed to be—without warning us, she proceeded to bake it, a pecan pie, forgetting the milk and eggs and nearly burning down the house in the process.

I remember the present I gave Effie that Christmas. I figured out the piano arrangements to a few of David Angel's songs, and I told her I'd play them whenever she wanted. Fatal move! For a year and a half I was never allowed more than a few feet away from the piano. But I like to think of that present now.

Sometimes, not often, Effie would talk to me about David Angel and tell me what he was like. They were uncanny, the things she told me. She couldn't have gotten them from those dumb magazines. She would talk mainly about his childhood on Long Island, name names and describe places. Effie had never been to Long Island. When I asked her how she knew those things, she would laugh and say she was making them up. Still, it was eerie.

I was curious as to why, in the crowds of rock singers and movie stars available, Effie picked David Angel. I asked her about it and she said it was because he was like her. That made me laugh—as if there were any resemblance between my shy little sister and that wriggling black-hearted fool. But then I thought about the time, equally unaccountable, when Effie had screamed in terror at Monet's painting of Rouen Cathedral—and I realized that all her life she had seen things that other people didn't. Things that weren't really there, perhaps.

As far as Mom was concerned, Effie's crush on David Angel had one supreme benefit—it got Effie out of the apartment. David Angel wasn't a star yet, so to get the 8 × 10 glossies and T-shirts and all the rest of the paraphernalia, Effie had to bicycle down to Westwood Village and look around.

Westwood is the friendliest town in the world—it surrounds UCLA like water does a pebble, and is always full of college students doing mime on the sidewalk to pay for their textbooks, and girls giving out free passes to their piano concerts. The streets are twisty, and the shops are bright as bathing suits. The whole village is crammed with record stores and bookstores and Indian-goods stores and health-food restaurants, each one playing music from a different radio station, depending on the taste each shop is supposed to represent. Effie, who hadn't been interested in exploring Westwood since we'd moved there, was now visiting it and discovering it and having fun in it, all the time.

At first she only went to look for David Angel memorabilia, but soon she got in the habit of having a glass of papaya juice at the health-food bar, or looking at the English children's books at Tomnoddy Faire. Sometimes she'd even stay to see a movie. Mom and I were delighted to watch her having fun again. We were delighted to see our Effie eased.

March 31

The feelings do die down. Now I'm beginning to think. I start to probe all the time at the edges of what happened, why it did. Even as I'm writing this, there are always the questions. Everyone tells me that it's over and that I must start "living again." But I can't until I make the confusion go away. I don't know who to blame. I cannot decide. I think sometimes that Mom was the villain, but other times that she was trespassed against so badly by us all. Dad and Stanley are sometimes the villains. Other times I am sure they never were. I was never, ever a villain; I cannot allow that. Tonight I am thinking that the villain was Effie herself, who did all this and caused us all the hurt . . .

11 P.M.

I found that tract this afternoon—the one that the *Turn of the Screw* woman pushed into my hand at the wake. I must have dropped it behind the sofa. I didn't mean to read it, even glance at it, but I found I had read the whole thing before I knew what I was doing.

It was about people who had been pronounced dead and then came back to life. I guess the real reason I kept on reading was because everyone described death as being so pleasant—embracing people you love, meeting this kind of bright light, etc. In fact, nobody who had "died" even wanted to come back to life again!

But then there was a report by a man from Florida. His wife had died of cancer, and he had shot himself in order to be with her again. He said what happened to him was awful. He didn't even want to talk about it, it was so bad.

He said he didn't end up near his wife at all, but in some misty, cold place, all alone. He was the only one in the whole pamphlet who was grateful to get back to life again. Then there were all these quotes from the Bible about what happens to suicides, how they're punished, wiped out, sent to hell.

Damn that bitch for giving me that tract. Oh, Effie, Effie. I know it's crackpot. I know that none of it's true. When you're dead, you're dead. Effie, I know you're all right. I know that you're not in that cold place. You're so gentle. I know someone is there taking care of you wherever you are, just as I was here, taking care of you on earth.

April 2

Mom is getting dressed to go out to dinner. She's drawing her bath—I can hear it through the wall. The Jameses made her promise to come to dinner with them tonight. I'm glad. She hasn't really eaten in a week and she gets thinner all the time. I told her it was selfish of her not to eat, but it's more than that. It's terrifying. She's slipping away from me, too. I told her to have a great time tonight. I didn't mean it sarcastically and she didn't think I did.

Mom had a few really bad months when Daddy first moved away. It's not surprising that they changed her a little. My mother used to pride herself so much on the fact that she was "upright." To her, maybe that meant a host of moral and religious things, but to me it always suggested her posture; "upright" like the figurehead on a ship that wasn't about to be knocked down by the waves. But during those first few months without Dad, Mom started being a little careless about the way she did her hair and not minding that she wore her clothes for days at a time. They never smelled or anything, but it was just so unlike her. And for me what mattered most was that she was suddenly slumping. She wasn't upright anymore.

It frightened me. I tried to make her take an interest again—forced her, really. I never let her alone. I just went on and on about things that had happened at school, friends I had. I guess I drove her crazy, but then again, maybe I didn't, because I'm not sure she listened anyway.

Then all at once she started taking an interest again, although not particularly in me. She was never home anymore. She started dressing right again and going out to lunch and movies with her friends. I hated them all; all those pointy women. I hated the thought that they had dressed up in their skirts and hats, and had made a reservation for two at the restaurant, thinking and knowing all the time that Mom would spill the whole juicy story to them. Which she did. Always. Sometimes I would come home from school and find them having tea in the living room, Mom in the middle of saying that Dad had never loved us, that he was as rotten as rotten could be. I started staying late after school so I wouldn't have to hear it.

Mom loved us. Of course. Effie and I both knew that. And looking back on those months, I have only pity and understanding for Mom.

There's one thing, though, that still makes me very angry to remember. It was around Christmas, and I wanted to have a party. Mom said I could. I made all kinds of decorations and baked cookies. Then I got the idea that Effie ought to invite some of the kids in her class, as well. She wouldn't have any of the responsibility of being a hostess and could have a lot of fun. Mom thought that was a great idea.

The party was planned for the day school let out for vacation. Effie and I were to be like Pied Pipers, leading the rest of the kids to our apartment after the last class. While we were away, Mom was to buy streamers and party favors and the like.

School was a blast that day. Everyone was excited about Christmas and the holidays—and, I hoped, our party. We were let out at last, and we were all so spirited that we ran to the apartment. When we got there the door was not only closed but locked, and Mom never locked her door.

I banged and rang the bell. There were forty kids crammed in the hall behind me, but no one said anything. Finally, Mom opened the door a crack and asked suspiciously who was there. I got so mad I started to cry. Mom threw the door open. She was in her nightgown and she started hugging me in front of the forty kids. She smelled funny.

"What kind of a mother am I?" she kept crying. "I heard on the radio about a rapist who escaped from prison, so I locked all the doors. Then I fell asleep. I forgot that you and Effie were still outside. My God, he could have raped you right here in the hall!"

"Mom, did you get the streamers?" Effie said anxiously.

My mother put her hands over her face.

Mom just called me downstairs. She's been packing away the things in Effie's room and wanted to know what she should do with the stack of David Angel records in the corner. Most of the stuff is going to Goodwill, and I was surprised Mom would even have to ask about the records. But I see what she means. We just can't give those records away—they're so incredibly Effie's. I said I would take them.

Though I wondered about it at the time, I really don't know what Effie felt about the way Mom was acting that winter. Because it was an embarrassing subject, we never talked about it except in an everyday, practical way. "What do you want for dinner, Effie? Mom's gone out."

Frankly, Effie didn't appear to be thinking much about it at all; she was busy with her own concerns. She had started liking Shaftsbury very much, better than our old school, and she really put herself out for good grades. Once she told me, quite seriously, that when she reached the ninth grade she wanted to try out for the cheerleading squad! And, of course, there was David Angel, whose records and posters and magazines took up more and more of her spare time as the winter went on.

In February, Mom snapped back to herself for a while. She remembered that she had two daughters and started trying to make up for the lost weeks by giving us extra elaborate meals, extra attention. I still have the satin and lace pillow she made me for Valentine's Day. But the balance had shifted between Mom and my sister.

In March, Effie started her fan club, and she now spent less time with Mom than Mom, at her worst, had spent with her. I knew Effie wasn't doing it on purpose, and I never once told her to mend her ways. Though I still stuck around Mom because I was her favorite, the way Effie was behaving seemed so wonderfully just, that it pleased me somewhere very bad, down deep inside me . . .

I'm thinking about Effie's fan club. It was the logical next step of idol-worship, I suppose, but I think everyone who knew my sister was amazed that Effie could actually bring a "Westwood Branch of the National David Angel Fan Club" into existence. She was dreamy and irresponsible, never the organizing type. Still, she did it all—applied to the National Head, went through channels, made calls, filled out forms, recruited other members.

She rarely bothered anybody else to help her. The only thing she ever asked me to do was make a few calls for her.

"You see," she explained, "sometimes it's very important that Effie Daniels sounds like a mature woman on the telephone."

I did my best to sound like a mature woman for her.

All that March, as I walked down the halls of Shaftsbury, I'd see signs, colored with Effie's familiar pink Magic Marker: *Join Now! The Official David Angel Fan Club! Questions? Ask Effie Alice Daniels, Homeroom 6.*

I always used to get a kick out of seeing those little pink messages. Then some wit got the idea of defacing the posters—drawing angels exposing themselves and so on, and I had to go around tearing every one of the damn things down before Effie saw them. She took things so personally.

How clearly I can see it. The David Angel Fan Club. Four solemn girls sitting in Effie's bedroom. David Angel loud on the stereo, Mom's cookies untouched on the floor.

"Can I come in?" I holler to the closed door. Sudden betrayed silence.

"We're busy!" Effie's panicked voice.

"Come on, Effie! I need my hair dryer back!"

Effie is cross-legged on the bed, her dress pulled down drum-tight under her knees. Her back is straight. She is playing with a plastic Chinese worrying toy and looks drawn into herself. Near her is Alexandra Carter. She ought to be a farmer's dimwitted daughter, with her set-apart eyes, bee-stung lips. She looks at me from under her half-grown-out bangs. Near her is Ginnie Fallon, Irish turned-up eyes, a body that spills over. She sits on the floor, I guess, because it doesn't make an embarrassing dent when she gets up. Last is Clara Didex, really well-dressed and sophisticated. I have the feeling she's a snob, but maybe I like her least just because she looks a little like me.

"What are you guys doing in here?"

The polite looks saying get out.

"Just give me my hair dryer, Effie." I am over at the dresser and feel like a wasp trapped in a car—all action stops when I am around.

"Well, sorry to disturb you." Even before the door closes I feel the relief that I am gone. It is melting through the crack. I hear Ginnie Fallon giggle. I know it isn't about me; it's just a giggle because they are alone again . . .

When I was ten years old there was a boy in my class called Joshua. Joshua was very small, with a narrow, secret face, and I loved him. For the record, he never noticed me at all. Every day I'd see him and every night I'd give Mom a minute-by-minute account of how Joshua had looked, what he'd said, what games he had played at recess, what I'd felt. One day, playing basketball, his best friend Steven pushed him down, and Joshua was sent home with a concussion. I wept all evening, out of love and fear for him, until my mother, to reassure me, looked up his number in the school directory and called his house.

"Hello? This is Alice Daniels, Susan's mother. I just called to find out how Joshua is. You see, I've got a weeping willow on my hands . . ." That pulled me up short, made me gasp. A *weeping willow on my hands* was what my mother called her adult friends who were having bad love affairs and came to her for advice. A *weeping willow on my hands* meant it was serious. It meant I was finally a woman.

It was like that with Effie's fan club. I knew it right off. The club wasn't a social event, the way most twelve-year-old-girls' clubs are, and it didn't degenerate into squabbling or cattiness or school talk. They were a riot together, Effie, Alexandra, Ginnie and Clara—like little old women, David Angel's grandmothers, poring over the information, careful and critical. It was no puppy love.

"David likes to spend time with his dates in quiet places, preferring the anonymity of *Lawry's* to a much publicized restaurant like *Chasen's*." Effie would read from the biweekly bulletin. I could hear her through the vent in my bedroom. "His date last Friday night was lovely Cheryl Tolman, model and would-be actress." A considering silence. Effie was showing the photo around.

"She looks insensitive. I don't like her looks. He doesn't usually go for redheads—she must have some special quality."

"I wish he'd stop going with actresses. They're *so* insensitive, usually."

The head David Angel Fan Club was based on Long Island, started, I heard, by David Angel's family. By the time Effie started her branch there were eight or ten others, most of them in New York or California. It was all very official; every other Tuesday, a big manila envelope would come: *Miss Effie Daniels, President, Westwood Branch, National David Angel Fan Club.*

. . . The envelope being disemboweled. The prongs at the back carefully bent forward, the handwriting on the envelope scrutinized. "They've got a new secretary." The staples delicately plucked out. One by one, the contents would be fished out: the yellow *Angel Review*, giving a day-by-day account of their hero's last two weeks, the sheet of facts and figures about him, the blue pamphlet describing the National Club activities, subscription information for teen-age magazines, mimeographed excerpts from articles on David Angel, photographs. The whole operation was pretty rudimentary in those early days. When I heard on the news a few nights ago about the sum of money the club had managed to collect for David Angel's grandfather, I was amazed at its size.

Then Effie would call up the other members: Alexandra, Ginnie, Clara, always in that order, and arrange for the club to meet that night. The girls would arrive at seven, driven by a tolerant mother or older brother, and would be ushered out at nine-thirty.

Tuesday nights, after the meetings, were fun. Effie was always in a thrilled mood—she reminded me of a coin collector who's been given some rare penny to pore over. Being President of the Club, she was allowed to keep the manila envelope each week. You can be sure that David Angel had done something splendidly fascinating to read about, and Effie was bursting with it.

"Oh, Susan, test me!" The nervous nail-bitten fingers rustling the papers in my face.

"What are you talking about?"

"Oh, Susan, you know."

And with a groan, I'd take the papers from Effie's hand and go through them.

"All right. Who went sailing with him on Tuesday?"

"His friend Harry."

"Describe what the drummer in his band looks like."

"His name's Ray-O Hall, he's got black hair. And he's got eyes just like that Mick Hanson you have such a case of!"

"Okay, Effie," I said sweetly. "You keep this up and I'm going to rip these papers of yours right—" She flew at me, laughing, protesting . . .

"All right, goon. Fill in the blanks. His favorite foods are blank and blank and blank bacon."

"M-mmmm, guacamole and—pecan pie—and *overcooked* bacon?"

"Oh, Effie—*Canadian* bacon!"

"That's not fair. I don't even know what it is."

"Just face it, you missed the question. Okay. Shirt size?"

"Forty long."

"Favorite book?"

"*War and Peace.*"

"*War and Peace?*" I was dying of laughter for about a minute after that one.

"What color is his house in Monterey?"

"Red."

"Is red his favorite color?"

"No. Gold is."

"Wrong."

"What do you mean, wrong?"

"It says here that it's purple."

"Well, they made a mistake. It's *gold!*"

Effie plows through her stack of ancient manila envelopes, looking for the supporting evidence.

"It doesn't matter, Effie; maybe he changed his mind. Lots of people do, you know."

"Not *David Angel*—he *never* changes his mind."

And she looked up at me with the most curious half-smile. A half-smile which was almost laughing at itself, I swear. I think of that half-smile a lot.

Mom was involved with Effie and her fan club in a different way than I was. My sister was so busy with her envelopes and photos that she had little time to spend with Mom those days, and Mom, although she'd never admit it, was making the best of the situation—she tried to use my sister's fan club as a way of getting close to Effie again. She baked cookies for the meetings, tried to make friends with the mothers of the members, offered to sew an official banner. Of course, Effie's fan club wasn't that kind of affair, but Mom was blind to that. Effie went on being not exactly cool to Mom, but acting as if she didn't realize that Mom was reaching out to her. I know my mother was depressed. Even the bad, deep-down bit of me wasn't happy about it.

In the middle of April, something happened that made things a little better for all three of us.

It was a Friday afternoon. Mom was off at an interview

for some secretarial work, and Effie and I felt like celebrating the weekend, so we bicycled to the Brentwood Country Mart for an early dinner.

Ever since we were babies, it had been the biggest treat of all to go there. The Mart is a whole nest of stores; toyshops where Effie used to buy her beloved mosaic kits, a dress shop where I got my first training bra, bakeries where we were given a free tollhouse cookie, rides where we put in a dime and were given one minute of noisy, jouncy ecstasy on the back of a cast-iron elephant. On my more poetic days I imagine that the whole history of our lives can be traced through those shops, from baby clothes on up.

But no matter what age we were, the high point of the visit was ordering lunch or dinner from all of the food stands. We would get ribs at one, move on to another for French fries, on to another for milkshakes, on to another for dessert. Heaven.

This particular April day I was standing in line to get the ribs, and Effie was finding us a table in the large plaza in the middle of the Mart. We hadn't been to dinner there for a long time—ever since we'd moved from Malibu— and the fact that the Mart hadn't changed at all during our absence made me feel very secure.

I paid for the ribs and walked to the table Effie had found. She was sitting without moving, as if she'd had a stroke and her face had gone feeble. I started to ask what was wrong, but I didn't even finish the sentence, because I heard Dad's voice somewhere behind me.

We had seen him a few times since the separation, but this was entirely different.

Effie and I left our ribs uneaten on the table and we walked with one mind into the old toystore. Dad didn't see us. Clearing a few dolls from the window, we could look out. My father was sitting at a corner table; we could barely make him out, but we could see the people he was with clearly: a woman, a little boy and a little girl.

The woman was very elegant. She looked as if she'd come to the Mart just for her kids' treat. I got so hard and sore then, thinking that Mom used to love the Mart as much as Effie and I did. The little kids were peevish, scrambling all over the place. Dad was speaking to them. We couldn't hear what he was saying through the glass, but he looked ill at ease, a man who wasn't very good with children.

We watched them until they left. Daddy swung the little girl onto his shoulder and she slumped there like dough. After they went, Effie and I didn't want to leave the toyshop.

April 6

I thought of something today which stopped me cold. What if Mom, Dad, David Angel had nothing whatsoever to do with it? What if it would have happened anyway? What if there was simply something "wrong" with Effie— something inherently flawed that made her do what she did? A mechanism to self-destruct at a certain age, a timer? And if there *was* such a thing in her, could I, being her sister, have it in me also?

April 8

I heard today, from her brother, that Alexandra is seeing a psychologist, that she's having nightmares, that she can't get over the guilt. Bravo.

God, I must be a monster, to write that about a fourteen-year-old girl. I'm turning into a monster...

11 P.M.

It gets harder and harder to live, it gets easier to write. I am always wanting to write this diary, but there's only so much I can say. I must make it last.

That May, soon after Effie and I saw Dad at the Mart, Mom met a man. I'm not exactly sure how she met Stanley—I mean she didn't come home one night and say, "I just ran into this wonderful human being." I knew something had happened, though, because Mom went back to ignoring Effie and me.

I first met Stanley at John and Marsha Hawkins' house. They were having a barbecue on the patio and Mom, Effie and I went out to join the other guests. A lot of people were in the pool, and one man was in a deck chair alongside it. He was wearing a terry-cloth robe and the hair on his legs was tangled with wet. He was throwing a rotted, dripping ball to the Hawkinses' two golden retrievers, and they were kissing his face and neck. Mom called out "Hello, there!" in a gay little voice, like she was surprised. The man turned around and was saying "Well, hello!" when one of the dogs twisted around and actually got its tongue right in his open mouth.

Once we had met him officially, Stanley started coming over to our apartment all the time. He was a real estate agent, and at first his excuse was that Mom was doing some work for him, and he just wanted to drop off some property listings. Then he started bringing steaks along with the papers, and soon Stanley was over almost every night.

Stanley was a big man; he was so tight in his skin that he looked like a plum, with the same orange veins. And he

had thick jellified hair that smelled like licorice. I had a
fancy that if I gnawed on his wrist, it was so firm and fat I
could suck all the juice out and he'd be left like a used,
lopsided enema bag. But it was easiest just to ignore
Stanley.

He tried very hard to make friends with me. Mom must
have told him I wanted to go to Northwestern, because
practically every time I saw him he'd make some comment
about it, saying, when I walked in wearing a bikini, that
I'd have to dress warmer than that to brave the Chicago
blizzards. He also must have overheard me complaining
to Mom about a French exam I'd taken; for two weeks afterward he'd say "Bonjour!" instead of "Hello," or ask
what I was looking so sad about. When I got back the exam
with a grade of B+, Stanley had nothing to tease me about
anymore.

I'd come home from school and find him on the couch
with Mom, watching television, or helping her make the
salad for dinner, something Dad would have sooner died
than do. I'd say "Hi, Mom" and kiss her, say "Hello, Stanley" and go straight upstairs. I never kissed Stanley, and I
never even called him "Stan," though he asked me to. I
knew he wanted me to kiss him also, and I knew Mom
wanted it, but I pretended not to know and never did it.

I don't think I ever for a minute hated Stanley. Maybe I
would have if he'd been forceful or good-looking, or tried to
"fill a father's place." I don't know. But I always did know
somehow that he didn't stand a chance with Mom, not
really. I was sure he wouldn't last for long, and that made
him harmless . . .

Effie liked Stanley. That was a surprise, a rather unpleas-
ant one, since she had always been Dad's girl above anything else. But she wasn't disloyal to Dad—with Stanley,
things were just different. She acted like a little baby, leap-
ing onto his back and hooking her legs around his waist or

sitting on his lap, when she hadn't sat on Daddy's lap for years. She would always give Stanley the kiss I refused him.

We are in the dining room.

"Stanley, what did you do when you were my age?"

"When I was your age, Ef? Well, let's see. For one thing, I was only in the fourth grade."

"The *fourth grade?*" Effie is cackling, she can't get over it.

"That's right. Old Stan here used to keep the teachers so busy with his mischief that they'd forget to promote him." Effie is laughing still.

"I guess mostly I was interested in girls."

Effie asks quickly, "What sort of girls?"

"I went for the ones that were popular. I figured there must be a reason why everyone liked them."

A long pause. "Would you have gone for me? I'm not so popular."

Stanley winks happily at Mom and me. "Are you kidding, Effie? How could I have passed up a beauty like you?"

Effie is on her feet. "You really think I'm a beauty?"

Stanley is smiling. "You better believe it."

Effie comes over to him and holds onto his arm. "Really —on your honor?"

"Really." He is still smiling because she is so earnest. The smile makes Effie suspicious.

"And what do you think about Susan?"

Stanley falls into the trap. "Susan is a beauty also."

Effie lets go of his arm, hurt and embarrassed.

"Oh, I see. Well, everyone says we both look very much like our dad, you know."

Mom gasps. Stanley is hurt also.

"I think you both look very much like your mother,"

he says firmly, "and she happens to be the biggest beauty of all."

Effie considers this. "Well—everyone says she and Daddy look a lot alike, too . . ."

Stanley used to take us to all kinds of places, and it was eerie going with him because they were places we had never been before. It was as if we had left our own lives and joined another one. Stanley was a golfer and used to drive us out to a dried-out course in Van Nuys. Neither Mom nor Effie nor I played golf, and we'd sit by the practice tees in a tidy row, watching Stanley get purpler and more plumlike as he'd smash out ball after ball. His arms would get very wet and white and the ruby ring he wore on his finger seemed to grow heavier and more glittering. Mom tried to play once, I remember, and made a big show of being too weak to swing the club.

Stanley also used to take us to this horrible Mexican restaurant. I don't remember the name, but it was too dark and didn't have air conditioning. I hated sliding into the booths. I always wondered what I might find in the corners. Once I got sick from some tamale I'd eaten there and spent the whole night throwing up. I told Mom that the food had made me ill, and she got mad at me. Because she knew I was really saying something bad about Stanley.

Once he took us to Balboa to go deep-sea fishing on a friend's boat. I had fun that day, because I was wearing a new pantsuit and three hired boys kept trying to get me to talk to them. But for Mom, the excursion was pretty tedious. She had taken along a novel and a delicate little lunch for us all. She wanted to enjoy herself, I know, but the fish Stanley caught started to smell pretty horrible, and Mom got queasy from the rolling and the harsh sprays of water. She put her head down on my lap and her arms around my waist, and she slept. She has such thin, baby hair. The saltwater spray soaked it right through until it was like a fragile seaweed.

Effie and I had been told early on that Stanley had once been married, and that he had two daughters, but we didn't meet them for about two months, when we came over to Stanley's house for dinner.

We weren't often invited. Stanley usually came over to our house instead—Mom didn't especially care for the things he liked; fish mounted on plaques, bowling trophies in the living room, and maybe he didn't want her criticizing.

This particular day as we arrived, there were two kids' bicycles parked in the front yard. I felt a little upset seeing them, as if I'd been tricked.

When we rang the bell the door was opened by a little black-haired girl, around nine years old. She was wearing a tank top and shorts. Since she was standing behind the screen door, it looked like she had a terrible checkered disease all over her body. When she saw who was at the door, she turned and walked right back into the house.

I could have predicted what the afternoon would be like. It was obvious that Stanley had made plans for it to be a "real get-together," but it was equally obvious that his daughters had made plans of their own. Right off, Stanley made us go for a swim, I guess hoping we could work off the tension. He had bought aquatic basketball and rafts and tubs, but nobody used them. We all just stood about in the water.

Mom was being gay. She proposed a game of Marco Polo and I got nostalgic, thinking of all the times we'd played it with Dad. But I agreed, and the nervousness of the day made me play better than I've ever played, before or after.

Sandy, the little girl who had turned from us at the door was It; within a few moments, she tagged Angela, the older girl. Angela was It now, and she managed to corner Sandy right by the ladder. Sandy was It again, and a few minutes into her turn she managed to make a good dive into the deep end to catch Angela, who was swimming away underwater. Since Sandy was supposed to have her eyes closed and Angela had been swimming very deep, I got suspicious. Sure enough, the next play, when Angela was It I swam about a foot away from her, trying to be caught. She should have tagged me in a second, but she didn't. I saw her eye open a fraction, then close as she realized who I was. She swam off in the opposite direction.

I waited until she reached the other end of the pool.

"I don't play with cheaters, Angela," I said.

Mom stopped setting up the barbecue table. Stanley froze in the middle of browning a frankfurter.

"I wasn't cheating," Angela called.

She disgusted me. "Yes, you were. You know you both were. Neither of you would tag Effie or me."

"Who are Effie and you?" Angela asked. She was standing up in the waist-deep water, and the straps of her bathing suit were cutting deep red marks into her shoulders. "I don't know any Effie and you," she said with slow and satisfied insolence, as if she knew the sentence by heart. "The way I see it, Sandy and I are alone in our pool."

"Get into the house, Angela!" Stanley shot out. Mom put her arm on his. "Oh, Stan, she's upset . . ." I could hear her murmur. I saw Stanley go weak between the strength of his anger and the strength of Mom's pleading. He stood undecided—holding up the frankfurter speared on the barbecue fork. He looked like a fat man in a cartoon.

Then he threw down the fork, strode over to the pool and yanked Angela out. Mom, shaken off, stayed by the table. Stanley half carried, half dragged his daughter into the house. Sandy and Effie stayed near the asphalt, not taking their eyes off the drain at the bottom of the pool.

The frankfurter quivered and shook on the abandoned barbecue fork like a gulping fish.

When I passed Mom's bedroom that night I heard her crying. But it sounded as if there were nothing new to it. I think she had also known that nothing could really work out between her and Stanley. Even at the beginning, she had never even tried to sell Effie and me on him. And he embarrassed her so often; when he'd make a stupid pun or pat her bottom "by mistake" in front of Effie or me, Mom would put on an aloof, pensive little frown, as if she were trying hard to remember who this Stanley person could be. But her crying was such an unhappy sound. I really hated to hear her cry.

After that, Stanley never came over again. Once the first few weeks were gotten through, I don't think Mom missed him terribly. I know Effie did, though. She never brought the subject up, but whenever Stanley's name was mentioned she looked like she'd just sat down hard on the sidewalk. When October came along, I was hoping that even though he and Mom had broken up, Stanley would send Effie a birthday present. He didn't, though, and I guess I never really expected that he would.

April 12

This morning Mom and I had the worst fight we've ever had. She wanted to visit the cemetery and I said I didn't, that there was no point. She said that I didn't love Effie, that I had never loved her. She told me I had always been jealous of her because everyone cared more about her than they did about me. I said, "Mom, think carefully—I'm all you've got left. You've driven away two men, you've made one daughter kill herself; don't wreck things with me now."

She slapped me. I keep on starting to pack up some of my clothes, but then I keep unpacking. There doesn't seem to be any good way out, no matter what I do.

LATER

Mom just came in. We both apologized for the things we said. I don't feel a whole lot better.

It's just so sad. It's so sad. I wish I could talk to Daddy, but he doesn't know anything. Are we such awful people? Is that why this terrible thing happened to us? Did Effie just want to get away?

April 15

Acceptances! Incredible relief. The envelopes came this morning. I got into UCLA, USC, Bryn Mawr and Northwestern. Didn't make Princeton. It's perfect, beautiful, knowing that I'm going to be getting out. It's my chances that are opening up. It's beautiful.

April 16

I don't know what's wrong with me. It's scary. Isn't there anything I can enjoy anymore? The college acceptances made me happy for a little while, and then I started worrying. It's all mixed up with what I was thinking about before—that there was a time bomb in Effie which might be in me, too. The great thing is to stamp it out. Defuse it—

isn't that the word they use? But how? I get absolutely crazy. I know I'm making more than just a choice of colleges. One college may mean safety, and one college BANG. But which is the safety and which is the BANG? Half the time I think it's one place, half the time the other. At Bryn Mawr I see myself ending up cheerful and capable and moderate. At Northwestern, I might turn out a little rarer, a little more lonely. I don't know. I hate not knowing.

At dinner, Mom said I ought to go to UCLA or USC and live at home. She said that would be by far the most sensible thing to do. She asked me please not to go away. When Mom said that, something freed itself in my mind and I was able to make one decision, at least. I must go away.

April 20

It was a very flat summer after Stanley left. We all felt it. Mom was out most of every day, seeing her friends, looking for jobs. Upright.

It was too hot and dull to stay home and I started spending whole days at amusement parks. It was almost as if I took them seriously. I went on all the rides and played at all the sideshows and lived on corn dogs. I'd never really cared for amusement parks before this, but now they seemed like the best idea in the world.

Sometimes Effie came along with me, but mostly she didn't. She had recently become very quiet, lethargic. That summer, she discovered persimmons. She'd sit in her room all day, reading, listening to David Angel, eating persimmons.

Effie was twelve and a half years old. From that summer, two things stick in my mind.

One happened on a Sunday morning in July. I was sleeping late and dreaming that a baby had just been bitten by a monkey at the zoo, and was crying. I woke up and saw that it was Effie who was crying. She had come into my room and was kneeling next to the bed. I said, "What on earth is it?," but she just sobbed on and on.

"Something terrible has happened," she said to me. I grabbed her and asked, "Is it Mom?," and she shook her head. In a moment, it came out in a loud embarrassed whisper.

"I got my period."

A few minutes later, of course, she had stopped crying and was laughing at herself. We went over all the stuff about belts and showers, and Effie was very factual and mature about it. We never again talked about her having called her period "something terrible." Now that we can't anymore, I am crazy to know why she said it. With all her romanticizing about David Angel, I had always assumed that Effie was dying to grow up. But maybe she wasn't at all.

The second thing which happened to Effie that summer came near the beginning of September. She was impeached as president of the David Angel Fan Club.

Throughout the summer, every other Tuesday as usual, Effie had been getting the manila information folder from the head fan club on Long Island. And always, it was her job to sort out the contents and show them to the other members. One Tuesday, along with the rest of the loot, Effie received an article supposedly written by David Angel himself. It was called "The House I Will Make For You."

Merely writing down the title like that begins to put me in a slow rage. The stupid article, the stupid club, my stupid, stupid sister.

I was crocheting on the sofa. Effie was standing over me, reading. "We will rise at dawn, you and I, and see a world untouched. The morning will be ours, my love, fields dipped in sunshine along the path to our house. It will be as if we are alone in the world. . ." Halfway through, there was a slip in her voice. I looked up from my crochet and I saw that Effie's eyes were streaming.

I really lit into her. I laughed at her, calling her an idiot, and said that the article was just cheap trash for the puberty market. I told her David Angel hadn't written a word of it, that some drip publicity man had composed every sentence, jeering at the stupid little girls who would fall for it.

I came on pretty strong. It really bothered me that Effie could be taken in by that idiocy. I guess I was ashamed of her.

I was folding some clothes in my room that night while the fan club meeting was taking place, and I could hear the girls' voices through the vent. They didn't sound like children that night. Their voices were gritty and brittle. I went to Effie's room to see what was going on. The door was closed, but their voices were loud enough for me to hear.

Alexandra was reading aloud in a prim little bray. "And in the evening, we will catch the geese as they pass overhead, their cry as short and strong as a haiku . . ."

"I tell you, it wasn't on purpose," I could hear Effie cry out, agonized. "It must have fallen out of the envelope!"

"Of course," said Alexandra. "Right into the bottom of your bedside table."

Effie had hidden the article. She had wanted to keep the geese and the mists all to herself. And so Effie Daniels, Founder and President of the Westwood Branch of the David Angel Fan Club, was impeached as president by unanimous, outraged vote.

The heavy, tired summer ended with the start of school, and it was in the winter that everything started racing past control. The divorce went through in October, and Dad started coming regularly to see us again.

That was something, yes. Having a dad. You could almost pretend everything was as it had always been; the loose skin on his hands, the backwards way he looked at his watch. You thought there was never a time without Dad. But there were his new clothes, which you hated, and you hated whoever it was that picked them out. And you hated the new car, although it was prettier and bigger than the old one. Every morning before Dad came I would think, It's today. And then afterward I would think, It was today. There was good in it and there was bad. Bad because it was only for a short space of time, an afternoon, an evening, and that was unnatural. Dad would take Effie and me out to museums, shops, meals. Almost like Stanley. Instead of just sitting and teasing and laughing as if he belonged to us. But it was good because he was good and we loved him.

Effie took the whole thing very well. I was really amazed. She seemed to have a great time when she was with Dad, but when it was over she didn't make a fuss or refuse to go home to Mom.

One incredible Sunday she even said she wanted to get back home early, to see a gymnastics competition on television. Dad looked pretty grim but he said that Sunday was his day to make Effie and me happy, and if going home was what made us happy, then he would take us there as soon as he could. I didn't want to go home, so I told Dad to drop Effie off and then he and I could have the rest of the afternoon to ourselves.

I held on to his arm all the way home. He just couldn't get over Effie. "She's really growing up," he whispered to me. I squeezed his arm again. It was nice to think that Effie was more able to manage her feelings these days. And

I must admit, it was nice being Dad's favorite daughter for once!

When we reached home, I scrunched up in the front seat to let Effie out from the back. But Dad stopped me. "Susan," he said, "why don't you go inside with Effie? We can make our afternoon alone another time. I'm really plowed under with work this week."

Effie didn't even watch her gymnastics competition that afternoon. She ran straight to her room and slammed the door. And I heard David Angel's music blaring from her record player until way past her bedtime.

There were big problems between Dad and Mom that winter. I have friends with divorced parents and they told me what to expect. The father being extra benevolent to get the children's affections. The mother feeling she can't compete, and resenting it. The children feeling used. The parents not talking to each other, or worse, talking with politeness poured over crushed ice. And all that came true with Dad and Mom and Effie and me.

After an afternoon spent with Dad, Effie and I would come home happy. He'd drop us off at the front door and we'd whisper our goodbyes, not knowing if Mom was listening in. He'd give us some message to remember until we next saw him; sometimes it was something to think about, like "All sunshine makes the desert," or sometimes it was something silly, like an Ogden Nash limerick, or sometimes it was just advice, like telling me not to diet all the time.

Then he'd kiss us, me first, then Effie, and we'd wait outside until he got into his car and drove off. Effie and I would then go inside the house, hoping we could get upstairs before Mom could see the booty we'd brought home. But she almost always caught us; sometimes right at the door, sometimes on our way up the stairs—once she came right into my room as I was putting away the new pocket-

book Dad had bought. Mom would always say the same
thing, in a hard, gay voice: "Well, how nice—presents! I
love presents! Let's see what you've got." And, hating it,
Effie and I would slowly untie the packages and show her
the new Jax sweater or book on needlepoint or Pappagallo
shoes. Mom would say politely, "Oh, how very nice."

Only once did I ever see her show what Dad's giving us
presents meant to her. Effie had been wanting a certain
leghorn hat she'd seen in a little shop along the Sunset
Strip. Although it didn't cost that much, Mom wouldn't
let her get it—she said it was too frivolous. Dad, Effie and
I were walking by the shop, and Effie pointed the hat out.
Dad said he was buying it for her that minute. Effie was
horrified, but the more she explained that he mustn't, that
Mom would be furious, the more he insisted. Finally Effie
started crying, but Dad still went ahead and bought the
hat. It was a real shock. Effie and I managed to sneak
the hat into the house, unnoticed, but Mom found it a
few days later in Effie's closet. When she saw what it was,
Mom's mouth seemed to lengthen into a slit like a cut.

"I think you know that I planned to buy it for your
birthday," she said.

But Dad did one thing that winter which was absolutely
perfect. Everybody who cared for Effie the smallest bit
knew it was perfect. Of course, looking back it doesn't
seem quite that way anymore, but that doesn't matter.

For the past year, needless to say, Effie had been inun-
dating Dad with stories about the wonderful David Angel.
She had only discovered him once Dad had moved out, so
Dad's was a fresh ear for her praises and exultations. One
Tuesday in December, I read in the entertainment section
of the paper that David Angel was beginning a nationwide
tour, and starting it off in Southern California with a small
concert. He would be in Santa Barbara that Saturday. When

I told Effie about it, she had fantasies about going, even
though David Angel was becoming very popular on the
West Coast and every seat for the concert had long since
been booked. Effie rhapsodized about it with me, she discussed it with Mom, she even called Dad and told him the
great news.

Friday night Dad telephoned and asked to speak to Effie.
I was on the extension and I heard it all.

"Effie," he said, "I got to thinking about that David Angel concert tomorrow night. It seems I know a lady who
knows a vice president of Discus Records; so, just for fun,
I had her call up and see if there were any house tickets
available." I could hear Effie's breath go in. "But"—Dad's
voice got very doleful—"the lady told me she talked to
the head of the company himself—and even *he* doesn't
have tickets for it."

"Oh." Effie's voice was barely audible.

"Don't you want to know *why* he doesn't have tickets?"
Dad asked her.

"Why doesn't he?"

"Because he's given them to you and me."

. . . I've got chills just writing it. Remembering, I'm
chuckling like a lunatic. Such screams . . . Effie was doing
cartwheels all up and down the hall, hugging everyone to
the breaking point. Finally she began to sob, she was so
excited, and I held her. I remember her body being so thin
and tight; her pulse as full of erratic motion as the Morse
code.

Though I had planned to go shopping the next day, I
decided to stay home where all the fun was. Every room
was jammed with activity, like in a dollhouse. In Mom's
bedroom, the sewing machine was groaning in little spurts,
as Mom took in the new blouse she'd bought Effie that
morning. I was in the living room, heating up the electric
rollers. A midafternoon snack was burning, unattended, in

the kitchen. Effie was taking a bubble bath, talking through the open bathroom door to the various members of the David Angel Fan Club, asked over especially for the great occasion. For the moment, all was forgiven.

When Effie left that night, we stood around the front door—Mom, me, Alexandra, Clara, Ginnie. I want to describe the way my sister looked that night: it gives me pleasure to remember.

She was wearing a long plaid skirt and a ruffled top. She probably imagined she looked like Lorna Doone. Sometimes when Effie was in play clothes and she'd be reaching up or running, I'd suddenly notice that she made a nifty figure, that there was a certain curve in her body or her arm and that maybe she'd grow up to be pretty. But in this outfit she looked childish and straight, as if her body were made up of angles like the plaid. Which doesn't mean to say she didn't look great. She did look great. Mom had put a little makeup on her, and Effie's eyes looked soft, like a stained-glass Madonna's. They even seemed to reflect light onto her cheeks—but that's silly, it was blush-on. Her hair was in a braid down her back and tied with yarn. I told her the bow looked like a tarantula, but she just smiled at me. Mom lent her her black velvet cape, which was quite a bit too large, so Effie had to stand very straight to keep it from dragging on the floor. Upright . . .

Mom and I were, of course, waiting up when Effie got home, though it was after midnight. The moment we heard Dad's car in the driveway, we leaped to the door and whispered loudly to Effie as she came up the walk. "Well? Well?"

And I have never seen eyes do what Effie's did then. It was as if the irises were the picture you turn in a kaleidoscope; they kept turning, shifting, switching shades, making flowers, making patterns . . . "Ohhh . . . oh" was all Effie said.

April 28

I was at school today, having my lunch alone on the bleachers. Miss Flynn from the counseling office came up and
said she wanted to talk to me. I'd never gone to see her and
I was surprised by how much she knew about me. She said
it must be terribly difficult for Mom and me to handle
Effie's death, and that she wanted to help in any way she
could. I said thanks, but we were managing fine. I tried
to go on with my sandwich, but she kept standing over me.

She said, "I wish your sister had come to see me," like
if she had, Effie wouldn't have killed herself. Then she
sat down and started asking these questions, real sympa-
thetically, real delicately. When did I first realize Effie had
psychological difficulties? When did my parents realize it?
What did we think had caused them? And she was especially interested in the trips my father had sent Effie on—
why did he feel justified in taking her out of school so often? Didn't my mother object? Didn't I see that the trips
might be unwise?

I thought I was going to start choking. I crumpled up
my lunch and got up. "Oh, dear," Miss Flynn said, "I see
I've upset you. Why don't you come to my office next week
and we'll talk about it." She looked almost satisfied, like
she'd caught a great big fish—the sister of a suicide. They
might even promote her to head counselor for that.

It is frightening to me how much I can hate. I hate that
woman for what she did to me. If she could only have seen
the joy that Daddy took in being able to send Effie to those
concerts. If she could have seen Effie's joy. I'd like to know
what Miss Flynn would have done in our place. Exactly
as we did.

6 A.M.

I'm so tired. I'm going to bed. I have a million answers to her questions, but they're coming out like excuses.

April 29

I feel better about it all. I called up the principal and told him what happened. I said he ought to fire Miss Flynn.

8 P.M.

I've been reading these last entries over and over, nonstop. They disturb me. I guess because I've asked those questions, too. About Dad sending Effie all around the country to concerts he knew nothing about. It isn't the sort of thing you just let go by.

But you do. You make the decision, and you just get used to it.

That spring Effie got one or two squibs about her in the paper, saying that Dad was sending her around the country so she could attend the concerts of her idol. David Angel was on tour for a month and a half. He must have done thirty concerts—Effie went to nine of them.

I guess, looking back, it *was* extraordinary. But it was what Effie wanted more than anything on earth. She absolutely lived for those concerts, and Dad loved making her happy—this sort of made up for his not being a full-time father. It made him feel important, too; arranging for house seats through his lady friend, booking hotel rooms, trains, planes.

Effie used to assure us that nothing bad ever happened

at the concerts, that they were the same as the first one, and that there was never any violence or drugs. But if there ever were, she assured us, she would come straight home.

And it didn't really interfere with school. Most of the concerts she went to were on weekends, and if they involved a plane or train trip, Effie could do her homework en route.

It did cost an awful lot of money to send her, and that got Mom mad. She said that if Dad were rich enough to throw away his money on trips, then he was rich enough to see that she got her alimony checks on time, rich enough for us to live in a nicer apartment. When she got really depressed, she'd use scare tactics to get me on her side against him. "It's either Effie's concerts or your college education, Susan; there isn't enough for both."

But I knew Dad would find a way for both.

I can't seem to make it stop coming out like excuses now. But back last year, it seemed a great, a glamorous thing to do.

It *was* exciting, getting Effie ready for those concerts. Almost as if she were the star herself. Getting her suitcase packed, making calls, reservations—and it was fun driving her to the airport. I always did that, because I like the airport.

Effie traveled alone. Dad couldn't afford to send two people, and Mom couldn't spare the time. Plus, I didn't want to go. But Daddy always made sure Effie would be well taken care of, in whatever town she was in.

Her schoolwork didn't even suffer. Effie always did well at school. I'm making excuses.

Mom and I did discuss the concerts, but it was strange —we never seemed to ask ourselves questions such as, Is it right to let a thirteen-year-old girl go away from home so often? Issues like that we just skated right over and concentrated instead on, Does Effie have enough clothes to wear? And what wattage hair dryer will we buy her? Some of the newspapers called Mom an irresponsible parent, but she wasn't. She was just very scared of losing Effie's love if she didn't let her go to the concerts. Mom never admitted this, but I'm sure it's the reason. Maybe she was weak or selfish, but even that damned Miss Flynn would have understood if she could have been there that Tuesday evening when the whole business started.

It was three days after the first concert. Dad called Effie again. She took the call on the extension in Mom's bedroom. Mom and I were playing Scrabble and eating homemade peanut brittle in the den.

Effie came into the room and said, "David Angel will be playing in Palm Springs this Friday—can I go?"

I remember her tone was very peculiar. She sounded gay and thrilled, the way she had about the first concert, but also wary—as if the concert weren't really such a surprise, as if she and Dad had discussed it already, as if she had a lot of prepared arguments ready if Mom should say no . . .

Mom did say no. She said that the concert had been a special, one-time treat, and that Effie must start settling back to real life now. Mom said that Effie couldn't miss school. Effie said that nothing important was happening that Friday. Mom said she didn't want Effie to go alone. Effie said there was only one seat available, and that Dad had already paid for it. The truth came out. Effie and Dad had already planned the whole trip down to the details, including where Effie would stay and who would drive her to the concert. I noticed I was beginning to sweat, and that it was smelling like peanut brittle.

When she heard Effie's speech, Mom put down the Scrabble tile she was holding.

"Well, well, a *fait accompli*," she said. I remember looking down at that moment and seeing, with a shock, that my mother had taken all the tiles and was rearranging them in crazy, neat little circles and stars on the board.

"Dad understands." Effie's voice was stiff and hard; she sounded like the stereotype of the teen-age girl. Then she yelled out, as if she'd lost all her control. "But I hate you —you never understand!"

Mom let the scream die away, and it was as if Effie hadn't been yelling at all. I was amazed by my mother. Every Scrabble tile had been made into a design, but her smile was a buoy, just bobbing along, not getting wet. Sweat was running down my armpits to my waist, the little drops were having a race.

Then, all at once, Mom put her arms out. "Oh, Effie, I understand," she whispered very low, and the whole room quieted down, like fur flattening. I could hear a motorcycle roaring somewhere along Sunset Boulevard. "I just hate your leaving me." Mom smiled at Effie then and nodded a slight, scared nod. Effie went into her arms.

And that weekend she went to the concert.

The Friday Effie was in Palm Springs, I was at school on my way to a biology lab when Miss Coppet, Effie's math teacher, called across the lawn to me. "Susan," she said, "how is your sister?"

I didn't know what she was getting at, so I just repeated, "My sister?"

"Yes; she's ill, isn't she? I presume that she is *ill*." Her face was a pit of suspicion. "She missed a very important test this morning."

What can I say? That Effie had lied to us, saying that nothing was happening at school so she could go to her concert? That Mom and I were the enemy? That the whole thing made me feel damn sick?

Of course I lied to the teacher, assuring her that Effie had the flu.

When Effie came back from Palm Springs, I had worked myself into a fury, I was so hurt. I told her exactly what I thought of her, I shouted at her for a half-hour about trust and lying and selfishness. I told her I thought her precious David Angel was making her into a person I hated to know. Effie was crying by this time. I was glad about it. Then she asked me if I was going to tell Mom and I said no.

"Anyway, I told Dad," Effie said, brightening up a little —she wasn't a total washout. "I told Dad about Miss Coppet and he said I'd done a free-thinking thing, and he nicknamed her Miss Cowpat. Isn't that funny?" But she was crying again.

Effie swore to me she'd never pull another stunt like that, so I forgave her. She got an A– on Miss Coppet's make-up test, I remember. I kept my word to Effie, and I never told Mom . . .

And it just occurred to me: if I had told Mom, it would have been Effie's last concert. An interesting thought. Which leads to the conclusion that, because I didn't tell her, everything that happened afterward might be my fault. Which is ridiculous.

. . . But I see I'm still thinking of those questions. What that Miss Flynn said about Dad and Mom and me.

Of course we watched Effie. Of course we watched to see if the concerts changed her in any way. We loved her. But it's hard to tell if a person has changed, and why. Everything on this earth is made up of a million elements, and if Effie was ever grumpy or unhappy or not hungry, it could have been due to the weather or a cold or an argument at school. It could have had nothing to do with the concerts.

But Effie *wasn't* grumpy and unhappy and not hungry. It seemed to Mom and me that she was the same as ever —perhaps a little more excitable than usual, a little more impatient, but that could be explained too. When you're thirteen, everyone of any other age looks stupid. And she still did well in school and she still loved art and she still loved Saturday-morning cartoons. A little more excited, a little more nervous, that was all.

But she was so happy. The concerts made her so happy. Looking back now, analyzing under the spotlights of that woman's questions, maybe Effie's happiness was also a change. It had become private. Always before, when Effie was happy, it was a boon to the rest of us because she was so lovely in her joy. I'm remembering her in the plaid skirt the night of the first concert, I'm remembering her stroking my bruised arm the night she told me she had a crush on David Angel. But in those later days she spoke little about the concerts, only assuring us that she had behaved herself, that nothing bad had been going on, and that she had had a good time. Her bedroom was right down the hall from mine, but it had become like the dormer corner of the bathroom at our old house. It was private—it was Effie's. As I passed her room I would hear her singing. Happy. But for herself only.

April 30

That April, during our spring holiday from school, Mom's older sister, our Aunt Kate from Nebraska, came to visit. She came with a brass trunk, a tin of the date cookies Effie adored, and a photograph album. I love Aunt Kate, even though I'm with her so rarely. She seems to mean family to me, in a way that even my mother doesn't. With

Aunt Kate I know that family can be a way of life. Out of her trunk she pulled a pair of hand-embroidered baby shoes and gave them to me. "For your first-born," she said. I loved that far-off first-born.

As often as we could, Effie and I would sit beside Aunt Kate on the sofa and look through her photograph album, careful not to bend the frail, thirty-year-old snapshots. We enjoyed the pictures of Aunt Kate at her first dance, and the funny hairstyles, but our chief joy was the pictures of Mom: the little blond-haired girl in the sprigged pinafore standing—upright—in front of the church or the school. We were greedy for the things that used to make up that little girl's universe; the doll she was holding in one picture, the horse she was riding in another. And Aunt Kate told us all the old stories—the ones Mom could never remember—about the days when our mother got sick eating blueberries or flirted with the banker's son. The time when she had no idea that, come one day, there would be a Susan and an Effie looking at her pictures.

Sometimes Mom would come from her sewing or reading and look through the album with us. She would soon walk away, though, since she had nothing in common with that little girl in the pinafore.

But Aunt Kate and I knew that the little girl was important, that she was a part of something already established—something that was my job to carry a little further along.

I think those days were among the happiest of my life. At night now, when I relax and put myself back into troubleless times, I'm always ending up in last April with Aunt Kate.

The concerts ended in early March, and Mom and I were full of self-congratulation. Everything had worked out beautifully.

Then, a few months after David Angel returned home to Monterey, he gave a special benefit performance. Naturally Effie wanted to go, and as a surprise for this special event, Dad even bought me a ticket.

Effie and I left for Monterey at noon and barely made it in time. We were staying at the Casa Munras Hotel and took two minutes to wash our faces and brush our hair. Then Effie insisted that we drive to the concert with the top of the car down, and our hair got messed again.

It was the most terrifying night I've ever gone through. Police sirens as we arrived, the hot squash of people. I lost Effie—she was whirled away by a thousand elbows, and I shrieked for her, frantic tears spewing in the crush. When I found her again I shook her and was frightened to find that she was so malleable.

I have been to shows before. *I have* been in crowds, but never like this. It was everything Effie had sworn, over and over, that it was not. She had fooled us all. The closeness, the interminable craziness. The audience tense like a cat. A band coming onstage and a wail growing from every part of the room, a wail without emotion, just a wail. There was a strong smell of drugs. The volume of the music was impossible, unbearable. Everyone shrieking at once, like a million car accidents. A few rows beneath us I saw a boy shoot something from a needle into his arm. The smells got more powerful, as if they were made by the music. The girl at the end of our row began to sob and hack. I could see her fall into the aisle, sobbing and hacking. I could see her head hit the floor. I turned to Effie, to get her out of there.

But Effie didn't look at me. Her eyes were bright and seemed yellow like the Cheshire cat's and the rest of her face faded away.

David Angel came onstage then, and there was no chance of leaving. Hot squash spilling from their seats, like lava in the aisles, trying to flow up onto the stage. There were policemen, I saw the clubs. I saw a boy go down.

Half-light. People were turning red to the hairline from the force of their voices. Against that red, their eyeballs were shiny and sticky. I touched my sister. She wasn't screaming, but her eyes had that same look. She grabbed my arm when I touched her. Then she started to scream.

Afterward Effie said over and over that it was all a mistake, that none of the other concerts had been anything like this, that she hadn't been lying, that it was all a mistake. Mom, too, after telling me that I always overdramatize everything, said, "You must realize, Susan, dear, that no two concerts are the same. After all, this one was in the papers. None of the others were."

But I just don't know.

May 1

I felt estranged from Effie for a long time after the concert. I felt I had been duped. I hated that feeling—I hated *her*. Mostly, it was queer getting used to the idea that Effie was growing up. I couldn't predict anymore what she was thinking, what she liked, how she would react. The private singing in her room.

It was the concert, I guess, that made me realize how much Effie was becoming herself and not me, and I felt lonely for a long time.

I also hadn't been noticing how physically grown-up she had become in the last few months. None of us had ever been able to predict how Effie would turn out. When she was three, she was so beautiful that a man from an advertising agency approached Mom about letting Effie do commercials. But when she was seven, her nickname at school was "Effie Dangles" because she was so thin and droopy. When she was ten, we were sure she'd turn out pleasantly enough, with a round face, snub nose, straight teeth. But at thirteen and a half, Effie was different from anything she had ever been.

She was pale and slender. She and her body seemed in such accord—I loved to watch her run. But she was so small that you felt afraid to touch her. Your arms felt too big around her. Her face was bones. She was like the Ghost of Christmas Past—half old man, half girl child. Startling shadows and curves in her face, and on them a delicate nose and mouth, very large hazel eyes.

"God, Susan, I'm the ugliest person in the world," she used to say. My sister was not beautiful, but she was watched whenever she moved.

May 18

School has suddenly turned into something precious. It makes me think of going to church on Easter Sunday. The air is soft and floating. Everybody's voice sounds beautiful —everyone is kind. It's so near graduation and parting. Every barnacle school has ever sprouted—fears, tediousness, winter mornings, exams—has been scraped clean away. You feel like you did the first morning of first grade, bouncing on the bed and expecting wonderland. You wonder if it's always been like this, deep down underneath. And we all eat lunch on the grass, sitting in one big circle and trading sandwiches.

This afternoon was lovely. After the last bell rang, everybody trooped out to the lower school playground as if it were the most natural thing in the world. We raided the little kids' ball cart and started playing games like kickball and jump rope. I got involved in a few hot matches of 2-square. I was champion of the world when I was seven. It seems I still am!

I felt good enough to make the final decision about college today. I thought once I put the envelope in the mailbox I'd know for certain if I'd made the right choice. But I still don't know.

May 20

Last fall Peter Kreske came into Effie's life. I suppose you could call him a boyfriend—he certainly considered himself one.

It's nearly midnight now, but I want to stay up anyway and write about Peter. It makes me giggle just to remember . . .

Peter Kreske was sixteen. He had been at Shaftsbury longer than Effie and I had, and he must have seen us a hundred times. Yet one afternoon near the beginning of school last year, Effie was walking down the corridor when Peter pulled her seriously aside. "I just want you to know," he informed her, "that I'm beginning to notice you."

A few days later he approached her at the cafeteria and asked for her telephone number. Effie looked in her purse for a piece of paper to write it down on.

"Oh, that's all right"—Peter waved her off—"I'll use this." And he wrote her number down on a twenty-dollar bill.

But he didn't call and he didn't call. I figured the twenty dollars had long since been spent. Then, late in October, Peter finally telephoned.

Peter's reputation before he met Effie was dubious. He was a loner. No one really knew him, so all kinds of vague rumors went around—one girl heard he had somewhat kinky sexual tastes, another that he was a motorcycle demon. After school he never joined the rest of us at the hangout, but disappeared the moment the last bell rang. We all assumed he was heavily into drugs and drink. I'd love to say that Effie changed all that, but I can't, because none of it was true to begin with. Peter had lovingly built up the rumors himself. He told me that before Effie, he had never had a date with a girl in his life. He couldn't even drive a car, much less a motorcycle; the smell of pot made him sick; and the strongest beverage I ever saw him drink was a ginger ale. I think Effie was a little disappointed when she found all this out.

Peter was a sweet guy, terribly sensitive, terribly romantic. But he took himself so seriously that it was very hard for anyone else to.

I remember one December night. Effie and Peter were going to the school production of *Antigone*, and afterward to the cast party, since Peter was friendly with the stage manager. In the middle of the performance, Effie came down with stomach cramps. She managed to contain herself until the end of the play, then asked Peter to take her home. Peter was a little angry at her for getting ill in the first place, but he asked his stage manager friend to take them to Effie's house.

"I've been looking forward to this party a long time, Effie," Peter said on the way, as she sat beside him doubled over. "I'm sure you won't mind if I go alone." Effie shot him one awful glance and wouldn't speak to him for the rest of the drive. Finally they arrived at our apartment and Effie stumbled out of the car. I opened the door to let her in.

"Effie!" Peter called out in a "Dying Swan" voice. "Effie!" But Effie didn't answer.

Peter got out of the car slowly and walked to the driver's side. "Jake." He laid his hand on his friend's shoulder. "Jake," he said in a faraway, heavenly voice, "this is a very hard thing for me to say, but I want to be dropped off here too."

Jake drove away and Peter turned to Effie. "This was one of the toughest choices I've ever had to make. If I had left you off at your house and gone to the party alone, I would've had a wonderful time and then I would've cried on the way home. I had a decision to make, Effie, and I made the right one. I, Peter Kreske, have become a man tonight."

Still and all, Mom and I were glad Effie had him. He was friendly, he was funny. Of course, he was very much in love with Effie, but that only reassured us all the more. He would never hurt her.

Peter was very jealous of anyone Effie cared about, including Mom, me, and especially David Angel. He had asked Effie to take the David Angel posters off her wall, but she had refused and he didn't dare insist. Still, Peter would have been glad to know that during the time Effie went out with him, she mentioned David Angel much less than before, bought very few articles about him, and only played his records a few times a week.

I wanted to tell Peter that at the wake, but what would have been the point?

Effie had a good time with Peter last winter. She used to laugh at him like crazy, but still they were together constantly, and he took her to a lot of places, showed her a lot of things. One aspect of Peter which could be taken perfectly seriously was his poetry. He was a beautiful writer and Effie was very proud of that. So they went to readings and discussions; he bought her a big book on Eliot and wrote a dozen sonnets about her. He also introduced her to Hart Crane, old Marx Brothers movies, peanut butter with Karo, and detective thrillers. Also, they hated the same things, and Effie, who loathed sports, was never forced into any healthful activity as long as Peter was around. He lived in mortal fear of bends at the pool, tennis elbow at the courts, and splinters at the Ping-Pong table.

Effie did not love Peter. There was just no room in her heart. I write this down with certainty, yet I find myself thinking of a photograph I found in her desk a few weeks ago. It was taken at a school fair. Peter is chasing Effie with a water pistol and they are both laughing like mad. Effie is looking so happy.

New Year's Eve, I came home from a party and found Effie sleeping in my bed. A note on the nightstand said: "Susan—Wake me the moment you get in." I didn't right away. I watched her sleep for a while. She was wearing a Lanz nightgown and every time she breathed, the lace on the wrist would stir.

When I did wake her, she sat up immediately. "Susan," she cried. "He asked me to marry him."

We stayed up talking until morning. We decided that the best thing to do would be for Effie to kindly, gently tell Peter that she was flattered immensely, but was too young to think of marrying anyone and that, under the circumstances, she thought it would be best if they didn't see each other for a while.

I got only two hours' sleep, but I didn't really mind. I felt closer to Effie than I had for a long, long time.

Peter came over the next day and the first thing that Effie the Brave did was burst into tears and flee upstairs. So big, patsy Susan was left with the joyous job of telling Peter that The Wedding was off.

I drove Peter back to his house late that afternoon. I was stringy and weak, hoarse and exhausted from my work of persuading Peter not to turn to heroin for solace, or volunteering for the Army. I had also managed to dissuade him from blowing up the school corridor where he and Effie met, from suggesting to the principal that Effie be expelled for loose morals, from telling every boy at school that she was sexually deformed. So I drove down Sunset, totally wiped out.

Peter sat beside me. He was pensive at first, but then, as we drove along the comforting valleys of Coldwater Canyon, his face became first calm, then slowly deepened into rapture.

"You know," he said soberly, "I have a feeling that today has been one of the most important days in my life. I had a decision to make—whether to set Effie free or to keep her with me—and I made the right one. Susan, tonight I, Peter Kreske, have become a man."

I spent most of my time at the wake with Peter. We didn't say too much. We just seemed to spend the time getting glasses of punch for each other from the sideboard. First he'd go and then I'd go.

May 25

My father never cared much for Peter. He didn't exactly put Peter down—except once or twice, saying that his T-shirts needed washing—but he was always arguing with him. Strange to say, Dad never chose to argue about the subjects he understood, like companies or ads; no, he was only interested in wrangling with Peter on those subjects about which Peter knew everything and Dad knew nothing . . .

Listening to Daddy argue, I felt touched and a little sorry for him. What is that truism about the old seal battling the young seal? I think Dad surrendered his little Effie only very, very grudgingly.

When I told Dad the romance was over, I expected him to be happy, but all he said was, "Well, Effie, now that you've had a boyfriend once, you'll never be able to go without one again."

"Oh, no, Daddy," Effie said. "I'm never going to have another boyfriend."

I couldn't resist murmuring that whenever I looked at her face, I couldn't help coming up with the same conclusion. Effie laughed and the subject was changed. But I had chills up my back.

I was remembering New Year's Eve when we were up until dawn talking about Peter. How Effie had sobbed and said that Peter was not what she was looking for. She had given up hope, she cried, of meeting the person who was right for her.

I suppose I should have laughed my head off at the fourteen-year-old goof, pointing out that she had quite a few years to go yet before she was technically an old maid. I suppose I should have told Effie about all the wonderful men she would meet in college—high school, even—and how she would pick the very nicest for her husband. But I didn't because I had the feeling Effie knew what she was talking about.

I still have that feeling. It is, as it was then, irrational and suspect. But the fact remains that though I've thought about it often, I have never been able to imagine the person Effie would have fallen in love with. She was such a strange little kid.

I sometimes find myself wishing that Peter could have

made her love him. A few more years would have ma-
tured him, and sooner or later he would have shaved off
those awful sideburns. And he would have been an important writer—I know it. And he worshiped Effie.

But whatever Peter felt for her, Effie considered herself
just his friend. Once I came into the dining room and
found Peter grabbing Effie, trying to kiss her. But she
pushed him off. "Oh, Peter, I don't want to do those silly
things!"

Silly with Peter, perhaps. But there was no one in the world
more misty-eyed than Effie. To me, love and romance
aren't everything. I understand words like *compromise, patience, adjustment* and *change*. But my idealistic, unreal-
istic, passionate little sister—what would have become of
her?

How dramatic I sound—like Effie herself. After all, she
was only fourteen—a baby. No doubt in a few years she
would have grown up and looked at the world with some
sense of reality. But I honestly don't think she would have.
And I wonder if anybody exists who was to have been the
person she was looking for. Anybody real, that is—for
David Angel, made up of publicity and celluloid, was only
somebody she imagined.

SATURDAY, 4 A.M.

Reading that last sentence over, I'm freaking out. I forgot
I'd even written it.

I've just finished watching a movie—*The Diary of a Mad
Housewife*. I turned it on to have company while I washed
my hair, but after about fifteen minutes I forgot about my
hair and just watched the movie, crying.

The mad housewife, Bettina, was Effie. She looked like

her, spoke like her, behaved like her. I don't know who the actress was because I missed the titles, but I decided around 2 A.M. that she's my favorite actress in the world.

I took that movie to heart like you wouldn't believe. Exalted, I acted as if Effie were the star, as if I were watching the story of her life.

Bettina found a husband, all right, but an arrogant, insecure, mixed-up bully. Seeing their relationship was almost like a sign, telling me that, in real life, Effie wouldn't have been able to find her ideal either, and that it was almost better for her to leave this earth before she went through what Bettina was going through.

Then, in the middle of the movie, came a character called George Prager. He was a playwright. I know this is crazy. I know I'm making this sound like a fairy tale, but as much as Effie reminded me of the woman in the story, George Prager reminded me of David Angel. Not simply in looks, but in the whole atmosphere he carried with him. I swear, even the story he told about his childhood sounded incredibly like something Effie had once made up about David Angel. I couldn't believe it—it was as if the actor who played George Prager had seen into Effie's mind, lifted out the David Angel who lived there, and put him up onto the screen.

I was so freaked out that I got the message of the movie backwards. I know George Prager was supposed to be a villain, just interested in sex and horrible to women, but I tell you, when he and Bettina got together, the hair raised right off my scalp. Of course, at the finish of the movie, you get the feeling that Bettina goes back to her husband, but I didn't care. I just blithely blanked that out and spent an hour inventing my own ending, with Bettina and George. How she finally frees him from himself, how they're going to end up all right together. It made me absolutely, ridiculously happy until four o'clock in the morning.

Wow. And then I came across what I wrote here about David Angel being simply a shadow in Effie's imagination. It's like lightning all inside my head. Maybe he *wasn't*. Maybe he was exactly what Effie wanted him to be.

SUNDAY

I just read this over and it sounds nuts. The whole thing was just a *movie*. It's just celluloid and publicity, for God's sake.

SUNDAY NIGHT

I just saw the *TV Guide*. George Prager was played by an actor called Frank Langella. Well, "Langella" is close enough to "Angel" for me to start freaking out again.

June 13

Behold the graduate! I am writing this with the gold-plated pen Aunt Kate gave me. The ceremony was lovely. Bishop Peters gave the address. I got the English award!! All the girls came around and hugged me. Mom looked beautiful. She had her new pink suit on. She gave me the Nikon I wanted! Dad came a little late, but he looked terrific, too. He gave me a string of pearls. I don't know how he ever afforded them. The graduation dress came up high on the neck, but I wore the pearls anyway. Afterward Daddy took a lot of pictures with the new Nikon and behaved really well around Mom. He even told her how beautiful she looked.

We all talked about Effie and laughed about how the sloppy little goof would have cried at the graduation. Later

on I went to the locker room to change, and I cried a
little too, wishing Effie could have been there.

June 14

I feel awful. Mom just took my temperature. It's 103. My
eyes hurt. It hurts to write. I'm in bed. Mom has drawn
all the shades. It's dark, I hate it. It's scary to be shut up
in a black box. Like Effie is.

June 15

Dr. Shirley came over, and he gave me a shot. I was feeling
so awful I didn't even flinch. Feel better now. Dr. Shirley
patted me and said, "You and your sister are the two best
patients I've ever had." I just remembered. He was the
one who signed the death certificate.

June 17

Effie wasn't really a good patient, but she liked Dr. Shirley because he had such soft hands. Right before Christmas, Mom sent her to him. Effie was so tired. She was always too tired. The doctor said it was not uncommon for
growing girls to exhaust themselves, and he patted Effie
with his soft hands and told her to eat lots of Christmas
candy and have more fun.

But Effie didn't seem to want to have more fun. And
she grew so thin. The bones in her wrist stuck out like

boulders. She spent most of her time looking through toys in the basement, things she'd had when she was two and three. I asked her about it once, why she was doing it, and she said she was trying to remember the person she used to be—that maybe the sight of the books and toys or the way they smelled might bring her back to it and she could start over. I didn't press her. I cannot say how heavy-hearted it made me feel, her wanting to remember what it felt like to be two.

Her schoolwork began to suffer at last.

We were over at Dad's, one rainy Sunday. It was right before Valentine's Day, and Dad had a card and gift for each of us. Effie's was a big tin of beef jerky. She adored the stuff but hadn't been able to buy much since the price started to zoom out of the range of her allowance. When she saw what was in the package, the whole day seemed to get warmer and sunnier.

"Dad!" she hugged him. "You remembered!"

"How could I forget?" he grinned at her. "Remember the time I came downstairs at three o'clock in the morning and found you solemnly eating a pound of beef jerky in the kitchen? You were fast asleep!"

We all laughed. And then I said, "You shouldn't talk, Dad. Who once drank a glass of juice a yard tall?"

Well, in just a minute we were all shouting over the others: Do you remember this? What about the time when? It was a lot of fun. We laughed so hard we all got stomach aches. I think we must have had more crazy things happen to us than any other family in the world.

Then, after a while, Dad straightened up and wiped his eyes. "Tell me something, girls," he said. All the laughter was drained from his voice. "We had a lot of good times together as a family. But I know you were both aware of how unhappy your mother and I were. You remember all the arguments and the fighting. But I sometimes wonder if we did the right thing by you girls—you don't wish we were still together, do you?"

In a second Effie was over at the sofa, diving into him, burrowing into his neck. "No! I don't!" she cried.

I added myself to Effie at Dad's neck. "Of course not, Dad. We're glad you and Mom found a way out. Before we had one unhappy home, and now we've got two happy ones. I call that a good deal, don't you?"

Everyone sort of gasped and wept and patted one another's back. We all felt better. Nobody wanted to get up, so we began a sitting-down game. "Name the Happiest Day of Your Life."

"You start, Susan."

"Well, there was one day when I was ten. I woke up in the morning, and I thought, This is going to be the best day of my life. And it was. Mom made pancakes for breakfast. I got a letter from my pen pal. Spring came. I found out I'd made the honor roll. I did my first handspring. Dad, you gave me a dollar, 'just for looking so pretty.' Nothing big happened—just a lot of little things went right."

"Serendipity," Dad said. "I think my favorite day was the first time I took you kids to P.O.P. You loved that amusement park more than Disneyland. You were just jumping for joy—Effie over her trip-to-the-moon ride—do you remember that, sweetheart?—and Susan with Popsie, the pink-polka-dot elephant. You two were pulling me along, each one in a different direction, and I knew that no matter how wrinkled and gray and tired I got, I had been blessed with a magic potion—in the form of two little girls who would see to it that I never got old."

Effie's whole face seemed to be smiling. She looked happier than she had in months, and gazing at her, I could almost see the ecstatic little girl Dad had just been describing.

"And what about you, Effie? What's the happiest day of your life?"

The look of bliss never left her face as she turned to Dad. "The happiest day of my life is going to be the day you and Mommy get back together."

It was the spookiest thing I ever heard. Dad and I just gaped at her. I was about to get angry, furiously angry because I thought Effie was trying to make a joke out of what we'd said not two minutes before. But then I saw her face and I couldn't be furious anymore. She wasn't trying to be funny at all.

June 18

A few days later, Effie and I were watching television in the living room. I had my first date with Fred Margolis that night, and since he was a basketball player, I was watching the sports news so I'd sound informed. I was also rolling up my hair in electric curlers, and Effie was next to me, spilling onto the floor and eating a chocolate bar. I was just lifting a roller off one of the red-hot stands when Effie screamed out. I dropped the roller onto my finger, gave myself one hell of a burn, and started to curse my sister out. But Effie wasn't listening to me; she just bounced up and down, whooping. "He's here, Susan, he's *here!*"

". . . mob at the airport," the newscaster was saying, "as hundreds of happy fans welcomed David Angel to Los Angeles. He commented that he plans to make his home in Beverly Hills for an indefinite period of time . . ."

"Wow," said Effie. "Wow wow wow!"

So he was here.

But it was a strange thing. For all of her *wow*'s, Effie

never once made an effort to find out where David Angel lived. You would have thought that she'd haunt his house day and night like the Headless Horseman, but she didn't.

And, come to think of it, Effie never made an effort to meet David Angel. Not at the beginning, when it would have been relatively easy, not at any of the concerts, not through Dad or his friends.

Maybe Effie sensed that her idol wouldn't live up to her expectations. And he probably wouldn't have. No doubt he's the bastard of the age. Still, I think of that *Diary of a Mad Housewife.*

You know something—if I had seen that movie a few months sooner, I just might have personally found out where David Angel lived and driven Effie to meet him.

But I mustn't think like that. I tell myself that even if I had seen the movie, I wouldn't have taken her to him. In fact, with all that sex and hurting going on between Bettina and George Prager, I might well have dragged Effie a hundred miles *away* from David Angel.

It was two weeks afterward. It started in such a stupid way. Lunch was over, and Mom and Effie and I were sitting in the living room, digesting. We all felt sleepy. Mom noticed that she had forgotten to turn off the light above the kitchen stove.

"How about turning off that light, Effie?" she asked.

Effie drowsed on the couch. "Can't you do it, Mom? You're closer."

One of Mom's eyes seemed to grow smaller than the other—a sign that she's angry.

"Effie, I asked you to turn that light off."

"Oh, Mom," Effie wailed, and flounced a pillow down. "You're the one who left it on, after all!"

Mom was on her feet in a second, going toward Effie. Effie was up then also, going toward the stove. But as she reached it, she mumbled, "Why can't you be like Dad? He never orders me around."

"Well, I'm not your father," Mom answered her with iceberg brightness. "But thank you for reminding me—he telephoned this morning and left a message for you girls. He says to tell you he's getting married."

I remember that my eyes became wet instantly, as if I'd turned on a bathroom tap. I remember seeing the hair stirring on Effie's collar and knowing how hard she must be shaking. Then she ran—first into a table which was still trembling from the impact half a minute later, and then out of the apartment.

I must have stayed in my room for three hours. It's funny how you can sneak up on yourself. Before that day, I would have sworn that I didn't believe Mom and Dad could ever get back together. But I believed it. Of course, I believed it all along.

My dad. I had never been his favorite—I knew Effie was —but he and I had had times, too, which nobody else knew about, times that were beautiful secrets between Dad and me.

I'd seen enough friends whose parents remarry. I know what has to be done. Establishing new connections, not oiling and maintaining the old ones. My times with Dad alone would have to fade out. I knew that.

I went through my drawers, looking for a pile of letters Dad had written me a few years ago when I went away to camp. I told myself I was looking just so I could reread them, but in the back of my head I knew I was going to throw them away. Mom never used to understand why, when I was a child and upset, I would tear out my favorite pages in picture books and destroy them. I could never explain it later, but that's what I was doing now.

I found the letters finally, and I threw them away.

I went downstairs to Mom. She was where I had left her

on the sofa. She wasn't moving at all. I was very noisy
and funny. I said a lot of things to tease her. She laughed,
and we talked for a long time, until we both felt better,
or at least said we did.

Then we started to wonder where Effie was. But we
made up our minds not to worry until it started getting
dark—after all, Mom's news had not been exactly pleasant,
and Effie was probably taking a walk somewhere, stamping
the sadness off. It takes a long time to become dark where
we live, and the sky got slowly dusky and grim like a relic.

By the time the sun had gone down, Mom was calling
everyone who might know where Effie was. But no one
knew—one by one they didn't know, and their startled
voices, on the phone, got Mom more and more upset.
Finally, at nine o'clock, she said, trying to make it sound
like it was something we did every day, "Well, shall we call
the police?" I'm the one who called, and when a reception-
ist asked if it was an emergency, I said, "I don't know."
That scared me more than anything, her controlled little
voice and the possibility that, yes, this was an emergency.

We got a sergeant on the phone. He asked a few questions and told us to wait a couple more hours, make some
more phone calls, and if nothing had turned up by midnight to call again. We took his name, Sergeant Frank Gilbert, and wrote it in the list of emergency numbers on
the wall.

Mom and I were afraid to use the phone too much, in
case Effie was trying to reach us, so we just sat in the living
room. I saw something horribly funny. No one, after all,
had ever shut off the light above the stove. I watched it
burn in its little globe until I could see it even when my
eyes were closed.

At ten-fifteen the phone rang. It had not occurred to
Mom or me to call Effie's friend Clara Didex, because
Effie hadn't been over at her house for nearly a year; but

it was Clara's mother on the phone telling us that Effie was there.

Although Mom and I had never been to Clara's house before, we found it with no trouble; it was the most brightly lit place on the block. Like a beacon. As we were walking up the steps, Clara's mother opened the door— she must have been waiting for us. "Hello," she said. "The girls are here and quite all right." She hurried us inside.

The living room was a large one. Effie, Alexandra and Clara were huddled by the fireplace, even though there was no fire going. My first reaction on seeing my sister was anger; I felt like a fist. I stared at her so hard I saw her double, but she wouldn't look at me. There was a wicker cat by her feet and she wouldn't take her eyes off it.

She didn't look like Effie. She was wearing a blouse I'd never seen before; it was all but transparent, and I felt nervous watching it. She had a narrow velvet ribbon around her neck. And her hair—Effie usually wore it straight down, or in a braid, but tonight she had done it as if for a dance— pinned up with little swirls and bobs. It must have taken her an hour to get it right.

Effie was staring at me now. All the black she had around her eyes made her look just like a witch in a picture book she'd had when she was tiny; it had scared her so much that Mom finally had to tape the pages together. But that's just what she looked like now.

"Thank you for your kindness," Mom said very nicely. "But if you don't mind, I'll be taking my daughter home now. Come, Effie." Effie followed us out of the house without remotely noticing Alexandra or Clara or Clara's mother. None of us said a word on the way home. It was as if what we had to say was too private for the car to hear.

The rest of that night was hell. Effie lay in her room with the door locked, crying. No hysterics. Just the bitter little sound that went on and on. But whenever Mom or

I knocked on her door, there was no nonsense about not letting us in. Effie unbolted the door right away, politely, and allowed us to come in and sit on her bed.

Her story was always the same, and she told it in the same straight, flat voice. She had left our house and had hitched a ride to Clara's. Alexandra had bicycled over. They had decided to go to Beverly Hills and shop. Clara had lent Effie a bicycle. They fixed up their hair, borrowed Clara's blouses and shawls. They had gone around to the shops. They had bought a hamburger. They sat in the park a little. They had an ice cream. When the sun went down, they had gone back to Clara's house. As a joke, they had not gone indoors, but had sat in the garage, talking. Clara stored her *True Romance* magazines there, and they read them by flashlight. At ten o'clock it had started to get cold, so they had gone inside, and Clara's mother had scolded them and called the other parents. Effie was sorry she had made us worry, and that was all that had happened. She swore it was. But Mom and I didn't believe her. Finally Mom called Clara's mother to see if she knew what had gone on, and Mrs. Didex said that Clara's story was exactly the same as Effie's. But it was infuriating, it was lunacy—because the moment we would leave her bedroom, Effie would lock the door and the bristly, stiff crying would start up again.

July 4

Today I met the woman Dad is going to marry. Her name is also Susan, but he calls her Sue. She is nothing whatever like Mom, nothing like Effie or me. She was friendly and seemed to care very much about making me like her. She was so light—she kept laughing. I have seen a lot of women like Sue, and I never thought that one of them would be brought into my life.

Dad was acting to her in a way that I've never seen him act before. He was a new person for Sue.

Mom is talking about moving to a smaller apartment, near where we used to live. She told me there would be a guest room where I could stay when I came to visit. It's an eerie thought. She's got her decorating magazines out. I wish she wouldn't do it. So much has happened in this apartment. She just can't leave it like that.

Life is going on, it appears. Picking up speed. First Dad, and now Mom.

The day after Effie ran away was Saturday. A group of us were going to watch the school volleyball tournament, and we had breakfast first at our apartment. Since the day was warm, we left all the doors open. Most of the kids were in the kitchen, but standing anywhere in the apartment, you could hear the softness of them—all the round, tanned girls in their pale dresses—and the hiss of cereal being poured into bowls. I was sitting on the living-room couch and I felt very much a part of what was going on outside me. I remember, curiously enough, thinking that that was what prophets say death is like—this being a part of everything.

Ed Hendries, a friend of mine, came in and turned on the television to hear a news program. His girl friend Donna sat down on the couch next to me. I was lying back, not really listening, when I heard the newscaster say "David Angel."

I looked up and there was a picture of him on the screen. I thought, why are they going to say he's living in Beverly Hills when he's been living here for a month? But the pretty blond newscaster said he had blown the back of his head away the night before, and was dead.

Next to me, I heard Donna cry out. I thought, Thank
God, thank God, Effie heard. I won't have to tell her. And
when I saw it was only Donna who had heard and not
Effie, I cried out also.

I told Effie while she was having her bath. She looked
at me for a long moment before she sank back into the
tub. She didn't cry at all.

The next few days the papers were full of the story. How
David Angel had been held on charges kept secret, how
had been involved in a dozen paternity suits, how he
had been heavily into drugs.

I couldn't help comparing those articles to "The House
I Will Make For You": *We will rise at dawn, you and I* . . .
and I felt sick and empty.

Mom and I tried to keep Effie from watching the news
and seeing the papers, but she watched and saw. I don't
know what we were afraid of—that she would find out what
her idol was made of?

Friday, March 18, Effie came down to dinner. She had been
eating snacks up in her room, so Mom and I were relieved
to see her. Not that we had been worried—as I said, Effie
had taken it very well. But still, when she came downstairs
at last, Mom and I were very gay. Mom made a fuss, talking about a play she was going to take us to on the
weekend.

As I recall, Effie only spoke about David Angel twice.
First she said he'd left all his money to his grandfather
on Long Island. Mom said that was something good, any-
how. Then Effie said she'd read he'd killed himself with a
Colt .45. Mom and I didn't know what to answer. Effie
went on to say that she had talked to Alexandra about it,
because her father had a Colt .45 under his bed in case of
burglars. He had said it was a painless way to die. So David

Angel hadn't suffered. Mom said again, that was something good.

The next morning I was driving Effie into Westwood to get our cousin Felicia a birthday card. We passed Alexandra's house, and Effie said that she had left her sweater there the last time she had been over—could we stop and get it? I said all right, if she hurried. She promised she would and got out of the car. I sat inside. The motor was running. I saw Effie ring the doorbell, and then, after a moment, Alexandra let her in. I waited in the car a few minutes, then I got out. I stood by the driveway. There were noises coming from the house. Then a noise like someone dropping a heavy drawer. I heard a scream that I told myself wasn't a scream, and after a minute, Alexandra ran out to me. She couldn't talk—she sounded like bad ventriloquism. She told me Effie had knocked her down and run into her parents' bedroom and locked the door. Alexandra had yelled, but Effie wouldn't come out. Then she heard the noise I had heard; the drawer being dropped.

Mom was there in five minutes, the police were there in ten. We called Sergeant Frank Gilbert. They broke the bedroom door down.

It wasn't the way that you read it was. With the gun in her hand, Effie looked like she was playing pretend, bang bang, being a gangster. I hope it was, as she said it should be, painless.

There was a little note, scribbled to me on the scratch pad. "Dear Susie . . ." She had never called me Susie in her life.

It's nearly dawn. I don't want to stop writing. I dread stopping writing, saying goodbye to Effie. But there is nothing left to write.

Oh, Effie, I'm never going to lose you. You're in this diary. I love this diary. I love it and I'll never forget.

August 3

I can't stand it. I read it over, the whole diary, and Effie is not there. God damn, she is not there. I want her so, but she has gone.

It is so cruel, *what she did makes no sense.* It's horrible not to understand, it is drowning. Why? Life without David Angel was so empty that she couldn't live. That's what she wrote to me in the note by the bedside table.

But it is lunacy. How could he be that important? She had never even met him.

I am looking through these pages, I am sweating because I cannot find more, because I cannot make the pieces fit. There must have been more—having to do with Stanley and Mom and Dad and Peter and me. A *real* reason, having to do with the Disneykins and the butterfly in the jar and the first days at Shaftsbury and the barbecue at Stanley's and her first period and playing Gethsemane and losing her shoe. And what happened the week before she died, when she was gone so long and never really explained what happened. More than anything else, I think, I wish she had told me that.

Or was there just that time bomb in her which may also be in me?

I wish so badly she were here. I wish she were here to hold me and explain, point by point, what David Angel meant to her, what he was in her mind, why her life was empty without him. I wish she were here to say she loved me and that, whatever the reasons were for what she did,

I wasn't one of them. I must understand, because if I cannot, nothing can mean anything.

I am thinking of that Christmas present I gave her—playing David Angel's songs on the piano. It was the best gift I ever gave.

September 5

Tomorrow's the big day. I arrive in Chicago at four-fifteen, and will be at Northwestern by six. I'm all packed.

I found this diary last night. I was surprised, reading it over. These days, what happened seems so much in the past that it has so much less power to hurt. What Effie did, she did, and it doesn't really matter why. I can never know why. I'm sure she never knew, either. But I do think it was brave of her to give a reason, at least a try at understanding.

There was no time bomb in Effie. She was only fragile, she just couldn't get along.

Unlike her sister. Unlike me.

I can't wait for tomorrow. I'm a bit nervous about finding my way around campus, but I can read a map so I'll be all right. Mom said to be ready at five; she is taking me to dinner and a movie tonight, so I'd better go.

I meant to throw this diary away, the way I did Dad's letters, but I changed my mind and I decided it's coming along with me to Northwestern. What the hell—Effie always did want to see the place.

Joey

RAY-O-HALL: I heard the news on television. It didn't seem possible, what they were saying. Then the camera stayed on a picture of Joey taken at our Madison Square Garden concert. I started to feel sick. And then they showed his house, and Joey covered on the stretcher. God.

PENELOPE BLAIN: There's a nun at school. We call her Old Black Angel. Everybody hates her because she always tells horrible news. When I saw her outside my room, I knew something was really wrong. But I thought it was Mom. Never Joey. He was the one who made me know that we are never really alone and lost.

APRIL DANZIG: I was having dinner at a little place with a bar in it. They said what had happened on the television over the bar, and I said to the fellow I was with, You may not believe this, but I used to be married to that guy who just died.

HARRY BARNES: Jesus Christ! Leave me alone, you bloodhounds! No comment!

PETER EDWARDS: Joey was only five years old when I knew him, and I haven't seen him since. But I've never forgotten him.

DEIRDRE BLAIN SHULMAN: What do I remember? The night of Mr. Sykes's party, when Joey hugged us all and said he loved us. That night I knew he was going to be a star. I wish it had never happened.

REBECCA MONROE: Sometimes I can still feel the softness of his hair. See his smile as he sang, and the shine that was always on his face. Oh, my love—your old green jacket . . .

The night before the day David Angel will die, the moon looks down into a garden. White in the night, a picnic table erupts with week-old sandwiches; a half-eaten chicken drumstick lolls against a small stone statue of Eros. In the swimming pool are beach toys. A cork-and-striped-canvas raft bleaches out in the moonlight, and three nervous balls of plastic start away at the faintest tremor of the water.

Past the lawn is a large dark house on North Rodeo Drive in Beverly Hills, California. Spanish moss drips, groping, over the roof. In the entry, a suit of armor stands sentry in the curve of the staircase.

To the right of the door is an uneasy, ugly room, filled with shapes like crushed sand castles. The purple satin on the bean-bag chairs is frowzy and worn. The fourteen-foot ceiling is black, white carpet is on the floor. A steel-and-chrome mobile dances in the corner, twirling a ghostly fouetté. And propped against the fireplace is a giant pasteboard cutout of a man holding a golden record and dressed all in white.

Down the hallway, over the ivory kitchen, the cold bathrooms and clothes closets, hovers the sweet scent of mildew.

On the second floor, one bedroom holds cracked shoes, books with broken spines, three-year-old *Variety* trade papers, shattered mirrors, scalded pots, a jumble of cardboard boxes.

The next room has been fixed up for a little girl. There is a ruffled white canopy bed, gold-leafed furniture, an eyelet bookmark in a copy of *Rebecca of Sunnybrook Farm*. But over everything lies a counterpane of dust.

Everything in the third bedroom is red. Red curtains swathe a steel four-poster bed, red sequin pillows huddle together on the couch in the corner.

A rippling begins under the red satin bedclothes and the moon gazes down . . .

David Angel turned over on his side. The touch of his cold hand on his cheek jerked him awake. His dark brown hair, brushed in waves for the public, was messy against the pillow. He rubbed his hands over his pointed white face. He looked like a cat. He was six feet three inches tall, thin, and he lay there like a lonely god.

He sat up in bed and touched the satin quilt that rose and fell around him in peaks. It reminded him of a story his Grandma Nana had told him many years before—about a little lame prince whose old brown cloak turned into a magical flying carpet and took him around the world. But David Angel knew that his quilt would not take him anywhere. It was not magical. It was from Bloomingdale's.

He sighed and squeezed his eyes tightly together. Usually he awakened to find cramps in his legs and stomach. But on this night he sparkled. It occurred to him that he might have been reborn in the night. He wondered, indeed, if he still had a body. He looked down at where his arms had once been and saw them there still, pale and quiet in the moonlight.

He threw off the quilt and stood up by the side of the bed. He was naked and the night was cold, but warmth sprang from his body like a force shield. He walked to the terrace and went outside.

He watched the stars. They burned smoldering holes into the sky. Although he was dizzy from holding his head back, he did not want to take his eyes off them.

He watched the two maple trees in the front yard whip and bend in the wind. He knew what they were saying to each other.

He wondered if it were true that every movement on earth, even the slightest twitch of a baby's finger, eventually changed the course of the universe. David Angel waved both arms back and forth in great swoops. "Okay, I've changed it!" he cried. The cocoon of heat around him had been dispelled and he was chilled, but he did not care.

"I've made it right again," he whispered.

He felt something soft batting against his naked legs—Glitter, his Siamese kitten. The little body on his ankles felt beautifully, almost foolishly dear to him. She whined and meowed.

"What's the matter?" Angel asked. "What's making my little baby cry?" He leaned over and petted her skinny haunch. "Did I forget to feed you again, Glitter? Oh, dear, forgive me. I guess I forgot to feed myself, too!"

He loosened the cat from his legs and, cuddling her to his chest, went into the red-tiled bathroom down the hall. Leaning against the sink were five ten-pound bags of cat food. He had bought them the day before, on sale. One by one he opened the bags and spilled their contents into the red sunken bathtub, which was nearly full when he finished; the room swelled with the pungent, brown odor. "There, precious—you've got plenty to eat now."

He tenderly lowered the kitten into the bathtub.

When David Angel went back into the bedroom, the first thing he saw was his guitar resting against the ottoman. He was sure it was an omen. He had not felt like singing the old songs for so long, but he had to play tonight.

He brought the guitar out onto the terrace and held its cold curves against his naked hips. He began to sing the song that had made him a star.

In the kingdom of ice at the back of the North Wind,
Adrian's daughter, intently listening
To the endless river/ shimmering tellings
Of fast-frozen poems/ Here is truth, here is beauty
Perfect, inhuman, ice crystals.
                              Light, my desire!

Adrian's daughter, sadly learning
Of the empty ballerinas fruitlessly turning;
Blind silver bullets sleeping in a gun
Until lovelessness fires them/ King with a
Scarred face/ He got too much of
The knowledge he thought he was seeking.
                              Light, my desire!

Triumphs and triumphs of light unfold
To Adrian's daughter. She screams to behold
The world she wanted/ Illumination!
Cruelty of the pale petals of reason
Crushing the flesh and ripping like razors.
The light burned her eyes out of her head.
O, give me the darkness instead, she is crying.
Now give me the darkness to crawl to and hide in.

The chance to dream of darkness.
Perhaps I'll dream of darkness.

David Angel sang the song over and over until his throat
hurt. And as the first blank of dawn came into the sky,
he went back to bed.

"Wake up. Wake up!"
The room was daylight-bright. Someone was shaking
him hard. David Angel opened his eyes. They felt as sore
as peeled fruit.
Randolph stood over him, his long nails nipping Angel's
shoulder. Randolph did not look well. There was a gray

sluggish undertaste to his dark-brown skin, and his eyes were shot through with an orange cast.

"The gentleman from *Beat* magazine is here," he said coldly.

"Oh, my God." David Angel looked up. He saw a fresh-skinned boy looking down at him, smiling.

"But, Randolph," David Angel whispered, "he wasn't supposed to come till three this afternoon. You promised! Not till three."

"It's three-thirty," the reporter answered brightly. "But if you aren't up to this, Mr. Angel, maybe we should forget the whole thing."

Randolph sprang forward. "Of course he's ready."

David Angel leaned back onto the pillows. *Oh, God!* he thought. *Relax.* The harmony of the night before lay in shreds about him. His heart beat in a clumping, abnormal rhythm. *Relax, mustn't make a mistake.*

The reporter sat down by the side of the bed, admiringly stroked the bed cover, then very professionally took out his yellow pad and pencils. Against the red quilt, they looked to David Angel like big bright Lego pieces.

"I'll start by asking you some basics," the young man said. "I've heard that your real name is Joey Danzig. When did you change to David Angel—and why?"

David Angel pulled the red sheets tight about his neck. "No," he said shortly. "My name has always been David Angel."

The lie could be easily exposed, but he did not want to think about that other, earlier time.

The reporter glanced up through his long bangs. "I see. But you were born in Westbury, Long Island, weren't you?"

"No." David Angel smiled. "I was born on Planet One."

The reporter chuckled soundlessly. "I get it! This must all be part of your new image! Your agent was telling me all about it downstairs—the new style you're moving toward. The upbeat lyrics, the more accessible image. He said you were even thinking of cutting a children's record. Pretty cute idea!"

He laughed again. David Angel's heart began to beat more confidently, and he grinned back at the young man.

"You look so much like an old friend of mine," he said impulsively. "Doesn't he look just like Ray-O, Randolph?"

Randolph did not answer.

The reporter blushed. "Mr. Angel, could you tell me *why* you felt you had to make all these changes in your group?"

Angel stiffened. He looked over at Randolph, who was in a chair by the window, trying to capture a minute particle of soil from underneath his fingernail; he didn't look up. There was a thick silence.

"Would you rather not answer the question?" the reporter asked softly.

"No, no," David Angel said hastily. He clutched the sheets tighter. *Relax!* The right response—he was so glad Randolph had made him memorize it—came flowing through him in a moment.

"We're making changes in the group because we feel we're at a period of growth. Our goal has always been to pull our fans in new directions, exciting and stimulating ones, not push them back into music that was worn out years ago."

"I'm happy to hear you say that," the reporter replied. "I've just been rereading a bitchy article about you in an old issue of the *Village Voice*. It said your last two albums have been the shittiest things to hit the market in years, and that within a matter of months your music was going to be as extinct as Herman's Hermits."

"I remember that article." Angel winced. "Well, it was wrong. All wrong! Wrong about everything."

"Your fans will be glad to hear you say that," the reporter smiled. "But do you really mean that your sales aren't down? I read that every time the stations play a David Angel cut, their ratings drop a point."

"All lies!" David Angel almost screamed. "The group is stronger than it's ever been. The only reason people think we're in a slump is because they believe lies like that article."

"What about the drugs you're supposed to take, and the women who're always around—and the canceled concerts and fighting in the group? None of that's true either?" The reporter seemed happy.

David Angel felt powerful and benign. "None of it," he said kindly. "And I'm damn glad to have the chance to give my side of the story."

The interview lasted half an hour. At first David Angel was reticent, but the reporter was so obviously impressed with his work that he began to relax. The young man's questions kept coming, and they began to vibrate within Angel's head, loosening ideas, memories the singer had forgotten were there. He spoke of them, diffidently to begin with, and then more and more eagerly. Theories of music, himself, a little girl he had once seen on a playground. Everything came out in a soft, then a strong, then a rainbow flow. David Angel felt confident that everything he was saying was good, and he was grateful to the reporter.

"Think you have enough?" he finally asked. The young man nodded enthusiastically.

"Good," Angel murmured. "I can tell you're nice, really perceptive. Not like that bastard from the *Village Voice*. Go home and say something good about me, will you?"

"Oh, I'll do my best, Mr. Angel, I promise you. He pumped Angel's hand earnestly. "Goodbye, and thanks so much."

Angel smacked his hand to his forehead. "Shit! After all this time, I still don't know your name!"

"It's Ludwin. Peter Andrew Ludwin."

After Peter Ludwin left, David Angel began to feel over-whelmingly sleepy.

"How did I do?" he asked Randolph.

"Just great."

Angel yawned contentedly. "It's crazy how much I wor-ried, isn't it? I guess you just got me spooked over how much this interview meant. But we've got nothing to worry about."

"Right," Randolph said, walking toward the door. "You get some rest now. The concert's at eight—I'll be by to pick you up at six-thirty."

"I'll be here, waiting."

After Randolph left, David Angel pulled a leather scrap-book from a bookcase by the bed. He flipped through it rapidly, looking for the article from the *Village Voice*. He found it at last. It was written by Peter Andrew Ludwin.

David Angel began to shake, so violently it looked like he was dancing. Five minutes went by. Ten. Betrayal! Why hadn't Randolph told him? He ripped the article to pieces, gulped in mouthfuls of air. Bright blood fell from his nose, pattered onto the quilt. He felt as if he had swal-lowed lightning—pain flashed and sizzled in his stomach. He shrieked for the maid, but Bella did not hear. He groped inside the drawer of his bedside table for pills. A watch and three books of matches fell onto the carpet. In his confusion he picked up something which Randolph had given him in case of burglars. It was cold and hard and he dropped it with a shudder. At last the right pills were found. He swallowed one, then another and, with difficulty, a third.

But the shaking did not stop. He poured a shot of Jack Daniel's down his throat. It did not help. Then he gave up and threw himself face down onto the bed.

Peter Edwards

Joey Danzig lived across the street from me in Westbury, Long Island, twenty-odd years ago. It was a pretty place, isolated and a little raw. Our block was full of tract houses and newly planted trees, young wives already pregnant.

I was five years old when my father got a job teaching at Hicksville Junior High School. We moved to Long Island from Brooklyn, and I found the new neighborhood a little too quiet. Walking across the empty fields, missing the crowded comfort of Christopher Street, an agoraphobia incubated that has remained with me until this day. I was also very shy. I remember my father having to pay me to introduce myself to the boy across the street.

It's strange, but I can remember Joey's house very clearly, and my own next to not at all. Joey's house was painted red, with weeds growing through the cracks in the driveway and garden furniture rusting on the back porch.

When I first saw Joey, he was in his bedroom playing with an Etch-A-Sketch. I bought that toy for my daughter not long ago, and it occurs to me that it might have had something to do with Joey; I know I remembered him as soon as I saw it in the store.

Joey was very small and looked undernourished. I could see his ribs through his shirt. And he was wearing short pants. To get his attention, I told him he was a sissy. Joey opened his eyes very wide and he looked at me without surprise.

"No," he said. "I'm Dracula."

For almost a year, I played with Joey every day—either at my house or at his. His imagination was immense. He made up myriad games that were enthralling during the day, but kept us both up at night. He taught me voodoo. He also liked to spy on the family next door, and we used to do alchemy in the garage. Anything was fair game for Joey. Years later, when I was an undergraduate, I made friends by teaching people some of Joey's games and pretending they were my own invention.

I've seen my relationship with Joey so often in the children that I teach today—the larger, slower children willing slaves to their smaller, quicker comrades. But Joey himself was unlike anyone I have ever known. Sometimes I imagine having a child like that in my classroom and ask myself how I would handle someone so highly strung, so precocious. I hope I could be helpful.

I remember that Joey was preoccupied with what he called the Angel of Death. His house was right beside the Long Island Expressway, and when the big Mack trucks rumbled by, the whole house would vibrate. Joey used to tell me that one day a big trucker was going to pull up at his house and ask Joey to fix him something to eat. Joey would obey, and the trucker would tell him to climb into the cab of his truck. Joey would have no fear. He would clamber up into the cab. But the moment his foot touched the seat, he, the truck and the trucker would disappear.

Joey was extremely moody. Almost manic-depressive, I realize now. Every evening he would become very unhappy and hide under the bed. I never knew why. And when he was happy, he would roll around on the floor, laughing and shivering.

He had a frightening temper. I remember once I was playing over at his house and my father came to pick me up a few minutes earlier than usual. Joey and I had been playing slapball, and he wanted to finish the game. He

jumped up and down on the sofa, screaming with rage because I was leaving. My father was amused, but I was
terrified.

I cared for Joey a great deal, as did nearly everyone else
in the neighborhood. Children were attracted to his fear-
lessness and fairness, and adults made a pet of him because
he was so tiny and so polite. Even my father, who had seen
all types of children, thought Joey was wonderful. That
bothered me, to be frank. Dad asked Joey what he wanted
for his birthday, and Joey named a brand of model rocket
ship he had seen advertised. My father, an impatient man
who usually gave up on something the moment it became too difficult to achieve, searched all over town until
he tracked down that particular rocket ship.

I seem to remember that Joey's family life was terrible.
Mr. Danzig used to beat him. When Joey first told me
about it, I didn't believe him until he took off his shirt
and showed me the round marks the notches of a belt
had made on his back.

Mr. Danzig was a plumber. He didn't get much business
—because of his temper, I suppose many of the housewives
were afraid to let him into the house.

But Mrs. Danzig was extremely friendly. She used to give
me apple juice, and she taught me how to say "Thank you"
in Polish—*dziekuje*. I still remember. She and Joey were
each other's life. Joey was not ashamed to kiss her, even
in front of other children.

Most clearly, though, I remember Darlene. She was huge,
six feet two, or so it seemed to me. Joey, who wasn't afraid
of the Angel of Death, was terrified of Darlene and she, in
turn, couldn't bear him. All he had to do was come into the
room, and she would attack him. She hated the way his hair
looked. She hated the way he walked. I remember once she
even said she hated the way he smelled.

Joey would run and hide. Once he answered Darlene

back about something, and she grabbed him by the legs with one hand and began dragging him to the closet. I became hysterical—started to scream and couldn't stop. Darlene grabbed me with her other arm. Joey and I were locked in that closet for nearly an hour. It was the only time I ever saw him cry.

What else do I remember? That Joey couldn't wait to start school. Looking back, I suppose it meant freedom to him, as it does to a lot of children. The first morning of kindergarten, I came by his house to pick him up. Mrs. Danzig had given him a red schoolbag, and he kept swinging it around and around.

Joey was a great success in school that morning. He even stood up in front of everyone and told riddles. The beautiful little girl beside me was craning her head so she could get a better look at him.

At recess we were lined up by size, and Joey, being the smallest, was first in line. We were inspected by our teacher, a pretty young woman whose name I don't remember. When she came to Joey, she ruffled his hair.

I'm afraid that was too much for me to take. I suppose I had been Joey's second for too long, and with the sadism typical of small children, set about hurting him in the most satisfactory way I could think of. I yelled out, loud enough for everyone in the school to hear, that I knew a secret, a terrible, awful secret about Joey Danzig. I felt extremely guilty when I looked at Joey's face—it was so white—but all the children were waiting expectantly and honor demanded that I supply my secret. I had to make one up quickly. Without much reflection, I whispered to the little girl next to me that Mrs. Danzig wasn't Joey's real mother—the dreadful Darlene was. The secret started down the line like wildfire, passing from blond head to brown, whispered by aghast and giggling mouths. Then the boy next to Joey said the secret out loud, very slowly. Joey started to shake. And then we all watched as he wet his pants.

Joey was out of school for three weeks. I went to his house every day to apologize, to explain, but he wouldn't come out of his room, wouldn't send me a message. Soon after, my father was offered a post at a girl's school in Nevada. We moved, and I never saw Joey again.

Throughout my life I have not allowed myself to think much about Joey Danzig, but from time to time I've wondered what happened to him. I became a teacher like my dad, and I could have guessed that Joey would turn out to be something glamorous and spectacular. He always said he wanted to be a stunt man in the movies, and when I read in the newspaper that he was David Angel, the rock singer, I wasn't surprised. Nor was I surprised when he ended up killing himself. For Joey lived desperately, even when he was five years old.

But I did want to see him again. I wanted to tell him that I made up the secret about Darlene just because I was jealous. I didn't realize until much later that it was the truth.

A shrill ringing filled the bedroom. It was the doorbell. The noise gonged through David Angel's head as if he were riding the clapper of a great bell. He gagged. Jumping out of bed, he threw on a robe of red silk and ran downstairs.

When he opened the door, he saw Harry waiting for him, enraged. Harry followed David Angel into the house and up the stairs. "You asshole!" he kept screaming, and when they reached the bedroom, he picked David Angel up under the arms and dumped him on the floor.

"I'll kick the bejeezus out of you for this! We've got a benefit in less than four bloody hours, and here you are, stoned out of your goddamn skull!"

David Angel covered his mouth with his hands. "Oh, no," he swore softly. "I haven't taken anything."

He tried to put his arm around Harry's neck, but Harry pushed him away. "Harry, you old bum," David Angel begged, "something's wrong. Tell me what's the matter."

"You're what's the matter!" Harry spat. "You stinking idiot. You look like hell, you can't sing—goddamnit, you can hardly talk. And we're getting pretty tired of your flipping out to Wonderland every time you see a fucking white rabbit!"

Harry slammed his fist onto the bedside table.

"I can't stand it anymore. I've had all I can take, watching you hit bottom. Oh, I was so sure I could pull you out of the quicksand. Old Harry could fix anything. But even with Randolph and Ray-O pulling along with me, you're

stuck up to your stinking neck and there's not a goddamn thing anybody can do."

David Angel shook his head and opened his eyes wide.
He stared at Harry in bewilderment. "I love the group,"
he said quietly. "You should know I wouldn't do anything
to hurt the group."

Harry snorted. "Oh yeah—I guessed that last winter,
when you made us change our name from 'The David
Angel Band' to 'David Angel.' Oh, you bastard—you bastard." He sank onto the rumpled bed, staring at Angel with
tired eyes.

David Angel shook his head. "You don't understand,
Harry," he said. He tried to put his hands on Harry's shoulder, but Harry jerked loose. David Angel watched him
sadly, blinking. "Remember when it all began?" he asked
suddenly. "That old garage we used to play in? Remember,
Harry? How great it was!"

"God save me from maudlin junkies!" Harry shouted. "I
quit! I quit your lousy fucking group."

David Angel kept staring at the floor. Harry's face con-
vulsed. "You don't care, do you? You don't care about me,
you selfish son of a bitch. I tell you I'm quitting, I never
want to see you again, and you don't care!"

David Angel staggered to his feet in protest and Harry,
out of control, knocked him backwards. A red china lamp
crashed into a handful of meteors. Lying on the floor,
Angel's mind abruptly cleared. "Fuck you, you bastard!"
he shouted, as Harry left the room and disappeared down
the stairs. "You fucking no-talent bastard. I don't need
you. *I'm* the star! You hear me, Harry? I'm the star!"

The front door slammed.

Angel lay there quivering. Hot pain flooded his stomach,
then it was gone. He breathed deeply and sat up. He was
relieved that Harry was gone—glad! Harry was dead weight

—anyone could see that. Now the group could have a fresh start. David Angel could begin to write the kind of songs he liked writing, play the concerts he wanted to. Record the sound of bells which sometimes lulled him to sleep.

But then fat, hot tears were spewing down his cheeks and frying on his face. His skin was dry, and the salt stung. He kept crying, stinging.

He crawled to the dresser and searched for the small packet of white powder. It was hard to fix, for in his eagerness the shaking had started again. At last it was done, and the warm stream fed and watered his body. He massaged his arm rapidly. His throat felt dry and he had difficulty focusing. He seemed to be whirling through space, then gently he fell to the floor near the ottoman. His hand struck the strings of his guitar, and the room was filled with the death chord.

He and Harry were sky-diving for the cover shot of the last album. It was fun, and the heavens seemed to scream to him over and over, *You're the star!* But each time, the wind would rip the words away like giftwrapping. And Harry let go of his hand.

Harry Barnes

I can't even go out of the house without some goddamn photographer or reporter getting on my back. How did we meet? How did we get the group going? What happened between us that last day?

Those are our secrets, Joey. You asked me if I remembered those days back in Westbury, before it all started to fall apart. You were always the one in charge of the poetry department, but I wanted to let you know somehow—I haven't forgotten.

FOR JOEY

Twelve years old.
Playing the guitar with my best friend,
Soaked to the skin by the sun
In an old garage.
He sang in a voice soft like moth.

His yawn smelled of peanut butter, mine of beer.
We talked parents, friends;
Being famous!
Concert halls and gold records
Jumped for a minute before our eyes,
Our bare backs resting on a pile of *Playboys*.

Sometimes it got dark quickly where we lived,
And the sun dropping like a warm, red coal
Made us shiver, remember homework.
We said goodbye, then ran off
Through the junk yards and the sadder parts of town,

Warming ourselves against the afternoon air.
Thudding and singing.

So. Well, I'm with you, man. Sorry you felt you had to leave so soon. I wish it could've always been like when we were kids. Joey, you were a great guy, a great musician. Wherever you are, knock 'em dead. And don't forget, man —*amplify*!

A timid knocking on David Angel's bedroom door. He started. "Yes?" he called, and Bella, his large blond cleaning lady, entered cautiously.

"Would you like me to do your room now?" she asked softly. "I didn't want to disturb ya. I know a big rock star's gotta have privacy to get in touch with his inspiration an' all." She peered closely. "Are ya sure ya're all right?"

"Sure," Angel murmured, gazing at the ceiling. "And don't bother doing my room."

Bella did not leave. "Mister Angel, there's another thing. My nephew, Clarence—my sister's boy—is coming here next week from Chicago. He's never been to California before. He wants to be a singer like you, Mister Angel—a star. I was wondering if when he comes out here, ya'd see him—just for a few minutes, ya know, and maybe tell him what he should do so's he can get started in on it."

"How old . . . how old is he?"

"Seventeen."

Angel laughed dreamily. Seventeen. "Sure I'll see him."

"Oh, thanks!" Bella clasped her hands to her breast. "I knew ya'd say yes, Mister Angel. And I know you're gonna like him. He's got this little group together, and he's got good looks, and his voice is nice, kinda like yours. All he needs is that first break."

David Angel sat up straight at the last two words. He frowned and stared down intently at his pillow. Superimposed upon it was the image of an angry blue-eyed young girl. Deirdre. Her hair writhed about her, blown by an unseen wind. David Angel sighed as Deirdre was blown away. A man's face replaced hers: Mr. Sykes, with his curly black hair and mustache. David Angel grabbed the pillow up off the floor and hurled it at Bella's head. She was gone, too. David Angel put his hands over his ears and began to whistle shrilly.

Deirdre Blain Shulman

Peace be with you, little bird. We shall not soon have another singer such as you, Joey.

Dead? He was too beautiful to die, but now I think he is beautiful in another incarnation. I dreamed last night I saw him riding on a golden pole.

Killed himself? Because he was so attuned to light and darkness. When the black forces came at him he couldn't seem to fight them.

We met in our wilder days. Waitressing at the coffee shop on Santa Monica Boulevard. A customer—a young man with long brown arms and slanted eyes. A boy, a very strange enchanted boy . . . He does not smile at me. Shyness stifles the communication between us. Please smile. I'll do anything to make you smile. He smiles. I sit down in the booth next to him. His voice is infinite. He draws it out of me, I tell him everything—my little town, Brimfield, Mass., dull like every little town, dull life, my rich daddy, wanting to get away. When all the other kids moved to L.A., I moved, too. I was just fifteen.

And my little girl. Baby bastard, love-child, Penelope. Never to be called Penny—materialism, a terrible thing to burden a child with.

Joey, a musician. I should have known that. I love his hands so. They are like spiders that spin webs in the air as he talks. He is new to California, came with his group the day before. He is going to be a star. I ask, and he takes me to meet his group, Harry and Ray-O. Harry asks if I know a place where the group can stay until they get rolling.

Our house. Sunlight coming in through the window. No Louis XV furniture. No furniture at all. Outside are the Venice canals, holding the water that never was. Washed-away boots and cans and babies sleep the sleep of the blessed.

Freedom days. Late up. Breakfast outside, so we can see the children going off to school. We wrap Penelope in a blanket, so she'll look like an old Indian. She wants Twinkies, but is discouraged. They are a dead food.

School days, school days. We know the importance of keeping our minds fit. Who will be the teacher today? Come form a circle, and see what book I take off the shelf. Why, here is a little message our friends the Krishnas have delivered into our hands. When did we get so popular, boys and girls?

Hearing Joey sing every afternoon. The notes like Penelope's toy blocks; building dreams onto the blanket I am resting under, building cities and plains onto the dishes I am washing. The songs he sings are from the back of the North Wind. He says he has been there. I believe him.

Talking at night on a blanket spread out underneath the stars. Penelope's succulent little head against my lap. Homesick little Easterners. I want Nathan's. Bagels and lox for me. Penelope, who is half asleep, says something that sounds like Brigham's ice cream. Hm-m-m, sounds to me like they're hungry, not homesick. I am the woman of the house, it is up to me to do something about it. Next day I bring a shoulder bag to the supermarket where I'm working now. And behold, I bring you home oysters in aspic, English mustard and Major Grey's chutney. Well, the employees' rest room is right by the specialty counter,

I explain to the boys. "I wish it were closer to the hot dogs," Harry complains. Men are so unappreciative.

I love you, Joey. I love you, magic man. You gave me some Baskin-Robbins coupons and on them you wrote: *To Wendy Moira Angela Darling, From the Lost Boy.* I told you later about all the flavors of ice cream I got, but I really didn't use any of the coupons. What was written on them was too precious to spend.

Joey says he cares for me. I am not caught up in vanity, I do not always have to buy things. It does not bother me when people swear. Joey says I'm great. I don't give a damn for what other people think, I'm free.

I try to be free. I try to be all the things I left Brimfield to be, I try to be what Joey admires. One day I find a picture in his pocket. A girl is bending over a French poodle. She wears a lace dress. She is not free. Afterward, I cry. I ask Joey who she is, he says her name is Rebecca.

I buy a razor that afternoon. I shave off all the hair on my legs. I start doing things again that I haven't thought about since I left Brimfield; making the bed in the morning, putting embroidery on shirts. Even wearing nail polish again. I don't envy Rebecca, because envy is a negative emotion, but from the way Joey looked at her picture, I know there isn't much hope for me. No, not much hope. But with Joey, I would take what I could get.

This hurts me a great, great deal. I am bewildered, scared. So much secrecy in Joey. Wrong, bad. A slender body closing in on itself is anti-life. I sometimes think he is not my soul mate after all—I do not understand so many things about him.

I know he is driven, but I cannot see why. He says he must be a star. I try and teach him about the golden road, the middle way, but he will not listen. He has put up walls.

He is only eighteen years old, yet he is an old soul. Sometimes in nightmares I see him in incarnation after incarnation, chasing after his star, never seeing it for the toy it is.

He writes letters to his grandmother back on Long Island because we can't afford a phone. He tells her he is living in a penthouse overlooking the Santa Monica Beach.

Night and day he talks about "the big break." How when the big break comes, he's going to do this and go here and say that. Oh, Lord! Where are his guardian angels? I send mine his way—I tell them to cry, *Easy, Joey; you get there a step at a time!* But Joey, he will not listen. He keeps on screaming, *Come on, come on, I'm ready!*

Well, the big break one sunny day came to Joey and to me all right, but what it broke was us, okay? I got myself glued together, took time, but Joey—I think a few pieces he could never put back together again.

A hot June day. Penelope sick, never enough money in the house. Joey stays with her, tells her stories until I say to hell with it, let's go somewhere. So we do. Playing tag, hopping on the bus. We get off near Doheny. A little store, I've never seen anything like it. Look at all those hats in the window. Joey points to one, the most beautiful hat I've ever seen. Straw with ribbons and lilacs. I feel Joey's thought waves are on Rebecca, so I quickly say a poem to dispel them.

> The broadbacked figure drest in blue and green
> Enchanted the maytime with an antique flute.
> Blown hair is sweet, brown hair over the mouth blown,
> Lilac and brown hair; . . .

Joey crying out in joy. His eyes like water in a crystal vase, I feel I am seeing so deeply into his soul that it singes me.

But an old lady comes. Chases us away. *Get out, get out you dirty hippies!* Joey's head is down, he stares, blinking at the dirt around his toenails.

Four o'clock. Oh, my God, Penelope should have had her medicine by now. Got to get home. Got to get home! No bus fare, got to hitch. Goddamnit, nobody wants to pick us up. Five-thirty, Penelope will be crying. Six. There's a big black car with blazing headlights and flags on the antenna.

It is pulling up. Is the President inside? No, just two regular men, one black, one white. Get in. We get in. Man, the softest carpet in the world.

Hey, the white man says to Joey, I don't usually pick up hitchers, but you and your sister looked so pitiful . . . She's not my sister. Joey's voice coming out real soft. She plays tambourine in our band sometimes. Hey? You got a band? The white man punches the black man's arm. Hey, M. J., he's laughing, we were just saying we wished there was a new sound around. You like music? Joey asks. I feel him getting tight on the jump seat. Oh, God, Joey, relax. Like it, sonny boy? I'm Ed Sykes, president of Clara Records, and this dude here is M. J. Watkins, who better get off his tail and bring me some talent.

Joey starts quaking. We're talent! he cries. I close my eyes in fear because he is so excited. Mr. Sykes laughs. That so? Well, maybe we can do something for you. I'm giving this little party at my beach house tomorrow night. You kids want to come along? Joey grabs my hand, he's so hot I look to see if he's on fire.

He spends all the next day getting ready. I help him take a bath, no easy matter. Poor little tub, the enamel all chipped away. Joey chatters on and on. I am worried about him, don't know what to do. The day passes quickly. Here we are at last, all dressed and ready to go.

And suddenly we're all hugging and kissing and crying.
Joey says how much he loves us all, how we are his family.
The tension and foreboding in me drain away before Joey's
loyalty and reassurance. It's a beautiful moment. Harry
says, You two look great—if you get a chance, why don't
you drop into a Woolworth's and take your picture in one
of those booths? I'll even spring for the quarter!

Fantastic getting to Mr. Sykes's beach house. Holding
hands with Joey. He is singing and swinging my arm around.
His joy begins to creep into me. When we get to the house
it is all lit up by torches like a Polynesian restaurant.

There are all kinds of guests and food and cigarettes.
Joey and I can't see so well, but we find a table with a
bowl of guacamole. We are so hungry. We eat nearly all of
it. Oh, hi, Mr. Sykes. Joey starts sweating. Hey, kids, I'd
like you to meet a few friends of mine. This is Vernon,
Lolly, our million-seller, Phil, borrowed from his soap
opera. You know M. J. Hi, hi, hi. Oh, and a special hi to
you, M. J., you old friend, you. Talking about movies and
music. Everyone friendly. Joey talking to Lolly like one
million-seller to another. I am so proud. Vernon comes by
in a minute and puts something in the guacamole to
make it spicier. Joey and I finish off the bowl, slow and
satisfying. Funny, but it doesn't taste any spicier to us. We
sit and look out at the party for a while. Then Joey turning
guacamole-colored himself. Deirdre, Deirdre, the lawn is
crawling up your dress! Hey, I think a dip in my Jacuzzi
would make you kids feel better. Mr. Sykes laughing, helping us along the lawn. It *is* crawling up my dress. Oh, God.

We can't undress, our hands won't do the things we
want. We're scared, won't come out of the cabana. Joey
covers himself up. These damn trunks are too short. But
I make him get out finally. I all my life wanted to lie in a
Jacuzzi.

So soft in there, so warm, Joey and I lying side by side, dreaming separate dreams. A jingling noise, growing and growing into bells in a cathedral. Wake up, Joey! Mr. Sykes standing by the Jacuzzi. M. J., Vernon, Phil, Lolly, behind him. Oh, wow, Deirdre, it's just like a magic trick. All their clothes falling off at once . . .

Running down the Pacific Coast Highway, so sore between my legs I can't go too fast. Joey's nose bleeding where one of them punched him. Cigarette butts, dirt, leaves swept up in my long skirt. I'm crying, trying to catch up to Joey. But he won't even look back. Finally I get so mad I start screaming. *It's all your fault—your ambition did this. Ambition like yours is a sin!* He stops walking and wheels around. *Sin, Deirdre? You talk about sin? I saw what you were doing—and you liked it, didn't you?*

The look on his face. Telling me there could never, ever be anything again between Joey and me.

We get to Venice at three. Nothing open but an arcade, two little kids playing pinball. One of them looks like Joey. My heart aches bad. I can't keep from crying. Joey puts his arm around me, comforts me at last. I cry harder. Come on, he says, we promised Harry a picture. He points to a little photo booth and we squeeze inside. I have to sit on his lap, it's so small. In the tiny mirror we can see what we look like. We are broken, scratched, red-bruised, bleeding. The light starts flashing. Smile for the camera, Joey tells me, and he starts laughing. I'm scared, for I can no longer see into his eyes. It's all blackness there . . .

Penelope and I went back to Brimfield a few days later. I had had enough of California. And it was time Penelope started school—I kept thinking about those private schools my parents sent me to, with the little gray uniforms.

God, I wanted Joey to say *stay*. But he only said he was glad for my sake that I was going back. I wasn't made to be free, he said. Some nice guy pampering me in a nice house, pretty clothes and enough money. Those were the things he wished for me. That sounded great. Only I wanted him to be the guy.

The group gave Penelope and me a farewell party. Joey got drunk and kissed me. But the next day he didn't remember. What we had had together got blasted away the night at Mr. Sykes's house. So on a blue day Joey took us to the airport and gave us big hugs, me first, then Penelope, because he loved her the most. He said he'd come to Brimfield and visit when he was a star, but he never did.

I got married a year ago to a T-shirt artist, and we're real happy. We live in the country, keep our own chickens. I wish Joey could have spent some time here—it would have been good for him.

When Joey became famous, I read all the articles about him, even though they didn't capture his spirit at all. People said he was caught up in the star publicity syndrome, but I don't believe it. Joey was always a very private person; I guess when he got to be a star, he pretended to be someone different than he really was. I also read somewhere that he was caught up in the whole power mystique, the money bit. That that was how he kept people under his thumb, how he got women. That's wrong, too. Joey didn't need any trappings. All by himself, without any money or any recognition, he had enough power to light L.A.

I heard from Ray-O right before I got married. He said that Joey was finally going back to his Rebecca. She mustn't have made him too happy, though, if she wasn't worth staying alive for.

Sometimes this plane we're on can be very cruel, but I know that Joey and I are destined to meet again in another life, and then it's going to be my turn.

But until that time comes, I know I'm going to miss him a lot.

From the living room downstairs, David Angel's steel-and-chrome grandfather clock forced out five emotionless chimes. Angel counted them. His heart jumped heavily, and for several minutes his body jarred with every breath he took. Five o'clock. Only an hour and a half until Randolph was due to collect him for the concert! Angel hid his face in his hands. The concert—how could there be a concert? There couldn't be, for Harry had quit. Hadn't he? He was sure Harry had quit.

David Angel pushed himself up. There would be a concert —a concert with cheering and flowers and supper afterwards, like in the old days. Better than in the old days! He would show Harry that he wasn't through yet.

Angel caught sight of the great dirty wash of envelopes on the onyx-topped desk near the window. The mail he had promised himself he would answer. He decided to start to work on the pile now. He had a little time, and he hoped his head would clear if he concentrated on answering letters.

Walking over to the desk, he kicked something soft and looked down quickly, afraid he had hurt his kitten. But it was only Glitter's rubber ball. Angel frowned. Where was Glitter? Now that he thought of it, he hadn't seen her all day. She was probably just out. She would be back. She loved him.

He went over to the desk and tried to pick up an armful of envelopes, but the letters skidded all over the floor. He gathered up as many as he could hold, finding he could manage three without too much trouble.

The first letter was from an attorney. It said he was being sued for attacking a television reporter and giving her severe lacerations. David Angel couldn't even remember any lady reporter. It had to be a mistake. He wouldn't have hit a woman.

The second letter was from April, dated two weeks before. She said that if he did not send his alimony check within a certain time she would have him sent to jail for contempt of court. David Angel threw down the letter and ran around the room, searching in every drawer and reaching into all his pockets. He was exhausted when he finished. He had found three dollars.

The third letter was from Penelope. She wondered why she hadn't heard from him in two months and hoped he wasn't mad at her. She told him she had tried unsuccessfully to be expelled from boarding school, and enclosed a poem she had written. Angel thought it was a good poem, and he decided to turn it into a song—that would thrill her,

He settled down to write it, staring down at Penelope's pretty round handwriting. He went through seven pages of staff paper, but every melody he came up with seemed to have been taken from one of the songs he had composed long before. No matter what notes he put down, no matter what introductions he invented, they began as new and ended as old.

David Angel tore up the sheets. Then, cursing, he tore up Penelope's poem. He had forgotten that her letter was written on the back. Then he went back to the desk and took a blue pill and two more shots of Jack Daniel's. That was all that was wrong with him—he needed to get up for the concert. He needed to trip.

He was aware that his hair was wet and sticking to his

face, like it sometimes got at the end of a concert, and he thought of all the kids who would come that night and how they would stamp their feet until he appeared on-stage. He swore he wouldn't be late this time, or have to clutch the microphone to keep from falling down. He felt so weak. Perhaps he'd call Randolph and say he couldn't make it. But if he didn't show, the kids would chant and scream and the whole auditorium would fill with hisses.

Feebly, he began to weep. "I don't think I can give this concert," David Angel confided to the red walls.

Of course you can. You're the star.

Penelope Blain

I almost went crazy when Joey died. I must have cried all day, through the night, and then it was the next morning.

Sometimes I think about him so hard I can't remember his face. I have a picture he gave me, and I keep looking at it. Except that when I try to think of him any way except like the picture, I get stuck again.

Mom and I and the group lived in Venice in a big apartment. We lived near the canals, and I was real scared of them. Once Joey made me go down into them. I was hollering, I was so scared. Joey said we were going to dig for gold, and we dug and dug, and I got so interested I wasn't frightened anymore. Then right on top of where we were digging was a big pile of chocolates made to look like gold coins. Okay, Pirate Penelope, Joey said, this just goes to show that you don't have to be afraid of *anything*.

After we came to Massachusetts, Mom married Steve, and after that I got out of hand and that's why I'm in boarding school. Sometimes Mom talks to me about the days when we knew Joey. She says they weren't good days like I remember, that they were terrible. She's cracked.

I loved Joey more than I'm going to love anybody else, ever. One time after I just started school here, things were really going wrong. I was more mature than the other kids, and they didn't understand me or anything. They didn't believe me when I said David Angel was my best friend, so for Open House I asked Joey if he could come and he flew out from L.A. just for me, and he made Ray-O and Harry come with him. I asked him if maybe he could wear one of the white jackets he wore in concerts, and he put on the whole costume for me, make-up, gold chains, everything. All the kids mobbed him. Even old Black Angel asked for an autograph.

When I grow up I want to learn to play the tambourine like Mom used to. I'm going to leave this old boarding school and go back to Venice. I'll find another group to play with and a best friend exactly like Joey. Except he won't kill himself.

"You're the star."

David Angel looked up. There in front of him, he could see himself upon a stage, bowing and smiling, his arm steady as he held the microphone, the inside of his elbows empty of needle tracks. The cheering the cheering the cheering.

David Angel on the bed felt a pain wave ride his stomach. "Just look at him!" he exulted. "He's beautiful!"

And suddenly he could hear the bells—the sweet, gay bells which made everything all right. They chattered and laughed, filled the room. And Angel smiled.

. . . Bells at all his concerts. Going onstage, facing an audience of kids. The auditorium filled, it was like looking at a fluttering white fan. No one applauded; only rang bells and lighted candles. It was heaven, like being in the dome of the great cathedral. The music swimming and swirling around him.

. . . Winning the first gold record. Holding the prize in his arms, the photographers taking pictures with heavy clicks. The lights from the bulbs teasing and nipping at the record, ricocheting off the gold in the chains around his neck. Gold flashing uneasily from place to place. He made a little bow for the camera.

. . . A phone call from a television anchorwoman. *Incidence of addiction to PCP is so high in teen-agers this year.* He was asked to go on television and speak out against it. The kids will listen to him, the anchorwoman said. Going on television with tears in his eyes because he wanted all the kids to get off PCP. After the show, lying down on the couch in his dressing room, exhausted.

. . . Seven hundred pieces of fan mail a day. People sending him requests, blessings, heirlooms, threats. Trying to read each letter, and failing. He decided it would be fairer not to reply to any of them. They were in heaps all over the recording studio. He piled them into one hill, climbed to the top and slid to the floor. Three quarters of the way down, he nicked his arm on a spur which a woman from Wyoming had sent to him.

. . . The move in December up to Monterey. Searching and searching for the red A-frame house by the water. Days spent in handfuls of brine-smelling antique shops, looking for furniture. Buying each piece with a sense of destiny—though he had never laid eyes on them, feeling that they were stamped "his," so that anybody else must step back, not daring to touch.

He walked often to the cypress forest and sat for hours on the cold ground. He built a fire, its snapping red fabric against the sucked dry crepe of the trees. He understood why the early men worshiped fire. He sat until it was hard for him to stand. Staggering home on stiff, trembling legs.

The house had little furniture. He liked it that way. He found a great many books in the back of a closet and in the attic, and those he read at night—Saroyan, Oscar Wilde, and someone called Elizabeth. He ate soup in rhythm to the Pentangle's "Light Flight."

He looked down at his clothes one day and saw that they were tinged with gray. He rejoiced, for the sea had weathered him.

. . . It was early in the morning at the beginning of spring. He had finished breakfast, spilled some Rice Krispies onto the floor, and was scooping them up into the

palm of his hand. He heard a fox scrabbling in the garden.
He looked up. His hand grew cold and stiff. He realized he
was the happiest person upon the earth.

The walls in the red room pulsed like a great heartbeat.

David Angel blinked. Then he sat up and took a deep
breath, flinging his arms up into the air. "I remember," he
whispered. "I remember how it was. You didn't think I
could forget, did you?" He buried his head in the bedclothes.
"Don't you know that if I could, I'd turn the whole thing
around and make it the way it was then?"

He raised himself on one elbow and glared at the wall.
"Why? Because I can't, that's why," he snapped.

"Why can't I?" He was appalled. "Why can't I?" He
sprang from the bed. He felt strong and clear and angry.
"Why not? Why not? Come on, you crazy old walls! What
do you say we go a few rounds?"

Ducking and bobbing, Angel began to box against his
opponent. He feinted, drew back and threw the hardest
punch he could into the fabric-upholstered wall. There was
an obscene ripping sound, and David Angel watched in
amazement as the wall deflated into crumbling plaster of
Paris and shredded satin.

"Jesus Christ!" And David Angel laughed until he was
wheezing and his eyes teared so much he tried to wipe
them on the carpet. "And listen here, man," he warned the
rug, "don't you start talking to me too!"

He pressed his face to the floor and lay there for a long
time. At last he rolled over. "I can do it," he whispered.
"Sure I can. I can make everything just the way it used to
be—Goddamn! What am I saying? I'm gonna make it
better!"

And joy filled his face.

"Better!" he cried, as he ran downstairs in three jumps

and dashed along the hall. "Better!" he cried, spinning about on the slippery floor. "The songs I'm going to sing" —he picked up a statuette from a side table and caressed it— "the way I'm going to dance, the crowds I'm going to draw!" He took down one of his gold records from the wall and threw it like a Frisbee.

"Hell!" he cried. "A year from now I'll be using these things as paper plates."

Then David Angel realized he was starving. He reeled into the kitchen. The shelves were scrubbed, but there was no food on them. The refrigerator door was open. There was no food inside, only three bottles of Coke. The last cook had quit two days before, saying it was bad for her morale to cook for a person who never ate. She must have cleaned everything out. Angel wondered why Bella hadn't told him what had happened. He guessed she had been afraid. Bella was the best maid he had ever had. She really cared for him, he could tell, and he vowed to give her a big raise the next day. He smiled, anticipating her joyous gratitude. And maybe he would also do something really great for Bella's nephew. He could call up Monique James at Universal. Sure! That's what he'd do. Monique would make the kid a star, and then Bella would always see that there was something good to eat in the refrigerator.

All at once David Angel felt so weak he doubted he could make it to the Premier Market a few blocks away. He searched hopelessly through the shining empty shelves above the refrigerator and beside the dishwasher. He looked in the garbage can. At last, in the closet with the vacuum-cleaner bags, he found two stale bagels. Swallowed with a little vodka, they wouldn't taste too bad.

A few bites steadied him. He felt his pulse flow on. He took the bagels into the living room and ate them before the large glass window. Everything looked tender and dewy outside. Julio, the gardener, was very conscientious. Perhaps he'd give him a raise, too.

David Angel did something he hadn't done for a long time—he watched the house across the street. He really liked doing that. Why was he always too busy to do the things he liked?

The house was the shabbiest one on the block, painted green with pink trim. There was a station wagon in the driveway instead of the regulation Mercedes or Cadillac Seville. David Angel always liked to watch the car being unloaded of its groceries or fishing equipment or picnic basket.

As he watched now, David Angel was amused to see the oldest boy—Frankie, his family called him—out mowing the lawn; nobody mowed his own lawn in Beverly Hills. Frankie was listening to a rock station on his transistor radio as he worked. David Angel smiled to think of what the boy would do if he knew who was living right across the street.

It was five forty-five. Beverly Hills was quiet. The children were home from school and ballet class. The women were drawing their scented baths in anticipation of their husbands' return. The cooks were making radish roses for cocktail trays.

Rodeo Drive was quiet also. But the young boy across the street, halfway through the lawn now, turned his radio up louder, indulging himself in a fresh infusion of sound. The first few bars of a song began to play. Frankie didn't recognize it, because it was a golden oldie from five years back. But when David Angel heard the melody he leaped from the couch and walked quickly out of the room.

The piano introduction was still playing when he reached the stairs. But by the time he climbed to the fifth step the lyrics had begun to sweep over the green lawns, and he was beaten. He sank down on the stairs.

When you were young
Your friends called you a fairy queen
And no one thought to disagree.
Did they?

Rebecca . . .

Rebecca Monroe

All through the night, I was remembering the touch of Joey's hair against the palm of my hand. I lay beside Bill, awake until dawn. Bill had gone to sleep angry with me. He could not understand why I had cried so hard at the news of a stranger's death. I didn't tell him that Joey was not a stranger.

This morning I whispered something that I have wanted to tell Joey for a long time—that though we have not seen each other for thirteen years, not a day of my life has gone by in which I have not thought of him.

The house is quiet. Everyone is asleep. I am in the kitchen, drinking coffee, pretending that once again I am the fifteen-year-old girl Joey Danzig fell in love with.

When I was fifteen, I was small, blisteringly shy, pale and ugly, at least to my own accusing and disappointed eyes. I held myself eternally up to a goddess in a song, someone tall and tanned and young and lovely. I lived in a big house on a hill in Old Westbury, New York. The house was filled with soft colors, old faded fabrics and a thousand other things I loved.

I didn't have any friends. I was the smartest girl in the tenth grade, as well as the shyest and the most ridiculous. When I did manage to latch on to a friend, I clung so tightly that the friend went away. And again I would be reduced to eating lunch in the deserted locker room. Anything to keep people from finding out that I was alone.

My real life took over when I came home from school every afternoon. It was then that I read, that I wrote in

my diary, that I put my arms around my body and danced
to the tunes Mummy played on the piano.

Mummy was the most beautiful, the most poised, the
most delicate princess in the world. But seeing her arrayed
in her perfections made me freeze beside her, turn to dust
inside.

I guess I needed to meet Joey.

Joey and I first saw each other that December, at my cousin
Merilee's Christmas party. I hated parties and didn't
want to go to this one, but Mummy made me go. She always made me go.

She dressed me up in my brown velvet dress, and I knew
all the other girls would be in jeans and sweaters. Mummy
knew it, too, but she liked upholding certain standards.

The party was nice. Ice cream and cake were served, and
I pretended we were all little children again. But when the
band began to play, everybody grew up and started to
dance. The shadows the dancers cast into the dimly lighted
room were monstrous. I fled into a corner, taking a bowl
of peanuts from one of the buffet tables with me. I
started eating peanut after peanut. If anybody should come
by to ask me to dance, I wanted him to know that I was
too busy eating to say yes.

Then I began to listen to the band. They were playing
a slow and gentle song, very like the songs the boy in my
head sang to me at night. Becky, he would chant, you are
beautiful, you are beautiful. I had not met him yet, had
been sure I would meet him in college. But when I looked
up from the peanuts, well, there he was.

My boy. With a white face, straight dark hair. His eyes
were black and alive, and he smiled as he sang.

For a moment it seemed as if he were smiling at me. I
couldn't breathe.

I watched him from my corner for the rest of the party.

In the breaks between songs, he drank glasses of punch, but he didn't look at me again. Afterward, when all the guests were leaving, he unplugged his guitar and jumped down from the platform.

Bye, Joey, one of the other members of the group called after him.

I came home, drunk on peanuts. I told Mummy I had had the most wonderful time of my life. She laughed and said she was glad she had made me go to the party. Then when I went to bed that night and the boy in my head sang out *Rebecca*, I answered back, *Joey*.

All winter long I thought about him. I dreamed up ways of finding him again, all the time fearing that if we did meet, he wouldn't even remember me. I thought about him so much that he took on almost mythic proportions, and I started disbelieving that he was even real. Yet everywhere I went, I looked for him.

It was a sad winter because my darling Grandpa died.

And then in March, I was sixteen. Mummy wanted me to have a birthday party exactly like the one she had had when she was sixteen, when all her boyfriends, promised that she would finally kiss them on that day, lined up around the block to claim their embraces.

I dreaded having a party, but Mummy looked so excited about it that I just couldn't let her down.

People said that Mummy gave the best parties on Long Island, and I was happy to let her arrange mine. Fresh flowers with ribbons were ordered for the tables, a tent was hired for the back yard, and caterers planned the menu. But Mummy made the dessert herself. She labored for two days, baking and freezing little coconut lambs, just because they were my favorite.

The last thing to be arranged was the band, and Mummy asked me if I knew any musicians. I froze up and couldn't speak. Mummy thought I was just bored, and she got very angry at me. She said I was spoiled and selfish, and that I hadn't helped at all with the preparations. I felt terrible.

Then, Tuesday afternoon, the sixteenth of March, I was in my bedroom doing some homework when Mummy buzzed on the intercom and told me to come downstairs —that the musicians she had hired for my party were here.

I went downstairs into the living room, and there was Joey.

I thought the sky had fallen on my head. I couldn't lift up my neck, and there were red cinders in front of my eyes.

Joey was sitting on the sofa with another boy from his band. Mummy was between them. The cinders left my eyes, and finally I could see again.

"So everything's settled," Mummy was saying. "Field Brothers will supply the uniforms—you are expected for a fitting on Tuesday at four o'clock. And I want to give you a down payment. Twenty dollars apiece should be fair."

She took two bills from her purse. "Here, Joey," she said, handing him one. "And the other for Harry."

"Forty dollars!" Harry cried. "That's enough to buy a mandolin!"

"And I'll learn to play it in time for Rebecca's birthday," Joey added politely.

Mummy smiled. When she turned and saw I was in the room, she came over and kissed me.

"I've got an appointment now," she told me. "But the boys are welcome to stay as long as they want."

I was so sick at my stomach I could hardly stand.

I asked Joey and Harry how they were, and they said they were fine. That took up two seconds, but then nobody said anything more. I asked if anybody would like a Coke, but they said no. Another two seconds.

Then Joey smiled at me, wonderfully, easily, just as he had at Merilee's party. "Harry," he drawled, "I think I saw a pinball game in the next room. Why don't you go and see if you can get any replays." His eyes sparkled a little bit. "Would that be all right with you, Rebecca?"

"Oh, fine," I said weakly.

Harry left. Joey and I were sitting across from each other. I picked up a crystal vase. In its prisms I could see he was still smiling.

"I saw you at Merilee Marks's party," he said. "I've looked for you ever since. You're so pretty."

So pretty! I dropped the vase, flowers and all. Joey helped me pick them up, and he mopped the spilled water with the table cloth. We sat down again. I felt so shy that I couldn't raise my head to look at him, but finally I did, and the Rebecca his eyes mirrored was tall and tanned and young and lovely.

"I see you like to celebrate holidays," Joey said, looking around. "You've got an Easter egg out."

I blurted out that it wasn't an Easter egg, but just a souvenir from Mexico. Then, afraid I had hurt his feelings, I said, "But I love Easter eggs. I saw the most wonderful one last week, a big chocolate egg with little sugar people inside. But Mummy wouldn't let me buy it. She said it cost more than it was worth."

Joey seemed interested. He asked other questions about me. It wasn't awkward at all; he even laughed a few times. And he made me feel that I was the most fascinating person in the world.

Harry came sauntering back into the room and announced he had gotten two replays on the pinball machine. "And I think we'd better be going now," he added to Joey. "I want to buy that mandolin before the music store closes. Let me hold on to your twenty dollars in case you lose it."

But Joey said he'd rather hold on to it himself. Harry shook my hand, saying he'd be seeing me again at my party. Joey also said goodbye, but he didn't mention seeing

me again. That made me very depressed and afraid. Then
he reached out and pressed something thin and crinkly into
my hand. It was the twenty-dollar bill Mummy had given
him.

"This is for you," Joey whispered. "I want you to buy
the chocolate egg with the sugar people inside."

I called Joey up on the phone that night. It took the
whole evening to get up my nerve, and when Joey answered
the phone, his voice was thick with sleep.

"Hello," I stammered.

"Rebecca," he said, sighing. "Next time, don't wait so
long to call."

It is Saturday morning now. I see by the calendar that
it has been a month since Joey died. I go into the den and
play one of his records. I have chosen the album carefully.
The last song on the first side is called "Rebecca." It is
my daughter Karen's favorite. "Mummy," she once said
to me, "this song is called 'Rebecca,' and that's your
name. Isn't that funny?"

It was the first song he ever wrote for me. We were walking along the beach together. It was very windy, and
sheets of hair kept covering my face.

"Hey, I wrote a song yesterday," Joey said. "Want to
hear it?"

> When you were young,
> Your friends called you a fairy queen
> And no one thought to disagree.
> Did they, Rebecca?
>
> You met a man,
> And married with a smile bouquet
> And with a rose and prayer book.
> Loving, Rebecca.

Your son was born
You held him and
Said "Wear my smile
When you're a man."

All flowers fade.
Why couldn't it have been a rose
Which died that spring, instead of you?
Fading, Rebecca.

Your boy grew up,
His smile admired by everyone;
But no one saw his smile to be
Your smile. Becky.

We sat down on the sand.
   "Am I really going to die young?" I asked him.
   "No."
   "And get married and have a son."
   "Of course."
   I couldn't breathe suddenly, and I felt very anxious. "But who am I going to marry?"
   Joey drew a diamond on the sand, then scooped it up and handed it to me. I took it, laughing, and he kissed me. My hands were full of diamond.
   Joey and I were together as much as we could manage that spring. I broke dates, cut classes—even lied to Mummy so that Joey and I could see each other. He seemed to need me so much. That was a little frightening to me. I was always afraid that by some clumsiness or thoughtlessness I would let him down. So when he needed to be with me, I was always there.
   Joey was different from anybody I had ever known. I was used to boys born into a world of wealth and rigid expectations. Sure, in high school there might be a little marijuana in the men's room, a little chatter about joining the Peace Corps, maybe even burning a draft card. But

these boys always came through. The day they were sixteen they appeared at school proudly driving their new Corvettes with a birthday bow on the steering wheel. And when they reached draft age, all they had to do was choose a college. Without exception they threw aside philosophy at Santa Cruz for pre-med at Stanford. And so they disappeared, and came back four years later, as their fathers.

But Joey was my vagabond minstrel, too filled with his own motion and excitement and information to even listen to the information other people might think he needed. He would talk to me about music, Mahler, the Beatles, rhythm, a certain brand of guitar, John Renbourn, a *Lied* he had heard the day before, the Doors album he was going to buy me the following week. He'd get so excited he made us both laugh. When I was with Joey, I would feel light-headed, like Alice in Wonderland, soaring up and up until I grew too large for my little house. Yet, Joey always protected me too, and where my interests were concerned, he could come straight down to earth. Of all the things he ever did for me, I think the one that touched me most was his teaching me how to drive.

And I think about his laugh—that warming, rich laugh that no one else could ever have.

At the parties Mummy gave in my honor occasionally, Joey never looked like anybody else there. The other boys would be in dark suits. Joey once arrived wearing a clean but wrinkled work shirt and a checkered bow tie, his hair parted in the middle like Scott Fitzgerald's. Mummy was absolutely aghast, but I loved it. I didn't quite know who Joey was pretending to be, but that didn't matter. Looking back, I don't think that Joey even knew he looked different from the other boys.

I loved him so much.

Joey took me to his house a few times, but they were not comfortable evenings. His grandfather kept asking me how rich Daddy was, but his grandmother was very nice when I spilled onion dip onto the carpet. I was a little afraid of her because she seemed so wise.

Joey seemed to want me to learn everything about him in that one evening. He showed me the room he had lived his life in, showed me all his old games and toys. He took me to the garage where he and Harry had first played music together. Joey, who could never stand still, was flicking at some chipped paint on the wall as he told me the story. I said he should leave the paint alone, because when the state made this garage into a museum, they would want the original color on the wall. I think he was pleased, because he stood still for once and looked at me with the smallest smile of wonder.

He loved to walk. It seems to me that we were always walking—walking along deserted boardwalks, walking under freeway bridges, walking in yards outlined by rusty barbed wire. I have an image of Joey, the corners of his mouth drawn down with concentration, carefully stepping over broken bottles and the pulp of newspapers.

We spent a lot of time at the playground near my house. We set off every Saturday morning, and we chased all the little kids away. The carousel was Joey's favorite ride. Sleigh bells were strung around it, and when he pushed the platform with his foot, the bells would start the cheeky peppering that Joey always said sounded like little laughing children. And we would lie back for a million revolutions, touching the dampness of each other's arms. Motion made him happy.

And he felt tenderly toward sunsets because he felt tenderly toward anything that was dying.

Something else Joey and I did together—we made each other sad. We never fought, but Joey got depressed so often. I couldn't understand why, but all his gaiety and hope would tumble away, and he would cry out that he was just fooling himself. He seemed to think, in those black moods, that we were not meant to be together and that only by having a great success in his music did he stand a chance of outwitting the fates and having me for himself. Vainly I would try to reassure him, calling out loudly that I would love him just as much if he were a drunkard on the streets, but he would just shake his head despairingly and leave. His grandmother told me that when Joey got sad like this, he would play his guitar all afternoon without letting up, until the strings broke and his hands were bleeding.

All this made a nervous wreck out of me. No matter how comforting my arguments to Joey had been and how much I meant what I had said, the moment Joey would leave me, I would be shrouded in a strange fear. It was so odd. When I think back on those days I picture myself walking within a cloud of my own making, as if the anxieties hidden inside me had forced their way out through my pores and glowed around my head like an aura, coloring everything I saw. When I chipped a dish, it meant that Joey did not love me anymore. If he couldn't talk for long on the telephone, I was chilled all day. And over my head broke a constant wave of things I meant to have said to him, wanted to say, couldn't say. And I always felt he would be taken from me, that we were not meant to be together, as he said. Every time we kissed goodbye, I clung to him as though he were going off to war. I knew I was never going to see him again.

And then, later at night, his dark mood gone, Joey would telephone me—normal, cheerful, inventing luscious scenarios that were always about our beautiful endless future together.

I would press the phone as hard as I could against my ear, and try to shut out everything but the safety of his voice.

He said we would be married, the moment I finished high school. We would move to California, to Monterey, to the red A-frame house we had once seen in a magazine. He would write music, and I would run a nursery school. In the afternoons we would go walking down along the beach. There was no doubt that he was going to be the greatest success of the decade, and we would have heaps of money from his records. For our first anniversary, he was going to buy me a painting I had loved in the 57th Street Gallery—Berthe Morisot's "Le Volant." Joey would put it above his piano, and the little girl on the wall would be his guardian angel. And in a few years we would have a child. Her name would be Karen. And she would grow up to be so incredibly happy. Like we were.

Such happy plans. It was sad that I could never really believe in them. Looking back, I am amazed at Joey and myself. That we could have been haunted by these misgivings, in the midst of the love we gave each other, was a feat of sensitivity worthy of the Princess and the Pea. And yet, once I sensed that there was danger, I was too stupid or too lazy or too blind to recognize where it lay. Joey was smarter. He saw. He knew my mother hated him.

I don't know why she did. He was so sweet, so smart. He loved me. With Mummy he was extra polite, but sometimes he spoke in a voice that boomed with feigned culture because he was nervous and wanted to make a good impression. Perhaps that was the reason Mummy's neck would flush a dark red whenever she saw him, the reason she would address him in her brightest, extra loud tones, as though she were speaking to a foreigner or a cripple.

About a month after Joey and I started going together, Mummy came to me, very serious. "Becky," she said, "I have always tried to teach you kindness, and I want you to know what a cruel thing you're doing, leading little Joey on like this. If you're not careful, he could get ideas about you, Becky, and you could hurt him very badly. But you're right in thinking he needs to know a nice girl—someone who could give him a little polish, make him a little more presentable. Cook's daughter is very sweet—just the right age for him, too. Wouldn't it be fun to set them up together? What an incurable matchmaker I am!"

When I didn't set Joey up with Cook's daughter but kept him myself, Mummy never said anything against it— but when I came home from a date, she would always be unreachable, locked in her room. Napping, the maid told me, even though I could hear the slapping of solitaire cards. And we never went shopping together any more, or sang harmony in the car. In May I was in the school play, and Mummy, who had formerly coached my every line, didn't even come to see the performance. And one afternoon in June when I was over at Joey's house, Mummy called there and told me to come home immediately—I had forgotten to feed my poodle. I asked her if just this once the maid could do it for me; I explained that Joey's grandmother had gone to a lot of trouble making dinner, and that it would be rude for me just to leave. But Mummy said she would give Sambo away if I didn't come home and feed him now. So Joey drove me home.

In the beginning, before I realized that Mummy's behavior had anything to do with Joey, I grieved for her and brought her little presents to try and cheer her up. Then when I realized who was upsetting her so, I got angry at Joey, accusing him of being disrespectful and ill-mannered. Then later I gave up and did nothing. I told myself that I knew, I absolutely knew, everything would be all right. Joey was so wonderful that Mummy simply had to come around some day; maybe the day Joey and I flew her to Europe in our private jet.

Now that I have a daughter of my own, I realize how

hard those months must have been on Mummy too. Even at that time I sensed that she did what she did out of love for me, out of not wanting me to make a mistake. But I let her walk over me and I can't forget that. I let her walk over my heart.

We were on our way to New York on the first day of September. It was a beautiful afternoon, and we had the car windows open. We had just stopped to buy apples at a roadside stand. We were munching and singing "Down in the Valley" for the first time in months. It all felt so wonderful, and I was so grateful that things were back to normal that I touched Mummy's arm and confided to her a secret. That the day after I finished high school, Joey and I were going to be married.

Sometimes in dreams I still hear the shriek of brakes as Mummy pulled the car over to the side of the road.

I was locked in my room for two days. The maids who brought me meals wouldn't look at me. Mummy came in the first night to talk to me. She held me pityingly in her arms and said that she had longed for me to confide in her for so many months. She knew the suffering I had gone through, she said. She didn't have to be told that Joey was emotionally retarded. She had known, almost from the first time she met him, that he was a very sick boy. She said that every time she looked at him, she wanted to slap him for hurting her baby Becky. Everyone had noticed the change in me, she said. The maids, her friends—even the hairdresser had asked her why Rebecca was so thin and unhappy lately.

I tried to speak, but she cut me off. She explained to me that Joey was after my money. She said he was a liar. She told me Joey was dangerous—unbalanced.

But she hadn't wanted to step in. She knew how important it was to let other people make their own mistakes. But it had gone on long enough now. It must be stopped. I was not going to marry Joey. I was never going to see him again.

I told Mummy I was going to kill myself. She told me to be her guest—that I would find sleeping pills on the top shelf of the medicine chest. I clutched her knees, but she pushed me away and left the room.

I got to a phone the next afternoon and called Joey. I yearned to be with him so much that I felt my body disappearing and traveling down the phone line.

Joey asked me if I loved him. He asked if I would do as he told me to, even though it would mean hurting my mother. I said I would do anything.

At midnight, Joey put the ladder up against my wall and came to get me. I was prepared for it, and yet I was shocked that he was there. My mind had done little else all day but imagine his taps on the window and my response. So many were the phantom taps, and so many the flights down the ladder, that their significance had blurred and softened. The real taps were so much louder. A thousand choices were narrowed down and simplified into the sound.

I took a few steps toward Joey, then I saw it was impossible for me to go any farther. Joey tapped again on the glass. I looked around at the suitcase I had packed, at the gloves on my hands. I think I had known all along I couldn't do it.

Joey's face was white on the other side of the glass. I saw that he had flowers for me in his hand. He was trembling so that I wanted to open the window, but I was afraid that a thousand changes would rush in with the night air and make me a different person. All courage and strength ran out of me. I just wanted to be a baby again. I started to cry until I could not see Joey's face anymore, and then

I jumped up and pounded on my bedroom door until Mummy unlocked it and I fell into her arms.

I keep reminding myself that I was only sixteen.

That was the last time I saw Joey. He moved to California soon afterward. He wrote me a few letters, which Mummy scanned first and then graciously handed over to me. He said he understood why I hadn't gone with him, and that he would be coming back to marry me as soon as he became a star.

But so much happens. I met Bill at college. He was a wonderful boy, and Mummy said he was the man she'd always dreamed of for me. It was a relief, a happy ending for all concerned.

Bill and I have been married for almost nine years. Our life is calm and certain, and there are no misgivings, no shadows. Sometimes I look back on how I used to dread growing up, and it seems a strange thing to be frightened of.

But I grow disturbed when I think that I am not the same person I was. The night air changed me after all, I suppose. Or perhaps I never was the girl that Joey thought he knew.

But it is a comfort to remember him. My sensitive, passionate, loyal Joey.

I don't know why he never came to see me again. I don't know why he committed suicide either. If I had climbed down the ladder that night, would it have been any different?

The heart I wear now is filled with Bill and my child. But there is a secret spring, and if it is touched the right way, it will open to reveal another heart, slightly smaller, slightly redder. Joey would recognize it, I am sure.

Ray-O Hall

Since Joey died, I walk around my room every night, thinking of things to tell him. No big secrets. Just little things, a funny story, maybe. Harry was the friend I was closest to, but I admired Joey more, I guess because he didn't swear or drink as much as Harry and me. He was just better, cleaner. I remember a lot of things; playing music in the old garage, through California and Deirdre, meeting Randolph, making it. We went to a lot of parties, played a few good jokes. And, most important, there was our music. I remember how crazy we were after those first concerts, fired up by the sound of ourselves. Especially Joey—when he left the stage he would be wet through, and his eyes would smoke and burn like klieg lights.

I met Joey and Harry on the same day, when we were all fourteen. They were sitting next to me at a school track meet, and the marching band was so awful that I got into conversation with these two guys. Joey told me they were musicians, trying to get a group together. When I said I was a drummer, Joey and Harry got up from the bleachers, dragged me out of the auditorium, and made me audition for them then and there in the music room. Afterward, when they asked me to join their group, I said I couldn't. I wouldn't tell them why, but Joey kept pressing me, and finally I told them I had epilepsy. Harry and Joey looked very serious. I felt really down, because as usual all the doors were closing the moment I said the magic word. Then Joey started grinning at me. "That's okay, Ray-O," he said.

"We wouldn't have it any other way. If you ever have a fit onstage, you'll be the wildest drummer in town!"

That got me for Joey, and the rest of his life I never felt any differently about him.

Everyone who cared about Joey has their theory about what made him kill himself. It's depressing to listen to all the things that have gone wrong in the life of someone you love. I have my theory, too. Not a theory, really, just a day when I saw Joey very unhappy. I've never talked about it, as it's very personal, but it would be a relief to tell somebody—somebody who cared about Joey the way I did.

It started back when Joey was sixteen. Our group played the wedding/bar mitzvah circuit in those days. At a Christmas party, Joey saw a girl eating a bowl of peanuts, and he was very attracted to her. Her name was Rebecca, and for months he tried different ways of getting to meet her. Finally, by chance, her mother called Harry up, wanting our group to play at Rebecca's Sweet Sixteen party. It just about killed Joey, he was so excited—and when he and Rebecca finally got to know each other, they fell in love right away.

Harry didn't think much of Rebecca. He used to call her "Redwood" for an unflattering reason I don't remember. I liked Rebecca, all right. She was always very nice to me, baking me chocolate-chip cookies and trying to set me up with girls. And she seemed to love Joey very much. I used to watch her when she heard him sing, and she couldn't breathe sometimes, she got so nervous.

Joey came to Harry and me one day and told us he had asked Rebecca to marry him. We were all pretty shook up. Joey was our age, but here he was taking a big leap away from us, doing something that belonged to the adult world.

A few months later, when we finished high school, we were all preoccupied with the future of our music. Harry decided that there was no chance for the group on Long Island, and that if we wanted fame, we had to go to California. Harry's folks agreed right away—in fact, I think they suggested the idea. Harry got kind of difficult to live with, sometimes. I was pretty excited about the move, seeing as how I was about ready to drift away from home, but my mom, she cried two days and two nights. But finally she let me go. Joey was the last one told, because Harry was scared to even broach the subject. He was afraid Joey would refuse to go. I knew Joey cared more about the group than that, but when Harry finally told him, he did refuse. He got very upset into the bargain, saying how dare we think he could leave Rebecca? When Harry and I were at the bus terminal that Friday, scared out of our wits, saying goodbye to our folks and getting ready to board the Greyhound, Joey came flying along the platform. Harry said, "At least he's come to say goodbye," but Joey had his suitcase with him. He didn't tell us why he had decided to come along, after all, but it wasn't too hard to guess that it had something to do with Rebecca.

Those early years in California did Joey a lot of good, I think. Being on his own toughened him up some. He got more forceful; he once beat up a guy who tried to pick his pocket. And all this confidence went to his music. Still, it kind of makes you lonely to see someone you care about, changing.

Those early years were enough to do it to anybody. We shared an apartment with a somewhat weird lady called Deirdre, and her little girl, Penelope, but after a while no one had a job and we got pretty hungry. Then we found this fleabag proposition called Rocker's Pier down in Venice. They wanted our group to play. It was a drug joint; it didn't

seem like there was one customer in there who could sit
up straight. Some people in there I could really have been
afraid of. But the ones who stayed conscious appreciated our
music, though only God knows how. After one of the cus-
tomers wanted to get it on with Deirdre's little girl, Joey
made us quit and we found another bar, Off the Farm.
There was a rotten spot on the stage, and one night during
"In My Life," Joey jumped around too hard and disappeared up to his knees into the Pacific Ocean. We moved on
again and got a job at the Bread and Butter in Hollywood.
This was the best yet; the audience had a little more class,
and there was this cook, Thomas, who took a fancy to Joey,
said he looked just like St. Sebastian. Thomas used to fix us
all real spicy tostados on the sly. We stayed at the Bread
and Butter almost a year and it was a good thing, because
we met Randolph near the end of it, and that changed the
whole tune.

In all that time we met a lot of girls, and there were quite
a few Harry and I went with, but it was obvious Joey wasn't
much interested. We asked him about it, and finally he admitted he was still waiting for Rebecca. Harry and I started
laughing, because we were both thinking the same thing,
that maybe Joey was not as changed as we had thought.
Once Joey told us his secret, he let us in on all his plans,
how when we were the number one group in America, he
was going to buy her a red house in Monterey, and a painting of a girl in a pink dress to put over his piano, then go
back to Long Island and marry her. I thought that was quite
touching, especially as I never thought we would be number one. It was strange that Joey never wrote Rebecca any
letters, and never received any from her.

Joey wrote a lot of songs those first two years called
"Rebecca." It caused a lot of confusion, so finally Harry
said, "Why don't you be like Beethoven and number them

'The First Rebecca,' 'The Second Rebecca' . . . ?" Joey laughed, and soon he started giving his songs other names. But I knew "Rebecca" was always the real title.

When our first and second albums took off, Joey finally bought his red house in Monterey. I used to love visiting him there. There wasn't much furniture, but it was very relaxing.

We always said we were going to get a lot of work done there, but we never did. We just walked around, looking at the little shops. We visited the house Robert Louis Stevenson lived in just before leaving for the Samoan islands to die. Joey and I said we wished we could have all been friends. We liked the way he looked and the things he owned.

At night we stayed up and read in front of the fire. Joey found a lot of books up in the attic and in the back of one of the closets; some were very quaint.

Spending those times with Joey really made me appreciate him. I even started thinking maybe I'd buy the house next door. Joey and I looked it over once, a nice white house. A bit steep in price, but what the hell.

In the first four years we were in California, we never went home for a visit to New York, but after we released our third LP, Randolph said he thought it was time to tour the country. Harry and I said that would be great. Joey didn't say anything, but he started playing fit to burst on the guitar. I knew he was thinking about Rebecca.

None of us could have guessed what kind of hell touring was going to be. A lot of fans, mainly girls, say to me how much fun it must have been to explore the country, but I give them a cross-eyed kind of look and just smile.

We did thirty cities in six weeks, but the only things we got to see were the insides of airports and hotels and concert halls. Up too early every morning, and then we all had to smile for the interviewers. *Do you like biscuits? Do you like blondes? Do you like Montana?*

All day long, until we had to leave, driving from one TV or radio station to another. *Do you have any interesting birthmarks? Do you believe in God? Do you like Seattle?* Oh, yes. Lots of fun. Lunch, with more interviews. Around this time every day Joey would start to feel the pressure and he'd excuse himself and be sick. But he couldn't lie down and disappoint all the interviewers who were waiting. *Do you have a drug habit? What bands do you listen to? Do you want to have children?* Lots of noise, crowds of kids wherever we went. Endless rehearsals; all the songs began to sound the same. A lot of tension; fights with the sound man, with Harry, the publicity agent, Randolph. Then usually I got to nap for an hour, because I was only the drummer, but Joey and Harry had to stay on their feet, answering questions. Real fun. Trying to get out for a little fresh air late in the afternoon and being followed by a pack of kids. In St. Louis, being hauled to the Chief of Police for being drunk and disorderly. Dinner, which Joey was too nervous to eat, accompanied by more interviews. *Do you think your music will last? Do you like Minneapolis?* Sometimes Joey would be sick after dinner, too. Then the sound check. Waiting in the wings for the audience to settle down. Every night we had to appease them by throwing out the same old sacrifice—ourselves. Something went wrong every time. Joey losing his voice, Harry's mike going dead, the lights not working, an earthquake in Sacramento, a fire in Albuquerque. The Grand Theatres, the Shuberts, the Palladiums. And in Chicago, the thing I had always been afraid of happened. We were in such a rush that day that I forgot to take my pills. During "Going Home" I started to throw a fit. Joey looked over at me, grabbed the drumsticks from my hand and pushed me over to a chair in the wings. He really cared about me, I know it.

Late at night after the concerts was the hardest time of all. If we were staying in town, it was bad enough fighting through the crowds to get to the car, and the kids outside the hotel kept us awake a few more hours. But if we were traveling, we had to spend the night in trains and planes. Halfway through the tour, Joey lost his nerve and even during the shortest flight he thought we were going to crash and burn.

Lots of fun, believe you me.

Around about Amarillo I really began to worry about Joey. I thought maybe he was starting to crack up. So while Harry and Randolph went out to dinner or to meet girls after the show, I got in the habit of staying with Joey in the hotel room. Sometimes I read to him, like we sometimes did in Monterey. Of course, I also read all the reviews and stories in the local newspapers about the group. That seemed to relax him, everyone writing great things about us. And if a bad review came along, well, Joey didn't get to hear that one.

I remember there was one story about a little girl from California whose father was sending her all over the country so she could go to David Angel concerts. Joey got all excited and told me to save the clipping because he wanted to send the little girl some house seats, but I lost it.

Then about the time we got to Tampa, Joey was suddenly full of energy. He wasn't even afraid of the planes now. He kept talking about going back home to New York and realizing his dreams after all these years; driving up to Rebecca's house, a star at last. And when we were in Chicago, we went to a big, quiet gallery, and this real cute saleslady showed Joey the painting of the girl in the pink dress he had spoken about getting a long time before. He'd hired somebody to find it for him, and when he saw it he said wrap it up. When I got a look at the price, I almost fell into another fit. But Joey had made up his mind he had to have it, and guess which sucker finally ended up loaning him some money?

You wouldn't believe what went on between Joey and this painting. He wouldn't play it safe and keep it in the hotel vaults—no, he had to have it with him every second of the day, in his bedroom, in taxis, in the concert halls, and he just kept looking at it.

Finally one rainy night we flew from Boston to La Guardia Airport in New York. When we touched down, Joey grabbed me around the neck. He was so happy. I didn't blame him. He treated our entourage to rooms in the Plaza Hotel that night. I was in the suite with him, and before I went to bed he came in and told me that the next morning he was going to see Rebecca. None of us wanted to tell him that maybe she wasn't living there anymore. I understood him wanting to stay up and talk about her, but at four o'clock I got so tired I fell asleep. At six Joey was on my bed, shaking me awake. He asked me if I would come with him. He was so nervous that I didn't think he could handle it alone—so I dragged myself into my jeans.

It took the limo over an hour to get from Manhattan to Old Westbury, and Joey was shaking the whole time. He pointed out street names, houses that he remembered. When we finally rolled up Rebecca's driveway, I thought Joey was going to have a heart attack. He was holding the painting, but I told him I'd take care of it for him; after all, I still had a ten-thousand-dollar investment in it.

The car stopped. The big house on the hill looked just

the same. Joey shook my hand and said, "Wait here; we'll be out in a few minutes." He rang the bell, the door was opened, he went inside. The driver kept the car running, and we talked about sports. But it got to be fifteen minutes, twenty minutes, and Joey and Rebecca didn't come out. I told the driver to shut off the engine, and I went to the house and knocked on the door. Mrs. Madison, Rebecca's mother, let me in right away. When I first met her she had been about the most beautiful woman I ever saw, but I must have been wrong. No one could change that much. She was all dressed up in some outfit that looked like a suit of armor, and her hair didn't move from all the hairspray. And would you believe eyes like blue granite? There was no looseness about her anywhere. I stuttered when I asked her where I could find Joey and Rebecca. She gave me this icy smile and pointed up the stairs. I mumbled thanks and started up. Then, on the stairwell, I saw a painting—a big portrait of Rebecca with a lot of white lace around her face and holding a bouquet of flowers with little ribbons trailing from them. I took the stairs four at a time and threw open the door of Rebecca's old room at the top of the steps.

The room was just the same as I remembered it, except Rebecca wasn't there. There was just Joey lying on her bed with his eyes closed. I touched him and he took so long to open his eyes that I got scared. But when he did, I wished that he'd kept them closed. His eyes were dead—just plain dead. I pulled him to his feet and led him downstairs. I don't think he even heard Rebecca's mother when she said that it would please her granddaughter to have an autographed record from David Angel. But I did, and I hated the bitch.

Joey didn't say a word on the drive back to Manhattan. This time I was the one who was shivering the whole way.

The concert that night was the best I think I ever heard

Joey give. After the show Randolph threw a party to celebrate the end of the tour. I was worried about Joey and
looked around for him, but I couldn't find him because
it was so crowded. When I asked if anyone had seen him,
Barney, one of the backup musicians, said he had been there
earlier. Barney looked like he had something on his mind.
I finally gave up looking for Joey and went back to the
hotel. I couldn't sleep, though. At four o'clock Randolph
called saying that Joey was in the hospital. He had bought
some stuff off Barney and had collapsed at a bar near the
hotel. I took the limo to Mount Sinai.

Joey was lying in a small white bed. I told him he was
lucky they got to him in time. Randolph told him never to
do it again. Joey looked up at us and said, "Never do what
again?," as if he really didn't know. I felt sick inside, because I'd always thought he was the cleanest and finest one
around.

He was never the same again. He sometimes seemed to
enjoy things, and he still did some good music. But all the
same, he started to slip. And kept slipping, and now he's
dead.

Uppers, downers, side-to-siders. David Angel found himself standing by the bar, pushing colored pills into his mouth. He was clenching the barstool so tightly that when he fell backward the barstool followed, clattering behind him. "I'm dreaming, just dreaming."

He did not remember getting off the floor or walking to the bar. That scared him. He poured vodka into one of the glasses April had given him for his twenty-fourth birthday, but the glass slipped and shattered on the sophisticated black surface of the bar. David Angel hit the fragments with his fist, and streaks of blood marbled his hands.

"Goddamn you, April," he said. He poured vodka over his hands to clean the cuts, and the pain made him scream out. "Why the hell doesn't somebody get me out of here?"

April Loeb Danzig

The Star and *Midnight* really paid some bread for all those stories about Presley after he died, so I've been working on one about Joey. I need the money.

My name is April Loeb Danzig. I was born and raised in Palm Desert, which is a little town down the highway from Palm Springs in California. I sort of liked it there, but there wasn't a lot to do. My pop helped grow dates, which is what everyone does in the desert. He was gone all day, though, and whenever there was something needed to be done, I had to do it: like the locusts came one summer and piled up on the porch and got in the cracks of the doors, and I had to sweep them away, even though their bodies crunched like crazy Martians crying.

Pop had two grown sons from the time of his first marriage, and they came to visit us about once a month. I don't feel like telling what they did to me, but they should be sent to jail for it.

So life went on with the sand and the dates and dead locusts. Then two years ago, my pop fell off of a ladder and broke his hip. He couldn't pick anymore, so it was my turn to get a job.

I decided to try up north because all my life I always wanted to travel. When I set eyes on Solvang, I know I'd found the place for me. Not everyone knows Solvang. It is a little town on the way between L.A. and Frisco, and it looks like something on a post card. Solvang is copied from a town in Norway, so the stores sell things you get over there, like aprons with beautiful embroidery on them and place mats with pictures of Mickey Mouse. It was all gorgeous—I went around looking at things in the shops nearly every lunch hour.

The job I found was making Swedish pancakes at a little restaurant. They gave me this wonderful uniform to wear. I remember exactly, it was red and had a black bodice and blue braid. I also wore a little hat. At first I was very glad to be making Swedish pancakes, because I saw it was a good skill to have. But now I know that every time I think about Swedish pancakes for the rest of my life, they'll remind me of David Angel.

He first came into the restaurant on the Fourth of July, two years ago. I remember the exact date because it was Independence Day. When this guy came in, I knew who he was right away, even though he had these big heavy dark glasses on, like he was in disguise. I kept looking at him, pretending I was doing something else. After a while I saw that every time I was staring at him, he was staring at me.

He ordered Swedish pancakes like everybody, and when I served them, my heart was pushing my chest out so much I was scared he could see it.

He kept eating my pancakes. Then he told me he had run away from home that morning. He said he had this recording session up in Monterey, where he lived, but he didn't feel like going to it, so he got in his car and drove until he came to Solvang.

"Oh," I said. "If you go to recording sessions you must have something to do with music."

"I'm David Angel," he said. He acted surprised I didn't know.

"I'm April Loeb," I said.

He started laughing. "You mean you never heard of me?"

I said no, even though I had all of his albums and had

his picture stuck on my bathroom mirror with Scotch tape. He said he knew it the minute he saw me, that I was so different and innocent.

The reason I lied like that is that in my favorite book, *Sweet Sensuous Fire,* the lady gets the rich man interested in her because she never heard of him. And David Angel sure got interested in me. He asked me if I'd like to go outside and see his car. I said I'd love to, but told him that I had another forty minutes left to work. He said he'd wait for me outside and there he was. His car was gorgeous. He asked me if I would like to go for a drive in it. I said all right. It was like a dream. We drove onto the freeway. Although I am not ignorant on subjects to talk about, I still couldn't think of much to say to this big rock star. He did all the talking. He said, "I want you to know that seeing you radiant in your dress and your long blond hair took my breath away. It's been a long time since I've known anyone as innocent and pure and good as you." It was really crazy.

He told me Joey was his real name and to call him that, but I like David Angel because it reminds me I'm with a VIP and not just another guy. He told me all about himself, how no one wanted him, how he was so lonely. That was so sad, to think that a big star that everybody loves could be lonely. I said that no one wanted me either, and that I got lonely all the time. I explained about my pop's hip and about everything in my life. Joey was very nice. He took me out to dinner that night, to Andersen's Pea Soup, and I told him restaurant secrets, like terms we use, and how we drop the food on the floor sometimes, then scoop it up and serve it just the same. Joey laughed; he didn't seem so lonely then.

The next morning there was a knock on my door. Joey looked more rested and he had on a beautiful blue cashmere sweater. He said he wanted to take me out to breakfast. When we're having bacon, he says yesterday was a real important day for him, that I'm the girl who's restored his faith in womanhood. I couldn't believe the way he talked. One day, two days, and before I have the chance to turn around, we're married.

It was a beautiful wedding. All my life I wanted a big one with a Val lace dress, and Pop to give me away. Joey was a doll about the dress, but he said he wanted the wedding to be a secret, so all we had was Ray-O, one of Joey's friends from the group, and Shelley, the girl who waited on the tables next to mine, making it legal. We did it in the judge's chambers. There weren't any flower shops open because it was late in the afternoon, but we saw a kid selling flowers down by the freeway and Joey bought him out, so I had more flowers in my bouquet than I can name.

I truly wanted to be the best wife to Joey. I can't say I knew him very well, but I figured being married was a pretty good way to find out. I don't think Joey thought the wedding was beautiful. He had his mind on something else even then, I could tell.

We went to his house in Monterey next day. I was glad because he told me all about how he loved his house, and I figured he was maybe homesick before. When we got there, there was this little black man ranting and raving at the front door. Joey started talking to him and forgot about me, so I had to lift the luggage Joey had purchased for me out of the car myself. But when I started to bring it into the house, the little black man starts shoving me and says I can't come in. He says he's Joey's agent and Joey's career is going to be ruined if it gets out that he's married. That got me mad, because I had been a good wife to Joey, so far, and I knew it was better than living with Pop on the desert.

Joey pushed his agent aside and he carried me over the threshold.

I was a little disappointed in his house, I must truthfully admit. Him being a rock star with lots of money, I had expected something a little more in the line of wealth, but his house was very plain with all this old furniture. There was even a brass spittoon on the floor—if I'd of known he liked them, I would have brought the one my pop had in his garage, since he was ashamed to keep it in the house. In a few months, though, I made the house a little more tasteful and warm with things I purchased —some were real collector's items, too.

Joey asked me to cook him some Swedish pancakes that first night, but I didn't have the right kind of flour and they didn't turn out.

That night was the Big Night. Joey and I got into bed and we fooled around a little, and then nothing. I felt real bad for him. I know how my stepbrothers used to worry about it when they dried up like that, so I used on Joey some techniques I knew. Joey didn't respond right, and I suspected he was shyer than I thought, so I tried some more things, but he got out of bed and slept the rest of the night in the spare room.

I really don't know what he wanted to get huffy for. I was only trying to help.

The next morning I met the other person from Joey's group, Harry. Harry was about the most handsome guy I ever saw, and even that first time I met him I disloyally wondered why he didn't make more of a splash with the fans.

So life went on. David Angel wasn't the greatest husband in the world. There wasn't nobody around for miles, just Joey and me, and Joey I never got to see. There was a little room where he wrote songs. He always kept the

door closed, but once I went inside when he was playing
the piano. There was this big painting over it, but the second
he saw me he pulled a sheet down covering it so I couldn't
see what it was. I went back in a few days when Joey was
out, and all the painting was, was a girl sitting. It wasn't
even very colorful.

Life was kind of dull. I'd go out at six in the morning to
swim in the pool and water the garden, but the rest of the
day I'd stay inside and read some books I found by an
English countess or something, Barbara Cartland. And I'd
eat like crazy. When I got tired of Barbara Cartland, I'd
fool around getting dressed and making up my face. Then
I'd do scrapbooks for Joey. I did sixteen of them. But
in all those articles about him and all the photographs,
I never really found out anything about Joey. I kept hoping he'd be like he was on that first date when he held my
hand, but he never was. When he'd come down to have
dinner with me, he'd just have that way-off look and if I
talked, he'd smile and say, "You're innocent and good and
that's the way I'll keep you."

Things just got weirder and weirder. There was a male
maid called Francis who was supposed to get me everything I wanted, but I could tell he took a disliking to me,
and I felt funny about asking him favors, so there were a
lot of things I did without. Once it was even my time of
the month and I wasn't about to ask Francis to buy me
feminine needs, so I sneaked outside the house when Joey
was writing songs, and I hitched a ride into Monterey. The
guy who picked me up was very sympathetic, but I didn't
tell him about Joey, just said I was married to a person
who was a little strange. He was kind enough to drive me
back to the house, and all I was doing was thanking him
properly in the car, when Joey came out like somebody
crazy. He started to beat me up and hurt me real bad. He
felt awful afterward, though, and cried and said he was a

wicked person and took me to dinner that night, somewhere public.

Joey did a lot of things people would call wicked, but
down inside I don't think he was really a wicked person. I
am more sensitive than most, though, and probably a lot
of people would condemn him. Joey began drinking a lot
and taking more and more pills. When he started using
the needle, I tried to make him stop, but soon I caught
on that he was a much nicer person when he was taking
drugs than when he wasn't, so I learned how to give him
the needle, and he said I did it real good. Sometimes the
drugs made him think strange things, though, like he was
made of iron and could run his motorcycle into a stone
wall. He was in the hospital for three weeks. He really
needed something for the pain then, and I was glad I could
help him. One other time he was drinking vodka, he had
this new Mercedes and he ran it into the back of a school
bus.

Joey got put in jail another time, when he hit a young
kid who wrote songs. Randolph, Joey's agent, came over
one evening and I heard him say the group wasn't doing
too well these days. He said maybe if Joey would stop
writing songs about insects eating up one another anymore,
the group would be back where it used to. Joey said he
liked writing songs about insects. Randolph said I'm bringing over another songwriter, he'll put us back where we
should be. The kid wrote two songs, and when Joey sang
them the group was number one again for a while. You'd of
thought that was great, but Joey got so mad he broke the
songwriter's nose.

Another weird thing really got me mad. For about the
last two months I'd been getting to know a nice girl,
who I met walking in the woods. She was a little retarded,
but at least she talked. She used to come up to the house
and see me when Joey was away and Francis was having

his rest. One afternoon when it was hot, I told her to take a swim in the pool. We were having fun, and then Joey came back when he wasn't supposed to. I got nervous, but he didn't seem upset like I thought he would be. Then I said, "This is my friend Becky" and he went real weird. I was just shocked. He jumped into the pool with all his clothes on and grabbed Becky by the hair and dragged her out. He was screaming like a loon, told her never, never to come back. Can you picture my humiliation? It was supposed to be my house, too, you know, and I wouldn't throw *his* friends out.

In the winter Randolph decided that Joey should get more in the public spotlight, with a whole new image. He was going to sell the house in Monterey so we could move to Beverly Hills. I was real happy about it, but I never saw Joey so miserable. This cute young couple came and wanted to buy the house, and Joey just stood there, not saying anything, like he was a zombie or something. And then that night he really flipped and he set the house on fire. The only thing good about it was that damned painting burned up with everything else.

I really don't know why Joey married me. I kept believing it had to get better, but it didn't. I don't know what I would have done without Harry. Harry was a living doll. He would come to the house while Joey was writing songs and talk to me. Ask me about Pop and everything. One day he said Joey didn't deserve a girl like me, but that I should try and understand that when Joey was acting terrible, it was just the drugs he took. Harry said that if I could get Joey to stop taking drugs, I'd see a new person, one that I'd really love. To tell you the truth, after about two months I didn't care so much about seeing that new Joey, because the one I was starting to really love was Harry. When the group was recording their album, Harry said he wanted me to come along. Joey hardly spoke to me the whole time, but Harry, he found me a seat and bought me M&M's and Cokes and anything else I wanted.

For my birthday Joey had Randolph buy me this old-lady dress from I. Magnin, but I got a real pearl necklace from Harry.

When I presented Joey the scrapbooks I had made, you'd of thought he'd be pleased, but he wasn't. He said he didn't want to think about those days and he ripped all the pages up and started kicking me. Later that night Harry came over, and I was bruised all over. When Harry started kissing me, I didn't do nothing to stop him. But Joey came in after a little while and when he saw us two together, he picked me up and threw me against the table in the dining room. That's all I remember.

I woke up in the hospital and Harry said he was taking me home to my pop in Palm Desert. Back with the dates, sand and the locusts. The whole time with Joey seems hazy in my mind, like it was a story I made up. But I didn't, and you can still see the scar on my face from where the corner of the table cut my cheek.

Harry comes down to see me once in a while, and I make him Swedish pancakes. Not one word from Joey the whole time except the alimony checks. Now I can't say I'm sorry he killed himself, because any fool could see he was in a lot of pain, but I can't say I'm glad, either, because once you've loved someone you just can't be glad, somehow.

I sure hope *Star* buys my story.

David Angel stood gasping by the bar. His senses had grown horribly acute, as had the pain in the cuts on his hand. There was a scuffling sound, and he looked up to see a face peering in through one of the lead panes by his front door.

"You've come," he whispered, almost afraid to breathe. And he waited for the sweetness of the bells.

The bells came, but in a knifing, brazen, furious squeal that made him cry and press his hands to his ears in pain.

Bells, bells, bells . . .

So many bells the day Joey was released from Mount Sinai Hospital. It seemed the whole world was calling and wanting to know if he had tried to take his own life. But he was clever—he skipped out and eluded them all. He wandered about New York like a tongue probing the cold, damp streets. Up near Columbia he found a woman. She was flat and white with freckles on her chest. She had never heard of David Angel. He lay glued to her body all night, smelled himself and was sick again. He felt her freckles branded onto the tips of his fingertips, damned spots.

Bells, bells, bells . . .

The cash register drawer popped out. "How'ya doin', Mr. Angel?" The girl who checked out his groceries teased, her long fingernails clicked on the machine. What was her name? She had worn panties of purple and gold.

There were women to pour like fountains on the places inside Joey where it hurt. Every day and night there were women. How they glistened as they poured him whiskey! How they glistened in the fire of pills! Ray-O came to visit, or Randolph or Harry, and they brought more women. Joey ached with readiness knowing that he could have any of them he wanted. He wanted them all.

Bells, bells, bells . . .

The alarm clock rang and he shut it off. Another night of no sleep. Nights lightened to days and there was no difference between them.

He suspected Randolph had taken up voodoo. One morning he went to the recording studio early and caught Randolph muttering incantations and pushing pins into a shirt. Joey shrieked because it was his shirt. He grabbed Randolph and punched his face in. Randolph sniffled that he was only sewing a button on. But all day long Joey fancied there was a red-hot pain pricking his chest.

The accountant and the head of Venue Records were always telephoning. It was so easy not to listen to the rough talk about debits and obligations to the public—so easy to push the voices back onto the receiver where they belonged.

Making music was no fun anymore, and when Joey went to the studio to rehearse, he brought a small mayonnaise jar filled with cocaine. The rule was that the group worked and worked until the jar was empty. He left the sessions, sometimes nearly a day later, every part of his body shaking like a child's rattle.

Pop goes the weasel.

He kept writing songs. All sorts of things came to his mind late in the night and he thought he was writing them down on a yellow pad. But in the morning he saw he had nothing down on the yellow pad. In fact, there *was* no yellow pad.

Bells, bells, bells . . .

"Five minutes, Mr. Angel." Randolph had made him sign up for a concert. He was scared. Something was wrong. Something about the kids out there—even from his dressing room he could tell they weren't the same kids who had used to come.

He went onstage. When the audience caught sight of him there was a blast of emotion so palpable and burning he thought his skin was going to peel off like the blackened jacket of a potato.

The audience: a solid roar, stamping with giant stamps, clapping, shaking the stage. Flash bulbs and strobe lights. He watched his fingers buck and bounce on the guitar like something from a jerking silent movie. What am I doing here?

He could not hear himself singing. Not a sound from the entire stage could be heard. The waves bounced harmlessly against the wailing wall of people, like a little girl throwing a foam-rubber ball against her garage door.

There were flashes of blue by the side of the stage that Joey couldn't understand. Then he saw that they belonged to a line of policemen, grim and heavy beneath him. As he began the second number, he saw something white shining near the cops. A young boy was trying to climb onto the stage, and the policemen were batting him down with their clubs. Joey screamed out to them to stop, but his cries sounded like part of the song.

Bells, bells, bells . . .

David Angel was in a storm at sea without a ship. Waves red with an incandescent light rose around him. He plunged sickeningly, his face contorted with the force of the descent, and rose again, hard and mindless, like something shot from a submarine.

"Help me!" he gasped, and his mouth was full of sharp, bitter water.

"Rebecca!" he cried as he went under. He was shocked to feel the saltwater waves prying into his nostrils and his throat. He must be dying.

He tried to think of what he could have done, of what he could have become. But the salt water flushing into his stomach told him there was no more time.

He went under for the second time. As the wave swept over his head, he cried out for Rebecca once again, in bubbles that sputtered and burst on the surface. He could hear the bells, bells, bells of hell ringing.

David Angel lay very still. He opened his eyes one at a time. Around him was his own living room. A small trickle of blood, a broken glass and an empty vodka bottle. Outside there was only the shrug of wind through Beverly Hills trees.

Then a small hand with bitten fingernails pressed the doorbell once again.

He sat up. He looked around him and exhaled in relief. Bells! Bells! It was only the doorbell! It sang again through the house. David Angel remembered the face peering in the window, and light broke across his eyes. He rose to his knees.

"Rebecca!" he cried hoarsely. "Rebecca!"

He jumped up, flew to the door, and with a yank, threw it open.

Waiting outside on the porch was a little girl. When she saw David Angel, she swayed and turned very pale.

"Rebecca?" David Angel asked brokenly.

"I'm Effie," she whispered.

David Angel passed his hand over his face.

"Hello, Effie." He smiled wearily at her. "Have you come to visit me?"

She nodded faintly.

"Rebecca must be grown up by now—but when I saw you, I was sure that . . . Rebecca loved Coca-Cola," he went on briskly. "Won't you come in for a bottle?"

As Effie passed through the door, he studied her more closely. She was frailer-looking than Rebecca, and her hair had none of Rebecca's curly shine.

"You're prettier than she is," David Angel murmured, "with a softer mouth and a nicer nose. She always said you would be."

"Who would be?"

"Karen. Our little girl."

"But I'm Effie," she said softly.

"Forgive me." David Angel pressed his hand to his head. "Please sit down."

Effie looked dubiously around the room. "This is your house?"

David Angel staggered backwards as if he had been struck. "No," he said. "It's only for a little while. I can't bear it here."

"Your house in Monterey . . ."

"All gone." He shook his head sadly. "All burned up. Nothing left of us. I don't even have a snapshot for you to see."

"I don't need one," Effie said reassuringly. "You had a blue-and-white kitchen, and a quilt with sailboats on it."

"How did you know that?"

"I know everything about you."

David Angel shook his head, startled. "That is scary," he cried. Then, catching sight of Effie's bewildered face, he grinned. "So you know *everything*; all the ins and outs of my life—is that right?" He tossed a sofa pillow at her. "Is that right, little Effie?"

She was trembling with excitement. David Angel could see the rapid rise and fall of her velvet choker. He was obscurely moved.

"How did you find me?"

"My friend Clara saw your house on a movie map. We came here on our bicycles. Clara and Alexandra hid in the bushes and I rang the bell."

"Here's your Coke," David Angel said. "Why don't you sit down? Here." He pointed to one of the bean-bag chairs. "This is the most comfortable."

Effie lowered herself into the chair and he smiled to watch her struggle to keep her skirt down. Why, there's nothing there to hide, he thought.

"So Clara and Alexandra are still stomping in my roses? What do you say we let them stay there a little longer? Serves them right for snooping."

Effie blushed. "But I was snooping, too."

"That's different. You're Effie."

They drank their Cokes. "Well, now you've come all this way to meet me," David Angel said, "what do you think of me?"

Effie did not answer, and he grew almost frightened. "That's all right," he said coolly. "You say you know everything about me—so you must know that I'm not as wonderful as they pretend I am."

"You *are* wonderful," Effie said.

He gazed down at her and felt as though a warm river had been let loose inside him. "Thank you." He smiled at her. "Does your family know you're here?"

"No."

"Would they be upset?"

"Maybe. But I don't care."

"You should care!" The smile drained from David Angel's face. "Your family should come first." Seeing that Effie looked stricken, he added more gently, "I didn't care either. But my grandma . . . I gave her this air conditioner—bought it for her birthday. It gets very hot in New York. I guess it worked too damn well. They called me up and said she had pneumonia." He turned his back on Effie. "I was going to fly back and visit her. I hadn't seen her since all this . . . since we made it. I bought out all the stores for things she liked—little bed jackets—but she died before I had a chance to give them to her." He turned back to Effie. Tears were running down her face.

"Don't worry," David Angel said wearily. "Your mom's not going to die."

"I know," Effie whimpered. "But the little bed jackets . . ."

David Angel started to reply, but in a moment he was heaving with sobs. "I wanted to tell Rebecca," he wept. Effie was crying steadily into the chair.

They both looked up at the same time. David Angel began to laugh. Effie joined in. They laughed until they were aching and spent.

At last David Angel reached forward and squeezed Effie's cold hands. She looked down shyly.

"Do you play guitar?" he asked her.

She shook her head.

"You should. You've got good fingers and you'd learn quickly."

"Oh, no," she blurted out. "I never learn anything quickly."

David Angel frowned and let go of her hands. He reached behind the piano into a mirrored cabinet and took out a chipped acoustic guitar. "Come here, young lady," he commanded. "You are about to see that you're wrong." Effie sat down beside him. "This was my first guitar." David

Angel ran his fingers along it. "Before this, I had to borrow Harry's uncle's ukulele. But after I told my grandma I wanted to be a musician, she bought this for my thirteenth birthday. And a little hat that the salesman told her all the musicians were wearing."

He named all the strings and showed Effie where to place her fingers. "Now strum." She strummed. "Terrific. You just played a C chord."

Effie smiled wildly. She bowed over the guitar and played her chord again and again. David Angel looked down at her translucent hands, puzzled, troubled. She looked nothing like Rebecca now. Stubbornly, she seemed to be walking away and standing apart from everyone else into a special corner of his mind that was hers alone. Then, to his horror, Effie's image blurred in his eyes and he was frightened. He fought to get her back in focus. When finally he did, he was wet from the strain. He sang "Blow Away the Morning Dew" softly while she played her chord, and he felt extraordinarily happy. "Keep that up, kid, and in a few months you'll knock me right off the charts!"

Effie dropped the guitar. It crashed to the floor. "Oh, *no*," she cried. "Never!"

David Angel moved toward her. "I'm going to write a song tonight," he said, "about a wonderful girl with wavy blond hair."

"Maybe," Effie said eagerly, "it could be like the songs you used to write."

David Angel went red. He could feel the anger flooding through his ears. "So you don't like the new songs," he said coldly.

"I hate them!" Effie cried. "They—they sound like you're in pain."

David Angel put his hands on Effie's shoulders. "I am in pain."

"No!" Effie cried.

David Angel smiled. "Does it matter to you?"

Effie hung her head and began to quiver.

"Stop that," he said sharply. "I'm not worth it."

But she kept on trembling. He took her face between his palms. "Hey, little Effie—would it scare you if I said I'd like to see you again?"

She shook her head slowly.

Someone rang the front doorbell.

"My friends." Effie bit her lip.

"That's all right," David Angel said. "I've got to start getting ready for my concert tonight." He walked her to the door. "I'll get you three tickets for the next show, but only if you promise to come back here tomorrow."

"I'll come," she whispered.

They smiled at each other.

"May I kiss you goodbye?" David Angel asked.

She lifted her face to his. He kissed her softly on the mouth. Her skin was cool and smelled of Ivory soap. Gently, lovingly, he reached under her thin blouse and touched one of her small breasts. He felt her stiffen. And then something—drugs, vodka, sleeplessness—sputtered and burst in his head.

. . . He didn't remember touching her, pulling her down onto the carpet. He didn't remember exploding inside, trying to free her from the little cotton panties. She was beautiful. Rebecca had come back to him.

But he did remember hearing the sound of screaming. The screaming of little girls.

A blonde and a brunette, dumb with panic, stood inside the door, wailing. Effie lurched from under him. Her eyes were ignited.

The brunette held out her hand to Effie, and Effie grasped it. The three little girls fled from him, heaped together in a frantic scrimmage. They fell toward the door.

The blonde was first. "Run!" she cried in a deep, sobbing voice. "Run! Run!" The brunette was close behind.
Effie, her face a soiled white, strained for the door.

What David Angel remembered most clearly was being
so dizzy he could hardly see, and screaming Rebecca's
name.

Effie paused on the threshold. She turned and looked
at him. Her eyes were ashes.

Then she was gone.

David Angel stood by the chair for many minutes and
then crumbled into it. Through the window he could make
out the three little girls pedaling madly away on their
bicycles. He knew Effie only by the color of her blouse.

Pills. Needle. Booze. Again and again.

At six-forty that evening, David Angel was on his knees,
vomiting into the toilet bowl. His hair was spiky and furious with vomit and tears. Bitter pools fell out of his
mouth.

When he finished he stood up and wiped his face.
He wondered why there was such a stench in the air. He
stared down inside his sunken tub. It was packed with
pounds of dry cat-food pellets. Near the faucet he saw one
still, gray ear and outstretched paw. David Angel picked up
Glitter's dead body from the tub and held it against his
chest.

Then he was sick again.

When Randolph came by at six-forty-five, he found David
Angel in his bedroom, sitting at the foot of the bed and
looking up at the moon.

"Joey!" Randolph called, coming slowly into the room

and standing over him. "Joey!" He touched David Angel's arm but Angel pulled away. "Hey man, it's time to go. I've come to pick you up for the concert."

"What concert?"

"The concert you're going to give tonight."

"I want to give concerts," David Angel said suddenly, "and one day I will. One day I'm going to be a star." a star."

Randolph was by the bedside, picking up the phone and dialing.

"What are you doing?"

"I'm calling Harry."

"Harry quit."

Randolph stopped dialing. "He couldn't have. He loves you."

"But he quit."

"Let me talk to him. He doesn't mean it."

"No."

"But you've got to give the concert, whether Harry's there or not."

"Why?"

"Because you're the star, man. Harry's not David Angel. He doesn't count. Only you count."

"David Angel? That's right—they were playing that song today on the radio."

Randolph was shaking him. "Tell me what's the matter, Joey! Tell me what's wrong!"

"Just a minute—just a minute. I'll tell you." Sweat dusted Angel. Randolph's face seemed to contract and expand before him, winking like a star. David Angel felt sorry and wanted to tell him what the matter was. But all he had in his mind were questions and no answers. There were so many questions—about a little boy's secret at school, a girl shaking her head from behind a locked window, a kitten, Swedish pancakes, a portrait on the stairs.

Five men standing beside a Jacuzzi. And a little girl bicycling away from him as fast as she could.

"Stop crying!" David Angel said sharply to Randolph. "How can I figure out the answer if you're crying?"

And then the answer came. It was something black and simple.

David Angel reached over to the bedside table. When he turned back, his face was red. "I wanted to ask you if this is loaded," he said.

"Give that to me," Randolph demanded.

David Angel laughed. "Now I know it's loaded."

Randolph reached out, but laughing even harder, David Angel pulled away.

"Let me help you!" Randolph was screaming.

David Angel spread out his hand and stared at it. One finger was Harry. One finger was Penelope. One finger was Ray-O. One finger was Rebecca. The last little finger was Effie. So he showed his hand to Randolph, but Randolph didn't understand at all.

David Angel drew all his fingers into a fist and crashed it onto the table. Goddamnit! Randolph still didn't understand and it was so simple.

"What have you taken? Tell me what you've taken."

The world looked very alive to David Angel. Leaves shivered with the ecstasy of early evening, the blue sky was so intense it made him shudder. He could hear the universe crying *Yes* all around him.

He smiled at Randolph. "Her name was Effie this time."

It was so important that Randolph be made to understand, but he just stood there dumb.

Then David Angel hit upon a way and was triumphant at last.

"See! See!" he cried, and raised the gun to his head and pulled the trigger.

Epilogue

There is a family living in the house on Rodeo Drive now. A banker from Tennessee, his wife and his little boy. The red and black furniture has been replaced by Early American reproductions. The refrigerator and kitchen shelves are always well-stocked.

There is a new carpet in the bedroom.

About the Author

MARY SHELDON, the daughter of novelist Sidney Sheldon and actress Jorja Curtright, was born in Los Angeles, and grew up there and in New York City. She attended boarding school at St. Clare's Hall in Oxford, and later studied at Yale University and Wellesley College, where she graduated in 1978 with honors in English. She is married to an attorney and lives on the North Shore of Long Island.